THE ASSASSIN'S LEGACY

THE ASSASSIN'S LEGACY SERIES
BOOK 1

LIBBY WEBBER

Dead, or Alive
Press

To request permission contact Libby Webber of Dead or Alive Press at DeadorAlivePress@gmail.com

ISBN 978-1-7377811-2-7 (hardcover)
ISBN 978-1-7377811-0-3 (paperback)
ISBN 978-1-7377811-1-0 (ebook)
Also available as an Audiobook

Book design by Libby Webber

Dead or Alive Press
Jacksonville, NC

www.libbywebber.com
www.libbywebber.com/deadoralivepress

For Moe, my very first fan.

PLEASE BE AWARE

This book contains topics that some readers may find triggering. These sensitive topics include violence against children, and the death of children. There is also mention, not in detail, of sexual assault and domestic violence. This book is recommended for 18+.

1

AERON

*A*eron glanced around the familiar hallway, the hardwood floors, crappy lighting, and fake potted plants coated in dust. Nothing about it indicated one of the world's most influential political players lived just on the other side of the faded wooden door in front of her.

She took a deep breath and smoothed out her skirt, fingers skating over the blade strapped to her thigh, the reassuring pressure reminding her this was not a social call.

"Showtime," Luke's low voice whispered into her earpiece. A surge of nerves jetted through her bloodstream. Should anything go wrong tonight, Luke and her brother, Decius, were perched in a sniper's nest and guaranteed her a swift death.

She pulled the earpiece out, tucked it inside a pocket on her bra, and knocked. Her heart pounded a few times before the practiced breathing calmed the nerves. This should be like any other mission, he was a target to be eliminated.

But it wasn't like any other mission. Shaun Brinks was a Legacy Member—a trained assassin like herself. And the man she was sleeping with. Shaun pulled the door open, hair tousled and his brown eyes blinking with sleep.

"Aer—I didn't expect to see you tonight."

She smiled and leaned against the door frame, fingers playing with the hem of her skirt. "It's been a rough night. I thought I could swing by for a drink and company. Unless you already have company." She peered around his shoulder, assessing if anything was out of place.

His smile broadened and he pulled the door open, letting her walk past. "You've set my standards pretty high. I don't think I'll be finding someone as extraordinary as you."

She gave an appreciative laugh, gaze remaining alert. The only thing out of place was a blanket on the couch he'd been sleeping on. "You know as soon as my father catches wind of this, you'll be dead."

He laughed too and headed to the kitchen. He pulled out two glasses and a bottle of whiskey. "That's the beauty of being a Liaison. I'm untouchable."

"Don't get such a big head. We take out the untouchables all the time."

He held out a glass of whiskey, but Aeron remained by the couch. Luke and Decius should be able to see her from their perch.

"What's going on?" His scrutinizing gaze roamed her body. She leaned against the couch, raising her eyebrows with a smile. The element of surprise would be necessary for her to succeed. He snapped his fingers, and Aeron's heart jumped. "Food. Of course. You need something to eat." His face lit up as he set the glasses down, turning to the stove. If there was something other than political manipulation that Shaun could have made a career out of, it was cooking. He turned on the burner, placed a frying pan on it, and pulled out a container of vegetables. She relaxed again. He couldn't know why she was here. "So, what happened?"

"Ever just feel like a hamster in a wheel? Wake up, train, kill some people, sleep, repeat."

"The training blues. You've got like two years of training left before you're released?" He glanced over his shoulder at her.

"Just about."

He returned his attention to the vegetables. "I get it. One of my team members was a Legacy Blood, like you. I never understood why they make you guys go through the Institute. You are born training. Chicken or fish tonight?"

"Fish sounds good." A small flick of her wrist released a throwing knife from her forearm sheath.

She took a measuring breath and flicked the black blade. It whirled end over end, and should have found purchase in the back of his neck, except he spun, frying pan deflecting the blade, sizzling vegetables dancing in the air. Aeron dropped, but his throwing knife glanced off her shoulder before she hit the ground.

He placed the frying pan back on the stove and picked up an onion, all playfulness evaporated. "You're out of your league, Aeron."

Aeron raised her hands, the next throwing knife held limply in her fingertips. A gesture of parley that could turn deadly with a flick of her wrist. Shaun picked a knife from the butchers block and began chopping the onion as she approached the breakfast bar, lowering her hands. She had wanted—no, needed the element of surprise.

"I know you don't eat onions, but they're my favorite." He pulled out a second cast iron frying pan and turned on a burner, never fully turning away. Smart man.

"So, what is really going on?"

"This isn't a social call."

"Your flying knife was a dead giveaway." He stopped chopping the onions, eyes roaming her entirety. She fought back a shiver. "Come on, Aer."

She held her silence. It would have been simpler to come over for dinner, sleep with him, and slit his throat as he slept, half naked, mouth slightly open, and arms splayed across the bed. Peaceful. But that was not who she was nor how she'd be remembered in the Legacy.

"This is strictly business, Shaun."

"All of it? Or just tonight?"

She detected the hurt in his voice, and a pang of regret gripped her for agreeing to help Luke with this last-minute mission. But the fact he had to ask...he was a secret she enjoyed—until tonight. "You know me better than that."

He nodded. "Just tonight." He tossed oil and onions into the pan, they sizzled in the high heat—too high to cook onions on. Aeron launched backward, covering her face as his hands closed on the two frying pan handles. He tossed the scalding food and oil towards her. She hissed, the bubbling grease landing on her hands and neck. He vaulted over the breakfast bar and swung again, this time, using the pans as weapons. Aeron dropped low and shot for his waist, bringing them to the floor. The searing pans touched her shoulders for a second—but long enough for her skin to want to crawl off her body. She jumped on top of him, straddling his waist. He swung the pans at her again. She covered her head, her outside arm taking another burning hit. He swung again and Aeron popped to her feet, the momentum of cast iron swung past her and carried Shaun to his side.

He abandoned the now cooling weapons and grab her ankles, yanking her off her feet. They scrambled, fists and knees and feet flying. Aeron landed on her back and wrapped her legs around his waist, crossing her feet to keep him from getting on top, but the flurry of punches barely let up. She brought her feet to her chest and kicked. He stumbled back only momentarily, and Aeron wiped the blood pouring from a cut over her left eye. The sharp pain of a knife sliced across Aeron's jaw and she stilled, breathing heavy. The glint of victory flashed in Shaun's eyes as he towered over her. An inch lower and she'd be dead.

He moved the blade to her carotid artery. She was out of her league and knew this could be a suicide mission. And Shaun had moved them out of the window view, so she was on her own.

"Who ordered this? Your father?"

"You think my father would let me sleep my way to a kill?" S.. scoffed. "If you're on the list, you deserve it. You know the Legacy never misses their mark. What are you into, Shaun?"

He shook his head, sighing. "Aren't you tired of blindly following orders? Wouldn't you want the option to say no?"

"We protect the innocent. I'll never say 'no' to that."

The knife let up a little. "Do we though? If given the choice, would you have said no to this? Tonight?"

She licked her drying lips. She did have the opportunity to say no tonight—this wasn't an ordered mission by her Guardian. But Luke had orders and needed help. She wouldn't say no to him either.

"C'mon Aer—why did they send *you*? No offense, but I'm slightly offended. I should rate at least a full member. Or a visit from your father at least."

Rage boiled beneath her gut. "Fuck you."

"Well, I did enjoy that." His face hardened. "This is just business, Aeron."

The blade stung as it broke the skin on her neck. She was not going to die like this. Securing the knife to her collarbone, she spun beneath him. Her legs shot skyward and clamped down on his neck and back, bringing her hips through his arm. His elbow popped; a spew of expletives escaped him as he fell over. Aeron held tight to his arm and hitchhiked to the top, swiping the knife from his fingers. She swung her legs around and drove her knee into his solar plexus, pinning him to the ground, the knife already slicing a thin line across his throat. He didn't give much of a struggle, just the half-hearted movements of a man who knew his fate—or maybe just accepted his fate.

"You don't want to do this."

He wasn't wrong. But it had to be done. Aeron let a smirk creep across her face. He was just a target who made the list. That was it. "Doesn't matter what I want, Shaun. The Legacy gets what the Legacy wants."

the Legacy."

ost of the Laws. I loathe my father. But I love my

Just-just think for a second, Aer. With me dead, nobody wins."

Aeron hesitated, the blade hovering beneath his chin. A dead Liaison would place a strain on the clandestine agreement with the government. A dead Liaison would create panic within the entire Legacy system. But he wouldn't be the first to stray from their mission. To take more than he gave. To put himself before the civilians. He would just be the first she had the honor of eliminating.

He jerked from beneath her, and her knee slid, slamming onto the floor, knife clattering out of her grasp. Before he could utter a word, Aeron grasped his chin, her other hand scooping the base of his skull. With a satisfying snap, his body went limp. The work wasn't done, however, and Aeron thread her fingers into his short brown hair, his empty gaze looking off into the distance. She gave herself a small shake. She retrieved the blade and pressed into his neck just below his right ear. Blood pooled onto the floor as she moved it from ear to ear.

She swallowed hard, his final words leeching onto her. From all accounts, Shaun was a damn good Liaison: honest, kept the Legacy on the right side of the missions, and liked by everyone she knew. Except maybe her father. But people kept secrets, even good people, and she'd seen firsthand how easily greed changed a person's priorities—Legacy or not.

She wiped the blood from her hand on Shaun's shirt and pocketed the throwing knife before pulling out her earpiece. "Complete. Heading out."

Silence answered. She checked the earpiece to make sure it hadn't been damaged in the fight, and stuck it back in her ear. "Dee?"

The earpiece remained silent. Hurried footsteps sounded on the hardwood floor outside the apartment. Before she could turn away, the front door sprung open, the frame splintering. Aeron shot backward, ducking behind the kitchen counter and out of their direct line of vision. Four men filed in, shouts of 'Federal Agents!' filling the room.

Fuck. Aeron dropped her head back. Being caught was a risk of the job, but usually held minimal repercussion—their network ensured they were never charged, and all traces of them erased from every system.

But she'd just assassinated the Liaison to the FBI.

She killed a federal officer and was alone, without an escape route or backup, while the FBI flooded into the apartment. She'd just eliminated Shaun. Sweet, funny Shaun who balanced the Liaison position better than any of his predecessors. And no one would be able to rescue her now. The best bet would be to get in sight of the windows—a swift death.

Aeron took a steadying breath, wiped the throwing knife of her prints, and slid it into a cupboard. Tugging at her shirt, which was already ripped, she stood, hands in the air, eyes wide. They pounced, pushing her to the ground.

"Please!" she protested. "He attacked me!" She hiccupped, tears now streaming down her face. Her arms twisted behind her back, and her face slammed into the ground, Shaun's dead eyes boring right into her. She hoped the blood and bruising she had endured mixed with the tears and her attire would buy her some time. But the familiar feel of zip-ties tightened around her wrists, digging into the skin.

"I'll take it from here." The deep voice sent a chill to her core, and Aeron struggled against the pressure on her head to look away from Shaun's blank eyes and toward the all too familiar voice.

2

LUKE

*L*uke settled into position on the rooftop beside Decius, the metal cool beneath his fingers as he adjusted the rifle. Their sniper's nest was lacking coverage, as in they had none. But if all went accordingly, he wouldn't need to fire a shot, and Aeron would have pulled off a kill even her father could be proud of.

However, he hadn't anticipated the possibility of Aeron knowing the target. Or how her knowing the target would enrage and knot his gut all at once. He kept his scope on Aeron's back as she leaned against Shaun Brink's couch. The audio may not be the best quality, but he'd heard enough.

"Did you know she was seeing him?" Luke asked his best friend.

"No. But if my sister wanted us to know, we would."

"This shouldn't bother me," Luke admitted, looking to Decius.

Decius smirked, eyes still glued to his sight. "I'm not getting in the middle of that. Once you're both done training, I'm sure our parents will lift the dating ban."

"I shouldn't have called you. Your father will be furious."

"Only if we fail. And Aeron doesn't fail." Decius turned to him.

"We didn't ask when you called, but I need to know now, what kind of mission is this?"

Luke licked his lips, looking away to scan the rooftops. He wasn't anticipating any interference—however, this should have been a solo mission, but if he wanted the man dead, Aeron was the best assassin for the job.

"My Granddad assigned me this task." Luke swallowed hard. He shouldn't have agreed. They should be preparing for training in the Maldives, not camped out on a rooftop. "I didn't think it was a good idea to tell our Senior Assassin 'No'—family or not."

"Damn. A Reaping mission from the top? Does that mean you're planning on leaving the team?"

"No." Luke shook his head. "I couldn't even do this mission without you guys. I wouldn't want to."

"Fair enough." They fell back into silence, listening to the fight unfold out of sight.

The hairs on the back of Luke's neck stood up. They were being watched. "Dee, we've got company." Decius didn't respond. "Dude." Luke glanced over, and the blood drained from his face. A green dot held steady on Decius' forehead, Decius' spotting scope directed to the adjacent rooftop. Luke moved his scope, scanning for the threat. His eyes fell on his mother, sitting cross-legged with a spotter scope and laser in one hand, her fingers pressed against her lips with the other.

"What the fuck."

"I could say the same thing."

Luke spun around. His dad stood behind them, shoulders set. "Where's Aeron?"

The urgency of the words fell heavy on Luke. "Finishing the job."

"Call her off." The order clear in his voice didn't matter, Aeron was unreachable.

"It's too late," Decius said, turning around too. "She's already requested extraction."

His father sighed, a disappointed sigh if Luke had to guess, and pulled out a cell phone. "It's too late…We'll be there."

His father snapped the phone shut, raking a hand through his hair. "It's time to go."

Luke scrambled back to his scope. Shaun Brink's apartment now hosted federal agents, but not a sound came from his earpiece. "Did you interfere with our frequency?"

"We don't have time for this. If you want Aeron out of there alive, we need to move."

Luke moved the scope to the apartment entrance, and more people filed in. "C'mon, man." Decius tugged at his shoulder. Luke pulled himself away from the scope, but not before catching a glimpse of the last person Aeron would want to come to her rescue.

3

AERON

"*E*nough." All movement froze inside the apartment, the command clear in the deep voice reverberating through the room. "Pick her up."

The floor disappeared from beneath her as the two agents stood her up and turned to face the man in charge. Her father's six-foot-tall frame towered over everyone in the room. She met his disapproving glare with one of her own. They could have sent anyone else to aid her. Anyone else who wouldn't make her feel like a complete failure, or hold this moment over her head for the rest of eternity. She could hear the ammunition now: "Too incompetent to save yourself."

"All this manpower, for what?" He scoffed. "Look at her? She can't be older than seventeen."

His gaze flicked down to the right as he assessed her. He needed her to remain quiet as he planted the storyline that would save her ass: an underage girl caught in the wrong place.

"And she's been on the receiving end of one hell of a beat down. Was that your men?" He turned to the agent closest to him.

"No!" The man replied, voice rising in defense. "No. When we arrived, we found Agent Brinks dead. She jumped out as we cleared the room. She's covered in blood, he's dead. We responded accordingly."

"I'm sure her lawyer will see it like that." Her father stepped closer, nose scrunched in disgust. Aeron's heart pounded in her chest. Was he mad? It was impossible to tell what was an act and what he truly felt. He looked away from her. "What's your name, agent?"

"Agent Waldorf." The man stood taller as he said it.

"Did you finish clearing the apartment, Agent Waldorf?"

"Of course."

"Even the hideaway closet in the master bedroom?"

"The what?" Agent Waldorf scanned the room, and Aeron heard two agents head back down the hallway to the bedroom. She dropped her head forward to conceal a laugh. The quickest way to clear a room was to make the men in it second guess themselves.

"Pass her over so forensics can get started." He held out his hand, palm up, gesturing for her to follow.

"That's okay. I've got it." Agent Waldorf stepped in front of her. Aeron had to give the man props. Bringing in a witness on such a high-profile case could launch a career, but most people were intimidated by the mere presence of her father. "Where did you say you were from again?"

"Do you suffer from short-term memory loss, Agent Waldorf?" He reached around Agent Waldorf and grasped Aeron's bicep. Nails dug into her skin as he ripped her forward and away from the two agents. "I'll be sure to speak with Special Agent Fox on your competency to retain the important details on such a high-profile case."

Before Agent Waldorf could even muster a retort, Aeron and her father moved through the growing crowd of people in the hallway. She looked over her shoulder, but no one was following. Her father pushed open the door for the stairwell, his hand not moving from her bicep.

They moved with haste down the stairs, passing only a few

people down the twenty flights, and he popped open the emergency exit instead of going through the lobby. A black Navigator idled at the curb, the rear door ajar. They paused only long enough for him to slice off her restraints before tossing her inside and slamming the door. She sucked a breath in as her burns landed hard against a body and turned, finding Luke and Decius looking contrite. Her father barely closed his own door before Luke's father, pulled from the curb.

Aeron straightened, rubbing her now raw wrists. Luke sat beside her, head buried in his hands, and Decius kept his eyes locked out the window. She reached across Luke, tapping her brother on the shoulder, pulling both their attention.

What the hell is going on? She signed in ASL.

Nothing, he signed back.

She glared. *Luke?*

He didn't answer either. He placed his hands on hers, turning them over to see the raw skin.

"I'm sorry."

"You should be," her father snarled.

Aeron looked up. Did he just come to her rescue *and* defend her?

"The entire Legacy operation could have been blown tonight," her father continued. "That man held the key to more successful covert operations than you can imagine, Luke. All that information, all those assets and missions—lost. And then leaving Aeron there with no plan of retreat and free to be used as a bargaining chip! What the hell were you thinking?" Her heart sank. Of course. His concern was not for her, but the reputation and vulnerability of the Legacy. But if what he said was true…her stomach rolled with sickness. She was just following orders.

"Enough, Drew." Luke's dad sent her father a warning look, but her father faced away from him, fuming. "I'm sure Luke has an explanation."

"Granddad called me. Said he needed this taken care of ASAP."

"That's your cousin Perry's job now, not yours, or Aeron's, son."

"I didn't think it was an issue."

"You didn't think at all," her father said. "And for what...to prove to your Granddad you're worthy of the five minutes he decided to grant you?"

John slammed on the brakes. Aeron braced against the front seat as the car came to a halt and John threw it into park. The two men exited the car, the vehicle shaking as they closed the doors. Aeron peered around the passenger seat, her father and Luke's toe to toe, faces contorted as they argued. Something was wrong—they never argued. Disagreed, yes. Often. Especially about the missions and training she and the boys should undertake. But she had never seen them like this.

"Are you okay?" Decius asked her.

She pulled her gaze back inside the car. Decius sat, shoulder's slumped, his usual bravado gone. "Yeah," she answered. "I'm okay." It wasn't the complete truth, but she wasn't dead or locked in an FBI interrogation room, so she could be worse.

"Why didn't you tell us?" Luke asked.

Aeron looked at him. "Tell you what?"

"That you were sleeping with Shaun?" He kept his eyes focused on her wrists, thumbs rubbing just under the raw skin, somehow bringing relief instead of pain.

Her cheeks heated and she pulled her hands away. "Because it's not your business who I'm sleeping with."

"I wouldn't have asked you to help...that was..."

"My job," Aeron supplied. "It was my job." But the whole experience left a sour feeling in her gut. Reaping was a high honor: confirmation you were the best of the best and able to eliminate other skilled assassins. But killing one of their own, and someone she *knew*...

"They're coming back." Decius sat back hard against the seat, Aeron and Luke following suit. The air thickened with tension as the doors closed.

"Do you understand the damage you've done tonight?" John asked, a seriousness in his voice she'd never heard in her twenty years. Aeron's tongue suddenly became like sandpaper. Even if she knew, she wouldn't have been able to speak.

Luke must have heard it too because he answered. "No." His voice was as low as his father's, but woven with fear, as if he'd made an awful mistake and realized his misstep too late. Aeron's eyes widened, catching the wrinkle of his forehead.

"Do you even know why?" her father asked.

Luke hesitated. "He wanted the FBI Director to know that the Legacy will not tolerate insubordination."

His father spit out an impressive number of curses in at least four languages she understood.

Luke's hands trembled in his lap. She twined her fingers with his and swallowed the lump rising in her throat. The car hooked a few harsh turns, and Aeron leaned in when Luke put an arm over her shoulder. "I'm sorry I asked Dee to drag you into this," he whispered.

"Don't be. We make one hell of a team." She leaned across his lap tossing to her brother. *What's wrong?* she signed.

Dad's pissed, he signed back, his expression hard. But then it softened as he signed, *but you fucking rocked it tonight.*

Aeron grinned. *I did. Don't be too jealous.*

Her joy dimmed, however, as the car pulled under a skyscraper, killing the mood. There was nothing special about the building, except it housed the deadliest people in New York City. John cut the engine, the doors remaining locked.

"Aeron, are you alright?" John asked.

She sat straighter. "I am." But was she? Physically, she'd taken harder beatings. Mentally, she'd have to unpack that another time.

"Well, you know where to find us, if anything. Luke?"

"Yes, Sir?"

"No more assignments that do not come from Mason. He is

your Guardian. Your Granddad has an entire army at his disposal. He needn't ask you for help. Is that understood?"

"Yes, Sir."

Aeron swallowed hard, wishing a lecture would be all that she and Decius would receive. They exited the car in silence, the group heading to the elevators. She glanced around the unusually empty garage, her heeled boots the only sound echoing around them.

Her father's hand grabbed her shoulder, stopping her from entering the elevator.

"Thank you," John said, nodding to her father. Luke gave a half-apologetic smile as the doors closed, dividing the Waywards and Sewards. The hand remained gripped on her shoulder as her father turned on Decius.

"What were you thinking!" The venom spewed from her father's words. "Did you have any idea who you were going after? Or did you just blindly follow him and then call your little sister in for bait? Did you think the recklessness would impress me?"

Aeron bristled at his use of 'bait' but didn't dare move. She'd been bait plenty of times. This had been something else—more of a betrayal. She swallowed around the knot in her throat.

Decius didn't move a muscle either, standing tall and mirroring their father's stance. "Since when do we leave teammates high and dry?"

"This wasn't a team mission. This was *Luke's* mission. You have no idea the damage the three of you have caused."

Aeron's mouth went dry, Shaun's words returning to her. *With me dead, nobody wins.*

"Stay out of the Wayward's family business." The growl that escaped her father reverberated down his arm and into her shoulder. She stepped away from him then, only to have him round on her; her guts twisted. His eyes raked over her, the bruises on her face tingling when he looked at them. His lip curled in disgust at the ripped shirt and too-short-skirt. He snatched her wrists, facing her bloody hands palm up. Pain rippled through the raw skin on her wrists, and her knuckles screamed when the heel of his palms brushed over the cuts. He dropped to barely audible.

"What if you were captured? You're not even claimed. There was no guarantee the Legacy would come to your rescue. Or was the plan to hope the boys had the balls to pull the trigger for you if things got out of hand?"

The knot in her throat prevented any words from replying. This mission, eliminating a Liaison, should have proven to her father she was worthy of the Seward Legacy, but it seemed to have done the opposite. He spun around and stalked to their car. She shook off Decius' attempt of comfort and followed, taking the back seat to herself.

"You were not there. Luke acted alone. I do not want to hear of this again."

"Yes, Sir." Aeron and Decius said together.

"We are breaking your training with the Institute early. Apparently, we have our own insubordination issues to manage before you come back."

4

LUKE

*L*uke brushed past his father into the apartment, slamming his keys down on the counter, the metal digging into his palm.

"We're not finished, Luke."

The door closed behind them. Luke ignored his father, gut still turning at the look in Aeron's eyes before the elevator door closed —fear.

"How long have you been working with your Granddad?"

"Huh?" He shook his head, pulling himself back to the kitchen. "I have never worked with Granddad before." And now he never would get another chance.

"Then how did you end up executing the FBI Liaison?"

Luke scratched his head, stalling. "Granddad called me into his office. Said Perry is out of town, and he needed something taken care of ASAP."

"Did you even think to call me? Your mother? Hell, even Mason?"

"I didn't really have time, Dad. He said you were on an assignment and if I didn't want to do it, he'd find someone else." Luke shrugged, leaning against the counter, the cool slab of granite sending a chill through his arms. "He's never asked me before. I kind of wanted to prove to him I could do it." The last part came out before he realized—but it was true. With his uncle dead, Perry had become his Granddad's first choice in all things Legacy related.

"But you didn't do it," his father said, tossing his keys on the counter and leaning next to him. "You brought the Sewards in. You had time to call the Sewards."

"He never said not to." A defensive, and childish response, but his father didn't admonish him. A heavy sigh escaped instead.

"Luke, Aeron would have been burned tonight if—"

"If what?" Luke asked. "How did you know where to find us if Granddad didn't tell you? Because that's what this is right? Keeping it a secret from him?"

"That doesn't matter. You put Aeron's life in jeopardy. And Andrew was right—you put the entire Legacy in jeopardy. The damage is irreparable."

His stomach dropped and he turned away. Aeron could have been executed. The thought that the Legacy wouldn't step in never crossed his mind. But it should have because she was not claimed by the Legacy yet. Aeron nearly paid the price because…because her father was a dick.

"Why hasn't he claimed Aeron yet? Secure her place in the Legacy?"

"That's not our concern."

"The fuck it isn't." Tension bubbled through his chest.

"How Andrew handles his family's Legacy is not up to us. What I need you concerned with is staying on track with your training. One more year and you can follow in your Granddad's footsteps. If that's what you want."

Luke remained silent. He wanted to lead his team with Decius and protect civilians from high-profile criminals who operated in the Underworld. He wanted Aeron to have the full protection of the Legacy. He wanted…he wanted Aeron. But that wasn't a choice that was up to him.

"You didn't even fulfill the mission yourself. He has zero patience for failure."

"Aeron had the best shot of getting him alone. He asked for a dead Liaison. That's what I gave him." Yet the nagging feeling of failure settled over him.

"Well, as far as everyone is concerned, you were the only one there. You'll get your credit." If anything, that made Luke's gut sink even further, getting credit for something he'd fucked up. The deep creases in his father's face indicated there was more to say, but he wouldn't be hearing it tonight. "Your mom is expecting us dressed and ready for the Institute's Gala in…" he glanced around Luke at the microwave clock, "two hours. Let's pretend for the night, this didn't happen."

The unsettled stomach stuck around as Luke showered, scrubbing the dirt from his hands. It was not how he envisioned ending this year. A long night of dancing and indulging in drinks; the party continuing at the club long after the backdoor deals and threats had been completed at the Gala.

A soft rap on his door pulled his attention.

"Luke?" his mother called through the door. "Are you ready?"

"Just about."

The door creaked open as he buttoned the jacket. His mother's green eyes glowed from the doorway, the purple gown she wore making them pop. With such a deep color on, it wouldn't matter what she wore—no one would look anywhere else but her eyes. It was how she managed to get weapons into the most secure areas. Even now, the elegant braid puffed around his mom's head most likely concealed a lock-pick and vial of poison. She never left home without a few provisions, even to a Legacy-hosted event.

"You look gorgeous, mom."

She smiled and picked up his black bow-tie making quick work of it. "You look very dashing yourself." Her hand rested on his cheek, and the storm inside him settled.

He turned to the mirror and grabbed a handful of gel, pulling it through his hair to tame the slight curls before following her out of the room.

His Dad waited by the open door. His matching charcoal tux to Luke's paired with a deep purple bow-tie. It suited his father's fair complexion, and Luke couldn't stop the smile from plastering his face. His dad's gaze never left his mom, like there could be nothing more important than her presence—a feeling Luke was slowly becoming familiar with every time he looked at Aeron, like nothing would stop him from giving her the world with a big gold bow.

Music crept into the elevator as they reached the rooftop, the sound dancing through the air when the doors opened. The Gala was hosted on the Institute's rooftop. Although not the tallest skyscraper in New York, the view over the city could be appreciated by even the most world-traveled.

"Luke!" Two sets of arms wrapped around his waist before he could make it ten feet. Gabe Woodsworth & Ben Finch beamed up at him. Luke smiled back.

"Isn't it past your bedtimes?" Luke joked. The Woodsworths and Finches were Legacy Blood families, like his own. The next generation of assassins.

"We are now old enough to attend the first hours of the Gala!" Gabe proclaimed.

"Did you see the trials this year?" Ben asked.

"You guys were awesome," Luke answered. "The way you took the sniper out with the acid balloons? Genius. You'll be beating our records in no time."

"Don't let Aeron hear that, she'll sabotage us!" Gabe said, laughing.

"I know for a fact she thinks if anyone can actually break her records, it would be you two."

Ben reddened, Gabe bumping his shoulder. "Thanks, Luke."

"I'll catch you guys later." Luke slapped hands with them, a quick secret handshake involving several punches and his epic death scene at the end. Luke looked up from the ground as they ran off, swerving between inattentive adults.

A hand reached down for him. Luke accepted his father's assistance and was pulled to his feet. "Those boys really look up to you."

"They're cool kids." Luke scanned the room. The Gala was the only place where politicians could rub elbows with the most vile Underworlders and no judgement was passed. The opportunity to set into motion the upcoming power moves happened right on this rooftop.

His father patted him on the shoulder. "He should be otherwise occupied tonight, however, if you see your Granddad—"

"I handled the Liaison alone. Gutted him like a fish," Luke answered deadpanned, to which he received a curt nod.

"She actually slit his throat. Go enjoy your team."

Luke watched him disappear into the crowd, the sick feeling in his gut not easing up. A light touch on his shoulder caused him to spin, hands coming up on reflex. "Shannon."

"Where's Aeron?" she asked. "We were supposed to get ready together, but she never showed."

"She and Dee went home early."

The freckles danced across her face when she scowled, her red hair, barely tamed, adding to the illusion of an ancient warrior. "What happened?"

"I couldn't say." He really couldn't.

Her petite hand slipped into his. "Well, c'mon. The gang is waiting over by the east wall." She pulled him along through the crowd, and a smile grew on his face.

"Are we free jumping tonight?" The question came out with more excitement than he intended, but a good run through the city would clear his head, and the east wall was the best place to jump.

"Only if Perry gets the stick out of his ass."

His feet stopped moving and he pulled his hand back. The green dress flared when she rounded on him, eyebrows raised.

"Perry's here?" The blood in his veins turned to ice.

"Where else would he be? Let's go." She took off, and he followed more reluctantly.

Cheers and hoots greeted him as he approached the oversized couches near the east wall, and even with irritation floating just below the surface, a smile found its way across his face. Perry sat like the king he was, Shannon on one side and her sister Keara on the other. Their normal crowd of eight was down to four. Perry's black tux was already skewed, and his light brown hair out of place. He'd probably just returned from a hook-up with one of the many affluent women at the party. His eyes crinkled in delight at Luke.

"About time!" He nudged Keara, who rolled her eyes, but bundled her oversized ball gown skirt and moved over for Luke to sit between them. "Where have you been?"

The question was meant as a conversation starter, but Luke bristled anyway. "I was running an errand for Granddad." He dropped down in the empty space next to Perry, and the crinkles on his cousin's face lessened a bit.

"Where's Dee and Aeron?" Keara asked, picking at her cuticles. It was going to be the question of the night. Luke scanned the crowd. Mr. Seward's absence would cause a ruffle throughout this crowd. It would be difficult to not miss his intimidating presence. Would it create doubt in the Liaisons, and who they represented? Would the FBI Liaison also be missed?

Perry nudged him. "Luke, did you hear me?"

Luke shook his head, rubbing a hand across the sore muscles in his neck. "No. Sorry. What did you say?"

A furrowed brow answered him. "Clear out guys." Perry handed Keara a hundred-dollar bill. "Grab some drinks." The ladies cleared out, Shannon's eyes lingering on Luke, but he ignored her.

Perry leaned back, crossing his arms. "What errands did you run for Granddad today?" A hint of accusation tinted his words.

Luke bristled. First his father, and now Perry, as if having a conversation with his Granddad was against some unspoken family rule. "Just an errand. He said you were on a mission and needed it done ASAP."

"You should have said no."

Luke stood up, the insinuation he couldn't handle a Legacy matter burning beneath his skin.

"Why is everyone upset that he asked me? I got it done."

The color left Perry's face. "What kind of errand did you run, Luke."

"The kind you were too busy to do." But the conviction evaporated from Luke. Secrets were not meant for family or teammates, and Perry was both.

"What happened tonight? The Sewards are missing an event like this, and your sourpuss ruining our celebration."

A chuckle barely escaped Luke and he sat back down, hands resting on the top of his head. If both his father and Perry were worried…

"I think I messed up."

"He called you in for a top-priority case. No one else could do it."

Luke shook his head, disgusted at his own naiveness. It happened exactly like that. "Basically."

"But you completed it. So, what's the problem?"

Trusting Perry had always been a no-brainer. They were closer than most siblings, even after Perry's father died and Granddad's attention zoned in on him.

"Whatever it is, don't beat yourself up. I failed my first test. You're supposed to fail the first test, but it sounds like you passed."

"I guess I did." The weight lifted from him a bit. Aeron and Decius were safe, and his Granddad thought he'd taken out a Liaison on his own. Nowhere to really go from here but up.

Perry's heavy hand clapped on his back. "I'm out of here tonight, and then this rag-tag bunch is yours to run. You've got new blood coming in, right? Focus on making the team strong and keeping them safe. I've done the dual role of Legacy heir and Team-Lead. I'll keep your seat next to me warm while you finish training. Trust me?"

The weight lifted from his chest. "Always."

"Good. Now let's go find the ladies, and toast to mine and Keara's graduation from this hellhole and our free dive into the Underworld."

5

AERON

*A*eron launched herself out of the backseat before the Navigator shifted into park. She slammed the door, funneling her outrage into the inanimate object.

Decius followed suit. "Hey!"

She pulled her arm out of range, his fingertips glancing off her elbow, and headed for the silver Lexus parked at the far end of their ten-car garage.

A firmer hand clamped around her bicep, jerking her around. "Where do you think you're going?"

"Anywhere but here." She tried to tug away, panic threatening to grip her as his hand tightened.

"There's no protection for you beyond these walls." He waved his hand around him, as if she was dense and didn't understand his meaning.

Aeron wanted to say there was no protection within them, but that wasn't true. Decius was there. "I don't need your protection."

"Then you should be sure not to leave this behind." He pulled her dagger from his belt and held the dull golden hilt to her. The vision of ramming it forward into his chest flitted through her mind, but he'd be expecting that, and she could already anticipate at least three different counters from their position. She ripped her arm free, took the weapon, and continued toward the Lexus, her heart hammering.

It could have been a scripted scene they were told to improv. The last four years she'd left without setting foot inside the manor. The first time, she'd been serious about leaving, only the team bringing her back. But each year after that, her father just let her go. His footsteps retreated toward the manor, and she took a deep breath, coming up to her getaway car.

Decius leaned against the front fender. "Aeron…"

"Decius…"

"At least wait until the morning, we haven't even been home five minutes."

"Three minutes longer than I need to be here."

He ran hands down his wrinkled shirt. "At least clean up those cuts and get something on those burns."

"I'll do it when I get where I'm going."

"And the blood on your hands?"

She didn't know if he meant figuratively or literally, but the fact he wouldn't meet her eyes paused her. An aggravated sigh left her. She tucked the dagger into her belt. "You look like a sad puppy."

He dropped his voice. "You're going to be close to the state line. At least try not to look like you were involved in a murder."

Of course. Her destination sat near the Connecticut/New York State line, out of bounds for Legacy Blood, and too close to the Legacy's Reapers for Decius' comfort. His overprotectiveness pushed aside the ache to be already gone. Aeron pried the dried bar of soap from the counter; it stung as it touched the open cuts. She ignored his silent stare as she scrubbed the stuck blood from her nail bed. Shaun's blood. A shiver ran down her spine.

"I'm not staying," she said, breaking the growing tension.

"I know."

"I'll be safe."

"I know."

She dried her hands on the stiff oil-stained rag hanging off the sink. An extra pair of clothes waited for her in the nearby closet, where she kept mechanic jumpsuits. But every second spent on the family property gave her father the opportunity to change his mind and stop her from leaving.

"This is the last home training before I'm full Legacy. I was hoping we could spend it like the good old days."

She looked up. What she wouldn't do to pretend they were twelve years old again and could run amuck at the town lake—maybe in the bars this time. "He would never let us. It'll be strict training for you. Threats of disownment for me. Being here—it's a constant reminder I'm never going to make it into the Legacy. My days are numbered, Dee."

"If you stayed, he'd see you're serious about wanting it." He hadn't raised his voice, but the words stung like he had. She wanted to be claimed, to take on the Legacy of the Seward's. To be an unseen hero.

"I'll see you, Dee." She patted his arm and offered a half smile.

He swallowed back the words she could see straining to come out and nodded, his hands tucked under his arms. The car purred to life, and she looked to him to open the garage door, ignoring the twinge of guilt bubbling in her gut. He knew this was going to happen. The metal track rattled above, and they exchanged a small nod. It was better this way. Safer, for both of them.

Aeron lifted her foot from the gas pedal, the Lexus slowing down as she rounded a bend on the long stretch of winding backroads. But there was no need, the spot where town cops normally camped out was empty, and she revved the engine again. One downfall of not driving a Legacy car meant she was subject to the same traffic laws as everyone else. The upside was, she couldn't be tracked.

As the wheels turned onto a gravel parking lot and the faded red barn came into view, a weight eased from her shoulders. She parked behind the barn, and cut the engine, taking several deep breaths before getting out.

The back door banged open. The outside light flickered on before she'd closed the car door. Aeron smiled, the cuts on her face protesting. Ernie's frame dominated the doorway, both arms sleeved with tattoos, and a large grease-covered hand holding the screen door open. His gut stuck out more than it did a year ago, and his salted-brown hair sported more grays than she remembered.

His wide blue eyes faltered her smile as he scanned her face, eyeing the fresh welts on her wrists and raw red skin on her arm. His lip twitched when he took stock of her outfit, and she looked down at the ripped and bloody shirt. Maybe she should have changed.

He closed the distance before she could and scooped her into a hug. "It is so good to see you."

She hugged him back as tight as she could and buried her face in his dirty, oil-stained shirt. He smelled like home.

He brushed a finger over her temple, and she winced in pain. "Let's get some ice on that, yeah?"

Aeron released a hiccupped laugh and nodded, wiping off her wet face before letting Ernie lead her inside. The farmhouse was a stark contrast to the manor. Warm, full of home-cooked meals, NPR on the radio, and mismatched furniture worn from use. Rita smiled from the stove, her dull brown hair tied in a messy bun at the nape of her neck, glasses fogging as she stirred a pot of fresh meatballs.

"Welcome home," Rita said.

Aeron offered a smile and plopped into one of the five empty mismatched wooden kitchen chairs, all of which should have been filled. Ernie placed two cups of steaming tea on the table.

"Here." He sat down next to her and handed over a bag of ice and ointment for her burns.

"What happened to the crew?" she asked, putting the ice on her temple and eyeing the empty spaces at the table. She'd take care of the burns upstairs.

"Rob was picked up for grand theft auto. We lost Cecile to a shoot-out a few months back. Zachary needed to settle up some debts up North."

Damn. Aeron liked Cecile. She reminded her of the new recruits at the Institute, eager, righteous, a little naive to the actual dangers of their lifestyle. And Zachary, well he'd been nice eye candy to have around.

Rita brought over two bowls of spaghetti and meatballs, and Aeron abandoned the ice to dig into the homemade food. The meatballs melted as she took a bite. The pasta was cooked to perfection. Proper diet is important for functionality of the body, but Rita's cooking was divine.

A voice behind her interrupted the meal. "I see you brought your appetite. Do they not feed you at the whorehouse you escaped from?"

Aeron choked on a piece of meatball. Tommy. If anyone could have been picked up or killed, it should have been him. He materialized from the stairwell, brown hair damp and blue eyes narrowed. She wanted to knock the smirk off his cocky face.

"Enough," Ernie said before Aeron could respond.

"Welcome home, prodigal daughter." Tommy bowed, shooting a dark look beneath his brows.

"It's nice to be home." She returned to her food, feeling less hungry than a few minutes ago.

"Where are you coming from?" Rita asked, eyes drifting to her wrists. The appeal of Ernie's was no one needed to know, or cared, where she came from. They asked very few questions about what condition she turned up in. There was only concern in the question —no expectation to spill her guts.

Aeron shrugged. "Nowhere impressive." She finished her food in silence, taking in every creak of the old building, the annoying slurps Tommy made every time he took a sip of soda, and the way Ernie's eyes barely left her, concern etched in every wrinkle.

With a full stomach, exhaustion seeped in. "I'm gonna shower and turn in. You didn't use all the hot water, did you?" she asked, pausing behind Tommy's chair.

"Wouldn't dream of it, Princess."

It would be so easy to snap his neck. She shook her hands instead and smiled at Ernie and Rita. They returned it with real smiles, the kind that crinkled their eyes and silently screamed they were glad she returned to them. She swallowed around the knot wanting to crawl up her throat. "Night, guys."

A rap on wood startled Aeron awake. The sweet smell of pine trees and motor oil greeted her senses, and she took several deep breaths. The knock sounded again.

She sat up, muscles aching. The patchwork quilt fell aside, the chilly air creeping in. "Who is it?" she called, a yawn accompanying it. She couldn't remember the last time she slept so soundly.

"Mason."

The restful feeling evaporated. "Just a sec."

She jumped up, and headed for the door, her bare feet protesting the cold hardwood beneath them. She crossed her arms, and paused, looking down at her sports bra and shorts. An appropriate outfit for training, but not for answering the door for her Guardian. She back peddled to the bed, tossing the quilt aside until she found the oversized T-shirt, and pulled it on.

She opened the door. Mason leaned against the frame, his black hair wild and his standard ripped jeans and gray t-shirt in place.

"You usually give me a few weeks before you show up," Aeron huffed, closing the door behind him. He moved to the center of the room, eyes always scanning. A queen bed took up the majority of the space, and a small desk with a faded wooden a chair served as a nightstand. This dingy bedroom was her safe haven, away from the Legacy—as away from the Legacy as a blood-member could get, and Mason ensured she stayed off the grid and away from her father.

"Hello to you too," he retorted, walking past her. "You were missing from the Gala last night. If it was just you…eh. But the whole squad?" He turned to face her, his brown eyes zeroing in on the fresh bruises on her face and wrists. "And it looks like I had good reason. Did your father…"

"No," she answered, but looked at them too. The redness had lessened, and scabs now decorated the area.

He shook his head. "You didn't have an active assignment, and when you left the boardroom yesterday morning you didn't have these." He reached out to inspect her wrists, and Aeron complied, his rough hands checking her injuries.

"Would you believe me if I said things got a bit kinky between the time we left you and before the gala?" She smirked, but his disapproving look lessened it.

"What happened?"

She pulled her hands back and took a seat on the bed. "I can't tell you."

His lips thinned. "Is it in connection with why you weren't at the Gala last night?"

She could lie to a lot of people—her life depended on her executing lies with perfection, but they would never get past Mason. So, she changed the subject.

"Since you're here early, does that mean you have an assignment for me?"

Mason dropped the topic too. "No. But here's an insane thought

—just stay here. It's a rare opportunity you have here to disengage. Take it."

"I'm ready to go," Aeron insisted. Shaun's death still buzzed through her system, and she didn't want to sit with it just yet.

His eyes flicked to her wrists, and he tapped his temple where her cut sat. "Even if I agreed, it wouldn't be until those heal up." She hated that he was right. He moved to leave, but turned back.

"Are you in trouble, Aeron?"

"Not yet," she answered, the heated conversation between Luke's father and her own resurfacing.

His eyes circled the room. "I keep your secrets. This secret, and any other you ask me to. It's my job to keep you safe. To keep all of you safe."

"I know."

"I can't do that if you lie to me."

She nodded, swallowing back the words wanting to spring out.

"I slid into Ernie's life to protect you. We could both be burned for this."

"My father didn't do this," she reiterated. On occasion, training sessions with her father went harder than what Mason deemed acceptable. A fine line existed between training hard and training dangerously.

"Then who, Aeron?" He came back over to her, the desk chair leaving scuff marks across the floor as he spun it. He sat down facing her, elbows on knees leaning in. "Sewards missing from the Gala. You showing up here like this? Not to mention the Legacy is up in arms over the death of the FBI Liaison."

"That was me," she whispered, the words slipping out before she could stop them—but she didn't want to stop them. "I killed Shaun."

"Excuse me?" Mason's eyes doubled in size.

"Luke and Decius called for backup. I went and was able to get in and execute." Her heart pounded in her throat. Why did she tell him?

"You killed Shaun?" He sat back, still staring. Not much surprised Mason, and a small balloon of pride began to stir in her chest, but was he impressed with her or shocked?

She continued. "It didn't go as planned. The FBI showed up before I could leave. I was pretty sure I was done. And then my father showed up. He and John were furious."

Mason dragged a scarred hand through his hair, the strands bouncing back in place. "Rightfully so. That wasn't sanctioned. Senior?"

Aeron nodded. She shouldn't be telling him any of this, but she also shouldn't be anywhere near the state line. "Luke said his granddad wanted to send a message about insubordination…I don't know." She released a long breath.

"Aeron—you must stay out of Wayward family business. You could have been burned last night."

She met his eyes, the irritation that surfaced when her father had said the same thing didn't resonate this time. Instead, the reality of what could've happened sank in. The risk factor of getting caught at Ernie's and burned was slim to none. Her father didn't look for her, and Mason kept wandering eyes elsewhere. But getting caught and burned by the FBI? She shuddered.

"How could Luke be so reckless?"

"He couldn't have known," she defended. "He would never…"

"I know." Mason nodded, but a pit in Aeron's stomach wasn't eased. "We need you to keep a low profile then—ah-ah!" He cut off her protests. "We'll get you back into the game when you return to the Institute."

"But—"

"I'm not bringing you into the city on the heels of Shaun's death. Even with our facial recognition and recoding software, good old-fashioned police work still comes out on top sometimes. We can't risk it."

He was right. But that didn't stop her from groaning. "Fine."

He headed for the door again, a little more weight on him than when he'd entered. "It was Luke's assignment from Senior?"

"Yes."

"But you executed?"

"I did." She caught the pride cross his face, the balloon in her chest filled again.

"Good job," he said and left.

6

LUKE

*Y*elling reverberated down the hall to Luke's room. He sat up, heart jumpstarting him awake as he strained to hear the words. His feet hit the ground and he fought the sheets from around his waist, mumbled swears leaving him. He couldn't make out the words, but if someone was yelling—he froze by the closed door.

"I'm done with it, John! It's been twenty-two years! Twenty-two years! We swore it would never come to this. We've failed twice already." It took a moment to realize it was his mother's voice, and he swallowed hard as his father yelled back.

"Then go! Bring her home if you think it would help." His voice cracked with emotion, and silence followed for a few moments before Luke realized their voices had dropped too low to hear. He cracked the door open.

"How?"

"We will figure out a way. Come here," his father's soft voice answered, and although Luke couldn't see them, he knew his father had pulled her in, while his mother's eyes closed, her ear pressed against his chest. Luke imagined just the sound of his father's heartbeat calmed her.

Steady footsteps came down the hall, and he stepped back seconds before someone knocked.

"Luke? Are you up?" His mother pushed the door open. He hadn't reached the bed yet, and his face flushed.

"I wasn't—"

"It's fine. Not the way I like to start my morning." She smiled. "We have some issues we need to discuss. Come join us." Luke followed, his mouth dry.

His dad stood at the kitchen counter. "Coffee?"

"Sure. What's going on?"

"We need to talk about what happened with your Granddad." His dad handed him a steaming mug of black coffee. "And what it means going forward."

Luke put down his mug. He'd forgotten last night—that Decius and Aeron had not come home to their Institute family residence, but instead returned to the family manor. That he'd set into motion something…but what?

"Why would Granddad ask me to do something so catastrophic? I mean, if eliminating Shaun Brink is that big of a hit…why?"

"That's what we're going to find out," his mom added. "A family meeting has been called. Eat something and get dressed."

He nodded and picked up the coffee mug, the contents not much cooler, and took a sip. His mouth tasted awful, the coffee coating the morning breath. He kept sipping until the coffee was the only taste. He should be proud that he accomplished the task—outsourcing or not. But a family meeting…the last time a family meeting was held was after Uncle Paul had died, to reallocate funds and responsibilities. And before that…he couldn't even remember.

Luke sat outside the boardroom. Apparently 'family meeting' did not actually include him. He sat on the floor in the marbled hallway across from the door, legs splayed out in front of him. The boardroom was fully secured, not a sound in or out. He leaned his head against the wall. What were Aeron and Decius doing right now? Training? Traveling? Their plan had been to travel abroad together after the Gala, to the Maldives. They should be laying out on the beach.

The elevator at the end of the hall pinged. There were a limited amount of people who had access to this floor of the Institute, and on some days it varied. Like today, only Wayward's were allowed access to the boardroom, and the only other Wayward's not here were Perry and his mom, Aunt Betty.

Luke looked toward Perry and gave a half smile as he stepped into the hall. "What's happening?"

"I wish I knew," Luke answered. "I was asked to wait out here. That was an hour ago. I feel like a damned toddler."

"Enjoy it," Perry said, sitting next to him. "Two or twenty-two, if Granddad's attention isn't on you, it's a good day. Want to tell me what happened?"

Luke dropped his head back again. "No." He didn't know where to start, or what his parents were telling Granddad. The knot in his gut wouldn't leave, however. Something bad waited just around the corner, he was sure of it.

The elevator pinged again. Luke snapped his gaze down the hall. Aunt Betty never left the family compound. If she was here...

Two women stepped off the elevator. The older one looked vaguely familiar, her brown hair pulled into a loose braid over her shoulder. She had a narrow face, sharp features, and her eyes... they were the same soft shade of brown as Perry's father's. The younger woman, who could only be a few years older than Luke, maybe twenty-five, had fiery red hair, with a full face, and softer features. But it didn't hide the gait or the way her gaze analyzed Luke in the same way.

Perry tensed beside him as the women approached. "I thought this was a family only meeting," Luke whispered.

Perry didn't answer. The older woman ignored them both,

approaching the boardroom doors.

"This is a family meeting. You'll have to come back later," Luke offered, standing up. The elevator may have glitched, but the boardroom would not. "I can pass a message along for you if you would like."

She looked over her shoulder at him and winked, before allowing the eye scanner to read her retina. The door clicked open. Raised voices escaped the room, and Luke's curiosity about who these women were faded.

"...need more time!"

"It's already been decided. The order is out."

As the door pushed open, the conversation halted. A gasp reached him. "Rosemary?"

"This is your grand plan?" his mother asked. "*This?*"

"So good to see you too, Mary." The door closed behind her.

The younger woman dropped to the floor next to Perry and leaned against his shoulder with a familiarity that stung.

"Guess the cat is out of the bag," she said, peering forward. "Hi, Luke. I'm Katherine, your cousin. Nice to meet you."

"I'm sorry, what?" Luke stepped away from the wall and stared down at them. He didn't have any other family. He couldn't have any other family. He turned to Perry for clarification.

"Her mom is...was?...my dad's twin. They've lived in D.C. Kind of the black sheep of the family."

Katherine cracked a smile. "Who you calling a black sheep?"

Perry bumped her shoulder and laughed.

"Okay..." Luke's mind spun. How had he never heard of them? What the hell have they been up to? D.C. was a no-zone for the Legacy. He settled on, "Why are you here?"

The door to the conference room opened before she answered. Rosemary smirked at Luke again as she strutted to the elevator. He shivered. Something about her set his defenses on high guard. Katherine scurried to her feet and followed.

"That was quick," she said.

"We're taking a field trip." Their Granddad exited next, Perry following suit to his feet. "Come, Luke."

Luke looked to his parents for reassurance, because after the debacle last night… he needed it. They nodded. The ride to the parking garage beneath the building was silent, each Wayward standing with their back to a wall of the elevator. The air was tense with unspoken words, but Luke didn't dare break the silence. In terms of where he fell on the family hierarchy, he was right at the bottom, and further down than he thought.

When they reached the parking garage, no one moved. Katherine sighed with annoyance. "Are we just standing here or…"

Granddad smirked. "After you."

Katherine nodded and stepped off first. Perry immediately followed, and Luke moved next, the instinct to follow his lead a knee-jerk reaction.

"Where are we headed?" Luke asked Perry.

"No clue."

"We're returning to the family compound." His mother came up next to him as they walked to the car.

"What about what happened with Shaun?" Luke shivered. He wanted to check on Aeron and Decius, he'd dragged them into the shitshow, they shouldn't be in trouble.

"It's why Rosemary is back. She'll be stepping in for the moment. No harm, no foul. Why don't you drive with Perry?"

His gut twisted again. "I'd rather drive with you, honestly."

"I think this would be a great opportunity for Perry to bring you up to speed on your Aunt Rosemary and cousin." She looked to Perry. His face darkened and he nodded.

"Yeah, of course. C'mon Luke, do I have a story for you." Perry headed to a Navigator, identical to all the other SUVs. Luke glanced back over his shoulder, but his parents were already strapped in their car. He begrudgingly hopped into the passenger side, and to his dismay, Katherine got into the back seat.

"What the hell." He spun around. "Who are you?"

She smirked from the back seat, arms crossed. She looked so much like Shannon. It was unnerving.

Perry hefted a sigh as he followed the other two cars out of the parking lot. "There is a lot to catch you up on."

"No there's not," Katherine said. "My mother moved to D.C. right out of the Institute, took a job with the government. Has had limited contact with the family until recently. She thought it best to keep her distance."

Luke didn't buy it. "How do you know Perry?"

"We came home for his dad's funeral, and Granddad thought it would be a good idea to meet."

He didn't believe a word that came out of her mouth. "Perry?"

"Yeah. That's pretty much it." He kept his eyes focused on the road. They were turning on to the highway. "It's not that big of a deal, honestly."

It seemed like a big deal. Every Legacy Blood member was always accounted for. Always tracked. No matter where they were, the Legacy could get to them. So how did two members of the reigning Legacy family just go off the map? Maybe it was because they were part of the reigning family.

"Oh shit!" Perry hit the brakes. Their vehicle swerved hard, Luke braced onto his seat, slamming into the door. The SUV in front of them flipped.... Once, twice, three times. Luke's heart pounded in his throat. That was his parents' car. He fought against the locked seat belt to unclip it, and threw his door open. Cars swerved around them on the interstate, horns blaring. He moved toward the crumpled vehicle, and two hands grasped him from behind. He fought against Katherine's arms, throwing elbows and twisting out of her grip.

He had to get to his parents.

Perry's hands shoved him back, but he kept pressing forward. A hard tug from behind brought him to the ground and dragged him behind the car door as a muffled blast rocked their car. Two bodies covered him, debris showering down on them.

7

AERON

"Hey, Princess."

Aeron looked up at Tommy from the wires she'd been stripping. She took Mason's forced advice and picked a project to work on. The complete focus it took to disassemble and rebuild engines kept her mind too busy to think about, well anything.

Aeron didn't answer. They had an unspoken rule to stay out of each other's way. She trusted him enough to do a job with him for Ernie, but not enough to sleep without her knife within reach—although to be fair she never slept without it in reach. She returned to the Impala's bad wiring without responding.

"I need to run into the city for a job."

"Okay." Did he want a medal? She'd weld him one just so she could work in peace.

"I need backup. You up for it?"

Aeron put the pliers down and tilted her head toward him. Nothing he said could convince her to do a job with him, and definitely not one in the city.

"No."

"What?"

She took a deep breath before picking her pliers back up. "No. I don't do jobs in the city, and you know that. Find someone else."

"There is no one else."

She caught the slump in his shoulders, and against her better judgement, she called out, "Wait." She stood, wiping greasy hands on her jumpsuit. "I'm not promising anything, but help me with this car, and I'll hear you out."

"What are we working on?"

"A custom rebuild. '67 Impala. It's not too bad, but I'm pretty sure the wiring has been eaten by mice."

"Let me see."

Aeron sat back as Tommy leaned into the driver seat. "Good thing is it doesn't run on a fancy computer. Makes this an easier rebuild." He dug around under the dashboard, tugging on wires.

"No shit, Sherlock."

He glared at her, and she smirked back.

"You work the wiring, and I'll work on the engine."

"Whatever you say, Princess."

The hours flew by, hip-hop blasting in the background at Tommy's request, the small T.V. in the corner muted for her. Flashing on the screen pulled her gaze up. The footage of a highway wreckage was gone and replaced with breaking news: 'FBI Director under investigation for death of staff'.

A chill rocked her body as Shaun's photo appeared in the upper corner, a professional picture in a suit and straight face, contrary to the smile he usually wore. Moments flickered through her mind, his laugh, lying in bed watching a movie, the snap of his neck beneath her fingers. Her eyes shut, trying to shake the memory—it wasn't allowed to surface here. Not at Ernie's.

The picture faded from Shaun to the Director, a snapshot of him avoiding the cameras. She scanned the crowd around him, picking out the Legacy members easily enough—expensive clothing, perfect postures, eyes that never stopped scanning.

Tommy moved to look at the TV too. "Always some scandal happening."

"Yeah," she answered, not really listening to him. Luke's dad said they'd fucked up. How badly had they fucked up?

"So, about this job…"

She faced him. "It's late. I'm going to finish up the car and we can talk about it tomorrow."

She expected an argument, but he met her stubborn gaze with cool understanding. "No problem."

Aeron expelled a long breath, eyes falling on the Impala they'd worked on. She could get a few more pieces of the engine out tonight.

She slipped into the rhythm of removing the mounting brackets, the wrench's rhythmic clicking filled the silence. She stilled at the sound of tires on gravel, heart pounding in her throat. The side door opened. Her grasp on the wrench adjusted to throw at a moment's notice. It was no knife, but it would buy a few seconds to grab the dagger from her boot.

Ernie's blue eyes peered from the dark, easing the knot in her throat.

"Good finds at the junkyard?" Aeron asked.

"Yeah. Brought home a '77 Z28?"

She let out a low whistle. "You're finally finishing up Bertha?"

"Let's hope so."

"Let me get this engine out, and I'll help you move it around back."

"No, no. I've got it." He grabbed a toolbox before heading back out.

She returned to cranking the wrench, the mounting brackets almost out. She should have known it was Ernie. No one would be looking for her.

A sharp rap on the door startled her. Aeron's hand slipped, slamming into the engine.

"Son of a bitch." She stuck the bleeding knuckle into her mouth and pushed the long curls out of her face.

"I guess if you live around the scum long enough, you begin to talk like them."

She spun, heart hammering in her windpipe. The side door stood ajar, a figure just outside blotting the light.

"I'm sorry," she called, voice wavering. "We're closed for the night."

He chuckled and stepped inside the garage, freezing Aeron in her tracks. Her father's dark form materialized from the shadows, his black slacks and long-sleeved shirt moving in the breeze.

"You're not happy to see me." He crossed his arms.

She swallowed hard. "How'd you find me?"

He ignored the question. "It's time to come home."

"No."

"I've allowed this long enough, now really." He reached a hand toward her. "Let's go."

"Go where?" Ernie appeared behind her father. Although her father's tall and lean frame seemed dwarfed next to Ernie's massive muscles, Ernie wouldn't stand a chance.

Her father turned and extended his hand. "Good evening. You must be Ernie."

Ernie eyed the hand, but didn't accept. Instead, he walked around and placed himself between her and the uninvited guest.

"What do you want?"

"I came to have a word with Aeron." His eyes glinted with danger, shooting past Ernie to Aeron. Daring her to say no.

Ernie's voice dropped low. "Who the hell are you?"

Her father's patience wouldn't last long. She brushed Ernie's arm before he could reach for the monkey wrench leaning against the closest toolbox. He looked back and she gave a slight shake of her head.

"I'm not going with you, Dad." She avoided Ernie's burning look and kept her eyes locked on her father, waiting for any sign of movement.

"You're leaving here one way or another."

"You heard her," Ernie said, grabbing the monkey wrench. "She's not going."

Her father's gaze didn't waver, but she saw the slight upturn at the corners of his mouth.

Aeron touched the cold metal in Ernie's hand, and he looked over. She shook her head again.

"I'm not letting this sorry excuse for a man come in here and—"

"And what?" Her father's voice slid out low and dangerous. "Come and take what is mine? I'd like to see you stop me."

Her gut plummeted. "I'm not yours. You've made that plainly clear the last twenty years."

"You don't have to go anywhere with him." Ernie placed a comforting hand on her shoulder. It was all the invitation her father needed.

He sprung forward. Aeron shoved Ernie aside, taking the brunt of the attack. She hit the concrete, the breath escaping her. She scrambled to her feet and crouched, waiting for the next attack.

"Stay back, Ernie," she warned.

"Like hell I will." He stepped in front of her again. Her father wasted no time striking at him. Ernie fended off the blows and Aeron watched in amazement as Ernie, strong but not necessarily fit, held his own against her deadly skilled father. She kept her distance, but Ernie would not last much longer. He shouldn't have even lasted this long—her father was playing with him. She picked up the forgotten monkey wrench and readied herself. Ernie's face was red and his breath labored, each block he offered barely covered his head in time. Her father changed tactics and aimed for the legs.

A resounding crack stopped all movement. A scream left Ernie as he dropped to the floor. Aeron leapt over his twisting body and swung the wrench. Her father stepped just out of reach and smirked. "Really?"

She abandoned the heavy weapon and landed a hook to his jaw. His head snapped to the side and her hand slid off his face. He grabbed it, pulling her forward, but she countered, breaking free. He attacked again and she moved in sync with the blows, left arm, right knee, right arm, duck. The technique was sluggish, but it kept enough distance between them so he couldn't get a grip on her shirt.

He backed her up against the Impala and she placed her hand in the open window, pushing herself on to the top of the car. Her feet had barely planted on the roof before they were swept from beneath her.

"Uh," she grunted, landing hard.

His steel grip wrapped her ankle. A well-aimed kick to his chest sent him back a few paces, and a smirk lit his face. Sweat dripped into her eyes, he was playing with her too. He could finish this fight in an instant. With feet beneath her again, she glanced to Ernie. He sat propped against the giant toolbox, a shot gun in his hand.

"Ernie, no!"

Her father pulled the pistol from his waist and aimed it at her, his eyes glued on Ernie.

"I'm a much faster shot, I promise."

"Ernie, put it down, please," she pleaded, wiping blood from her lip.

"No." Sweat dripped from his pale brow.

"We need to get you help," she countered.

"He's fine." Her father waved a hand in Ernie's direction. "It's a clean break. He'll live. Now you, are coming with me."

"Why?" she asked.

"Do I need a reason?"

She glared in response. Showing up here had been a power move, and she wasn't going to bend the knee that easily.

He changed tactics. "Do you know who she is?" he asked Ernie.

"She's trusted you with her real name—quite an achievement. But do you really know where she comes from? Who she comes from?" He walked over and squatted next to him.

Ernie glared. "From the bruises she appears with, I can only expect a jackass with no respect for women or children," he said, spitting at her father's feet.

The humor drained from her father's eyes. A knot tightened in her stomach as he leaned in close. "She is the daughter of one of the deadliest assassins on the East coast. You should check your tongue before it is ripped from your mouth."

"Dad!" Aeron begged, but he ignored her.

"I do not beat my children. I train them." He landed a hard blow with the butt of his gun to Ernie's temple, rendering him unconscious, and returned his attention to her. "Enough of this. We're leaving."

Her anger flared. How dare he show up here, disrupt everything she's built. "No." She jumped down, kicking the gun from his hand. It skidded beneath the car and she charged, the need to strike, to draw blood, to kill, the only thing in her mind.

He side-stepped the rash move. Grabbing a fistful of shirt, he swept the feet from underneath her and slammed her into the ground. She sucked in a breath, pain radiating down her spine. He dropped a heavy knee to her ribs, securing her to the ground. He became heavy and impossible to move. Struggling to find space, panic clouded her mind. It would be effortless for him to choke her unconscious and drag her back to the manor.

"Imagine if you trained like your brother. You could probably take me out."

"Shut-up," she ground out.

"Make me." The taunt stung. She hardly ever trained with him anymore.

He shifted, his knee and full weight driving into her sternum. She sucked in a breath and held it, afraid he'd crush her lungs if she didn't.

He lifted his weight enough for air to fill her lungs. His hazel eyes locked on hers. "There's been an accident."

Her breath did stop then. If Decius wasn't here... "What kind of accident? Is Decius—"

"No."

Relief raced through her body, and she was grateful he'd removed his weight. "How did you find me?" she asked, defeat creeping in.

"Tracking chip on your dagger."

Her eyes fell closed. She should have seen it when he handed back the weapon she would never shower without. Her mother's dagger. He sat back, giving her space to reach into her boot, grasping the decorative gold handle, worn smooth from years in her mother's possession. Flipping it over, the almost invisible round sticker winked at her in the crappy garage light.

"You need to come home."

"Why?"

"John and Mary are dead."

The contents of her stomach threatened to come up. "The car accident on I95."

"It was no accident." The words reverberated in her head.

"Luke—is he?"

"Alive, for now."

Relief washed over her until the recognizable sound of a shell being chambered into a shotgun stopped their conversation.

"Need a hand, Princess?" Tommy crouched next to a half-conscious Ernie, gun poised to fire.

Without hesitation, her father dropped on top of her, a shield against the glass raining down from Tommy's shot. Rage burned in his eyes.

"Dad." She tried to calm him. He snatched his gun from beneath the car. With the agility of a fox, he stood and aimed at the two men. Aeron scrambled to her feet, grabbing the back of his shirt. He was going to kill them. In one swift movement he spun, grasped her hair, and returned his aim, using Aeron as a shield.

"We're done here," he said, backing toward the door, keeping Aeron in front of him. She grabbed onto the hand tangled in her hair to release the tension and locked onto his arm, pulling it close.

"Aeron," Ernie called. She could see the distress and confusion in his face.

"Let go of me," Aeron yelled, trying to pull away. When he didn't let go, she stepped back and turned, pulling him closer and rotating her body, squeezing the arm into her, locking it in an armbar.

He released her immediately, and she stumbled forward. "We put them to rest in a few days. If you aren't there…"

She flinched. If she wasn't there, Luke would bury his parents alone.

The shotgun wavered in Tommy's grip. "You don't have to go, Princess."

"Aeron—" The word alone said everything Ernie needed to. It conveyed more affection and concern than her father had mustered most of her life.

She bit her lip, eyes jumping from her father to Ernie and Tommy. "I'm sorry, but I do. I need to go."

"He's lying," Ernie said, eyes pleading with her to stay.

She glanced back at her father, impatience clear in his stance. But the traces of bags beneath his eyes, and the fact he didn't kill them and drag her out of the garage spoke volumes.

"I'm sorry." She turned her back on them and followed her father out of the barn and toward a forest green Audi parked at the edge of the driveway. She took a final glance at the barn—to the only taste of freedom she'd known.

Anger boiled inside her, and she slammed the door. She never asked for any of this, and she sure as hell never asked to be an assassin's daughter.

"You can never come back here," he said, starting the car. "You've placed them in danger."

She crossed her arms.

"Aeron—"

"You placed them in danger," she spat. She was already in deep shit, might as well get it all out. "Why did you have to show up here like that? You could've just been normal about it. Make a phone call. Send Decius."

He pulled onto the street.

"Besides, no one will come looking for me if I'm not there. I'm not that important. I'm an unclaimed child—soon to be a name on a hit-list for SERE training."

"You're my flesh and blood—as long as you breathe, someone will always be looking for you, claimed or not."

"What is that supposed to mean?"

"It means that you can't just run away from this life, Aeron!" He slammed his hand down on the steering wheel.

"Why should I have to sacrifice what I want?"

"And what is it that you want?" No malice tainted his words, only genuine curiosity.

What did she want? Life at the garage with Ernie and Rita? She found them because she couldn't stand to be with her father. Life in the Legacy? She thrived there with Decius, Luke, and Shannon— but it came at the price of working under her father; of constantly failing no matter how hard she tried. She never failed at the garage.

"I don't know," she admitted.

"We've all made sacrifices." His voice softened as they turned toward the highway. "It's the price of this life."

"What have you ever given up?" she spat. A thick silence followed her words, and she ignored the sweat that formed on her brow. She looked over, but darkness swallowed his face.

"Dad—" she tried to rectify herself, but his answer was barely a whisper.

"Some sacrifices must remain unspoken, Aeron, or they lose their value."

8

LUKE

*L*uke's eyes remained glued to the door as mourners filed in to pay their respects. He needed to keep his gaze on anything except the black caskets behind him. Who knew so many people would show up?

A small hand tugged on him, and he glanced down. Bright blue eyes of the Finch twins, Olivia and Sarah, looked up at him. "We're very sorry, Luke."

Luke squatted down and wrapped the girls in a hug. It was hard to hold himself in check, the small girls sniffing with sadness.

"Thanks girls. Where's Ben?"

"Off with Gabe, like always." Olivia rolled her eyes, wiping her nose.

"Girls!"

Luke looked up. Shelby Finch hurried over, her husband, Joe, on her heels. Luke stood up to greet them, another Blood Family.

Joe reached out a hand, which Luke accepted. "Condolences, Luke. They were amazing people."

Luke nodded, unable to answer. The girls darted off, Shelby and Joe following after them. Luke scanned the room again, landing on Katherine.

"Hey, cuz," she said, reaching for his arm. He pulled away, hugging his arms around him. "Do you need anything before I disappear?"

"Have the Sewards arrived?" His raw throat protested the words, his voice raspy from the tantrum he'd thrown the night before, yelling and screaming in a drunken rage.

"Not that I'm aware of."

A flash of red hair at the entrance jump started his heart—Shannon. She'd know where Aeron and Decius were. Abandoning Katherine without a backward glance, his feet moved before his brain, and he stumbled through the crowd. Hands and words of sympathy slipped over him. Reaching out a shaking hand, he grabbed on to Shannon's shoulder. She spun, green eyes widening and her small arms wrapping him in a hug. He pulled her close as the weight he bore in his chest burst out, and he choked back a few sobs.

"Have you seen them?" he asked, face buried in her hair.

Her head shook beneath his chin. "They'll be here. C'mon, let's get some air."

"Aeron too?" He couldn't fathom doing this…saying goodbye to his parents…without her.

She nodded and grabbed him by the wrist. He blindly followed, gazes of peers and mentors glancing off him until the humid summer air engulfed them, but it was less stifling than the people inside. He took a few deep, painful breaths, the knives in his chest not easing.

He leaned against the cool brick wall, the deep, measured breaths filled with pain, consuming all thoughts. In. Out. In. Out. They weren't really dead. They couldn't be.

Shannon's fingers drew light circles on his shoulder. Breathe in. Breathe out.

Hurried footsteps reached Luke's ears. Decius rounded the corner and stopped short. His normally cheerful smile and mischievous eyes were nowhere in sight. The distance between them vanished and Luke was wrapped in a bone-crushing embrace.

"I'm sorry," Decius whispered. "I'm so sorry."

Luke nodded, unable to choke back the sobs as he'd done with Shannon. When they finally broke apart, Luke wiped his face. His gaze found Aeron standing behind her brother, hands tucked in the pockets of a black dress, and her long dark curls pulled into a knot on the top of her head. The intense swirl of pain ebbed the moment his eyes met hers.

"Hey." She stayed planted to the spot, chewing on her bottom lip.

A smile found its way to his face for the first time in days, and he wiped at his wet cheeks again. "You made it."

"Of course." She returned the weak smile, stretching a recent cut on her lip. He closed the distance between them, catching her chin gently and running his thumb beneath her lip, catching the small trickle of blood before it could start. She looked away, color flooding her cheeks, and pushed at his hand.

"Stop, it's nothing." Her arms wound around him, and he pulled her into his chest.

The pain for his parents pulsed into anger, and he glanced to Decius. He shook his head at Luke's silent question, mouthing *Later*. Luke nodded, returning to his deep breathing, the scent of her hair filling him, easing the torrent that churned beneath his surface.

"I'm so sorry, Lulu."

The use of her childhood nickname for him sent tingles through his body. It had been years since she'd called him that. She squeezed him again and let go. He reluctantly dropped his arms and stepped back, stuffing his hand in his pockets.

"Thanks for coming guys," Luke said.

"I'm sorry we couldn't be here earlier." Shannon placed her arm across Aeron's shoulder. The sight further lightened Luke's heavy heart, and he managed a small nod. His parents might be dead, but he still had a family right here.

Perry rounded the corner, stopping short at the group. "They're waiting for you."

Luke nodded, but his feet seemed cemented to the ground.

"C'mon." Decius wrapped an arm around his shoulders, giving a reassuring squeeze.

"Yeah," Luke agreed, a deep breath fueling his courage. "Let's do this."

A mass of people crammed inside every corner of the Wayward ballroom. Two walls of people dressed in black highlighted the only path forward; toward his parents' caskets. His feet refused to move. Decius' arm urged him forward.

"I can't do this," Luke whispered. "I'm not ready."

"Yes, you can." Aeron gazed up, her arm looped through his. "We won't leave you."

With his two best friends at his side, Luke started the tortuous walk toward the front of the hall, all eyes on them until they took the designated seats in the front. Aeron's fingers slipped through his and held tight.

The service lasted an eternity, and Luke didn't hear a single word of what people said in honor of his parents. He did know that Aeron's right hand had at least seven small scars and a handful of fresh cuts across the knuckles as if she'd been in a fight just yesterday.

Her hand slipped from his. Luke looked up—they were in the family cemetery behind the house.

"Where are you going?" Panic rose in his chest.

"Your granddad wants just the family right now. I'm not going far—I'll be right behind you."

He'd rather she stood across from him but nodded as she walked away, her hand trailing up his arm as she passed. Perry took her place.

"It gets better," he said.

Luke ignored him. Without Aeron by his side, nothing could distract from the black caskets now poised over the open ground, waiting to swallow them whole. He couldn't see the bottom of the hole from this angle. How did they dig so deep?

A slight shove jerked Luke's attention away from the gaping hole. He looked up. Perry held two roses out to him. He took them, glancing around confused. The roses—the caskets—he'd missed the final words. It was time to send his parents off. The few steps forward seemed lightyears away. He placed the first roses on the caskets, opening the procession, each dropping another rose and offering words of condolences he couldn't process.

His hands remained on the caskets as they began to dip into the ground and he crouched until a chill assaulted his hand as they fell out of reach.

"C'mon, man. You need to at least move from between them, or you are going to get knocked in." Decius yanked him to his feet. Luke's legs nearly gave out, and Decius supported him to the end of the rectangular spaces.

They plopped to the ground, Luke dropping his head between his knees and grabbing the back of his neck. How did this happen?

He surveyed the cemetery, generations of Wayward's laid to rest. He should be laid to rest with them. He should have been in that car.

His gaze found Jack, the groundskeeper, standing near the trunk of a massive oak tree, shovel in hand. "What is he doing?" He clambered to his feet. "What are you doing?" Luke called out.

"I'm waiting to fill the graves, Sir," Jack answered.

The words rebounded off of him. "Excuse me?"

"Your parents were the most generous people I knew. They deserve more than a machine dropping dirt on them."

Luke's voice caught in his throat, unable to say anything.

"Do you have extra shovels?" Decius asked. Jack nodded, retrieving two more from the truck. "C'mon." He pulled Luke to his feet.

The three of them worked in silence. Each scoop of dirt into the never-ending hole filling the void in his chest only a smidgen. Time stood still until the ground finally leveled off, the world suddenly dark around them. Luke leaned against the shovel, his breath coming in short bursts.

"My deepest condolences for your loss, Mr. Wayward—"

"Luke. Please call me Luke."

"If you need anything at all, Luke, I'm here. Please don't hesitate."

"Thanks," Decius said for him, as the words refused to leave Luke's mouth, and he only managed a curt nod. They were soon alone again, and Luke took a seat, the shovel falling to the side.

"I forgot to give him back his shovel."

"I'm sure he doesn't mind. Just leave it there; he'll find it in the morning."

He nodded, not giving the shovel a second thought. The fresh dirt mounds pulled the darkness from around him, encapsulating every fear he ever had. Being locked in a burning building—waking up to a locked empty house—losing a teammate in a mission—his parents dying before he had the chance to have his own children. Each a very real possibility in their lifestyle. But dying like they had —not even on official business, but in a stupid car accident—never crossed his mind.

"I'm going to find Aeron. You'll be alright?"

Luke nodded, the quiet dead around bringing stillness to his mind. People could believe the dead were at peace. But the dead weren't quiet—they were silenced—suppressed beneath the pounds of dirt to keep their secrets from surfacing. What secrets now lay beneath his feet?

9

AERON

*A*eron found Luke sitting beside his parents' grave, right where Decius said he'd be.

The ceremony ended hours ago, the grievers and gawkers long since departed. Aeron slipped off her heels and walked through the grass, taking a seat beside his still form.

"Luke," she said softly, "you can't stay out here all night."

"Why not?" Luke's raspy voice tugged at her.

Yeah. Why not?

"Did you know they stayed with me? The first night we moved back to the family compound when I was eight?" He squeezed his eyes shut. "I couldn't sleep without the sound of the city. They slept in my room. They stayed with me."

Her chest tightened. "Would you like me to get some pillows? Hot chocolate? Whiskey?"

He gave a small laugh, but it didn't reach his eyes.

"Just stay with me?" The words broke, and he dropped his head.

"Of course." She reached across his shoulders, and he leaned in. The silence surrounded them as his tears seeped into her dress. She closed her eyes, her own tears falling.

"Aeron."

Aeron's eyes shot open at the slight touch to her shoulder. She reached up, grabbing a fistful of fabric, and pulled it in close.

"Hey," a familiar voice whispered. "It's me."

Releasing the death grip, she blinked the sluggishness from her eyes. The dawn light barely peeked from behind her brother, leaving his light brown face in shadow.

"Dad's looking for you," he said, squatting beside her. A chill flooded her veins—she'd been out all night. "I told him you were keeping Luke company, while I ran inside to grab some coffee, but..."

She nodded. He put the cups of coffee down to help her up. The first rays of sunshine brushed his face, accenting the dark circles beneath his eyes. "You stayed up all night?"

"I didn't want him to find you out here alone, but Luke didn't need me last night." She smiled in appreciation and glanced down at Luke's sleeping form. His hair stood up in every direction, and she leaned down to brush it away from his eyes.

"How did this happen?" She stood and turned to Decius. "Losing Mom was hard enough, but both?"

"You would throw a party if Dad died."

"I'd probably go to jail for being the one who did it."

Decius chuckled. "Luke's not alone, Aeron. He has us."

"I hate this life," she retorted, a swell of emotion attempting to drown her composure. She took a deep breath and hesitated before leaving.

"I'll wait with him," he said, answering her unasked question.

She picked up her shoes and brushed the dirt off her dress before heading back to the main house of the Wayward Compound. Her father stood in the rear gardens, a hushed argument passing between him and Luke's granddad.

She ran a hand over her curls, aware of how messy she

appeared, and inched forward, her bare feet masking her approach, and she caught a few words from her father.

"...who better than me, Elijah?"

"Don't be a fool, Andrew. I need you on the front lines, now more than ever."

Her father's back stiffened and she crept forward another step.

"Of course. I just thought—"

"Don't let the sacrifices be in vain. I would hate to require more of them, should our priorities not be aligned." Mr. Wayward's head snapped in her direction, a smile creasing his face, eyes twinkling. "Aeron."

Aeron continued forward to mask her eavesdropping. "Mr. Wayward. Dad."

Mr. Wayward held out an arm, and Aeron leaned in for a hug, his embrace tight. "How are you?" he asked.

"I'm well, Mr. Wayward," she answered, stepping back and smiling at him.

"My dear, on such a day like this, I'm reminded of how few I still call family, so please—it's Elijah." He slipped a hand beneath her chin and tipped her head side to side. "You look more like Maureen every day." Aeron's stomach flipped at her mother's name. "She would have been proud of you. How is Luke?"

"He'll be okay," she answered, unsure if he was looking for a status report on one of his assassins or the emotional state of his grandson.

"Good. You should join us for breakfast." With a slight nod and a glance at her father, Mr. Wayward disappeared back into the house.

Her father crossed his arms, a glare boring into her. "Where were you last night?"

"With Luke. Where else would I be?"

"Aeron, we've been over this. You cannot be involved with the Waywards."

"He's grieving. I promise you we were not rolling around on top of the fresh graves."

Her head snapped to the side. Her cheek stung where he struck, and the hair fell across her face, shielding her tears from sight.

"Aeron." The regret seeped into the soft way he said her name, but she kept her face down. "Get your brother. This is no longer a safe place for us."

"What do you mean?" She looked at him.

"We need to leave."

"Aeron?"

She jumped. Luke stood at the garden's gate, and his eyes jetted to her cheek. Aeron dropped her hand and quickly dipped her head forward, her hair covering the mark. His features darkened, and he hopped the gate, rushing toward her. "Was that your father?"

"Where?" she asked innocently and took a step away from him to look toward the house.

"Aeron!" Decius called as he ran up the hill. She looked past the hurt look on Luke's face and straight to her brother. Decius' eyes barely flicked to the rising welt before he said, "I didn't realize I got you so hard this morning when you woke me up. Keep a better guard next time, or you know…just don't wake me up."

She forced a laugh, and Luke's sour expression lightened a bit. Decius raised an eyebrow at her, and she shook her head at his concern.

"I think breakfast should be served soon. Are you hungry, Luke?" Aeron asked, her fingertips brushing his arm.

The darkness returned to his features. "No. I'm not." He pulled away and headed inside without another word. Aeron watched until his shadow was out of view. It wasn't fair to lie to him, but she couldn't burden him at the moment with the truth.

Aeron dropped onto a nearby stone bench, her head in her hands. Decius knelt in front of her and gently lifted her chin. He brushed her hair back, sucking in a breath.

Her stomach dropped. "That bad?" She winced when his thumb grazed the skin.

"Well, he had on his insignia ring. I can see the outline." Aeron looked at the identical ring which he wore. He dropped his hand and took a seat beside her. "What did you say to him?"

"Because my words are enough to warrant this?" She pointed to her cheek.

"That's not what I meant."

She released a long sigh. "I know."

Aeron endured the uncomfortable ride home to Seward Manor in complete silence. The one time Decius tried to break the tension, their father's look sliced the words before they finished forming.

She had expected a lecture to last the entire three-hour drive, but the silence made knots in her stomach. A soft snoring sounded as Decius slept against the window, a small dribble of drool escaping his mouth. She nudged Dee with her foot, rousing him as they pulled onto the family estate. Their father retired to the house without a backward glance, and they exchanged an uneasy look.

Aeron scanned the unused cars in the garage, some broken, others in need of TLC. Most had been involved in nefarious acts and therefore compromised.

"What are you thinking?" Decius asked.

"That I need to stay busy or I'm going to be dead before this training is over. Which car do you like best?"

He raised an eyebrow and looked around the room. "Um…that gray Audi over there."

"The A6?"

He nodded. "Why?"

"Want to see what I do at Ernie's?" Her stomach flipped as the suggestion came out. Life at Ernie's stayed there, untouched by her harsh reality of life. Well, at least it used to.

"Yeah. I'd like that." His smile eased her nerves.

"Does it start?"

He shook his head. Aeron didn't even change out of her dress.

She popped the hood of the Audi and began poking around. The day sped past them, and it felt almost normal. Maybe she could survive here, as long as she stayed in the garage.

"You're really good at this," he said, laying out car parts on the drop sheet as Aeron finished cleaning them.

She looked up, his genuine joy pulling her back to their childhood. "Thanks."

"Ah hem."

Aeron nearly dropped the bearing she'd been cleaning. Her father stood in the doorway, eyes surveying the mess before landing on her.

"My study."

Words couldn't form around the sick feeling rising in her throat. His expression gave nothing away before he turned and left. Not looking back at Decius, she placed the bearing down and followed him into the house. She hadn't lived at home in years, but the last time she'd disobeyed her father inside his house still haunted her dreams.

His long legs and no-nonsense gait left her far behind. By the time she caught up, he was standing beside the large bay windows in his study overlooking the family cemetery. She paused in the doorway and waited while he swirled the amber liquid in his glass without much effort. Minutes ticked by. Finally, she rapped her knuckles on the open door, waiting.

"That is the hardest part of what we do, isn't it?" His voice carried across the room, and he caught her gaze in the window's reflection. "The waiting." He turned around. "The planning can be exciting—playing a chess match with an unknowing opponent. The execution is exhilarating—the adrenaline and the power you wield. But the waiting—it's excruciating. Come in and take a seat, Aeron."

She nodded, remembering a ghost of a lecture he gave her on waiting as a child in this same room. She followed the path she'd worn into the carpet from the door to the straight back chair in front of his desk.

"Ah hem."

She looked up. He gestured toward the extravagant black couches near the fireplace. She moved to the couches and hesitated before sitting as straight as possible on the soft cushion. He refilled his glass and sunk into the oversized armchair across from her. She fought not to fidget under his unmoving stare, the cool leather less comforting than the familiarity of the hard, wooden chair, begging her to sink back and fall asleep.

She held his gaze, biting her lip against the urge to look away. With a small tilt of his chin, shadows from the fireplace contorted his features. Goosebumps spread down her arms; she averted her eyes. It was a reminder he was more than an angry, unappeasable father. He'd killed hundreds of people without a moment's hesitation.

They remained in silence as the second hand ticked on the grandfather clock.

It chimed ten.

Then eleven.

Then midnight.

She kept her eyes focused on her hands. Dirt and grease clung to her cuticles. She took deep breaths, the smell of motor oil fumes which seeped into her hair and clothes bringing her back to Ernie's. If she could hold on to the feeling of peace…

The clock chimed one, and Aeron's eyes fought to stay open. Something cold touched her cheek. Her hand shot up to grab on— an arm. Her father held a cloth napkin with ice in it. She hadn't heard him get up. He placed it against her cheek again, and she accepted it, her heart beating a mile a minute.

"I did not realize I had moved so fiercely." He reclaimed his seat across from her. "There are some things we need to discuss."

Aeron bit her inner lip, fighting back the questions and comments wanting to pour out. That was the closest he had ever come to apologizing to her. He never apologized, not for the time he'd broken her wrist—or her nose, and those had been accidents. She leaned back on the couch and adjusted the ice.

"I have about two years left to claim you as part of the Seward Legacy. Seal your life to the Legacy. However, you are also free."

She stared at him. "I don't know what that means."

"The last five years I've let you leave. You've sped out of here and I prayed you wouldn't return. I kept thinking: this is it. This is the year I pushed her hard enough, and she'll leave. Yet you always return to the New York apartment. Why?" He stared at her, the question sincere in his gaze.

"I couldn't leave Decius behind," she answered softly, although she was sure her heart thrummed louder than her voice. Did she hear him right? He wanted her to leave and never come back?

"Your mother's heart," he said, nodding his head.

Her chest constricted—it'd been years since she heard mention of her mother from him. "I had hoped that when I went down there tonight, you'd be gone again because it would have given me no other options. But—here you are."

"Dad." Her heart was going to break out from her chest. She should have left—found Mason and begged him to find her a new safe house. Was he going to incite a Legacy Hunt and turn her over to the Institute? Would he just kill her right here and be done with it? The only exit was the door behind her and the hidden passageway behind the bookshelf he was currently in front of.

He held up a hand, mouth set in a frown and eyes looking up from the golden liquid in his glass. "You believe that I think you're a failure, not worthy of the Family Legacy. Can you blame me? You run away to that garage and pretend you are not nearly as important as you are—hiding like a scolded puppy. You act like a meek girl playing on the edges of the Underworld—when we both know you are capable of decimating the vile creatures within."

She swallowed around the lump. "I can explain…"

"But you are a Seward. A formidable opponent. Outspoken. A leader—the boys have always followed your lead. And you make a difference in people's lives through tremendous sacrifice, with little concern for yourself—a true Legacy heir if ever there were one."

Aeron's mouth became dry. He'd just offered her more than a passive-aggressive compliment. Did he intend to claim or kill her? She couldn't keep up.

"Not being claimed feels like a punishment, but you truly are closer to freedom than the rest of us."

"Freedom?" The word slipped out, and she bit her lip to stem the flood of words begging to come out. They were free. They were the freest people on the planet with limited consequences and unlimited resources.

"Yes. It's what your mother wanted for you. Freedom from the Legacy." Her chest seized again at her mention—three times in one day and twice in less than five minutes from her father. He took a deep breath. "I didn't just come to the garage because of the funeral. I came because I was afraid the price your mother paid thirteen years ago would be placed on your head if I could not account for your whereabouts. I need you in this house to keep you alive, Aeron."

"The price? It was an accident, Dad."

A humorless smile touched his lips. "It wasn't an accident. It was an intentional car wreck."

Aeron's breath caught in her chest, heart pounding so hard it would break through at any moment. "What? Why? Why would someone do that?"

"Why was she murdered, or why would the bounty be placed on your head?"

The questions seemed absurd.

"Both," she whispered, every nerve in her body screaming to change topics. She didn't want to know. She didn't want to think about this—her mother.

"She never wanted this life for you. The last thing your mother asked was for me to take you as far away from the Legacy as possible. She'd rather you grow up in a foreign orphanage than here."

Her mouth fell open. "No."

"Your mother planned to leave with you before you were born, and I agreed."

Tears burned the back of her eyes. "Why didn't you just send me away then, after she died?" she asked softly. "Honor her request? Would have made life easier for you." He'd always hated her. She was never good enough. Never enough. "It's not like I'm doing you any favors around here." She pressed the heel of her hand against her eyes to stop the tears. "If you want me gone, I'll leave."

"Aeron." His voice was distant compared to the roaring in her ears. She'd spent the last thirteen years of her life busting her ass to earn his approval. Thirteen years of feeling like a failure. Every. Single. Day.

"No." She stood up, wiping at the rouge tears. "I can't believe…" He grabbed her wrist, but she tugged away and tripped against the couch. She tumbled toward the floor, emotionally and physically exhausted. She saw the coffee table's edge but couldn't move quick enough and squeezed her eyes, bracing for the impact. Instead, her body jerked to a halt, an invisible force pulling on the back of her shirt. Cracking her eyes open, she was barely centimeters from the edge of the table. He pulled and sat her back on the couch.

"Sit." His voice didn't hold a commanding tone but a rougher, raw sound. "Please." Aeron met his blood-shot eyes, the hazel eyes so much like Decius' and her own. She nodded, and he went on. "Your mother begged me to let you go. Send you away to keep you safe from Mr. Wayward, but I couldn't. You've always had the capacity to be ruthless, Aeron. I pushed you harder, and you rose higher every time. I realized, what better way for you to be safe than to be able to protect yourself? Your mother begged me to let you go, but I don't regret for a second that I didn't."

A hiccup escaped her, and she wiped her nose, mind reeling. Her mom. Mr. Wayward. The Legacy. "I don't understand."

He downed his glass of whiskey and looked up at her.

"The Legacy killed your mother."

"No." She shook her head. "No, that doesn't make sense. Mr. Wayward is family. Why would he allow it? Why would he not investigate?"

"The same reason he did not investigate Paul's murder and the reason he will not be investigating John and Mary's deaths, ruling them accidental. He ordered them."

A short laugh left her. What a ridiculous accusation. Mr. Wayward—kind, friendly, dare she say father-like to her. But her father seemed gravely serious.

"Dad, are you telling me Mr. Wayward killed his own sons?" The words barely escaped her mouth, the thought preposterous.

"Yes."

"No," she said, shaking her head and walking away from him. "That is impossible."

"I promise you it is very possible. He's killed many people to get what he wants. His own father included."

Aeron couldn't wrap her mind around the idea. "We do Christmas with the Waywards every year. We take vacations with them."

"No. We did Christmas and vacations with Paul and John. We happened to have a sociopath tag along to make sure we weren't trying to escape the Legacy."

Escape the Legacy? The hammering in her throat prevented any words from forming. She leaned back into the couch, sinking down on the sofa cushions.

"Why?" she asked. "Why would he?"

"Because he's greedy. Anyone who stands against him does not live to tell about it, or live long, at least.

"It began to unravel shortly after Luke was born. Elijah—Mr. Wayward—killed his father and threatened to take the children and start a new Legacy if John and Paul didn't fall in line. It made no sense. Killing his father, perhaps to gain control. But start a new Legacy? He already ran the Legacy."

He released a shaky breath and ran a hand over his hair,

smoothing the dark curls that had become misplaced. Finally, he sat in front of her on the coffee table where she had almost face-planted and leaned forward, elbows resting on knees.

"I cannot deny that I agreed to your mother's plan. I love your mother and I would do anything she asked of me." The hurt stayed plastered on her face. He looked away.

"When Elijah caught wind of our plan to sneak you two away, it forced us to put it on hiatus. When you were eight, I saw an opportunity for you two to disappear, and by the time questions would be asked, you'd be long gone.

"What about Decius?"

A broken sigh left him, and a bubble of sadness rose inside Aeron. "For you and your mother to disappear while on a missionary trip is one thing. For my oldest son to go too would send up red flags."

"How do you know it was intentional?"

"I didn't, at first. But the next week, Seamus had a recon mission go sideways—he barely made it home. He'd been making the papers for your departure. I knew then." He stood and paced in front of the fireplace.

"Seamus…Seamus Gale. Shannon's father?" Aeron didn't need to try too hard to picture him: sandy hair, bright blue eyes. Shannon had a picture hanging of him in her room in New York.

Her father nodded.

"I remember the night you brought him back here," Aeron said hoarsely, closing her eyes against the memories. The screams of pain from a grown man. Shannon, her best friend, crying as her father fought for his life. The blood—there was too much blood. It was one of her most vivid memories. She opened her eyes instead, trying to get the images out of her head.

His long breath pulled her back into the present, but he looked heavy all of a sudden.

"How do you *know*, though? That Mr. Wayward is…" she couldn't bring herself to say it.

He paced for a few moments. She could almost see the internal debate wrestling inside him. Finally, he nodded to himself.

"Okay. I need you to trust me. Can you do that?"

She nodded. Not that she could trust him—but she wanted answers.

"Follow me." He poured another glass of whiskey before leaving the study. Aeron jogged to keep up. They retraced her trek from the garage, and she paused in the entrance. Was this some kind of test?

"Dad?" He didn't turn around, his brisk pace taking him through the garage. He stepped over the car parts she'd lined up and did not stop until they were face to face with the garage wall. The bare, solid garage wall. He'd lost it for sure. "Dad?"

He turned toward her, and for a split second, she swore he forgot she'd been following him.

"There's nothing here."

"Illusions. Much like what we've been living," he said.

What? How much whiskey had he consumed? "Listen…Dad."

He held up a hand and pulled out his keys, pointing them at the wall. Aeron stifled the urge to ask what the hell he was doing when a grinding noise came from the wall, and it *moved*. Well, slid would be more appropriate. Crunching and grinding echoed as the drywall broke away from the ceiling, revealing a small storage area that had been sealed away.

Aeron's eyes doubled as she stepped toward the dark room. With another click from his keyring, lights slowly focused on the only thing in the room: a crumpled blue sedan.

Her feet moved her forward—the lights bringing more focus with each second. Not just blue—baby blue. Her mother loved baby blue. She moved around the car, taking in each dented, scratched, crumpled area. She froze when her gaze fell to the back seat—a pink booster seat—*her* pink booster seat. The awful children's music rung in Aeron's mind—the smell of her mother's coffee tickled her nose.

"I'll never get my hands on John and Mary's car—I'm sure it's been completely demolished by now. But I managed to get a hold of Mom's car before it was demolished. You want proof, Aeron? Tell me what you find."

She found her voice wouldn't work, burning in her throat so intense she could puke. He began his retreat, leaving her alone with her mother's killer.

"Does Decius know?" Her heart contracted. He remembered their mother with such detail, jealously used to flare inside Aeron when he would talk about her. Those days had been few and far between the past five years.

"He'll be on assignment for the next few days." That would be no, then. "Happy hunting." His footsteps rebounded off the empty room—a room much larger than she ever imagined.

10

LUKE

*L*uke looked up from his sketchbook at the slightest sound, expecting to see one of his parents checking in—but his parents were dead.

Dead.

If he repeated it enough, maybe the reality would stick. Katherine leaned her petite body against the door frame. Everything about her irritated him, from the obnoxious red hair to her ripped jeans, which eerily mirrored Aeron's favorite pair. She was the perfect marriage of Aeron and Shannon—it unnerved him.

"What do you want, Katherine?"

"We're leaving in the morning. My mom wanted to know if you're packed and if you are going to bring anything to the car tonight."

"No."

"Is that no you're not packed or no you—"

"Get out of my room."

"I'm only trying to be helpful."

"Can you bring my parents back?" Her face blanched. "Then you can't help."

"I'm not trying to be a jerk, Luke, but your parents knew the risks, just like the rest of us."

"Dying in a car accident isn't a *risk*." He spat the foul word out. "It's a tragedy. I'm not going on this 'family trip'. Get out."

"Suit yourself."

Luke swallowed back his anger as she disappeared from view. Who cared what Granddad thought. This mess started with his Granddad and his 'special assignment'. If he had just said no—he would be training in the Maldives right now. He dropped onto the rumpled bed, drawing a deep breath, the scent of Aeron still surrounding him from their night-long vigil.

The sensation of eyes on him pulled his attention back to the door, prepared to start swinging if Kathrine had returned.

"If Aunt Rosemary—"

But Perry waited just outside the threshold. "You're going, Luke." Perry's blue eyes bore into him. "You're going because I'm not going by myself."

Luke released a mirthless laugh. "If you want a wingman, ask Katherine." He closed his eyes, taking another intoxicating breath. "I'm not packing because I'm not going."

Silence answered. When he glanced toward the door, Perry was already gone.

Something soft landed on Luke's face. He shot awake, feverishly looking for the attacker. Katherine stood at the foot of his bed, a smirk dancing at her lips.

He turned away, trying to return to the dream, where this past week hadn't happened.

"You're done luxuriating in misery," Katherine said. "Don't worry about packing. We'll buy you new stuff. Just brush your teeth."

He took a deep breath, sitting up. A single day without someone reminding him what happened was all he wanted. But the Legacy didn't stop because a person, or two, died.

"Just a heads up—Granddad is pretty moody this morning. I don't know what happened, but I said you were getting ready." She picked at her cuticles. "I know you probably haven't trained with him much, but when he gets like this, it's easier to just agree and move on."

Luke raised his eyebrows. "What do you mean?"

Katherine met his question with a frown. "I'll see you downstairs."

A sick feeling in Luke's gut bubbled as she vanished. He'd never spent much time with his Granddad. Education at the Institute always came first, and any spare time found him with Decius and Aeron.

He sighed and trudged toward the bathroom. Anywhere was better than staying here, feet from his parent's rooms. Worst case, he'd hop a flight and return to the New York apartment early—maybe Aeron would be there too.

But the idea of any thing good happening disappeared as Rosemary Wayward's shrill voice assaulted his ears before he could reach the dining room. "I look forward to the day I can take a shotgun to your face, Betty. You were the worst thing that happened to my brother."

"They've been at each other's throats since she showed up with Kat." Luke jumped, spinning around to face Perry. He brushed past Luke, interrupting the cat fight. "Morning!"

Luke followed. The women sat on opposite sides of the table, the tension between them hovering over the food. If he'd had an appetite, it disappeared into the animosity circulating the room.

"Morning," Luke offered, picking at the fruit platter.

"Good morning, Luke." Aunt Rosemary's voice plucked at his heart, and his small appetite completely disappeared. It had been like this for days. He would wither away at this point, but it didn't matter. "We leave within the hour. If you need to finish packing anything, I'd do it now."

He nodded, putting his untouched bowl down and retreating from the room, words unable to get past the lump in his throat.

"Seriously? Is compassion that difficult to muster for your grieving nephew? 'Pack your things,'" Aunt Betty mocked. Luke left the argument behind, returning to his room. The idea of bringing a picture of his parents flitted through his mind—but he settled on a sketch pad for the flight.

Perry was asleep before wheels up, and Katherine plugged her iPod in and ignored the world. Luke stared at the blank page in front of him, the need to sketch anything at his fingertips, yet his mind refused to focus. He sipped at his water, his eyes getting heavy. Maybe he was tired. His head drooped forward, and he forced it back, staring at the overhead compartment.

The water bottle slipped from his fingers, a shadow falling across his closed eyes.

His Aunt Rosemary's voice was the last thing he heard before the darkness took him.

"See you in a few hours."

"How much did you give him, Rosemary?"

"Enough."

"Granddad, he hasn't eaten in almost a week. Mom—what were you thinking?"

"Do we need to call someone? Or—"

"He'll be fine, Perry. Just sit with him until he wakes up. Seriously. It's not like I killed him."

"Granddad—"

"He'll be alright, Perry. Kathrine, come with me. Rosemary—"

"FBI headquarters."

A door closed somewhere nearby. "Hey. C'mon, wake up

already." Perry was shaking his shoulder, but Luke couldn't open his eyes. He couldn't move at all. What happened to him? Last he recalled, Aunt Rosemary handed him a drink and...

He fought to open his eyes, and his body jerked in response.

"Luke!"

He convulsed, his body on delay receiving his brain's message. When his body stopped moving, he dragged his eyes open to meet Perry's frazzled face.

"Holy shit. Luke, are you alright?"

He nodded, his head moving in slow motion. Every nerve on fire.

"What the hell." Katherine's voice echoed through his head. Perry disappeared, and a scuffle registered in Luke's mind.

"You promised! I'm going to kill your mother if anything is wrong with him."

"Get off of me!" Something shattered, Luke struggled to sit up but two sets of hands guided him back down.

"Easy, killer," Katherine said. "I'll call in some help."

"No. I'll handle this."

"I'm not my mom," she snapped.

Luke's eyes opened, the dizziness settling, and he sat up. Perry's wide stare melted into concern.

"Hey—how are you?"

"I'mfine." The words slurred, and Luke tried again. "I'm. Fine. She—drugged me."

"Why?" Katherine's genuine tone surprised him.

Luke blinked a few times, the image of his aunt handing him the drink. "I don't know." The words came easier.

"Idiot."

"Shut it." Perry glared across the bed.

"I-di-ot," she repeated, her head moving side to side with each syllable.

Perry poised to lunge, but Luke brushed him back. "What do you mean?"

"You shouldn't be here. What happens here isn't child's play." She plucked her phone from the nightstand and left.

Luke's chest buzzed with indignation. Child's play? He was the youngest in the room at twenty-two, but there was nothing child-like about him.

Luke rubbed his face, every nerve-ending fried. "This cannot get any worse. Can we just hop a flight and go back home? Maybe Mrs. Gale will let me crash there."

Perry shook his head. "The Gales are in Haiti. Plus, Granddad confiscated our passports and stuff when we landed."

"He what?"

"It happens every trip. You've never been on one of these, but…" His frown mirrored Katherine's that morning.

"What am I missing, Perry?"

"It will be better coming from—"

"No. You convinced me to come on this trip. You tell me."

Perry crossed his arms. "You would have come anyway, and Granddad is much easier to handle when you just go along."

"Whatever." Luke's muscles begged him to lay back down, but he ignored them. "Where are we anyway?"

"A compound in Washington."

"D.C.? D.C. is neutral "

"Welcome to the other family business."

Other family business? What the hell was going on. "I don't even care. I'm leaving." He didn't move from the bed, though. His body still shook with small tremors from the ill-intentioned drug over dose.

"Just wait until he gets back. It will make more sense."

"No. I want to be gone before he gets here." Luke pulled himself off the bed this time, taking a swig of water from the glass on the nightstand. The hydration gave a bit of relief, and he looked for a water jug. The hotel room, because they were definitely in a hotel room, was standard. Sub-par even. Luke sat on the only bed beside the only nightstand. There was no TV. No dressers. No desk. "When will he be back?"

Perry leaned back, interlacing his fingers on his chest. "No clue."

"I'm going to shower."

"Luke—"

He ignored his cousin's calls. This trip was not voluntary. His parents would never send him here. He shouldn't be here. The shower washed the stale plane musk from his skin. Wrapping the warm towel around his waist, he wiped the mirror to get a clear look. He rubbed the coarse stubble on his face when a thought hit him: he had nothing with him. No razor. No clothes. No passport. He grabbed his filthy jeans from the bathroom floor and felt the pockets. No wallet.

"Damn it." He charged back into the room.

Perry smirked from the couch. "Realizing a minor flaw in your plan, cuz?"

"Where's my wallet?"

"Like I said. You're not going anywhere."

Luke's hand palmed his forehead. The ache in his muscles had let up, but a piercing pain started behind his eyes.

"What the hell am I supposed to do?"

"Stop trying to fight it."

"Fight what? Being kidnapped by my own family?"

"Luke—"

"I hate this. I hate the stupid Legacy and its stupid rules, and that we're expected to just do whatever he says! Well, guess what, I'm not going along with it." He tossed his hand up.

"We don't have a choice."

Luke stared at him. How could his older cousin—the person he looked up to and trusted without question just nod and drink the kool-aide? "What happened to you? You never took orders before."

"What happened to you? Since when do you *not* follow orders?"

Luke crossed his arms.

"This isn't the Institute. This isn't home. In this reality, you follow orders or you die." The mimic of Katherine's statement irked Luke.

"Just give me some clothes. I'll figure the rest out on my own." He'd walk back to New York.

"No."

"I'm not joking, man. Give me some clothes."

Perry stood. "No."

Indignation burned beneath Luke's skin. Everyone kept telling him no. No—your parents didn't make it. No—they're not coming back. No—you can't grieve, you have to come on the family trip. No. No. No. He vaulted over the bed, taking his cousin off guard. His fist connected. Perry stumbled back, knocking over the chair.

Perry rubbed his chin. "Don't pick a fight you can't finish, Luke."

"Give me some damn clothes." Perry didn't budge. On his best day, Luke could take Perry, but today was not his best day. It didn't matter. In a few furious moments, Luke entangled his cousin, who outmaneuvered him. Perry slipped his arm beneath Luke's chin from behind, locking his arms. Six to ten seconds was all Perry needed to put him out. Grasping his cousin's arm, he tried to make space as the pulsing in his head increased.

The door opened. Perry's hold decreased a smidgen, and he turned, dragging Luke with him. The towel snagged between them, and it was the towel or his neck, so Luke kept his hands firmly in place.

Katherine stopped short. "Is this really what you boys do to pass the time?"

"Get off me," Luke ground out. The pressure tightened for a millisecond before vanishing. Luke dropped to his knees, coughing, and scooped up his towel.

Perry ignored him, already facing Katherine. "What's going on?"

"We need to work fast. My mother wants you out of D.C."

"Shit. After all I've done, I'm still a pawn between them." He paced the small area, raking a hand through his hair. Luke racked his memory. He'd never seen Perry like this: terrified.

Luke returned to his feet, securing the towel again. "What's going on?"

Katherine's gaze bored into him as if deciding he was worth answering. He stared back, tired of being pushed around. She smirked but didn't answer.

"Perry?"

But Katherine continued as if he hadn't spoken. "It's better than dead, which she wanted, now that Luke…" She grabbed Perry's arm, halting him. "He was sending you home. I suggested the Villas and reminded him you have been more valuable when your not at home. Go to the West Indies."

"He won't let me go there. Not with your history."

"*My* history. Not yours. We need to at least try. Gunnar is there. He'll have other contacts for us."

Perry nodded, still pacing, a hand running over the back of his neck.

"She wants you gone, Perry, and he's too busy to care where to."

Katherine looked back to Luke, smirking. "I told you, you should have packed a bag."

Luke's patience died. "What the fuck is going on?"

A silent conversation shot between his cousins before Katherine answered. "Do you trust Perry?"

"With my life." The words left him without hesitation.

"Perry?"

Luke sent a pleading look, realizing the answers he wanted depended on what Perry said.

"That's not fair, Kat. He has no idea."

"Do you?"

Perry licked his lips before answering. "Maybe."

"I can't gamble with maybes."

Perry tossed his hands up. "Why bother asking if you already made your decision?"

Luke swore a growl escaped her.

"Find some clothes," she ground out. "It's time to get you

acquainted with the area, and understand what's expected of you in the upcoming weeks."

Luke dropped into a chair. What bizarre nightmare did he wake up in? What other secrets did his parents have?

Something soft landed in his lap. Clothes. "Guess you get to go out after all."

"What about you?" Luke looked up. He was about to be left here with people he didn't know or want to know. "Are you just leaving me here?"

"I don't have a choice, Luke. Trust Kat. I do." He patted Luke on the shoulder, hugged Katherine, and left the room without looking back.

Kat dropped onto the bed, laying back, hands tucked behind her head and shoes just barely hanging off the bed. "Get dressed. We're going shopping."

Luke followed Katherine through the busy streets. He would not stay without Perry. Finding money, and a phone to call Aeron or Decius was priority one. It was easy enough to get what he needed in such a crowded area. He drifted into people, bumping, collecting, and apologizing. Two wallets, a phone—which he turned off immediately—and a pack of gum. His breath tasted nasty.

A hand closed on his arm. He spun, yanked away, and then took a step back. His Granddad towered over him—hand held out.

"Give them to me."

Luke swallowed hard. Katherine called for him, but he couldn't answer around the rock in his throat.

"Lucas Benjamin Wayward. You hand over what you took, now."

Even if he wanted to, which he didn't, his muscles refused to cooperate with him. The spark of anger in his Granddad's eyes froze him in place. It was like he was five years old being scolded for stealing extra cupcakes—except much, much more terrifying.

"Granddad! I thought you had meetings." Katherine's voice

became lighter and sweeter than Luke had heard before, but his breath started again with her by his side.

"I thought I'd better see how my grandson was adjusting. Good thing, since his babysitter didn't catch him pickpocketing half the city."

"What?" Kat reached for his pockets. Luke didn't bother fighting —he was out numbered. He raised his hands as Kat pulled out the wallets and phone.

"Seriously?" she whispered. "Are you trying to get killed?"

Luke shrugged. Stealing had never been his thing, but it wasn't something to normally get killed over.

"Granddad. I—"

"Katherine, I don't even know where to begin."

"I. I um—"

The glare that froze him turned on Katherine; she fell silent and stepped back.

"I want to go back home," Luke blurted out, Katherine's fear propelling the words from him.

The look swiveled to him, and Luke stepped back too. "You are home. Wherever your family is, Luke, is your home. Get used to it."

"No."

Katherine stepped in front of him as if shielding Luke from the piercing glare. "He'll fall in line. He just needs time."

"You either keep him in line, Katherine, or I will be lending you to Rufus...and Rosemary can handle him instead."

"I said I'll handle it. Have I ever let you down?"

"Good." Their granddad turned, melting into the crowd.

"Where did he go?"

"I don't know," Katherine answered, turning and walking in the opposite direction. "Let's get you some clothes that fit and some food. There's a lot you need to be caught up on."

Too many stores and an absurd amount of shopping later, Luke adjusted his jeans beneath the cafe table. Katherine insisted on his new wardrobe: jeans with a shirt that was a cross between a t-shirt and a dress shirt, sporting just a few buttons at the top. To be honest, the look suited him better than his khakis and polos.

They ate in silence, Luke aware her eyes never stopped scanning for more than a second. It created a pit in his stomach, readying him to be attacked from behind at any moment. He pushed the plate away, no longer hungry.

"Katherine, what's going on here?"

"We're eating lunch."

"No. I mean in D.C."

"Nothing." She pushed the chicken around on her plate. "A lot."

"What does it have to do with the Legacy?"

"Everything. I'm not going to tell you. One, because I don't trust you. And two, because Granddad will know. And you're safer if you don't have to lie."

Luke rubbed his forehead. "I feel like I've been dropped into an alternate universe."

She gave a small laugh. "You have. I'm truly sorry about your parents. I know they never wanted this for you."

"You knew them well?"

"I knew them well enough to know I should have never met you in this lifetime."

Luke pushed the food around on his plate. "Thanks."

"For what?"

"For not lying to me."

"I'll never lie to you, Luke." She dropped money on the table and stood up. He picked up his shopping bags and followed, unsure of their destination but not wanting to get caught alone.

11

AERON

*T*he aroma of coffee reached her nose before she saw her father. Aeron pushed the dolly out from beneath the wreckage and looked up.

"The brake lines were loosened. And it's hard to detect, but a small puncture was in the fuel line. Hell, if the lug nuts had been loosened, I'd say they just Googled most common ways to tamper with a car. The computer system is fried though—and if I was going to cause a crash, the computer system would be the most reliable way."

She accepted the bowl of fruit he offered and enjoyed making him cringe as she started eating—hands filthy and all. "The car was tampered with." The car. She couldn't bring herself to say *Mom's* car.

"I've tried getting the digital records—we weren't as concerned with our own safety and accountability back then, nor was the technology nearly as good as it is today."

"What about Luke's parents' car?" she asked, wiping the watermelon juice from her chin.

"There's a black space 24-hours before the crash. It's been

labeled as 'technical difficulties'. Elijah has shut down any requests for further investigation."

Aeron nodded and leaned against the broken car. She'd started digging through this killing machine the second he'd left last night and hadn't stopped—stopping allowed her to think about Decius—Shannon—Luke—her mom. She needed a lid on all of it to get her answers.

"I believe you—the accident was no accident. But it still doesn't prove it was Mr. Wayward."

"Clean up and meet me in the training area."

She stared after him, exhaustion weighing her down. She didn't want to shower or train—she wanted answers.

After a short shower, a fresh pair of sweatpants and a tank top, she found herself standing just outside the training room's open door. Five years ago, she'd walked out of that room, hopped into one of the cars in the garage, and left. She couldn't remember the exact reason why, now—just the overwhelming feeling of resentment.

The sunlight filtered down into the room from the skylight inviting her in. Tendrils of dread crept up her spine as her feet touched the padded floor. The room looked exactly the same. The scaffolding against the rear wall nearly touched the five-story high ceiling. A shiver raced through her as her gaze passed over the array of weapons and targets and landed on the door to the Disciple room, hours spent holding stances and positions, electric poles placed an inch from the body which sent shocks if touched. She owed her life to the training done in there, but it would be a lie to say her skin didn't twitch at the thought of it. She folded down on the mats near the kicking bags, and the door slammed shut—the lock sliding into place. Her father leaned against the inside of it.

"You're late."

Her heartbeat quickened, and she jumped up. His casual demeanor had vanished, replaced by the intensity that sent her running from home in the first place. He lunged from the door, and Aeron stumbled back, tripping and rolling out of his reach. She pivoted, running to the scaffolding, and began to climb, not looking back.

They always received an objective when training—evade the pursuer, follow the target, or engage the threat. But without an idea of what he expected or why he had asked her to come here, she fled. He grabbed at her ankles. She climbed higher. Grab, pull, grab, pull. She hauled herself out of his reach, trying to make it to a platform twenty-two feet off the ground. Her hand grasped its edge when fingers wrapped securely around her right ankle. With a swift tug, her grip slipped. Her stomach plummeted as he released her ankle, and she flailed her arms, reaching for the metal structure. The irrational thought he planned to kill her in a training accident jetted through her mind right before her body slammed to a halt.

She sunk her teeth into her lip to stop the scream from escaping as her shoulder popped out of the socket—her father's fingers wrapped firmly around her wrist. Heart pounding, Aeron looked up as he pulled her close enough to reach one of the bars with her foot.

Ragged breaths left her. She found the bar beneath her weight, and grasped one of the poles with the free hand. He didn't immediately drop her arm but lowered it slowly as he brought himself down beside her. A moan escaped her as the pain increased, sweat dripping down her temples.

"Why didn't you reach for me?" he demanded. She leaned her head against the pole, the cool metal a blessing against her flush face.

"I didn't think you were going to catch me," she said between gritted teeth.

"I told you to trust me."

He balanced himself on the two-and-a-half inch surface. Placing one hand on her shoulder, he grabbed her arm with the other, and she braced herself as he rotated and pushed her shoulder back into place. The pain seared for a moment and then decreased to a dull throb.

"Thank you." She rolled her shoulder a few times, the blood flowing normally.

He took a seat beside her, rubbing the back of his neck. "I assumed you knew we were racing to the top. I used to do this exercise with your brother."

Her face reddened at the foolish mistake.

"I remember watching," she admitted, following his quick change of subject. For a moment, it seemed as if he held *concern* for her. "I'd sneak in after you started lessons and watch you train him."

"Yes you did. You hid in that wardrobe over there, next to the knife targets."

She looked up in surprise. "You knew?"

"I did. I always knew when you were somewhere you shouldn't be. As long as you were learning, I let it slide."

Her eyes drifted toward the wardrobe, thinking of the many hours spent huddled inside. Deep gouges covered the wood from stray knives missing their targets, quite a few with her just behind the door.

"You work too hard trying to prove to me you belong in this business—you do belong. I knew when you were seven that you would be a formidable assassin. You out-did your brother at every turn, but you have your mother's heart, Aeron.

"You would let yourself burn before you let an innocent bystander get any blowback." He looked out over the training area. "I don't have the proof you want. Just my word. John and I have—had been working on gathering evidence for years. It's what got Paul killed. It's what got John and Mary killed."

"And Mom?" It was barely a whisper. The word stale in her mouth. She hardly remembered her. How could she feel this kind of sadness over a person she barely knew?

"Your mother was a message for me, just like John was a message for me: Fall in line."

She rubbed her shoulder, eyes roaming around the training room, looking anywhere but at him. Entering this room again never crossed her mind. But here she was, having a semi-heart-to-heart about a taboo topic with the man who made her feel completely worthless for years—the monster of her dreams.

"Let's get some ice on that shoulder." He slid to the ground. Aeron followed much slower all the way back to his office. Two steaming mugs sat on his desk, an ice pack next to one of them. She paused in the doorway, waiting for permission to enter.

He shuffled papers around the desk—the sight of him not in a suit, but workout shorts and t-shirt did not fit the room. He caught sight of her as he sipped his coffee and waved her in. "Don't just stand there—come in."

Her stomach lurched; the casual nature was a tone she could not get comfortable with. The edge in his voice lacking...like a barrier had fallen when he opened that wall in the garage. Aeron joined him, waiting for the other shoe to drop—for the facade to fade. But he dropped into his chair, and she followed suit, the hard chair comforting in the bizarre dream she seemed to be existing in. He slid the ice pack across the desk, and she accepted, the cold a pleasant sting to her shoulder.

"What proof would you need? Because if I cannot convince my own daughter, how can I convince the entire counsel that the Senior Assassin is killing his own?"

"Irrefutable proof. Raw audio or video."

"What about documents?"

She shook her head. "Too easy to forge."

"Digital?"

"Too easy to manipulate—if you know what you're doing."

"You want video or audio proof, which cannot be linked to any type of wi-fi because it will be deleted as soon as our programs detect facial or audio samples matching that of the Legacy members?"

Shit. "Yeah." Her resolve began to fade. They lived in an invisible world—one that would protect them from law enforcement and media. It also protected the Legacy from itself, apparently. "I see your point."

The corners of his mouth turned up in triumph.

"Let's say I believe you—why is he killing people? Why murder Legacy blood—his Legacy blood?"

"Money."

She arched an eyebrow. "That's stupid. We have access to unlimited funds."

"Not exactly." He leaned against the desk.

"Okay…"Aeron said, realizing just how limited her understanding was of how the Legacy was funded. Everything she had ever needed had just been provided.

"We've had access to an exorbitant amount of money, but it's shared with all the Legacy Blood families and members. It provides for everyone, so it belongs to no one. Not everyone likes to share." He took a long breath. "There is a section of the Legacy which is no longer a servant of the people—it's transformed into a multi-billion-dollar corporation—Legacy Inc."

Aeron's mouth fell open. "That goes against everything. It's against the Laws to even take a bribe, let alone a cash deal for murder."

He nodded. "That's true." He grabbed the cup of coffee and took a sip but then stared longingly at the bottom.

"How do you know all this?"

He lowered the mug to the desk, sitting up straighter. "I'm not proud to admit it, but I helped build it, Legacy Inc. We—John, Paul, and I— didn't realize the implications of what Elijah was doing at first. But after he killed his father, the threat to our children was extremely valid. As Senior Assassin, without his father as opposition in the Board, what he said went. As Legacy-blood, we belong to the Legacy. As claimed Assassins under the law—we belong to him and therefore must follow him. It's why I never claimed you, Aeron. By blood, you are bound—but never by law."

Thoughts would not stop fighting to get out of her head first. Surely Legacy members realized they were killing innocent people. It's obvious even when taking a guilty life that some are paying for much greater sins than others.

"How can no one know?"

"Because he's done quite the job of compartmentalizing over the past ten-years. A single leader is in charge of a handful of members. That person reports to someone in charge of a handful of leaders, and so on up the pyramid. No one knows anyone—almost no one. Shaun Brinks knew."

The blood drained from Aeron's face. "What?"

"We were working together, an angle to stop Elijah. Obviously we know how that ended."

"I didn't know." Shaun's final moments resurfaced, her hands shaking with the memory. *Who ordered this? Your father?* "He thought you ordered the hit. He said 'With me dead, nobody wins'."

"With Shaun off the table, we lost a lot of leverage on Elijah. He knew which blood families had already joined Legacy Inc., and which were eliminated."

Her face paled, and she removed the ice pack from her now numb shoulder. "Eliminated? As in…"

"Dead. Unless they got on board—and some did."

Then where were the members coming from? It was drilled into them as children to take pride in protecting innocent lives. It was hard to imagine shedding that skin just for money, although she knew it happened. But an entirely new corporation?

"They're working with the Underworld," she realized. "There is an entire corporation of Underworlders here in the states?"

He looked into his coffee cup again, as if the liquid would magically refill itself. "The D.C. model is well established. Elijah now has his sights set here. John and I…" a long sigh left him. "We were trying to convince him to take D.C. and leave New York to us. We'd stay out of his way, and he'd stay out of ours."

"He said no?"

"He said yes. And John and Mary were dead three days later." His voice cracked on the last word.

Luke. *Luke.* "Luke—we have to get him out of there."

"Aeron—"

"If there is an entire corporation set on killing anyone, we're the enemy!" She stood up, looking for something...anything to keep her hands busy.

"I've been waiting. Like I've said, the waiting is excruciating."

She grabbed the pillows off the couch, her hands needing to be doing anything as her thoughts for Luke's safety raced around her mind.

"Aeron," his voice was light at first. "Aeron!" he said a bit sterner. But she ignored him, the need to do something overtaking her. Luke—did he have any idea how much danger he was in? Rough hands spun her around. Her eyes widened as her father grabbed her right hand and placed a gun in it. She stilled, fingers wrapping around the cool grip.

"I need a favor, Aeron." His voice was barely a whisper. He placed his hand over the gun in her grip. "Will you help me take down Mr. Wayward before he destroys us all."

Aeron gazed at the gun in her hand—a family heirloom. A masterpiece. The ivory grip beneath her fingers worn down by generations of Sewards, the gold inlay insignia now dull. It weighed heavy in her hand, heavy enough to be loaded. She looked up at her father, who stepped back, eyes trained on her, waiting for an answer.

Luke needed her, but more importantly, she needed Luke. She couldn't imagine doing this life without him. If there was even the slightest chance he was in danger, she'd do whatever it took to protect him.

"Yes."

An unamused laugh sounded from him, "So you believe me?"

She paused—fear wrapping the panic that had grown in her stomach. She racked her brain for a logical reason he would lie to her. He met her inquiring gaze with grief, hung in bags beneath his eyes and supported by an unshaven face. The weight of losing his best friend.

"I do. Now tell me, how do we save him? How do we get Luke out?"

"Getting him out and saving his life are two completely different things, Aeron."

"What?"

He rubbed his forehead. "First and foremost, I need your complete trust. Saving Luke's life is not going to be easy or heroic, if that's what you're thinking. It's going to be messy. You're going to have to get messy."

"I know that, Dad."

"Do you? Because once you commit—once we commit to this— there is no going back. There is no getting out and becoming a mechanic." His lip curled on the word. "We become enemy number one to both Legacies and the Underworld. It will be kill or be killed."

"I'd do anything to keep him alive." The words left before she thought them through, yet she wouldn't take them back. A life without Luke? That was no life at all.

The intensity of his gaze faltered. "Then I don't need to ask how far you will go for him."

They stood in silence for a few moments, Aeron waiting for his instructions, but he stared off into the fire.

"What happens now?" she asked.

"We train, and then you return to New York. Reintegrate into the Institute, go about your business as normal. And wait."

"Normal? You want me to be normal? I know things now... things that change everything."

"Mr. Wayward is dangerous, but as long as Luke is kept in the dark, he's safe."

Aeron swallowed the lump in her throat. "We should tell Luke. He should be aware of how dangerous Mr. Wayward is."

"Not yet. It's us against an invisible army, and without hard proof to stand on, it would be suicide. It's not like I can make an accusation and hold a trial. Elijah has the entire Legacy Inc. at his beck and call—none who give a rat's ass about our Laws. And then there are those stateside that have already turned."

"What about Decius? He should know. Mom was…" The words stopped in her chest. Their mother was everything to him.

"Decius needs to be in the dark, for now. The less you both know until I need you to, the safer it will be for everyone—Luke included."

"Why?" she asked again. She felt like a toddler, learning about the world for the first time.

An aggravated sound escaped him. "Because if I'm killed, I need him to be focused on the best interests of this family and protecting you. Decius will go to hell and back to defend you. When you need him, he will be there. It's better to keep him out of it until there is no other option."

"That doesn't make sense! Luke is his best friend; they're like brothers. If anyone can—"

"Can what—convince Luke his Grandfather is unstable and killed his own children?" He laughed. "It is not going to be Decius. It will be the girl who sat by him at his parent's grave and held him while he cried."

Her cheeks grew hot. "I will not—"

"Let's not pretend this isn't the entire reason you are willing to do this. You now have my permission, with a few stipulations."

Aeron's heart leapt for the briefest moment. The idea of her and Luke, although dreamt about, never seemed tangible. Hands brushing and sitting too close on the couch were the extent of their forbidden relationship. Men were used as assets—a means to an end in any mission.

"Stipulations?"

"You cannot, under any circumstances, allow Luke the slightest hint that something is out of the ordinary. His parents just died.

He's vulnerable and has months with Mr. Wayward. We must assume he's deep within Elijah's circle by now."

She had no idea what that meant, but the look in his eyes when he said it left a vice on her heart.

"We need a running tab on his whereabouts and conversations. The more information we have, the better chance we have."

"How do you know Luke will be back at the Institute?" It sounded as if Mr. Wayward had swooped him off to a prison.

"He knows that's where Luke feels most comfortable; he'll need to make Luke feel secure—in control."

"What's his end game?"

He released a long breath but didn't answer. Aeron tried another angle.

"Who else knows? Are the other families trying to stop him?"

He hesitated, a hand absent-mindedly rubbing the back of his neck. "He's the Senior Assassin, Aeron. He says fire, we shoot until he says otherwise. When John and I started investigating, the Joneses had already been eliminated."

"The entire family? But they have...had young kids—a lot of young kids."

He nodded. She placed the gun on the table beside her untouched glass of whiskey, her hand feeling too light without it now. It wasn't just Luke's life in danger, it was all Legacy Blood.

"Do you really think we can get Luke out?" she asked, heart hammering in its cage. "Do you think we can save the Legacy?"

He gave her a measured look before nodding. "I will do everything I can to save Luke. I made John a promise to protect Luke, but you have my word, I will die before I let the lunatic hurt him."

Her father's word—not a promise, an oath.

"And the Legacy?"

"I think we should focus on staying alive first."

12

LUKE

"Whoa." The word slipped out as they approached a stretch of Rowhouses near Capitol Hill. The three-story, brownstone Queen Anne homes were identical, with their rounded turrets and individual porches. To an untrained eye, it would be easy to pass it off as multiple multi-million-dollar homes. But Luke's eyes traveled to the roofs, where even from the ground, he could see the running paths created for travel.

"Yeah. It has that effect." Katherine's scowl pulled his attention away from the Victorian architecture. "C'mon, you can stay in Perry's rooms."

"He's already gone?"

"Most likely." She pulled out an old flip phone to double-check.

Exhaustion crept in on Luke as they entered the fourth entrance from the left. A blinding hallway greeted them and the Victorian mystique of the exterior was replaced with a rigid, sterile interior. He followed her to a slim staircase which led to a halfpace with stairs leading to a more open second floor. People hurried around them, most nodding at Katherine and giving him a wary look. No one stopped or questioned them, but a few did give her a wide berth. It reminded him of the Institute, and homesickness pushed away his growing awe.

They went up the stairs and through a labyrinth of hallways and secret passages. After the third time going downstairs to go up another set, he conceded there'd be no way to find his way out on the first attempt. They finally entered a door down a deserted corridor. The open room had a similar setup to Aeron and Decius' wing at their manor—a shared living area with two doors leading off to private rooms. His gut churned at the thought of them. He wanted to go home.

"Living quarters are located throughout the building, although unless you live in them, you won't know they are there, so don't go snooping around, or you might get shot." She headed straight to the door on the right. "There is a dining hall in the basement that is open all hours, or you can just eat whatever is in Perry's room. He always has food stashed away."

Luke's heart jumped to his throat, the reality sinking in that he was stuck here with no guarantee he'd ever return to New York. "Katherine?"

She glanced over her shoulder, a weariness in her eyes he hadn't seen before.

"Thank you."

She nodded and retreated. He pushed open his door, dropping the shopping bags to the floor. The large room hosted a grand fireplace opposite an ornate king bed that did not match the institutionalized atmosphere of the building but did match the grander feeling of the outside. A desk, a single dresser, a mini fridge, and a small sofa near the window were the only other pieces of furniture in the room. It could have been a mock room for any high-end hotel advertisement. Luke neared the window, opening the curtains. The view overlooked a courtyard in the rear of the Rowhouses. He rested his hand against the cool rock which made up the windowsill and outside wall.

His stomach growled, and he moved to scope out the mini-fridge. He pulled out the unopened milk, checked the expiration date, and retrieved a glass from the desk where an envelope sat, addressed to him. He poured the milk before opening it.

Luke—Had the fridge stocked. Coffee and snacks are in the top dresser drawer. Sorry I couldn't stick around. If you need anything else, I trust Kat can provide you with the essential survival needs.
-Perry

Essential survival needs…Trust Kat to survive. Great. He dropped the letter to the desk and downed the milk before investigating the two doors on either side of the bed. One—a walk-in closet with a few pieces of clothes and training gear. The other—a bathroom complete with a grand shower, a stand-alone tub, and double sinks. It was nicer than his bathroom back home. The idea of jumping in the hot water sped momentarily through his mind, but he returned to the king bed and collapsed onto it, asleep within seconds.

Light flooded into his dreams, pushing them into the darkness. Luke scrunched his face trying to hold on to the feeling of…of…

"You're not going to be able to sleep your time away here. Granddad wants you in the training area in an hour." Katherine's voice blasted away any good feelings he may have had, and he pulled a pillow over his head.

Home. It had been a feeling of home. "I'm not going anywhere."

She tugged the pillow away. "It wasn't a suggestion. Get dressed."

He rolled over, his body groaning in protest. She was already in workout clothes, hair braided down her back. "What if I just don't go?"

"You'll go, even if I have to make you go. I'm not incurring his wrath because you don't want to be a part of this family."

He smirked at the mental picture of her dragging him around the castle. She grabbed the blanket from beneath him and yanked, pulling him to the floor.

"Ouch." He rubbed his elbow. "What was that for?"

"Get dressed, or so help me God I will—"

"I got it!" He put his hands up in surrender and got to his feet.

"You have ten minutes." He made a face as she left and kicked the blanket off.

After a shower, and some cursing, while he dug through the shopping bags, he left the room with an oatmeal bar in hand. His irritation level lowered a smidgen when Katherine met him with a smile in the living room.

"I knew those would look good on you."

"Where are these training areas?"

"There are several, but the one we're going to is on the roof. Now pay attention so you can navigate this place on your own. I'm not a babysitter."

With a full night's rest and a clearer mind, Luke realized the secret passageways were steel-lined halls built just behind the drywall and activated by Katherine's retinal scan.

"Who has access to the passages?"

"Blood only."

"You, Perry, Granddad, and your mom?"

"And now you. It's a tight-knit group."

"Are there cameras?" he asked. They exited into a deserted hallway.

"Everywhere. Stop thinking what you're thinking. You're not going to get out of Headquarters without him knowing."

They stepped onto the roof. From the outside, it looked like an oversized rooftop conservatory. But inside—his jaw dropped. He slipped his shoes off and bowed before stepping onto the matted floor. It spread halfway across the building and then transformed into a massive warrior course.

"Wow," Luke said.

"Glad you could make it." His Granddad sat cross-legged off to the side, wearing a blue gi. Katherine bowed beside Luke and tossed a gi at him.

"Suit up."

The next three hours were a blur of punches, sweeps, and submissions. After being thrown to his back a final time by Katherine, Luke gulped for air, sprawled out while his Granddad stretched a few feet away.

"You need more discipline, Luke."

He nodded in response, feeling better than he had in weeks, the physical contact filling a hole he didn't know was there.

"I didn't hear you."

Katherine nudged his leg.

"Yes, Sir," Luke said, sitting up.

"You will train here every day for at least three hours."

"Yes, Sir," Luke answered, his mind buzzing with adrenaline. His body had craved the physical workout, his mood boosted. This wasn't too bad. Maybe he just needed to get back into a routine.

"Now, you might be wondering why you are in D.C. Your father was the successor to the Legacy. With his untimely death, we are in a precarious situation."

Luke's mouth went dry.

"Without an heir to the Legacy, there are rumbles from below; people looking to step in. But I think this gives us an opportunity to change the way the Legacy operates. Make it more…profitable."

"What do you mean?" Luke's pulse quickened, his gut pinning him to the ground. He had gone an entire three hours without thinking about his parents. Instead of being slightly reminded, the Legacy seemed to be collapsing without them.

"Right now we need to keep a public face for the Legacy and establish the line of succession. What you see here?" he looked around the room. "This is Legacy Inc.—a branch of the Legacy no longer bound by the Laws. A business model, if you would. We don't just serve the public here. We make profits. There aren't Laws governing the way we live or act. Instead there's a code of conduct agreed upon by a single person who chooses to work within Legacy Inc.—not an entire bloodline."

"What are you saying?" Luke's throat had become dry.

"If I have a suitable replacement, I can stop the scrambling from below in the Legacy. If I have the right replacement, we can turn the Legacy around—into Legacy Inc. I want that replacement to be you."

Luke's eyes widened. "I'm sorry, what?"

"I want you to help me bring the Legacy into the 21st century."

Luke swallowed the knot in his throat. He must have misunderstood. His Granddad said profit, but the Legacy didn't protect the people for profit; they did it because it was an honor, a necessity. "Who does Legacy Inc. serve?"

"Technically, they will work for you."

"What if I don't want it?"

A hoarse laugh escaped his Granddad. "You will. You need focus. You need somewhere to channel all that anger and pain. Don't worry about the obstacles. Right now, I'm more concerned with stopping the inevitable uprising that is occurring as we speak. This operation is a hundred times more successful and profitable than the Legacy. I built this. Your Aunt Rosemary built this, and one day, it will be Katherine's, while you run New York. Don't you want to be a part of something so revolutionary?"

No. As impressive as it all sounded, Luke didn't want to be a part of it. His parents never wanted him to be a part of it. In some fantasy world, he'd run away with Aeron, away from both their Legacies. This was the opposite of that. This should be Perry's. His Granddad's gaze bore into him, and fear coiled in his stomach, reminding him of yesterday in the streets. Only one answer would let him walk out of this building.

"When you put it that way, of course."

"Then it's settled." He clapped his hands together and stood up, bowing as he stepped off the mats and exited the building.

"What did I just agree to?"

Katherine smiled. "You agreed to not being killed today."

He helped her up, and they moved slowly toward the edge of the mats, both battered and bruised. But she didn't answer his question.

"Why isn't Perry being groomed for Senior Assassin?"

She just shrugged.

"What's with you two?"

She raised her eyebrows. "What's with you? I thought you were all mopey and 'send me back home'?"

He had been. But if all he had to do was show he could play nice to get back to New York, he'd take it and worry about the rest later. "You said that's not an option, right? And if all goes accordingly, I could be home before training at the Legacy resumes. So, I'm going to 'stop luxuriating in my misery' and start doing something." A smile tugged at his lips, and he changed back into his clothes.

Katherine left without a backward glance, but it didn't bother him. If he had to be in D.C., then at least he'd be training.

"Duck!" Luke swung a broken two-by-four. A sickening crack resounded as it connected with the man's skull. He crumpled next to Katherine on the ground, and Luke hated the pleasure the growing pool of blood gave him.

He offered a hand up, but she turned, rolling over the unconscious body and digging through his pockets. Wallet, phone, multiple weapons.

"Is it there?" Luke asked, taking each item from her. She shook her head and rolled the body over again, checking the waistband.

"It's not here."

"It has to be. I saw it being handed off to him." Luke pocketed the items in his hand and moved to the feet. He unlaced the combat boots.

"What are you doing?" She raised an eyebrow at him.

He tugged them off, rolling down the socks. A small paper fluttered to the ground. Luke held it between his fingers, a smirk crossing his face. "Mission accomplished. Let's get it home."

They blended into the busy streets toward the Rowhouses, Luke aware of anyone who could be working for Granddad. Unsure of the guard situation in the front of the buildings, and after a swift argument, the ten-foot wall in the rear seemed the safest bet. No guards greeted them as they snuck back into the property. The clock chimed the hour just as they entered Granddad's office, chests heaving.

Luke waved the paper between his fingers and held it out. "Mission completed."

"And without a second to spare." His Granddad's voice didn't hold a bit of admiration. Instead, Luke caught the disappointed furrow above his eyes, a look he'd become quite familiar with. He placed the paper on the desk and retreated beside Katherine.

"Two of the bodies you left were already discovered, and you were spotted by a sniper going over the rear wall. You may have retrieved the information but failed the mission."

Luke held back a groan. They had yet to complete a successful mission. Each time he gave them conflicting feedback. Leave the bodies, hide the bodies, push through the barricade, stealth is the only way to survive. No matter which of them took the lead, they failed.

"Bull," Luke spat, irritation fueling him. "You gave no such parameters."

"They are not parameters. They are expectations, Luke. I am grooming you two to take over this organization. Now, I expected these mistakes from you, Luke. The Legacy has failed on many fronts. But you performed your first test better than anyone I've seen —you *have* the potential." He rounded the desk, and the small bubble of hope popped in Luke's chest. He needed to prove he could do this so he could get home—but it was Aeron who belonged here, she took out Shaun. "I expect better of you, Katherine. *I've* trained you better."

Katherine's cheeks burned beside him.

"It's my fault," Luke offered. "If I'd listened to her judgment, we would have been back hours ago."

The older man's gaze bounced between them. Did he believe the lie?

"I have a grand vision of you two working seamlessly together, so figure out how to do that. Dismissed."

Luke didn't wait to be told twice, following Katherine without looking back. Neither of them spoke until they reached the top of the stairs.

"Why did you do that?" She looked up at him, disbelief pulling her jaw down.

"Do what?"

"Lie to him. He'll find out. He always does."

"So be it."

"I thought I would be calling Perry and breaking the news of your death." She walked a few paces and turned back around. "Thanks for that, down there." Her voice lightened. "But it's not necessary."

Luke rubbed his sore shoulder. "It was. And I'd do it again."

"You were in direct violation. There will be consequences."

"So be it."

"Do you trust him?" She leaned against the wall and crossed her arms. Her red hair, no longer in a neat braid, frizzed around her head.

"I want to go home. He's my only ticket. And honestly, he hasn't given me a reason not to. You don't, though."

"We have a long history of bumping heads."

"Well, I don't want to be bumping heads because I want to make it back to New York. So, how do we complete the missions?"

She glanced around. "Want to go for drinks tonight?"

The offer caught him off guard, but it was an olive branch, and he accepted. "Yeah."

They went their separate directions, Luke heading to the room. A figure leaned next to the closed door, and his shoulders tensed. He'd gotten off too easily downstairs. The hulking frames of his Granddad's lackeys, Cage and Dave, pushed off the wall as he approached.

"Mr. Wayward wishes to have a word. Now," Cage said.

Luke exhaled a short breath and ran a hand over his head. "Yeah. Let's go." He followed without protest, back the way he'd come. Kathrine, nowhere in sight, was excluded from the certain punishment which awaited him.

Dave held open the study door. Luke brushed past and jumped when the door slammed shut. He took his position standing in front of the grand desk again, hands clasped behind his back.

"You wanted to see me, Sir?"

"You lied to me. It was equal parts screw-up on that mission." He put his pen down and leaned back in the chair.

"I did, Sir." No point in lying again.

"Take a seat, Luke. I have something I've been meaning to discuss with you." His granddad sat back, and Luke dragged a high-back armchair over to sit and crossed his arms.

"I know things haven't been easy this past month." Luke stiffened at his words. "Your parents' untimely death has been harsh to digest, especially for you, although you have made great strides in your training."

Luke said nothing. He kept his eyes on a rip in his pants, mentally building the wall in his head a bit higher and tuning out his granddad. The past month had been rough, but he hadn't thought of his parents much, and he didn't want to start now.

"I wanted to wait until I knew you were in a better place, mentally, to speak of this. Your parents' demise was no accident."

Luke stopped building and looked up. Did he just say... "Excuse me?"

"Ah—I've got your attention now. Don't you think it's suspicious they died in a car wreck on a sunny day? Your father was an elite driver."

"Accidents happen," Luke said, but a pulse thrummed through his body.

"Not like that. I've had both the Institute and a private forensic team all over this, and there is evidence of foul play. I can take this to the Board, but I wanted to give you the choice." He leaned forward, resting his chin against his intertwined fingers.

"The choice of what?" Blood pounded in Luke's ears.

"Justice or revenge." The words hung in front of Luke as if written in the air.

"You—" He swallowed. "You know who did it?"

Granddad nodded. "This betrayal comes from within the Legacy, Luke. The antiquated laws have not been kind to us, and the usurp for power is not unexpected." He sat back, one hand rubbing his chin. "The Legacy will be torn to bits before it's over, and the Institute as you know it will cease to exist. I need someone by my side who understands what we can be with some change. Someone I trust, and who better than the son of the most recent people targeted?"

Targeted. The word reverberated in his mind. Someone killed his parents. Someone in his life decided their need for power trumped his parents' lives. The pounding in his ears ceased. Whoever made that decision sealed their own fate. The Legacy's justice offered a swift death. Luke wouldn't be as kind. He returned the measured look.

"What will it be, Luke?"

The second hand on the antique clock ticked, each beat securing Luke's decision. He straightened in the chair.

"Revenge. I want revenge." Stillness overcame his racing mind, grief being overshadowed by a quiet rage. He needed to remain in control, show Granddad he could handle whatever he threw at him.

"Good."

"Who's responsible?" He held his breath. Who would be so cruel? So selfish?

"I have a list."

Luke swallowed around the profanities begging to come out. "I thought you said you knew."

"I need someone I trust to confirm it for me. We're dealing with a painfully patient person. This wasn't a crime of passion—these murders were strategically spread out over decades, and I've followed many false leads. They have a network. They have funds. Besides, we also have the Laws to consider—they are a Legacy."

"But you just said the Legacy would fall. Why bother with the pretense?"

"In order for a smooth transition of the rest of the members, we must show good faith."

And he must show good faith to play the game. "What do we do then?"

A pile of dossiers moved across the desk toward him. "We study."

"*A*eron!"

Bang. Bang. "C'mon, Aeron. Open the door!"

She rolled over and looked at the clock. It was either twelve noon or twelve midnight. The blackout curtains on her windows prevented her from knowing which. The door burst open.

"Rise and shine, lil' sis!" The curtains parted. She rolled away from the harsh light and groaned.

Noon. It was noon.

Decius wasted no time digging through her wardrobe. A pair of sweats and a tank top landed on the bed. "Let's go."

"Go where?"

"Get up. Dad wanted us in the training room a half hour ago. You sleep like the dead."

Killing people tended to have that effect on her. She pulled a pillow over her head again, every muscle crying in protest. Training with her father had proved to be just as taxing on her mind as on her body. Where the chase and combat came second nature to her, getting inside a person's head was far from natural.

"Did he say why?" she mumbled.

"I didn't ask." She peeked at him from beneath her pillow fort as he dug through her closet, boots and high heels scattering the floor. "Where the hell are your sneakers?"

"It's fine. I'll get them." She ran a hand over her head, crusted blood creating a clump in her hair. "I just need to shower."

His smile faltered as his eyes bore into her. She made sure the dried blood wasn't visible.

"What does he have you doing?"

"Huh?" she asked, buying herself some time to think of a good answer. Rule number one: complete trust. Rule number two: Decius must know nothing of what they do because they were doing more than hunting. Most assignments they'd tackled were not Legacy sanctioned.

"Dad. You leave for days, sometimes weeks on end. And when you come home...it's just I don't remember training being so intensive."

"We're training—just like you wanted me to, right? I have several years to catch up on, I guess. Mostly, I need to keep my mouth shut." The lie slid off her tongue too easily, and her stomach turned. She had never lied to her brother before. He had always lied for her. Protected her. The look of slight amusement in his eyes confirmed she fed him the line perfectly. Her stomach dropped. "Tell him I'm in the shower. I'll be down in fifteen."

The soft thump of knives imbedding in wood greeted her in the training room. She leaned against the wall for a moment, eyes falling closed; her head throbbed. She'd hit it on a cement wall— well smashed it into a cement wall—during an attempt to take on two bodyguards while her father drugged a man and stole some paperwork in a back alley in New York. The altercation over the file could have been avoided—an electronic copy of that file existed, and hacking worked without needing her skull bashed in. Unfortunately, learning to judge perspectives needed to be done in person, and stealthily stealing a file didn't send quite the same message as a petite woman taking out two oversized adult males.

"Are you just going to stand there?"

Her eyes flew open. Decius stared at her from across the room. She joined him next to the throwing knives, circling her tight shoulders. He picked up a black blade and threw. It landed left of center.

She plucked a silver, palm-length blade off the table and stood beside him. She held it next to her ear, the small blade comfortable between her fingertips, took a breath, and threw. It landed next to his, in the center. She smiled up at him.

He laughed. "Try doing that with a rifle."

"Just because I don't like to doesn't mean I can't." Something whizzed past her ear and landed with a solid thud in the bull's eye. She looked over her shoulder, hand automatically checking her ear. Her fingers became slick, and she wiped it on her pants without looking, eyes on her father.

"You okay?" Decius asked. He avoided looking at their dad and touched her ear.

"She's fine."

"I'm fine," Aeron agreed, brushing off his hand.

"I am not bringing you here to slack off."

"Who's slacking off?" Aeron asked.

"Aeron—" Decius started.

"No," she interrupted, grabbing a knife from the table and throwing it without a pause. Metal scraping metal sounded as the knife imbedded centimeters from their father's blade. A smile danced across her face, she'd been honing her accuracy for the last three weeks non-stop.

"Damn," Decius murmured.

"Don't inflate her ego." Her father walked past them to the target and yanked the weapons out. "We have much work to do before Institute-training resumes in a few weeks."

"You have nothing to worry about," Decius said.

"We'll see about that." He dropped the knives on the table. "Let's play a game of Cat and Mouse. Aeron, you start here." He returned to the target, hanging a fresh one up with ten x-marks. "You must hit each mark before you can join us. Decius, you'll need to evade me until she can come to your rescue."

"My rescue?" Decius asked.

"Yes." Her father laid out twelve knives. "Aeron, this is what you have to hit your marks. I will have these—" he held up three knives, "and Decius, you have nothing."

"If we lose?" Decius asked.

Her father smiled, a gesture that would have sent her running months ago. But each day, he dropped his guard with her a little more, and she understood that look: she and Decius presented a true challenge.

"We won't lose," Aeron assured.

"I wouldn't count on that. Suit up."

Aeron and Decius moved to the wardrobe and pulled out two thick leather vests to protect against serious blade injuries.

"Don't worry about me," Decius whispered.

"I never do," she replied. "I'm not sure what he has planned if we lose, but I don't intend on finding out." They moved to their respective starting positions, Aeron at the table with the knives and Decius near the door.

"Three…two…one."

Aeron's adrenaline surged as Decius sprinted to the scaffolding. She released a deep breath and turned to focus on the target. She picked up the first knife, placed it next to her right ear, and paused. The target was one she'd trained on the past week, with the left hand. She'd struggled with the awkward angle. A challenge inside a challenge. She switched the knife to the other hand, brought it up, and released it. It struck the first X. She continued, striking each mark with precision until the ninth one. The blade landed too far right.

"Damn it."

She took a deep breath and shook out her left arm. A shout of pain met her ears; Decius had fallen from God-knows-where. She wiped her palm on her sweatpants and threw again: too far to the left. Sweat dripped down her face. With only two knives remaining, she swapped hands, the knives sinking dead center of the targets. But she had none left to bring with her.

She pulled one free from the target anyways and tucked it inside the vest. Panic crept up her spine. The room was empty. A distant shout pulled her eyes to the propped side door. They'd taken the exercise outside.

The deserted grounds were far too quiet, and she scanned for any sign of them. A disgruntled neigh echoed from the barn, and Aeron swore. She hated the barn, but sprinted across the open field toward the red building only to hear Decius yell from much closer. She stopped and looked around. Where would Decius lead him? A splash: the lake.

A laugh bubbled up and she raced toward their old summer oasis. The lake harbored a climbing tree they would jump from. Decius walked along the thick branch hanging over the water. Their father, only ten feet off the ground, looked up at him.

"Checkmate." A giddy smile fought to cross her face.

Her father looked down at her, and for a brief second, she thought she saw approval. He jumped from the tree without warning. She misjudged the distance, victory already cemented in her mind, and he landed on her. They tumbled to the ground. He held fast to her vest. They somersaulted, and he gained control, landing on top of her. He removed a knife from a sheath on his forearm. Aeron crossed her wrists, trying to push his hand away from her.

"Aeron!" Decius yelled.

"You lose," her father said simply, leaning his weight down. She didn't have the upper body strength to push him off. Instead, she let him lean down and bucked her hips up, using his weight and momentum to flip him off of her. He rolled over her head, and she latched onto the knife, trying to pull it from his grasp. The momentum betrayed her, and he continued the movement until she ended on her back again. She tossed her hands up in surrender.

"Disappointing." He stood and kept the knife pointed at her, pulling another out to point at Decius, who had jumped from the tree's vines. Her father sucked on his teeth. "You lost."

Aeron sat up, pulled the knife from her vest and threw it. It sailed past her father's head and lodged into the tree behind him. He spun to face her, eyes wide. A red mark appeared on his cheek, and blood spilled from the wound.

"Dad!" She scrambled to her feet. "I'm—"

"Go." His voice, although soft, held a familiar dangerous tone.

She remained rooted to the spot. "I didn't mean—"

"You did. Because you either have impeccable aim and meant it, or shitty aim and didn't. Which is it?"

Aeron took a shaky breath. "I meant it."

"Aeron," Decius said, warning her to be quiet.

"And I'd do it again." She gained confidence in her words. He wanted her to prove herself—prove her loyalty to him, and the first step was to show she could lie to Decius. This was the perfect opportunity. "I'm done, Decius. I want out."

"You can't be serious." Decius' brow furrowed in disbelief. He moved toward her, but the knife to his chest halted him. He glanced down for half a second before continuing. "You are the best assassin the Legacy has seen since Dad."

Aeron barely caught the flash of pride cross her father's face before he turned toward Decius. "Don't be ridiculous. She may possess the skills, but Aeron lacks the tenacity to be one of us. At best, she can be labeled a *spy*. If you want out, it will be at twenty-two when you are disowned. I have two more years to make you or break you. I own you until then. Get out of my sight."

Bile rose in her mouth, his words searing open old scars of torment and disappointment. She hadn't meant her words at all, but had he? She retreated, careful not to turn her back on him until she was out of sight.

She waited in the study, swirling a glass of whiskey and taking small sips in front of the fireplace. The amber liquid burned all the way down, and she savored every second. The need to convince

Decius she wanted out of the Legacy hadn't seemed that big of a deal when her father instructed her until Decius' disbelief danced in front of her eyes. The doors burst open, and she jumped up at her father's disheveled appearance.

"What happened?" She put her empty glass down and moved closer.

"You gave quite the performance. You passed."

"I passed?"

"Your brother challenged me for the head of our Legacy."

"He what?" Her heart jumped into her throat. How could Decius be so foolish? If anyone had witnessed, it would be death if he failed. "Why would he do that?"

He rolled his neck, popping and cracking audible from across the room. "He's afraid for you. I believe his exact words were 'If you disown her, you disown me. If you hurt her, I will kill you.'"

Aeron nodded. She wasn't proud to deceive him. He would die to protect her. "I would have been afraid too, just a few months ago."

He picked up her empty glass from the coffee table without a word and filled it. It amazed her how easily he tossed back the drink and refilled the glass again. The burning sensation still coated her mouth.

"I don't understand why we have to keep up the charade." She dragged a hand down her face.

"Yes, you do. Come help me over here."

She moved to the desk, looking over the documents he shifted around. Most of them were financial records for the remaining Blood Families. "Any luck finding out who may be in his pocket?"

"Not yet. I put feelers out to the Finches and the Smiths to see where they are, but I haven't heard anything yet."

"And the Gales?" she asked.

His eyes cut to her and she swallowed the urge to back away. He hadn't mentioned them since that first conversation, but Shannon was her best friend—she needed to know if she should be worried.

"The Gales are neutral."

"What does that mean?" Neutral? Like Mrs. Gale knew about it? Or was she off limits to Mr. Wayward as well?

"You head back to the City tomorrow," he said without answering her. "Remember, everything is the same."

"Yes, because god forbid we have a functional relationship." She caught the smirk on his face, but he didn't respond. "What if he's not there?"

"Luke will be there," he assured. "Elijah won't rock the boat that much with the Board—or Luke."

They finished re-stacking the papers in silence. He moved to the safe behind a slide-out bookcase to the left of the desk, and Aeron headed to the door.

"Aeron?" he called.

She paused in the doorway, looking over her shoulder. Her stomach was a series of knots, and she couldn't form words. Within the week, she'd be back in New York with Luke—she hoped.

"It'll be worth it."

14

LUKE

*T*he dossiers splayed across Luke's bed represented all possible suspects in his parents' murder. He'd spent the last week cross-referencing the dossiers with all on-record missions, financials, personal statements, and anything that could determine if they belonged in the capture, kill, or safe pile.

A knock on his bedroom door pulled his attention from the coded documents. His eyeballs stung from staring at the stark pages, reminding him he hadn't moved for far too many hours.

"Yes?"

"You got a second?" Katherine called through the door.

He tossed a blanket over the documents, his knees protesting his request to move. He leaned his forehead against the cool wood.

"What do you need?" he asked.

"Can you open the door? I don't really want to have this conversation through a piece of wood."

He sighed but opened it a crack. He'd blown her off for drinks last week and avoided her since, the search for his parent's murderer the only thought fueling him. She pushed past him, storming into the room.

"Kat!" He jumped back, putting himself between her and the bed. "What the hell?"

"What does he have you doing?" She peeked around him, and he glanced back to make sure the dossiers were hidden.

"Paperwork. I'm doing a lot of paperwork and research. Showing him I can start from the bottom and work up."

She glared but didn't respond.

"What do you need? I'm busy."

"I can see that since you're wide awake at four in the morning. You haven't left your room in four days. I wanted to make sure you weren't dead. And since you're up, I can only assume you've got too much work to handle."

"I'm good," he lied. Was it really four in the morning? He was drowning in information he couldn't process any more, but he needed to be finished in a few hours.

"Sure you are. Well, I can't sleep. Come spar with me?"

"I really shouldn't." He looked back to the bed.

"Trust me. You need a break. I've worked with him my whole life. He can work for days straight on cases. That takes time to learn how to do. Come roll with me and let your brain sleep for a bit."

She arched an eyebrow. It reminded him of Shannon, and then Aeron. He needed to get home. He let out a long breath and ran a hand over his face. He wasn't going to get any more work done right now.

"Alright." He pulled on his sneakers and a shirt and locked the door behind him.

The roof-top dojo was empty. They changed into gis and stepped on the mats. Kat wasted no time in attacking. His legs were in the air and his back on the ground before he had a chance to blink. He fended her off, countering every indicator. The cool demeanor was gone, replaced by a fierceness that unsettled him. They moved from Jiu-Jitsu to Muay Thai and everything in between. Katherine's intensity drove all thoughts from his mind as he fought back, and he realized how similar to Aeron she was. So he gave her what she needed—an outlet. After nearly removing his arm and getting him to tap from submissions for at least the fifteenth time, she dropped to the mat, chest heaving. The silence stretched on, their breathing evening out until she got up to change.

Luke watched her. He'd just experienced one of the most intense training sessions of his life, and not a word had been spoken.

"What was that about?" he called before she could leave.

"Your evaluation with Granddad is coming up. Perry asked me to make sure you're prepared."

"And?"

"You'll be fine."

"Is that all?"

She met his gaze from across the mats, her rage gone. "I needed to let off some steam. Perry is usually here to help. But since you have replaced him, I settled. You can go back to being Granddad's lapdog now." She left.

"Shit." He jumped up, realizing they'd spent nearly two hours sparring, and he didn't have any answers for his Granddad. He raced back inside to the piles of documents. It was nearly seven. After showering and devouring some stale bread from his leftover dinner, he had thirty minutes to formulate something out of the heaps of paper on the bed. An underlying connection. Something.

"Damn it," he muttered, picking up the dossiers.

His Granddad nodded when he entered, gesturing to drop the papers on the desk and join him for a drink. Luke accepted the glass of dark liquid but didn't drink it, his stomach in knots.

"I couldn't find a connection," Luke said, cutting right to the chase.

The older man chuckled next to him. "I know."

The knot in his stomach tightened. "You...you know?"

"You're trying to put the puzzle together, but you can't. It's like there's a single thread missing."

"Yes." Was he just locked in his room for days looking at an unsolvable puzzle? He bit the inside of his cheek, tamping down on his first instinct to yell. He needed to play the game to get the reward. "Are there any more files I could look at?"

"I was hoping you would have found what we needed without this file." He picked a dossier off the table and held it out. "I'm jaded in my perception of this. And I was afraid my personal feelings were clouding my judgment. Since you were unable to find any rational conclusion in the other files, though, then I'm afraid I was right in my conclusion of who killed your parents."

Luke took the large dossier: *SEWARD*. His heart skipped several beats.

He flipped it open, scanning the codes. Every question, every hole in the other dossiers suddenly connected. Missing money, timeframes that didn't line up, swiped missions. Bile rose in his throat when he turned the page. WAYWARD, JOHN/MARY: Deceased. He nearly dropped the file: A picture of his parents sprawled across the pavement, number markers around the scene. He wanted to pull his eyes away, but he couldn't. The overturned Navigator in the background. The skid marks. The pools of blood beneath his parent's broken bodies.

"Luke." The deep voice pulled him back.

"Mr. Seward killed my parents?"

"The evidence points that way."

"No. That's not possible. There must be a mistake."

"It's no mistake."

Luke shook his head. "There has to be another explanation. He's family."

His granddad's fingers peaked beneath his chin. "I didn't want to believe it myself. He *is* family. But the evidence doesn't lie."

Luke flipped through the pages, not wanting to see the connections but unable not to.

"It's strange that his wife and your parents died in the same manner. A car wreck. Not very original, but makes a believable cover if no one is digging."

"You're not saying…"

"Keep flipping. You'll see."

Luke obliged, scanning the names at the top of each section until SEWARD, MAUREEN appeared. He flipped back and forth between the two cases, the similarities eerie.

"Maureen was like a daughter to me; I know her case inside and out. I had suspicions about what really happened, but there was no substantial evidence. When we finished the report of your parent's deaths, I knew it was no accident."

"How do you know it was him?"

"I didn't. Not right away. Maureen's death changed him—he became withdrawn. Secretive. Paranoid. The weeks before your father died, he confided in me. He believed the accident was a cover for the real cause of Maureen's death—abuse. I tried to corroborate the accusation, but it's been so many years, and Mr. Seward is an intimidating man. No one would confirm or deny."

Luke's fingers began to tingle. This couldn't be real. This was another test.

"He killed Maureen and your parents figured it out. What started as self-preservation has turned into an all-out war on our family. On the Legacy. Until your parents died, I had no idea how deep his treachery went. It's deep, Luke."

The tingling intensified, and he realized his hands were shaking. "Aeron and Decius, are they in danger?"

"I don't know. The motive, the abuse, is based on rumor, but the evidence does not lie. He's had ten years to raise them as he wishes. They could be in on it for all we know."

A hysteric laugh left Luke. "No. You must have your intel wrong. Mr. Seward would never…" But the confrontation between Aeron and her father at the funeral returned to him. She never talked about home, and Decius rarely had praise for his father.

"Luke?"

His parents had put a noticeable distance between themselves and Mr. Seward the past year. They'd opted out of summer training —unheard of in the past seventeen years.

He returned to the dossier, reading between the coded lines to decipher the forensic evidence. From what he knew, forensically speaking, the two accidents were identical. And in the days leading up to the deaths, both parties were involved in a public argument with Mr. Seward, where threats of violence had been tossed from his lips. Not the damning evidence Luke wanted, but threats in the Legacy could not be taken lightly. A verbal threat was as good as a death warrant.

"He's building an army, Luke. Every document in there has evidence that he has been planning to overthrow our family for a very long time. He's just declared war on us. If it were just the accusations, I would allow the Board to intervene. But he murdered my children."

"Uncle Paul?" Luke raised an eyebrow.

"You didn't think we were unfortunate enough to have two accidental deaths in this family, did you? No. He must have stumbled on to Mr. Seward's intentions years ago, but it was your parents who discovered his connection to Maureen's death."

"Why did he kill her?" His voice cracked on the last word. Decius never really got over his mother's death.

"She tried to take the kids and leave the Legacy. Take them away from the abuse is my guess. I would have offered safe-haven had she confided in me."

Luke's gut sank, catapulting bile into his throat. If she took the kids, Luke would never have gotten close to Aeron and Decius. Mr. Seward would have lost his Legacy. But she did die, and his parents rallied around her murderer, supporting him. Aeron's hatred of the Legacy Laws must be a constant reminder to her father. The fear in her eyes the last time he saw her surfaced. She was in danger.

"How do we make him pay?"

A triumphant glint met him. "We eliminate the competition.

Take out his known associates. Then we make him feel the pain of losing his family. And finally—"

"What?" Bile coated his tongue, and he swallowed it back. "His family? You mean Aeron and Decius?"

"Yes."

"No." Luke stood up. "No. You can't."

"Luke—"

"They are all *I* have left. *She* is all I have left."

Granddad arched an eyebrow. "She?"

Luke hesitated. They weren't an item, but the thought of something happening to Aeron—his fingers itched to break something. "You can't hurt her. She's more important to me than anything else."

"Even revenge?"

Luke sat back down, a deep sigh leaving him as he grasped the back of his head. What the hell happened to summers on the beach and island hopping?

"Luke—"

"I want him dead. I do. I will kill him myself, and I will help you destroy his mutiny. I will help you transform the Legacy. But I can't let you hurt them. They've suffered enough at his hands."

"How touching," he scoffed. "And what of my revenge? Is my loss less valid than yours?"

"Of course not."

"I want that scum to feel every ounce of misery we feel, Luke. I want him to question the motives of everyone he works with. I want him to *pay.*" He rose to his feet, towering over Luke.

"He doesn't even care about her!" Luke shouted back, scrambling for the words to change his granddad's mind. "She hates him."

"How do you know?"

"I think," Luke's voice dropped to a whisper, but even when the words left his mouth, they felt true. "I think the abuse wasn't only towards Aunt Maureen."

"And why would you think that?"

"Because I witnessed an altercation between them after the funeral. And she lied to me about it."

"That is a heavy accusation, son. The Laws—"

"Who cares about the Laws. They're stupid." Living free from the Legacy Laws put into perspective how restrictive they'd lived. His parents were dead, and someone would pay.

"I'm glad you see that. However, we have to function within their bounds—for now."

Luke nodded. Abuse was not tolerated in the Legacy. They stood for the greater good. But it would explain Decius' overly protective nature toward Aeron.

Granddad leaned back, crossing his arms. "This changes things. If what you say is true, then maybe adding her to our arsenal will be a better approach. I mean, *if* he doesn't care and she truly hates him, then she will make a great asset to use against him. She could have access to everything we need."

Luke released a breath, the tension in his shoulders easing. "And Decius?"

"What about him? I will spare one. Not both."

Tension wrapped back around his shoulders. "She'd never forgive me if something happened to him."

"He allowed his sister to be harmed at the hands of their father. In my book, he's just as bad. He should have challenged or come forward. But cowardice is a worse crime here. For all we know, he is working with him to destroy the Legacy."

"Or he could be suffering the same as she is. Granddad—"

"Enough."

The glint in the older man's eyes was final. Arguing would do Luke no good. He needed to figure out how to protect Aeron and Decius. Treason on this level would be a chess game; there would be time to plan. Right now, he needed to stay in good graces.

Granddad picked up the dossiers and returned to the desk. "Are you going to help me take out your parents' murderer, yes or no?"

"Yes," Luke said, biting back the stipulations on the tip of his tongue.

"Good."

"And Aeron?"

"No harm will come to her on my end—as long as you stay on task."

As long as you stay on task. She wasn't safe. Not by a long shot. He'd only managed to put a temporary hold on her execution.

"And Decius?" Luke held his breath.

"I will determine his fate once I have more information and know where his loyalty lies, with their Legacy or the new one. Inform Katherine your training is complete. Both of you be ready at six a.m. It's time to show you what we really do here."

Luke swallowed the acidic taste in his mouth, afraid vomit would resurface if he responded. He left without being dismissed and made it to the stairs before retching—three, four times. With hardly any food in his system, the green-yellow liquid burned as it came up.

"Luke?"

He wiped his mouth. Katherine's pale face confirmed he looked as bad as he thought he might, vomiting on the stairs.

"What happened?"

He opened his mouth a few times, but no words formed, and she helped him up the stairs.

"So, your best friends' father killed your parents—his best friends— because they discovered he'd killed his wife, also their best friend?" Katherine paced the worn ground in front of the couch. Her bare feet filled the dip as if she'd walked miles in the tiny space.

He nodded. They'd retreated to their shared living area, Luke not wanting to sit with this information alone in a dark room.

"With friends like that, it's no wonder the old Legacy is crumbling."

"You're missing my biggest problem. I don't care about the Legacy or Mr. Seward. I mean, I do…I want to see him suffer. I want to make him suffer. I'd go over there right now and beat the living shit out of him if I could. But Granddad—he has a different agenda, and it includes killing Aeron and Decius as payback, if I can't get them on board."

"I'm not missing it. I'm just trying to wrap my head around the treachery they grew up in. It's bound to have an impact. How sure are you that they aren't aware of it?"

"Kat—I've lived with them for longer stretches of time at the Institute than they've lived with their father. And even over breaks, we spent all of our time together. They believe their mother died in a car accident. It took one glance to know the 'accidents' were caused by the same person. If they knew, then…"

"What about bringing Aeron into the fold? It's an option, right?"

"And leave Dee to Granddad and your mother? Never."

She nodded and continued pacing. "How sure are you that he did it? I mean, from what you describe—he's an asshat, sure, but murderer? Traitor?"

Luke's face flushed with irritation. "I saw the dossiers—the evidence is damning on its own. I may not have believed it, but add in the avoidance of their father and the fact I *witnessed* an altercation—what else do I need?"

He traced the cuts across his knuckles, the thought of his fist against Mr. Seward's face hovering below the surface.

"Just make sure he's paying for the right sins. We're trained to fabricate this stuff. If you're wrong, about any of it—"

"I'm not wrong."

Katherine scoffed but dropped the subject. "Get your shoes on. We will regret this in the morning, but let's go get that drink." She pulled on a pair of shoes and motioned him to follow.

They snuck out of the property, Katherine catching him several times before a guard could spot him. Once over the wall, he kept pace with her.

After an hour of aimless walking, they slipped into the side entrance of an apartment building and headed up the stairs. Luke remained quiet, filing away every question that popped into his mind. Where were they going? Who'd she signal on the street? How could they successfully sneak off the property without casing the security team in broad daylight but fail the past three training missions?

They stopped outside the third apartment on the fourth floor. Katherine gave two sharp knocks and a whistle. Two whistles and a sharp knock answered, and she opened the door. A shabby apartment greeted them, the distinct smell of lavender wafting out. Katherine stopped just inside the threshold, putting her hand up to stop him, and pointed to a tripwire.

"Dominic? It's me and a buddy. I'm going to step over the line. If you shoot me, I will kill you nice and slowly, understand?"

A soft click followed by metal sliding across the floor answered her. Luke spotted a loaded magazine on the floor. His stomach knotted when she stepped over the line and picked up the magazine, but no shots rang out. He followed, more hesitantly, closing the door as he did. The rest of the room came into view, and Luke's eyes widened as he took in two entire walls of computer screens. For an off-the-grid setup, it was almost as impressive as what they had at the Institute in New York.

Beneath the constant movement on the wall sat a short, stocky man. His black hair was untamed, and brown eyes searched him from behind glasses.

"Who is this?"

She ignored his question. "Get Gunnar on the line."

Dominic eyed Luke with suspicion but punched away on one of his many keyboards. All but the middle screen went black, and a dark, blurry figure appeared on the screen.

"What's up?"

"It's me," Katherine answered, slipping second nature into an island dialect Luke couldn't place.

"Cher—how are you?" The concern in his voice echoed through the speakers.

"Never better."

Even through the blurriness, Luke saw he didn't believe what she said.

"Where's my cousin?" she asked.

"Haven't seen him in two days."

"Shit."

"What's the word?"

She rubbed her chin, irritation in her eyes. "When will he be back?"

Gunnar shook his head. "Don't know, Red."

"Alright. Have him call when he gets in."

"What can I help with?"

"Just stay available and off the grid."

"You know we're not sitting back on this." Gunnar leaned closer, his dreadlocks falling forward, and he pushed them back.

"You're already doing enough." Kat's voice softened.

"It's not just your fight, Katherine."

"But it is my world. And if another one of you dies…"

"Then we go out fighting."

"Gun—"

"Shay would never forgive me." Kat's back stiffened. "There has only ever been one word he manages, and that is your name. Now I don't know if he understands me and just can't communicate or if you are the only thing he can remember. But I cannot let you take this on yourself."

A long breath escaped her. "I'll keep you updated."

The screen went dark, and Katherine tossed the loaded magazine to Dominic. "This is Luke."

Dominic looked him over once and then began plugging away on the computer, screens lighting up as if Luke's sudden arrival was nothing more interesting than the arrival of the Sunday paper. Katherine moved to the small kitchen and pulled out two bottles of beer, opened them, and held one out. He accepted.

"Do you know why Granddad is the most feared assassin? I'll let you in on a secret: It's not because of what he does out there, but what he does in-house. Short of killing us, he will go to any lengths to ensure we stay in line."

"What do you mean?" Luke took a sip of the cold drink.

She kept her eyes on her bottle. "Between the ages of twelve and seventeen, I spent time in the West Indies on a quaint little island, completely off the grid. I was young. I met a boy. It was instant chemistry, and while my mother made deadly deals with mercenaries, I fell in love. When it was time to leave, I wanted to stay, and I convinced my mother that I could be a liaison in the area. It was the simple matter of keeping the locals in check and managing the contacts of the West Indies. Being able to stay with Shay was a bonus—or so I told myself."

He kept his gaze glued to her, the sudden life history catching him off guard. He took another sip of his beer, waiting for her to look up. But she stayed focused on the fake hardwood floors.

"Granddad said I needed to leave. He had bigger plans for me back home, and there was no need for me on the island. I said no. I wanted to stay. I thought maybe he saw me as too young for it and wanted to prove I could do the job."

A slight laugh escaped her, and Luke's chest tightened. Those exact thoughts had run through his head the first time Granddad had given him an assignment to kill the FBI Liaison. It had caused a rift with his parents he never had a chance to fully repair.

"It didn't take long for Granddad to find out my true motive for staying. I was ordered to break his heart, make him forget all about me, and come home. I did and left that night. A week later," her voice caught, and she cleared her throat. "A week later, Shay was found. Disoriented and beaten almost beyond recognition."

"What happened?" Luke whispered.

She wiped the tears from her cheeks and sniffled. "That's what I wanted to know. I stormed into Granddad's office. Irate. Demanding to know what happened to him. Me, a seventeen-year-old child, demanding the Senior Assassin answer to me about someone I should have no connection to anymore." She took a sip of beer and met Luke's eyes for the first time. "Granddad said—he said when he gives orders, they aren't meant figuratively. He had personally tortured him. Electrocuting until his heart stopped. Then revived and beaten. Repeatedly. Until his brain could no longer form a coherent sentence. So, he couldn't come looking for me.

"He'd recorded it. Forced me to watch it, over and over and over until my tears finally stopped falling, and I agreed it was what needed to happen." Silence fell, a look of torture on her face Luke would never forget. He couldn't imagine having to watch that happen to Aeron.

"What did you do?"

"I fell in line. I did everything I was told. I never asked questions. And as far as Granddad is concerned, I learned my lesson, embraced the life, and became the best apprentice to follow in his footsteps."

"Kat…"

"You can't…you can't witness something like that—the brutal torture and reoccurring death of the person you love. Every time he stopped moving, I was *relieved*. I thanked god he was dead. And then they brought him back to life. Over and over."

She was lost in her own nightmare, staring out the window over his shoulder. "Katherine. Why are you telling me this?"

She swallowed hard and looked back at him. "Because this is what he does. If you can't be broken, then you're a threat. And he will find what breaks you. There's a reason we are always on display as his first family here. Because we are the example of what happens when you fail. And there is nowhere we can hide. Everyone knows us. Knows our faces. Knows our demons. Your parents kept you hidden for good reason, Luke. Aeron and Decius are in grave danger. He will use Aeron to make you do unspeakable things, and you will do them because his threats are anything but idle."

His throat tightened.

"You can't trust him, Luke."

"I can't afford not to," he whispered back. "You just told me the horrors that await us. I did this. I put her in the crosshairs, and she has no idea how much danger she is in."

"Keep it that way. You can't let her know what's going on because then she is no longer a pawn for him, and she will suffer beyond imagination, and you will be forced to witness it. Then, and only then, will she be removed from the board."

"What do I do? Just sit by and pretend everything is fine? That I didn't just gamble her life?"

"Help me." The words were soft, but there was a slight plea in them.

"Help you what?"

"Help me, and Perry, and our rag-tag crew. We're taking over Legacy Inc."

A laugh escaped Luke before he could stop it. "You're already taking over Legacy Inc. by the end of next year."

"No. I'm the fresh young face to the company. A new generation. But no one will really be in control of anything until he is dead. Let me rephrase: We're overthrowing the current regime to stop any more unnecessary deaths.

"The original Legacy was built on honor and created to protect the people against corruption and evil. Yeah, it has its faults. But Legacy Inc. is built on corruption and is nothing but evil. Too many lives that should have been protected have been taken instead—all for profits. It needs to end. There needs to be a balance between the two."

"Are you crazy? It's suicide. Do you know the ramifications of taking out the Senior Assassin? There are protocols. Hidden sects. You'd be dead in a week."

"No. Well, maybe before—but not anymore." She shook her head, and a heavy sigh blew through her lips. "You just changed the game, Luke. Granddad is focused on taking down Aeron's dad and making you the face of the Legacy. We'll have a window. You want to protect your friends? You need to be the closest to your enemy. Are you in?"

Katherine kept her face neutral while Luke processed her offer. There wasn't much to think about. Agreeing to help Katherine locked him in to a mutiny that would almost guarantee death. But it was the surest way to keep Aeron and Decius alive, and he would go to hell and back to keep them safe. Worst case scenario, they all die. Best case scenario, the Legacy is reset, and he and Aeron could walk away. There really wasn't any other answer.

"Yes. What do we do?"

15

AERON

*A*eron dropped her suitcase by the marbled breakfast bar in the New York apartment and gazed out the wall of bay windows. The view used to calm her nerves, remind her there was someplace safe other than Ernie's.

"I forgot how beautiful it is here."

She spun at the deep voice. Luke's tall, muscled body leaned against the empty door frame, his brown eyes dancing in the sunlight.

"Hi," she said softly and glanced around him to see if Decius was there. She'd counted on having the team to buffer their first inter-action post-funeral and post-secret-keeper for her father. Having her father's approval to date Luke should make things easier, but her fear for his life dampened her excitement.

"Can I come in?"

"Of course." She waved her hand awkwardly. "Why wouldn't you be able to?"

He shrugged his shoulders, joining her by the window. They watched in silence as the ant-sized people scattered around Central Park in the rain.

"How are you?" she asked, desperate to have conversation

moving between them. It was a stupid question. His parents were dead—he was terrible.

"I'm...I'm good."

She looked, but his eyes remained focused outside. He did look good. The dark circles beneath his eyes were gone, and his complexion glowed with a summer tan.

"I'm glad," she said, bumping his shoulder. "It would be depressing if you were moping around here while we tried to run missions." That caught his attention.

He gazed down at her, his eyes clear and hard—controlled.

"Lulu. It's okay to be mad. And sad. And generally pissed off right now."

"I already did the five stages of grief," he said. "I don't really want to relive them."

"There are seven."

"What?"

"Seven stages of grief: denial, anger, bargaining, depression, acceptance, vengeance, and body disposal," she said seriously, thinking of the growing body count she intended to stop.

He stared at her and then released a roar of laughter. The deep sound filled her, his crinkled eyes and how he clutched his sides warming her. It seemed a lifetime ago she'd seen him smile.

"Oh," he said, catching his breath. He placed his hand on her shoulder, small chuckles escaping him.

"What'd I miss?" The musical voice sounded over Luke's laughter.

Shannon smiled from the kitchen. She placed a bag of groceries on the counter. Aeron's own smile broadened at the sight of her best friend. "Luke—good to see you. Decius ran down to grab the rest of the bags. Want to give him a hand?"

"Sure," he said, escaping the apartment before Aeron could protest.

"Hey, stranger." Aeron moved to help her put food away. "How was your break?"

"Better than yours," Shannon said. She placed some fruit in a bowl on the counter, and her eyes flickered to Aeron's cheek. The scar on her cheek from the funeral was barely visible, but it wouldn't slip past her best friend's scrutiny.

"Who told you? It happened after you'd left." Aeron opened the fridge and began putting the vegetables inside.

"Luke asked what I thought."

"And?"

"And I said he should ask you, if he was all that concerned."

Aeron released a deep sigh. "It wasn't as bad as last summer. How's your mom?"

"Still in Haiti. I had hoped after the funeral you would come with us. It would have been fun."

"Yeah, medically attending to sick people, in a third world country…I think I had more fun."

"You could have helped build houses and done hands-on work," Shannon said with a laugh. "Trust me, my mother would never let you near a sick person with a needle. You would end up stabbing them in frustration."

"This is true," Aeron agreed, ignoring the guilt that pinged in her chest. "It was just your everyday training-in-hell at Seward Manor, though."

"Well, I got to run surgeries all summer."

A smile spread across Aeron's face. Since the age of seven, Shannon spent every second away from the Institute training with her mother to be a medic. At sixteen, she was training in surgery. It's been Shannon's dream to be performing surgeries with her mom—saving people was her calling.

"That's fucking fantastic, Shan."

Shannon beamed and tossed a paper bag at her, and Aeron caught it with deft fingers.

"Your lifeline."

Aeron spied a cell phone inside.

"It's already programmed and everything."

"Thanks." She placed the phone inside her luggage and rolled it near the hallway to her bedroom. The door opened, Decius and Luke dragging more luggage.

"Jeesh, Shan. What do you have in here, cement blocks?" Luke huffed. He dropped the duffel bag to the ground with a thud.

"Don't be ridiculous," Shannon said with a smirk. "That's my combat gear."

He rolled his eyes, smirking. If Aeron had not known his parents were dead, she could almost believe everything was normal. After unpacking the food and placing luggage in the respected rooms, they gathered around the breakfast bar, Decius grabbing each of them a water. He'd remained quiet, heaviness hanging on his shoulders.

"Everything okay, Dee?" she asked.

"It's just weird—only the four of us and Justin this year."

"We still have our connections," Luke said.

"Yeah, but it's not the same."

"We have fresh blood coming in," Shannon reminded them. "She's young, but she'll be valuable. We need a bio-chemist on the team now that Keara's gone."

"Wait, you mean you didn't like my makeshift bomb?" Decius said with feigned innocence on his face.

Shannon turned beet red, and Luke choked on his water. "No, Dee. No one liked your makeshift bomb."

Decius let out a roar of laughter, Luke joining in once he could breathe again.

"Alright," Shannon said, no hint of amusement on her face. "You guys can go now." She walked over to the door and held it open. "Goodbye." She pointed a finger out the door.

The two boys, still laughing, headed for the door.

"Later," Aeron called out.

Decius waved without actually looking back. Luke paused in the hallway and caught Aeron's gaze, a slight smile directed at her.

"Later, Aeron," he managed before Shannon slammed the door in his face.

"Shan!"

"So...you and Luke? This the year you guys break Laws?"

"Maybe," Aeron said, her face warming at the thought. "If I didn't think my father would kill me."

"Decius wouldn't let him. Speaking of, who gets to break the news to him? His best friend or his sister?"

Aeron scrunched her nose and stuck out her tongue.

"It is weird not having Keara around—she always had people coming and going. It's quiet."

Shannon agreed. "I think this is the first time in recent history this apartment has only housed two members."

"How do you think the new recruit will be?"

"Young," Shannon answered. "She's only sixteen."

"That's it?" Aeron only remembered part of the trials at the end of May. Her mind had been on what Ernie's would have in store for her. "I don't remember the last time we had someone that young, not Legacy-born, on the team. Was she that impressive?"

"Every training-team of the Legacy put a bid on her."

"That's right. Decius made the executive decision to extend the invitation. No wonder he's stressed."

"Pays to be Legacy-blood every once in a while. I'm going to turn in; I'm not fully back in this time zone." Shannon yawned. "I'll see you in the morning."

Aeron retreated to her room, dropping her bags to the floor. The phone Shannon had given her buzzed, 'Lulu' flashing across the screen.

"Hello?"

"Just making sure Shannon gave me your number and not one to an escort service like she did last year."

"Maybe this is a dating line," she joked as she sat on the bed. "Maybe this is the direct line to my side job."

"Very funny, Ron," he said. She could hear the exasperation in his voice, but the use of her childhood nickname heated her from within. Only he was allowed to call her that growing up. "I just wanted to be sure."

"How does it feel to be back?"

"Like home."

"The apartment or the company?"

"Both," he said.

Her heart thumped. "How was training?"

"It was training. Not all that great." He lapsed into silence.

"Any plans for this year?" She asked, not wanting to get off the phone.

He let out a rough laugh. "Yeah. Apparently, my Granddad is expecting me to run the Legacy next year." His voice was thick with contempt.

Any doubt about her father's accusations was slowly ebbing away. "You don't want to?"

"I don't know what I want anymore."

They fell into silence. She never imagined feeling awkward talking to him, but she wanted to run across the hall and tell him how much danger he was in. Yelling erupted from his end of the phone, and her heart jumped. "What's going on?"

"I think Decius needs help in the game room. Later."

"Later," she said, not sure he even stayed on long enough to hear her.

The boardroom echoed around her. Aeron thought the apartment felt empty, but the vast boardroom, lacking Perry, Keara, and Josh, was worse. Decius checked his watch next to her.

"They should be here any minute."

Aeron gazed at Luke across the table. He sat too straight, posture screaming not to bother him, his eyes focused on the table, lost in thought. He seemed different. Harder. The armor he'd built around himself was nearly visible, and she wanted to strip it down, wrap him in her arms, and take him far away from here.

"Hey."

She turned to Shannon and raised an eyebrow.

"Stare any harder, and you might as well be wearing a sign saying, 'Fuck me on the table,'" she whispered.

"Shut up," she laughed.

The doors finally swung open. Silence echoed again, and they straightened in their seats as Mason entered, towering over the brunette behind him. He directed the young girl to take a seat, her petite frame dwarfed by the high-back wooden chair. Unlike most Guardians, Mason didn't wear button-down shirts and ties at the Institute. His jeans had rips in them, and he wore a plain gray T-shirt with a black zip-up hoodie.

And unlike the usual calm Aeron felt when seeing him, the blood drained from her face when his eyes met hers. Her exit from Ernie's garage flooded into her mind. Tommy; Ernie.

"Fuck," Aeron said, a little louder than she intended, her heart racing. Mason's eyes stayed on Aeron for a few moments before greeting everyone in the room.

"I trust you all settled in nicely?" Mason asked, passing around a stack of dossiers. "Lesley, I would like you to meet your team. Decius, your team lead." Decius waved his hand. "If you need anything, he will be able to assist you. Aeron," Aeron nodded in their direction, "and Shannon, your new housemates. We also have Luke and Justin." The boys waved, and Lesley's tense smile responded. "Over the last three months, you have met other trainees like yourself. They were recruited in a similar fashion to you and joined of their own choice. They train year-round. You, however, were selected by this team."

"I'm sorry, selected?" Lesley asked. Her eyes snapped around the room, and Aeron caught a hint of the girl they'd seen on the roof last year. Her mousy appearance of just fourteen or fifteen melted away, and the calculating sixteen-year-old slipped into place.

"Your recruitment video." Decius adjusted in his chair, leaning forward on the table. "Your calm demeanor and use of the chemicals around you were impressive. "

Lesley nodded, her eyes landing back on Mason. "You may have seen them around, usually in a hurry and most likely covered in blood. However, this is *the* elite training team of the Legacy; the descendants of the original Legacy Families, along with a few select others."

"Oh." Lesley's eyes doubled, and Aeron fought not to groan. The celebrity factor of their lineage was the one downside of bringing in fresh blood. In all fairness, though, if she'd just been recruited to a top-secret program with the purpose to protect civilians at all costs, meeting the children of the founders would be pretty cool.

"It also means you get an unreasonable amount of leeway in your extracurricular activities," Justin added, trying to lighten the room the way Perry and Josh would have. "And we live off-campus." He wiggled his eyebrows.

Aeron couldn't think about clubbing or any number of the shenanigans they used to get into—things were serious this year. Luke was in danger, and there was the real possibility of her becoming enemy number one to the Legacy.

Shannon scoffed beside her, but across the table, Luke fist-bumped him, forcing a laugh.

"It's not that great," Decius said, getting into the conversation. "I mean, we do have to do our own laundry."

"And our own cooking," Luke added.

"You mean I do the cooking," Shannon clarified, and Aeron could almost hear her eyes roll.

"Don't forget we also have to actually make it to the Institute after long training nights. It's not as good as being able to just roll out of bed and be here." Decius grinned.

"Except for the partying," Luke said.

"And the ladies," Justin piped in, nudging Luke, who fist-bumped again.

"Or gents." Shannon leaned forward and glared at the guys. "You act like you are the only ones who get laid. Seriously." She looked at Lesley. "Unless you prefer the ladies, then those too."

"Enough, enough."

"Oh, c'mon," Aeron chipped in, forcing herself into the conversation. Everything needed to appear normal. "You like it when we bring in fresh blood and you get to show us off." She tried to meet Mason's eyes again, but he skillfully overlooked her.

"Oh yeah. I get to show off my overgrown teenagers, who are three times as much work as any other team in the Legacy. Do you know how much bull I put up with being your Guardian? Of course, I'm damned proud of you guys. You could have turned out so much worse. Remember the Roberts' boy?"

The room filled with laughter and hoots, Lesley's gaze trying to take them all in.

"Alright, alright! Back to business," Mason called, sobering up as he opened the file. "Your assignment is a Watched Target, so be prepared for a moment's notice on this one. Also, be ready for several individual assignments, since this one isn't going to have much activity on it."

"Watched?" Decius flipped through the folder. Aeron opened hers as well, intrigued by the unconventional first assignment. Watched Targets were unpredictable targets—they weren't for trainees, even elite ones. However, Reaping missions weren't for trainees either. What was their Senior Assassin up to this year? She moved her gaze from the coded document titled 'Wilks' to Luke, the only person who didn't seem interested in their assignment.

Decius closed his dossier. "Any reason for the sudden change of pace?"

"I didn't ask," Mason answered. "But, I'm assuming because you've proved successful on many active cases, and let's be honest —it may help keep you all out of trouble if you know you can be summoned at any minute."

"I doubt that," Shannon said, and Aeron laughed, the atmosphere filling with the obnoxiousness of years past.

"I have an announcement." Luke stood up so fast his chair skidded back almost a foot. Everyone snapped their head toward him, and Aeron's heart began to race. "I know I don't have to do this formally, but since we are all here—I'll be taking on a double duty as my Granddad has asked me to train to take my father's place." The room went silent. "But my commitment to the team comes first, always. I just wanted to let everyone know." The world seemed to drag him down with this announcement, but her heart fluttered, realizing he had confided in her first.

"Who's your Granddad?" Lesley asked.

Aeron didn't think the room could have fallen any quieter, but she was wrong.

"Luke's Granddad is Mr. Wayward. The Senior Assassin of the Legacy," Mason supplied. Lesley's mouth fell open.

"I think it's admirable," Mason commended. "You'll make an amazing Senior Assassin, and I know your team will do whatever they can to help."

Luke bowed his head and sat down, eyes not meeting any of them.

"Is that all?" Decius checked his watch. "I was thinking we could go get some dinner. Want to join us, Mason?"

"No. But thank you. I do need to borrow Aeron for a few moments, though. Here." Mason slid a flash drive across the table to Decius, the digital files for their first case.

"Text me where," Aeron called after them as they filed out the door. Her stomach rumbled, and she checked her own watch: 8:30. "How did it get so late?"

"Morning meetings ran late, pushing everything back. You guys must have been waiting easily two hours after your first few meetings for this one."

"How is—"

"I requested you for standby on an assignment. Unfortunately, your father has denied the request." Mason's eyes crinkled in the corners, and Aeron's guard went up.

"Of course he has."

"Everything going okay at the manor? I thought that…"

Aeron trusted Mason with her life and her secrets. He'd taken over their Guardianship five years ago after their lifetime Guardian, Sarah, had died in the line of duty. He'd become more than a Guardian; he'd become a friend. "Yes. Better than it has been."

"Good. I was concerned until I saw you at the funeral. Working with your father is a good thing."

Aeron leaned against the table and crossed her arms. "How do you think Luke's handling it?" She raised an eyebrow at him, but he shrugged his shoulders and tucked his hair behind his left ear—a conversation for another time, in another place.

"Here." He pulled out a small envelope from his back pocket. It would be a lie to say her stomach didn't flip for the briefest moment.

"From you?"

"No, your father." The flip catapulted to her throat. Aeron unsealed the envelope and pulled out a black business card. On one side an intricate 'S' was scrawled, on the other an address and time —a calling card. She rolled her eyes. It was too late to meet him now. She'd have to call him when she got home to the burner phone tucked under her bed for communicating with him.

"Thanks." She left the boardroom, pausing only to drop the folder in the shredder by the door. The vibration of a text or phone call jumped in her pocket, but she ignored it and raced down the flights of stairs and out a side door, heading for the subway. The screech of the train reached her ears, and she raced down the steps, but missed boarding by just seconds.

"Great." She glanced around the unusually deserted Monday night platform and perched herself at the edge of a bench. She should at least call Shannon and let her know she was heading home. A noise by the stairs paused her movement. Raising the phone a little higher, she caught a reflection on the black screen—two males behind her. They leaned against the wall facing away from her. She relaxed a little as the next train sped in.

Aeron fumbled her phone, dropping it on the ground, and allowed the guys to go first. They entered a middle car, and she headed to the back, where there would only be one entrance to watch. She took the seat at the rear of the train to get a clear view of all the cars ahead. She put her phone in her breast pocket and leaned back as the train moved forward.

A female voice cried out and Aeron shot to her feet, heading for the other car. The men from the platform towered over a cowering girl, clutching her bag. Her short blond hair stuck to the blood on her forehead.

"Please, I don't have any money," she cried. The men laughed, and Aeron slid into the car behind them.

"You heard her. She doesn't have any money."

The men spun around, and a pulse of pre-fight adrenaline spread through her like fire. The two white males sported hoodies and baggy jeans and weren't much taller than her, though, in her five-inch heels.

"Hey, sexy," the one on the right said, his eyes roaming her body. "Want to join this party?"

"Not particularly." Aeron caught the girl's eyes—a bright, star-tling blue. Aeron jerked her head to the side, telling her to get out. She stared for a moment before coming to her senses and scurrying away.

The men watched her go with disappointment, then turned their attention to Aeron, adjusting to block her from leaving the way she'd come.

"What are you doing traveling on the subway, alone?" the one on the left asked.

She dropped her gaze. They'd done this before. The men—they could only be a bit older than Luke, maybe twenty-four—moved closer to her, close enough for her to catch a whiff of their drugstore aftershave. They kept their hoods up, masking them in shadow, but she didn't need to see their faces.

"He asked you a question," the one on the right said and took another step closer. The cheap cologne stung her nose. "It's not polite to not answer."

Aeron snapped her eyes up to the man closest to her and glared. He froze—the look she inherited from her father tended to do that.

"It's not polite to speak to a lady that way," she said in a voice that matched her stare. She needed him to move a bit closer. He did. Aeron shot her left hand forward, grabbed the strings of his hood, and yanked. The fabric closed tight around his head. She pulled down, her knee coming up to meet his face. He tried to pull away, but her grip remained on the strings, and she made quick work of crossing them in a knot behind his neck. The other man stood rooted to the spot as his friend struggled to free himself, shocked by Aeron's sudden movement.

"I'd run," she said. The words snapped him into action. He whipped his hood off and charged at her. A laugh escaped her while she nimbly avoided him and eyed the other man—he was almost free. She kicked at his face. Strong arms snatched her from behind, pinning her arms and squeezed as she tried to drop her weight down. The hoodie had concealed his muscles, so instead of burning her energy, she stilled, and he squeezed his arms tighter.

The leader ripped his hoodie off. "Clever trick," he spat, "but you should have run."

Aeron smiled at the blood flowing from his nose, and the adrenaline pumped again. "I don't run," Aeron said, trying to contain the mirth in her voice. "Do you see how high these heels are?" She aimed a kick at him, nearly catching his nose again. "You can't run in these."

The muscular man squeezed her tighter, and she found it difficult to breathe. The other man took another step forward and traced a hand down the front of her suit jacket.

Aeron spit in his face, and he backhanded her. She tasted copper and smiled. She could finish this fight in moments. A single opportunity was all it would take, but now that her blood was pumping, she wanted a fight more than she needed to finish one.

"Do you like it rough?" A twisted smile lit his face. He pinched her face between his fingers and thumb, leaning in to kiss her.

Aeron pulled back and tried to wriggle away, but Muscles held fast. She continued to fight until her skirt slid up past her mid-thigh and then let out a breath and slumped down, making herself heavier.

"See?" the leader said, leaning into her. "All that did was make you tired. His hand ran up the side of her exposed thigh, inching slowly to the hemline.

Aeron laughed again. Not a frantic or hysterical laugh, but a deep, humorous laugh. There were many types of vermin she enjoyed eliminating, but eliminating men who took advantage of women and children took the cake.

"What's so funny?" he demanded, grabbing her chin.

She answered by driving a small dagger into his forearm. The struggle had allowed her skirt to rise enough to grab the throwing knife hidden there. He whirled back in pain, and she dropped her heel onto the in-step of Muscles. She dropped to the ground. The leader pulled out his own knife. With a quick kick, it skidded across the train. Aeron reached into her boot and pulled out her longer, deadlier dagger, and pushed him against the side of the car, the blade to his throat. His eyes widened, and she could feel the panic rising in him, fueling her.

"Muscles. You come one step closer, and I will kill him." He stopped in his tracks, and another burst of adrenaline pumped through her. Now that she could see both clearly, they were related in some way—cousins or brothers—it didn't matter because it worked in her favor. They would not risk the other's life.

Aeron dug the dagger deeper, drawing blood. She couldn't keep her smile from widening as he let out a whimper.

"If you wanted money, all you had to do was ask," she said. "It wouldn't have helped. I would have told you no and kicked your asses anyways. But the polite thing to do is to always ask."

He didn't speak but took raspy breaths beneath her. The train slowed, and she looked around, surprised she hadn't missed her stop. The right thing to do would be to kill them now because they would do this again, she had no doubt. But logistically, there were too many cameras and not enough exit strategies.

"This was fun, boys," Aeron said. "We should never do it again, because there will be no mercy." She flipped her dagger and swung her fist, knocking the leader out with the hilt.

She turned to Muscles, who remained rooted to the spot. She slipped the knife back into her boot. "I'd knock you out too," she assured him, "but someone has to carry that pile of crap home." She thrust her finger toward the unconscious lump on the floor. The train came to a stop. "Next time someone says run—run."

Movement on the platform caught her attention. The petite blond exited the train. Aeron hurried after, but she disappeared.

"You're welcome," she muttered to the empty air.

"Aeron!"

She spun. Her father stood by the open door. His eyes raked over the ripped suit splattered in blood and the bloody lip she hastily wiped up. His nostrils flared in disapproval. "Dad!"

"What happened?" His voice was tight, eyes taking in the scene from the train doorway. The warning sound chimed, and she tugged him away so the doors would close. It wasn't the first time she'd been harassed on the subway. Certainly wouldn't be the last.

"Nothing. Some Underworlders thinking with their dicks and not their brains."

"Why didn't you kill them?" He pulled out a napkin and handed it to her. She accepted and followed him to the street, heading toward the apartment.

"If I killed every man who crossed the boundary line from just creepy to asshat, I'd have a higher body count than you, and the Legacy would spend their days cleaning up my messes."

He looked over at her, brows furrowed. "Seriously?"

"Seriously. What are you doing here?"

"Our meeting." The envelope. She'd completely forgotten. "When you receive a sealed message from me, follow the directions."

"Our meetings ran late. I didn't receive your message until about twenty minutes ago. And then there was that whole assault thing on the subway."

They fell into silence when they reached the building. Instead of entering the lobby, Aeron and her father moved to the alleyway. He jumped, his long arms and torso giving an easy reach to the fire escape ladder. He pulled it down for her, and Aeron quickly scaled it, moving with ease from level to level with her father right on her heels until they reached the rooftop.

The view was always breathtaking from the rooftop. This one was nowhere near as high as the Institute's roof, but Aeron could see a whole possibility of travel from here.

"Why can't I train with Mason?" she asked abruptly. She had no idea the purpose of this meeting, but she needed to know. However, standing next to him and overlooking New York City, the question seemed childish as it escaped her lips.

"If you would like to load up on assignments, I will arrange it," he said, lip curled in disgust. "Why do you think I said no?"

"Because you hate me." It was an automatic response. Being back in the city, away from him, around her team, made it easy to think that way. His eyes widened slightly, and the heaviness in her stomach doubled. "I mean—"

"No, don't take it back." He rubbed his head. "I realize only a few months ago you would have gladly pushed me over this ledge. That is a difficult instinct to shake, and even harder when I keep telling you we need to keep it that way while asking you to trust me." He stepped back, touching her shoulder to turn her around. "Mason has been working closely with Perry and Mr. Wayward over the past few years. I handed off the message to him as a test to see if he would deliver it and if he would read it."

"So, what? You don't trust him?"

"It's complicated. John and I asked him to get closer to Mr. Wayward, but so much has happened. He's been in deep for several years. I can't be sure where Mason's loyalty is."

She pinched the bridge of her nose, trying to imagine how life would be different if she'd just returned to the garage instead of saying yes to her father. She trusted Mason with her life. How could she convince her father? Her eyes snapped open.

"Mason knows about the garage."

His voice dropped dangerously low. "Excuse me?"

She swallowed hard. Breaking the Laws herself is one thing. It could be chalked up to a one-time deal if caught. Being caught breaking them for several years would be a Family Legacy infraction—the whole family would pay. "You didn't know? I assumed you knew he knew where I was. I thought that was why you never looked."

"We've been over this. I couldn't look, Aeron." He gazed out over the city, darkness swallowing his expression.

"He's kept me safe. He's broken Laws to keep me safe. If he wasn't on your side—our side—why would he?"

"Quiet." He paced back and forth, hand running over the back of his neck. "Take the assignment with Mason. But if he is in deep with the Waywards, I want you far, far from him, understand me?"

She nodded, feeling heavier than she had just minutes ago. For just a few hours, she nearly forgot they were on a deadly mission. "What did you need to talk to me about?"

"What have you learned from Luke?"

"He's being groomed to take over the Legacy next year," Aeron supplied, leaning against the wall. "He wants nothing to do with it, but his Granddad is adamant it needs to be him."

His father nodded. "You should encourage that."

"What? I thought we were trying to get him out."

"The deeper Mr. Wayward has him, the less likely he will try and hurt him. I'll be in touch." He retreated to the elevator, and she followed, a bit slower. The doors closed, and she stared at her father's reflection.

"This is not what I imagined—having a functional relationship with you."

"Welcome to the family business," he said, not a hint of humor in his voice. She caught a slight smile that brightened his face. The elevator went down one floor and opened. Decius stood next to her doorway, arms crossed.

"Aeron?"

Her body stumbled forward as her father shoved her off the elevator.

"If I ever catch you talking to that mechanic-trash again, I will burn their garage to the ground—with them inside," her father spat, signature glare in place. She had a moment of confusion but grasped on to Decius before he could lunge forward. A look of hatred colored his light brown features as their father disappeared from sight.

He turned on her, his eyes wide.

"What did he do to you?" he demanded, running his finger over her face, checking for any serious injuries. "I was going to let you know we changed our plans, but when you didn't answer, I figured you were just coming home."

"He didn't do anything. This was some jerks on the subway," she said and brushed his hand away.

"And Dad just happened to be there?"

"No. I met Dad in the elevator. He found out I've been talking to the guys at Ernie's, even though he forbade me after the funeral. He wanted to be sure I got his message." Another lie too easily told.

"Aeron—"

"I'm fine, Decius. Just drop it." She moved past him and pushed the door open, heart pounding from the emotional whiplash her father just gave her. Why did he suddenly swap the narrative?

All eyes turned to her—pizza halfway to their mouths. She froze in the doorway—her clothes bloody and disheveled.

"What the hell happened to you?" Luke jumped up from the couch and was beside her in moments.

"Nothing," she responded. "I would have straightened myself out if I knew you were here."

"Would have?" he said in a dangerous voice which warmed her in a way she didn't expect. "You shouldn't have to."

"I'm fine, guys. I'm more pissed about my outfit," she added, trying to lighten the mood. She pulled off the torn shirt and walked over to the kitchen, dropping it in the garbage and grabbing a bottle of water.

"Yeah," Lesley put in, concerned eyes on her. "There's no way you're going to get that blood out. Is this normal for you guys?"

Aeron smiled at her, and Luke laughed. "Not really. I'm going to change. There better be some left for me when I get back."

She tore off the remains of her beloved suit. She hardly ever wore heels and skirts, but if she had to dress nice, this had been her go-to outfit. She tossed the rest in the garbage and pulled on a pair of loose sweat pants and a tank top—she'd shower later. Aeron pulled her hair into a messy bun as Shannon walked in.

"What the hell happened?" Shannon demanded. "You could have called. Texted. Anything."

Aeron gazed at her best friend, her green stare ablaze with fury and her hair dancing like wildfire around her head.

"I'm sorry," Aeron said. "Shan, I wasn't even thinking—"

"That much is obvious. You may be the best of us, but accidents still happen. Look what happened to Luke's parents."

Aeron held her furious gaze until Shannon looked away, wiping the moisture from her eyes.

"Aeron, it's hard enough all summer not knowing if the call I finally get is for your funeral. Keep that in mind."

Her heart skipped. Shannon knew the tremulous relationship she had with her father. The lengths Aeron went to prove she could be part of the Legacy. She had witnessed Aeron's complete breakdowns, afraid she would never be good enough for her father's approval. But this summer had been different. She'd thrived, and learned some scary shit, and understood for the first time why her father was how he was. She'd been happy—and couldn't even tell her best friend about it.

"I really didn't mean to," Aeron said, looking out the window. She wanted nothing more than to spill her guts. "I just…"

"I know."

"Pizza!" a voice yelled down the hall. "Are you decent?" Luke appeared with his eyes covered and a box of pizza.

Shannon rolled her eyes and shot Aeron a grin. "I'll let you get some food. You're cranky when you don't eat." She paused next to Luke on her way out. "We're decent; you can open your eyes."

Luke slowly removed his hands with a grin and offered the box of pizza to Aeron as if it were a silver platter. "Your dinner, my lady."

She snatched it from him and sat on the loveseat by the window, grabbed a slice, and took a huge bite. Luke sat beside her, holding the box open. Pizza—her ultimate comfort food. She devoured two slices before noticing he wasn't eating.

"Aren't you going to eat any?" She grabbed a third slice.

"I already ate. I hid this box just for you."

"Thanks." She let out a satisfied sigh and leaned against the window.

He moved the box to the coffee table and sat beside her. They stayed there, shoulder to shoulder in silence. Her eyes drifted closed. Luke brought a calm with him—a peaceful silence she enjoyed with few people.

"What are you thinking?" His voice rumbled with exhaustion.

Her thoughts swirled around, digging deeper for where he stood with his granddad to telling him the truth about what happened to his parents. Instead, she turned into him, placing her ear against his chest, the thrum of his heart a steady anchor. "I'm thinking I'm really glad you're here right now." She fell silent, listening to the steady heartbeat beneath her.

He must have thought she'd fallen asleep—and she let him think it. He gently slid strong arms under her, cradling her against his chest. She breathed slow and deep, taking in his earthy scent. He laid her on the bed, brushing a few stray hairs from her face, and pulled the covers over her shoulders. He flipped the light off at the doorway.

"G'night, Ron," he said before she drifted off to sleep.

16

LUKE

*L*uke's phone chirped from the coffee table, and he opened Katherine's message: *He's pissed. Tonight. Midnight.*

Great. Just what he needed, to be on the lookout for blind attacks while attending training, keeping Aeron and Decius alive, and trying to take down the mutiny lead by their father. He shot a thumbs-up back to her and closed the phone. He shouldn't have left the airport after landing, but he needed to see Aeron.

He jumped as a door banged open. Curses flew from Decius, and he slammed everything that touched his fingers.

"What the hell, man?" Justin scoffed.

"Dee. What's wrong?"

"I should have stayed behind and waited for her." He dropped on the couch. "I can't believe I just…."

"She's good," Justin said. "I know I wouldn't want to come across her alone in a dark alley."

Luke laughed, but Decius just gave a small nod, his eyes focused on the corner of the coffee table as if it had attacked his sister.

Justin's phone buzzed, his eyes lighting up like they did every time one of his girlfriends called. "I'm going to take this. Night, guys."

"We leave at seven tomorrow morning," Luke called after him. He waited until the door shut before turning on Decius. "What happened tonight?"

Decius stood and began pacing, his face contorted as if struggling to find the words describing his turmoil. "I really thought this year would be different. She trained all summer with him."

"She what?" Luke's stomach dropped. "I thought she ran off to God-knows-where."

"She came home for the funeral and then stuck around. It terrified me, Luke. They were gone for weeks at a time while I ran missions. She was battered and exhausted. But she never complained, and she was *training*. I thought for sure he'd claim her. That I could have a year of not worrying about her. But they had a huge blow-up—I challenged for head of the Family Legacy." He laughed, rubbing the back of his head.

Luke remained quiet, letting Decius get whatever he had bottled up off his chest. Challenging for Head of Legacy was not a laughing matter.

"But tonight—I don't think Aeron was 'attacked', and if she was, it's one hell of a coincidence." He looked up, eyes bloodshot. "My father was in the elevator with her. I never thought he'd become violent, but...I don't know, Luke. I don't know what to think anymore. I'm the Legacy; I trust him with my life. But I don't trust him with Aeron's. She's too much like our mother—he was never the same after she died. He pushes her away, shuts her down. He always has."

"What do you mean?" Decius had never spoken ill of his father. And he always kept the relationship between Aeron and their dad close to his chest, venting enough for Luke to understand it was rocky.

"I don't know anymore." He dropped to the couch again, head cradled in his hands. "I think I made a mistake taking a step back. I think things have gone way south, but she won't confide in me."

Luke's stomach knotted itself. He wanted to tell Decius the

truth—that his father was a murderous traitor. But he'd already pissed Granddad off enough. Priority one was Aeron's safety.

"I can take her out and see if she'll let her guard down."

Decius' steady gaze met his. "Are you asking permission to date my sister?"

"I—no! Yes?" The question caught him off guard, and his cheeks burned. It wasn't a secret he had feelings for Aeron, but the precocious balance between his best friend and dating his best friend's sister hadn't yet been officially tested. "I want to make sure she's okay." He hadn't envisioned this conversation happening like this, but Decius' laugh lifted the embarrassment from the air.

"Sorry, man," Decius said, sobering up. "You left the door wide open." He moved to the breakfast bar, and Luke followed, taking a seat next to him. "You are the only person I trust to keep her safe," he half-whispered. "I'm not ready to leave the program and leave her behind. I'm not ready to work side-by-side with him."

Gears spun in Luke's head. Decius never spoke about *not* wanting to take over the Family Legacy.

"Imagine life without the Laws." Luke planted the idea.

His best friend raised his eyebrows at him. "If only such a thing could happen. If you can get her to talk, go for it." He stood, a hand on Luke's shoulder. "I'd take a hundred bullets for you, and I have killed too many to count saving your ass. But if you break her heart—"

"I'll hand you my gun so you can kill me yourself."

"I was going to say I won't be able to protect you from her, but —that works too."

Luke waited until he heard Decius' door close before leaving the apartment. The meeting with his Granddad started in fifteen minutes.

The security guards waved as he passed the desk in the darkened lobby. Luke waved back and stepped onto the elevator. The Institute never closed, but used an apartment building as a cover, allowing it to buzz all night. With each passing floor, a soft bell sounded. It was late enough to whiz past the floors containing the training areas and classrooms. He anticipated stopping at medical ward, which dominated the entire fifth floor, but it continued climbing, six through ten speeding by as younger trainees and families slept in their apartments. A knot in his stomach grew as the numbers climbed past the offices and holding areas, slowing to stop at thirty-eight. He placed his hand against the doors for a concealed scanner to read his palm print before they'd open.

A bleak, tiled hallway greeted him. The tall ceiling bounced the sound of his footsteps, announcing his approach. The office doors swung open, and Luke fought back the urge to roll his eyes at the dramatics. Dave's recently battered face contorted as he glared at him. The sight lifted Luke's mood.

"Let's move it, Wayward."

"Your face looks so much better, who should I send the compliments to?" Luke grinned as he passed.

"Shut your mouth."

"He's upset this is a family-only meeting and was just leaving." Katherine was sprawled on the couch in a way only she could make look elegant. Except for the dark circles beneath her eyes.

"Where's Granddad?" Luke flipped off Dave as the door closed.

"Retrieving Perry from house arrest."

He nodded, guilt trying to worm into his mind about Perry being forced to leave D.C.

"What happened to Dave?" He pushed her feet to the floor, dropping beside her.

"I'm not sure. He was keeping tight-lipped about his secret mission, but it didn't go quite as he expected."

She shrugged and shot to her feet as the door opened. Perry entered, followed by their Granddad. The three cousins took their respective spots in front of the desk, at military ease, waiting as the Senior Assassin took his seat.

"It is good to have my grandchildren all in one place again and all on the same page. I've caught Perry up, but I want to be sure there is no confusion.

"The most important priority is identifying and eliminating all threats to us. When all is said and done at the end of this year, Katherine will be returning to the D.C. Headquarters. Luke will be sitting where I am sitting. And Perry will be joining me as we look to expand our empire across the world."

The three of them glanced at each other, Perry's face paled while chewing on the inside of his lip.

"Before we can do any of that, we need to take care of the imminent threat—the coup d'état that has formed, causing the death of at least one of each of your parents—both in Luke's case."

Luke fought the urge to look at Katherine. He'd had no idea Mr. Seward killed her father. To be fair, he never even asked about her father.

"I only just confirmed the evidence, Katherine. I know it's been something you have asked about for a long time."

"Who?" she asked.

"We won't worry about the who—they will be dealt with as we chip away at their army." His gaze fell on Luke, a warning reminding him the information he wielded was highly classified, and there'd be no mercy for sharing it. Too bad Luke already confided in Katherine and Perry about everything.

"What's our first objective?" Luke asked, wanting to get this meeting over with.

"I will call you as needed. At the moment, the rest of your team, Cage, Dave, and Alexis, are getting acquainted with the city and how we are running things here. If this gets as messy as I believe it will, the Legacy will fall hard and be ready to rebuild with Legacy Inc."

Katherine fidgeted beside Luke, a question wanting to get out, but she knew better than to ask.

"You may turn in. Luke, I need a moment."

His shoulders tensed like a whip to his back as the office doors closed behind his cousins. Should he try and explain why he left the airport?

"I thought we made progress in D.C." He folded his fingers. "I thought you were on board with all of this."

"I am on board, Sir."

"How is your young lady? Safe and sound?"

Luke didn't answer. Aeron's disheveled state and Decius' anger afterward popped into his mind.

"There's been an incident."

Silence met him. "Interesting. When?"

"Tonight."

"You're sure it was her father?"

"Yes, Sir."

"Well, I will do what I can. But, she ultimately has to join us of her own accord."

Luke nodded, not trusting himself to keep his tongue in check.

"Good. Now that your worries are at ease, I have an assignment for us. We're going to be visiting the Legacy families. This is expected as I'm grooming you to take over in my position. What we will be offering is asylum and transition into Legacy Inc. for two things. First, any and all information on Mr. Seward's activities over the years. The second is a bit more complicated. In order to dissolve the Legacy and rebuild, I need all assets returned to the Legacy."

"You mean property, money, weapons; all of it?" Luke asked, his forehead creased. No one would willingly hand those over.

"They will receive monetary reimbursement with the understanding a gag order is in place."

"A gag order. We're paying everyone off to leave the Legacy and then never speak of it again."

"Well, you know assassins—it's hard to stay out of the business. There will be job opportunities for those who accept my terms of transition."

"And if they don't?"

"What do you do with a fly that just won't leave, no matter how many windows you open?"

Luke swallowed the lump in his throat. He didn't plan to transition anyone. He was going to kill them all.

"Almost no one will make the transition, Luke. Especially the Blood-families. We are where we are because of their willingness to blindly follow the Laws of men long dead. And honestly, I believe most of them are allies of Mr. Seward. We're fighting a giant here."

"Katherine and Perry?"

"Need not know of any of this just yet." He looked down and shifted papers on his desk. "Your father would be proud of you. Go get some rest."

Luke gave a weak smile before leaving but didn't believe for a second his father would be proud. He met an empty hallway, Katherine and Perry not sticking around any longer than they needed to. He checked his phone—an address.

His cousins sat in front of a corner store, cups of coffee in hand. Perry passed him one.

"Kat says you're caught up."

Luke nodded and took the top off the coffee to let it cool. "We need to talk."

They started down the deserted early morning streets, making sure they weren't being followed.

Luke couldn't hold his question in much longer. "Kat, when did your father die?"

"I'm not completely sure. But I know my mother killed him."

Luke choked on his coffee. "Then why…"

"Because Granddad doesn't know I know. I overheard my mother and him arguing one night—I was eight. I didn't understand then what was being said, but when I got older, I put the pieces together. It's a sensitive topic with her."

Luke stopped and stared, not sure if he should apologize or say anything at all.

"I've long since come to terms with it," she assured.

"Why did he lie about it then?" Luke asked and continued walking.

"Because she's a wild card," Perry supplied. "It's how he will keep her invested in this."

"What do you mean?"

"I asked about my father over the years, piecing together what happened. Granddad has never had an answer for me. I'm not essential to this task force; I volunteered so we could work together on Legacy Inc. 2.0. He doesn't want me to get bored and request to head home."

"Is that the name you've decided on?" Luke asked. "2.0?"

"No," Perry cut in. "We are not calling it that. Speaking of…"

Luke checked again for eavesdroppers before relaying his mission to them.

"He's recruiting and eliminating at the same time," Katherine said. "This is perfect. He's doing the dismantling for us, and without the Legacy Laws to worry about, we will have more time to focus on the endgame. Luke, you need to sell out on taking over the Legacy. Whatever is necessary."

A pit wobbled in his stomach. "I know. And I will, but I need to know Aeron is safe."

"We'll keep her safe," Perry promised.

"And Decius?"

"You have my word," Katherine agreed. "You know," she added thoughtfully, "if you're positive he isn't working with his father, and Granddad doesn't want anything to do with him, maybe it's time to offer him a place with us."

"I'll think about it." Decius would help him in a heartbeat—but then he would have to tell Decius the truth about his father—and how his mother really died.

"Where are we on funds?" Perry asked.

"I've been working with one of Granddad's financial advisors, Wilks. I've had him assigned to the team as a Watched Target, a way to keep him safe. Granddad thinks I'm being proactive."

"That's actually brilliant," Perry said.

"Thanks." Luke thought it was the perfect solution to his triple life. "I've managed to convince him to set some funds aside for us. He's not completely flipped yet, but as soon as he is, we'll have access to all the Legacy financials Granddad's been skimming."

Katherine nodded. "Good. And the dismantling will keep Granddad distracted. So, with you accompanying him, and Perry, you doing whatever it is you're doing, we basically have eyes on Granddad at all times."

"Great," Luke said and downed his coffee. "Just what I've always wanted to do, babysit."

17

AERON

*A*eron's body ached from lack of use the past few days, and the late-night pizza sat like a rock in her stomach as she ran. The exhilaration of running in the city, though, was dampened only by the semi-toxic air. Free-running in the country was possible, but the city provided unending obstacles to vault, scale and jump from. Building tops to fire escapes to parking garages to Central Park—Aeron let the world fall away from her as she let nothing halt her forward momentum. Sweat dripped as she bounded up the stairs back home.

Shannon, dressed in a pants suit and heels, stood at the stove making breakfast. Aeron nodded to her and, sweat-soaked and slightly out of breath, moved the coffee table in the living room and began her post-run workout. Her arms ached from holding the plank while her abs burned from knee thrusts. She pumped out an extra set of mountain climbers and jumped to her feet, grabbing a bottle of water and yogurt from the fridge.

"Why are you killing yourself before morning workout?" Shannon asked.

Aeron leaned against the counter, swallowing a mouthful of

yogurt, her heart rate decreasing. "It's a new training I started. I'm just keeping up."

The door swung open, and the boys filed in. Aeron's eyes appreciated Luke's formal attire of a pin stripe suit, and she became hyperaware of her sweat-drenched workout clothes. "Closing some deals today?"

"Don't start," he said. "Dee hasn't shut up about it all morning. Granddad's newest request — 'proper attire'."

"I like it," she said.

"You'd like anything he wore—or didn't," Decius teased. Aeron's cheeks grew hot, and she chucked the water bottle at him, which he caught with a smile.

"Breakfast is on the counter," Shannon said, eyes narrowed at them. Justin and Decius bee-lined for the kitchen, but Luke leaned next to Aeron.

"Early morning run?"

"Yeah. You should join me sometime."

He grinned. "Have you checked out the dossier we got yesterday?"

She shook her head, having forgotten all about it after she shredded it. "Are we going to the Institute today or recon?"

"Institute," Shannon answered instead.

"Damn," Aeron muttered and finished her yogurt. "Let me get cleaned up."

Fifteen minutes later, she returned in her favorite jeans, stretchy for flexibility with rips across the front of her thighs, and her well-worn sneakers—even though they were only a month old. She tugged at the hem of a loose-fitting white tank top, making her skin look more sun-kissed than normal. Luke gave her an appreciative look from across the room, and her stomach flipped.

"Where's Lesley?" she asked, looking around the room.

"Getting ready," Shannon called from the kitchen, piling the dishes in the sink.

"First day as a Noob, she's bound to be nervous," Decius added.

The small, mousy girl from yesterday must have gotten lost in the apartment. The girl who exited Lesley's room looked confident, almost fierce. The jeans and generic top were gone, replaced by some of Shannon's clothes if Aeron had to take a guess. Black Leggings and a soft pink tunic. She looked like an Upper East-sider.

"Looks amazing, right?" Shannon asked. "I figured she could use an updated look."

"Welcome to the team, more officially today." Decius held out his hand. She shook it, a nervous smile on her face. Shannon handed her a banana and a yogurt.

"You'll have to eat on the ride. We're running late."

Ropes hung from the six-story ceilings of the gymnasium. Rock walls adorned the sides, and halfway up, an observation deck sat behind a one-way glass mirror. The interior boasted both antiquity and high-end equipment. Steel scaffolding, like the kind Aeron used at home, dominated the training area connecting platforms and ladders. Beneath, a running track circled the padded floor where a number of walls, inclines, and half-pipes sat, waiting for students to conquer.

Aeron reveled in the obstacles around her. Every discipline under the sun could be taught at the Institute, depending on the instructor in charge. Aeron preferred Parkour as her method of training. It transformed the flight instinct into a usable device.

She scanned the room. People had broken into groups doing kinesthetic workouts, precision jumps, and various vaults—definitely breaking a sweat. She leaned on a platform, waiting for Mason.

"How are you?" he asked, making his way over to her. In a building full of assassins, it was safe to assume everyone was listening. The Institute might be a safe place to talk about proper killing methods, but there were eyes and ears everywhere.

"That assignment you requested me for?" She tested the waters. What was he willing to talk about here?

"Yes. Your father approved my request last night. We can set up a meeting later. It's not a life or death case at this point."

"Good." She wiped her hands on her sweat pants and looked around the room. "What do you have for me this year?"

He turned to the obstacles around them. Mason understood she lived and breathed the challenges around her and provided what she craved.

"There are sixteen silver flags numbered in Japanese hidden throughout the room. Retrieve them in order. You have fifteen minutes—go."

Aeron hurried out of the locker room. She'd finished her exercises after everyone else and was running late to the lecture hall. She opened the door to the stairwell and collided smack into someone coming out.

Two strong hands grabbed her shoulders, steadying her before she fell. She spotted the pinstripe suit Luke had on this morning and smiled, but the smile faltered as she met the ice blue eyes of Mr. Wayward, his tall frame dwarfing hers. She could see the finely defined muscles beneath his tailored suit, and his commanding grasp secured her in place.

Anger flared in her chest, but panic overshadowed it. This was not the Enemy Number One she had envisioned all summer. Aeron struggled to understand why her father feared this man— she did not remember him as scary. But every nerve shook from the sudden pulse of adrenaline, and she tried to twist out of his grasp. He released his grip. Her heart pounded, and not from the near fall.

"Apologies, Aeron. I'm in such a hurry these days. How are you?"

Aeron stared at him, eyes wide and taken off guard. She had expected him to attack her, accuse her of treason. Something.

"I'm well," she answered tersely. "My father has me on a tight training schedule."

"So I've heard. Does he finally recognize your potential? Are there whispers of you being claimed?" His eyes glowed with curiosity. The taunt stung. Most Legacy-blood children were claimed as soon as the Law allowed, at ten years old.

Her heart continued to pound as she mulled over her two options: 1. Pull the dagger from her belt and stab him here in the stairwell, or 2. Play along. Aeron gave a small laugh, falling into the role of the naive unwanted daughter she realized Mr. Wayward believed her to be.

"I'm just trying to survive—I only have a few more years."

He leaned against the wall in front of the stairs, blocking her path. Aeron looked past him and then down at her watch. She was really late to the lecture now.

"Am I holding you up?" He straightened.

"I'm just late for the first day of lecture."

"Let's walk and talk, then." He held his arm out, pointing up the stairs. "Shall we?"

She nodded and tried not to flinch when he placed a hand on her shoulder. Clenching her fists to control her shaking hands, she moved beside him and hoped he hadn't noticed.

"You know, your father's Legacy is not the only option for you," he informed as they started up the stairs. Her mouth became dry, and she didn't answer. "As Senior, I have a lot of pull with the Board. I can make things happen—or not happen."

Aeron physically bit her lip to stop herself from responding while her stomach turned. She wanted nothing to do with his type of pull.

"What other options are there?" she said instead.

"Well, I know one person who'd be happy to have you on our team."

She stopped and looked at him, startled. He kept his hand on her shoulders and smiled down at her. Was he courting her to leave her family?

"Do you mean claim me under your Legacy?" she asked. "Can you do that?"

"*I* could. Technically there are a few loopholes I can dig out of the archives. But with only a few years left, there's a quicker option."

She raised her eyebrows at him, her heart still thumping as loudly as when she had bumped into him at the bottom of the stairs.

"You could always marry in, Aeron."

She would have thought him joking, except for the twinkle in his cold eyes held no mirth, which frightened her more than if he held a gun on her. She stepped away and gave a nervous laugh. Marriage was never an option; Luke's parents and her dad had made that clear at a very young age. But his parents were dead, and her ticket into avenging their murder was right in front of her.

They stopped on the fifth-floor landing, and he pulled the door open. "I insist on walking you in. I would hate for you to start off the year with a bad impression."

"Thanks." He followed her into the Medical Ward. He paused outside the door, gazing down at her again, and brushed a cold finger across the tiny scar her father had given her the morning after the funeral. She did flinch away this time.

"You carry such weight in your eyes, Aeron. Your mother would be so sad to see you like this. If you ever need a safe haven, our home is always open." He opened the classroom door, and she entered, her heart lodged in her throat, her mother's name not as warming from his lips anymore.

"Dr. Sherwood, please excuse Ms. Seward's tardiness," Mr. Wayward said as Aeron took her seat. "It was my fault."

Aeron did not look back at him, but the door closed, and Dr. Sherwood continued her lecture on some life-threatening bacteria and ways to botanically treat the symptoms. A knot formed in her stomach. How dare he speak of her mother. She clenched her fist beneath the table, digging her nails into her palms. The conversation ran over and over in her head. If he had made that offer before the summer, would she have accepted? Yes. She would have given anything to be out of her father's reach. But marriage?

She tried to dislodge the sensation of his hands on her shoulders, but the commanding feeling would not budge. Instead, she thought of the work she'd done with her father. Planning to take Mr. Wayward down for his crimes was one thing in theory. To see the man, be cordial to him, and step into a cover of her former self was downright terrifying and left little room to be infuriated.

Something brushed her arm, and she jumped.

"Are you okay?" Luke asked, offering her a hand up. She ignored it and stood, looking around the room as everyone filed out. She'd missed the entire lecture.

"Yeah. I'm just not feeling well."

"Want me to walk you back home?" he asked. She looked up, trying to see past the pinstripe suit that no longer looked appealing. His soft brown eyes eased her fear of impending danger. Could the answer to their obstacles be as simple as marrying Luke? She released a shaky breath.

"No, I'm fine. I think I overdid it this morning on an empty stomach. I'm just going to catch a cab home. Cover for me?"

"Yeah. Okay," Luke said, walking with her back to the stairs.

She split off when they reached the lobby, making a break for the front doors. Shannon caught up with her.

"Everything okay?"

Aeron nodded, the knot in her stomach threatening to end up on the lobby floor. "I just need some air," she said and rushed outside.

Aeron hailed a cab, telling the driver to just drive.

"I need a destination, ma'am," the man said, pulling away from the curb.

She pulled out her phone and a few hundred dollars, holding money out to him.

"I don't care where you say you're driving me; just drive." He nodded, and she sat back, fiddling with the phone. She needed to call her father. She needed to see him. Ring. Ring. Ring.

"Dammit, Dad." She dialed another number.

Ring. Ring. Ring— "Yes?"

"I need to meet. Now."

After a momentary pause, he responded. "Third safe house. Fire Escape." The line went dead.

She looked out the cab's window. The building was only a few blocks from them.

"Hey! Pull over!" she called. The driver stopped and looked at the meter, which read $11.25, and then up at her. "Go get yourself some lunch, or buy your wife something nice," she said, and hopped out onto the sidewalk.

Once inside, she did a quick inventory of the unfamiliar room. The tiny studio apartment held zero personal effects but an insane amount of expensive computer equipment. She dropped into the computer chair, leaning her head back.

"What happened?" he asked.

"I saw him." Her voice slipped out low. "Mr. Wayward."

He said nothing, his gaze intent on her.

"Why is he suddenly so intimidating?" Aeron wondered.

"Because I took his mask off. What happened?"

"In a nutshell? He suggested I abandon the family and marry into the Wayward Legacy."

"He what?" her father said with a small laugh. She might have laughed too at the shock on her father's face, but she couldn't shake the feeling of Mr. Wayward's ice-cold finger on her cheek. She closed her eyes and shuddered.

"What did you say to him?" His tone serious as he moved from his position looking down on her to squatting in front of her.

"Nothing. I mean, once I realized he hadn't a clue what I knew, I stepped back into the "me" from before. He asked me how home was."

"What did you talk about. Tell me everything."

She reiterated their conversation. "He touched my cheek," she placed her hand over the spot. "Then he mentioned mom and assured me that if I needed 'a safe haven their home is always open'." She shuddered at the cold that crept into her skin.

"He thinks I beat you." It wasn't a question. She looked up at him and caught the slight smile on his face. "You should encourage that."

"No, Dad, that's not a good thing."

"Yes—he thinks I beat you and that I'm never going to claim you. It means Luke is confiding in him. Otherwise, he couldn't have known that I lost my temper at the funeral. And I bet Decius spit some choice words at home last night after the elevator incident."

Of course. His sudden change in behavior made sense. "You set that up? You wanted Decius to have something to tell Luke, to see how far it would travel." She hated how much she was keeping from Decius these days.

"I saw an opportunity."

She swallowed the indignation that swelled up.

"Where are things with Luke?"

"Seducing a mark is much easier when you don't know them personally and don't actually have feelings for them," she answered.

He nodded. "Go clean yourself up." He pointed to a small bathroom in the corner of the room. "We need to train." He pulled her to her feet and handed her some black clothes. "These should fit."

She stared into the impeccably clean mirror above the sink. What if she had taken his offer at the end of the summer to leave the Legacy? What would she be doing right now? She shook the ridiculous fantasy out of her head before it could form and pulled on the clothes—black sweatpants and a t-shirt that fit pretty well.

He gave an approving look and left the apartment. She followed. They went up one more floor and entered the room directly above her father's apartment. It had been transformed into a sound-proof martial arts training area. She slipped her shoes off before she entered and looked around in wonder. The floors and walls were adorned with mats. Dummies and pads were neatly laid against one wall, and a row of punching bags hung from the ceiling near the opposite wall.

"This is nice," she said. Although the studio was tiny, it was more than enough room for them to train.

"This is where we will be training for the rest of the year. I'll give you the keys to both apartments."

"Mr. Wayward, he's stronger than I thought," Aeron said, walking around the room.

"He's the oldest assassin in the Legacy. He didn't get that way by twiddling his thumbs."

"I need to be stronger." The sensation of his fingers around her arms still seemed fresh.

"Then let's begin."

After four hours of training, Aeron's body begged for a break.

She charged him in a last-ditch effort to bring him down, and he easily swept her legs from beneath her.

"Ugh," she grunted and dropped her hands above her head on the mat in defeat. Her body hurt on every inch. She wiped the sweat from her face and laid there. Her father sat beside her, breathing as heavily as she was.

"Not bad." He tossed a water bottle. It landed on her stomach, and she moaned, grabbing it as she sat up. A raised bruise on her arm caught her attention. It would be a nasty one.

When they returned to the apartment, she had five missed calls. "Damn. They're probably looking for me."

"Who?"

"The team—mainly Luke, I'm sure. I'm supposed to be home, sleeping off not feeling well."

"Tell them you went for a run. Here." Her father pulled a black hooded sweatshirt from the back of the computer chair and tossed it at her. "Wear this to cover up the bruises."

She looked at the jacket; it was small enough to fit her but had a Darth Vader picture on the back.

"Whose is this?" she asked, holding the image for her father to see.

"Ah, that would be Ivan." He looked a bit uncomfortable.

"Is that whose clothes I'm wearing too?"

"Yes. He's an apprentice of sorts," he said, as if training a civilian in a tiny studio apartment was protocol. She raised her eyebrows.

"He's my techie. You'll run into him here at some point, so I might as well tell you, so you don't accidentally kill each other."

Aeron looked at all the electronics again. Her father was skilled in many areas, but computers were never his forte.

"Fair enough." She flipped the jacket inside out and accepted the keys.

"Aeron," he said, halting her in her tracks. "Getting closer to Luke will help us with Mr. Wayward, but that doesn't mean what you're feeling is not genuine. You're doing this for the right reasons, and this is a rare instance where you can actually enjoy the job."

"Is this you approving of a boyfriend?" she joked.

He kept his face serious, and Aeron laughed, but his next words dampened her spirits.

"If you have any reservations, any at all, now is the time to step back. We will find another way. But you need to be all in with him, or all out. Anything in between will get you both killed."

Aeron nodded. All in or all out seemed like such an easy decision, except all in came with lies, and all out came with a death sentence.

It was nearly five o'clock when she reached home. She checked her reflection in the mirrored elevator doors for any sign of her bruises, tugging the sleeves of the black hoodie. An empty apartment greeted her, though, and she hurried to her bathroom to enjoy a shower. She let the hot water beat into the sore muscles, pain stinging when the water hit an open cut.

She pulled on sweatpants and a long-sleeved shirt, threw her wet hair in a bun, and went to the kitchen for pain meds. As she opened the cabinet, a note on the fridge grabbed her attention.

Dinner across the hall —S

She downed the pills and headed over. They looked up when she entered.

"I'll check it," Justin continued, "but that is not a real place."

"How do you know?" Lesley asked, eyes moving from the glass table that doubled as a touch screen to Justin.

"I have several lady friends in that area."

Slight disgust crossed Lesley's face before she could mask it. "Why would they give us a false address?"

"Make sure we're thorough in our research," Decius explained. "Our dossiers are usually full of mistakes and misinformation. They can give us all the details, but the missions are designed for maximum learning potential."

Aeron took the open seat beside Luke on the couch while they dissected the dossier. Her father was right. What was the point of trying to save Luke if she couldn't enjoy the reasons she wanted to save him?

Thankfully, he no longer wore the suit but a pair of lounge pants and a white t-shirt. He wrapped his arm around her, and she leaned.

"How are you feeling," he whispered.

"Better," she admitted. She dared a glance to Decius. He watched them with a curious look but said nothing. She offered a smile, and he nodded back.

"What do we know about the security in his office?" Shannon asked.

"Nothing. But we know he favors red-heads."

Shannon scowled.

"I'll go with you," Aeron put in. "You still have the wig from the Diplomat sting?"

"Yeah. That was a nice look for you," said Shannon.

"We'll go this Friday," Decius clicked off the screen, the table returning to a black surface. "Justin, scope out that address tomorrow and get started on our covers." Justin nodded, and Decius pulled out his wallet, extracting a gold credit card—holding it out to Shannon. "Keep the spending under wraps, got it?" He held it out to her. She grabbed ahold, but he held tight. "Under $3,000, Shan. Justin, keep that in mind while creating the aliases." He didn't release the card until she gave a confirming nod—one that was completely contradicted by the smile on her lips.

"What about me?" Aeron asked.

"You're escorting Lesley to training," Decius said. "Mason and the others will be expecting someone to show up."

"Dammit." Aeron would have argued, but her body ached too much to care at the moment. A day of lectures would give her a chance to rest.

Luke laughed. "What are we doing?"

"We're going to check out the bar and canvas the area."

"Recon. Sweet."

Aeron closed her eyes and listened to them chatter.

Decius continued to answer every question Lesley could come up with and explained what they each would be doing as part of their job. Not everyone recruited to Legacy had to become an assassin, except the Legacy Blood. They each were recruited because they offered specialized talents that benefited the Legacy.

She tuned him out and listened to Luke's heartbeat. His breathing and steady heart rate lulled her to sleep.

"Hey," he said softly, shaking her shoulder.

"Mm, hm."

"I bought you something. Want to see it?"

She smiled and nodded but remained in her spot.

"I need to get up to get it," he said, humor in his voice.

"Later then," she said.

"Have you eaten?" he asked.

"Not yet," she admitted.

"I was going to make some dinner. Salad sound good?"

She nodded again. He gently picked her head off of him and stood up.

She opened her eyes. Everyone was still in conversations, except Justin, who was nowhere in sight.

Shannon took Luke's spot, bumping shoulders with her, a sly smile on her face.

"So," she whispered. "When did that happen?" She raised her eyebrows in Luke's direction.

"Nothing's happened," Aeron said. But the small barrier that held their relationship platonic was deteriorating.

"Yet." Shannon leaned back into the couch with a smug look.

Aeron looked at her best friend—the one person she confided everything in. The wall that started crumbling between her and Luke was slowly building up between her and Shannon.

"What did Mr. Wayward want this morning?"

"Just asking about my dad," Aeron said.

"That poor man. All of his kids dead. Good thing he has Luke and Perry."

"He seems to be handling it just fine," she said, a bit sharper than intended.

"How would you know?" Shannon asked curiously.

"He just seems to be putting a lot of pressure on Luke."

"He is graduate—"

Aeron clapped her hands over her ears, a sudden ringing of the fire alarm blasting through the apartment. She followed Decius to the door, slipped on her shoes, pulse racing, and they descended the stairs with the other tenants. She didn't detect a hint of smoke on their descent and slowed her pace.

In the lobby, Aeron paused, searching for the fiery hair of Shannon. The Institute supplied them with an emergency evacuation plan—Aeron never read hers. She caught a glimpse of red slipping through a side door and followed—but it wasn't Shannon.

A woman of similar build ran back up the stairs, her short red hair bouncing around her head. Luke called for her, and she slipped back into the lobby.

"Luke!" she called for him. "Lulu! Over here!" She jumped and waved her hand in the air. He pushed his way through the crowd.

"What are you doing?"

"Not now," she said, cutting him off. "I saw someone running back upstairs. Tell the others I'll be right down." She pecked him on the cheek and headed back to the stairwell.

Aeron could hear the footsteps echoing into the blaring noise several floors above her, and she took the steps two at a time, easily catching up. The red-haired lady continued to the top floor—oblivious of anyone following her. Aeron waited for the door to close before peering through the window. She stopped in front of their apartment door, attempting to open it. Two more people emerged from the adjacent doorway at the end of the hall, and Aeron pulled back, bumping squarely into a solid body. A strong arm wrapped around her waist—not her mouth or throat—and a familiar scent assaulted her nose.

"Two more with duffel bags just entered from the other side," Aeron said, hoping he heard her over the blaring alarm.

"I'm guessing there isn't a fire." A chill ran through her as his breath caressed her ear.

They peered through the window again, the intruders now trying various tools on the apartment door—her heart forgot how to beat. She didn't recognize the woman, but she'd fought those men before.

She leaned forward to get a better look, Luke peering over her shoulder, and the comfort of him behind her pooled in her core. He pulled away, though. She looked back, his face pale—as if he'd seen a ghost.

"Do you know those guys?" she asked.

He shook his head. "Do you?" he countered.

"Yes." She said, avoiding his gaze and looking down the hall again. "These are the two guys who tried to jump me on the train." Luke went rigid.

"I thought your father…"

"Did Decius tell you that? I told him he had nothing to do with what happened."

"What do you want to do, Ron?"

Aeron leaned back, aware of how close Luke was to her, his arm still wrapped around her waist.

"I want to know why they're here and who that redhead is."

"Let's leave them," Luke suggested. "Once they get it open, the reinforcing door will be engaged. Maybe they'll get in before the door drops and get stuck."

"Or maybe they'll get away, and we won't know who they are. I should have killed them when I had the chance," Aeron said, peering forward again, Luke's hands loosening to drop perfectly on her hips. "Do you have your phone?"

A crash sounded from the hallway, and the alarm stopped blaring. Aeron covered her ears to ease the ringing, and Luke pushed her behind him as he looked through the window. "Well, the security door is down, and we have company coming this way."

Not needing to hear anything else, Aeron let Luke push her toward the railing. She looked over, straight to the bottom floor.

"Follow me," she said. "Let's get them a few floors down."

18

LUKE

*L*uke swore as Aeron launched herself over the railing. He counted as she fell four floors before grabbing a landing, swinging herself down, and rolling out of sight. He followed suit, landing next to her as the door crashed open above them.

"Why did you pull me back!" Katherine's voice snarled.

"I'm sorry, I didn't want you to be crushed to death." Cage's voice stirred hatred in Luke's chest.

"The whole point was to get in before the security door fell, you idiot!"

"What good would that be if you're dead?" he snapped back.

"Well, you screwed up again, and I prefer the quick death of a steel door than whatever he may have in store."

Luke silently agreed with her, but more importantly, why the hell was she here? Aeron motioned for him to follow, and they crept down the stairs ahead of the threesome.

"What he doesn't know won't hurt us—so let's get back, and it will be like this never happened," Dave said.

"If you think he won't find out about this, then you're about as sharp as a bag of balls." Katherine spat.

The footsteps above them stopped, followed by the distinct sound of fist hitting flesh. Luke and Aeron paused on the fifth floor as two solid thuds echoed through the stairwell.

"Enough!" Dave yelled.

"Shut it." Katherine's tone left no room for argument.

"You are lucky you are related to him, Kat. I would have finished you a long time ago," Cage retorted.

"I'd like to see you try."

The need to turn around and defend Katherine battled inside Luke, but he followed Aeron to the second-floor hallway. She peered through the small window, and Luke stared daggers as they passed.

Aeron tugged on his arm. "Hey."

He avoided her gaze and leaned against the door, running a hand down his face while trying to steady his breathing. His double —no triple—life was starting to intersect—exactly what he was afraid of.

"What's wrong?" she asked.

"Your attack on the train—it wasn't random."

"I guess not." A heaviness settled over her.

"What did they want on the subway?" The thought of Cage and Dave touching her made him clench a fist.

"Nothing. They were harassing some girl. I intervened, and it got out of hand."

Blood drained from his face, the urge to race out the door and break Dave's face begging to be indulged.

"Are you sure they don't seem familiar?"

"No." He met her gaze, still as a statue. "Why would they?" She looked away first. He hated lying to her. "Who do you think sent them?" Luke probed as they headed back upstairs, opening the door to the top floor.

"No idea."

"Your father?"

"Why would he? Besides, if he wanted me dead, he'd do it

himself," she assured, but it didn't reassure him in the least. "Maybe I pissed off the wrong Underworlders on the train."

Underworlders—she handed him a perfect cover, for now. The girl's apartment door stood open. A steel security wall had dropped from the ceiling.

"Guess we'll have to wait here."

"Or you could come back over here," Luke called from next to his open door. "Would you like to come in, my lady?" he asked, bowing slightly.

Her smirk warmed him. He wanted to keep that smile on her face.

"You know, I still have to give you your birthday present." He disappeared into his room, ignoring the protest. The silver-wrapped present sat on the nightstand, he grabbed it and hurried back to the living room, palms sweating.

She sat cross-legged on the couch, her curious gaze smiling from across the room. "What is it?"

"Open it." He sat across from her, biting his lip. She tore at the wrapping, and a plain white box fell into her lap. The anticipation ate at him as she slowly opened it. He'd spent weeks searching for an underground steel maker who could craft the blades as small as he wanted. Her gasp was everything he wanted it to be—and worth the several heads he smashed to find the guy.

"It's beautiful."

"It's carbon steel and double-sided, so be careful. One side is meant to be used as a block support and the other as a weapon. May I?" He scooted closer and picked up the cuff bracelet. The elongated S's wrapped her left wrist.

"Fits like a glove," she said, smiling.

His eyes moved from the bracelet to her profile, basking in admiration. He wanted to kiss her. He wanted to do a lot of things with her. But mostly, he wanted to keep that smile on her face.

"Thank you." She added, turning to face him. "I love—"

He closed this distance between their lips. The soft, delicious taste of her did not disappoint, like a fresh garden fruit. She leaned into him, and Luke wrapped her in his arms, pulling her closer. The empty present box tumbled to the floor, and the apartment door banged opened.

Luke fumbled back as Aeron tumbled to the floor as if to retrieve the fallen box—but no one noticed them. He straightened his shirt and wiped at his mouth, looking back at the intruders, positive his face betrayed his cool demeanor.

"There you are," Decius said, holding the door open.

"Where else would we be?" Aeron responded, back on her feet.

"What happened to the security door?" Shannon asked, falling back into the armchair.

Aeron met his silent question with eyes wide. He would have told them in a heartbeat—if the trail didn't lead right back to him.

"Aeron forgot her dagger," he interjected before she could answer. "She ran back up to get it. I followed to warn her about the new security door, since we all know she doesn't read the manual, but…"

Decius' questioning gaze bore into his sister, and Luke recognized his mistake too late. Aeron didn't even shower without her dagger within reach—she'd never have forgotten it. It was probably strapped to her leg at the moment.

"Lucky it didn't kill you," Justin said. "Did you see the diagram in the handbook?" He shuddered.

Luke tugged Aeron's wrist to sit down again, avoiding her gaze. Conversations started back up, and planning resumed. But he couldn't concentrate. All he wanted to do was retreat to his room and call Katherine or pull Aeron in his room and finish that kiss. A knock on the door silenced the room.

No one moved. Luke looked to Decius, who shrugged. "Who is it?" Decius called out.

"Mason. I'm being polite. Open the damned door."

Decius jumped to open the door. Mason's cool demeanor was replaced with red cheeks and heavy breathing.

"A phone call—that's protocol, yes?" He eyed each one of them around the room, landing lastly on Decius.

"It's my fault," Decius admitted. "Sorry."

"It's fine." He brushed his wild hair back from his brow. "I rushed over when the alert about the security door came in. Did you see those pictures in the handbook?" He shuddered. "What set it off?"

"I did," Aeron said beside Luke, backing up his original claim. "I left something inside and went back for it."

Mason's eyes narrowed. Luke caught Aeron giving the 'Seward stare' back. Mason looked away without arguing.

"The door's been lifted," he said. "A phone call next time—yes?"

They all nodded. Decius waited until he was sure Mason was gone before turning his own stare on Aeron.

He took a seat across from them, eyes intent on his sister. Luke excused himself to help Shannon in the kitchen, who had also slipped away from the siblings. His eyes did not leave their silent conversation of facial expressions. He'd seen it often enough growing up to know Decius would fill him in when he was ready.

Decius tilted his head to the right.

Aeron shook her head.

He tilted his head to the left.

No.

He raised his eyebrows.

She swallowed hard, then shook her head.

Decius slammed his fists down on the arm of his chair, and Luke jumped. Irritation shone from Decius' eyes as he sucked on his teeth, storming off. Aeron jumped when his door slammed, and she stood too, bee-lining out of the apartment.

"Shit." The tomato exploded in his hand, soaking into his shirt. "Aeron," he called, heading after her.

"I'm not hungry," she called, closing the door behind her.

Shannon appeared in front of him, hand on his chest. "Give me that."

"What?" He tried to move around her.

"Your shirt. It's going to stain."

"It's fine," Luke insisted, but she continued to block his path.

"Give it."

"Whatever." He pulled his shirt off, wiping his hands on it and dropping it into her hands, before racing after Aeron.

He pushed the other apartment door open.

"Shan—I'm just tired."

"I'll tell her when I get back," he said, closing the door. "We should talk about tonight."

She spun around, moisture in her eyes— eyes that lingered on his bare chest for several seconds, sending shivers down his spine.

"Um—where's your shirt?"

His cheeks burned, and he suddenly felt naked. "Oh, I, uh...got some tomato juice on it. Shannon swore it would stain."

"Of course she did," Aeron said with a tense laugh.

They needed to talk about tonight. About his other team being out for her blood. About why he lied to their team—it would be the perfect time to gauge her reaction and why she lied too. And they needed to talk about the kiss. The delicious, sweet taste of her lips. But her tense stance against the counter pulled his attention to the most important issue.

"I should have asked you if you wanted to tell them."

She downed her water and then pulled out a second glass and a bottle of whiskey. Pouring them each a decent amount, she dropped into a stool at the breakfast bar and held a glass out to him.

He accepted and sat beside her.

"Why didn't you tell them?" she asked.

His face screwed up as the warm liquid assaulted his mouth, and he stared at a crack in the kitchen wall. He wasn't ready to drag her into a crazy double life.

"The lie about the dagger was terrible—I was a bit flustered." He looked sideways at her with a grin. "I had the feeling you didn't want everyone to know there might be a bounty on your head and went with it."

Bounty on her head. If he brought her into the fold now, how could he explain Cage and Dave? Granddad was making this impossible.

"You sure do know how to kill a mood," she joked but pinched the bridge of her nose, taking a few deep breaths.

"Hey." He pulled her to his chest, his head resting on her soft curls. "It will be fine. We'll figure it out." He breathed deep, the sweet fruity scent of her invading him and chasing out any coherent thought. His fingers slipped beneath her chin. "And if you want to tell, we can," he whispered and kissed her again.

The kiss wasn't soft this time—but hungry. Her fingers jetted across his bare chest; chills raced through his core. She turned into him, and Luke wrapped her arms around his neck, dropping his hands to her waist. Her legs wound around him, and he scooped her up, moving them toward her room, breaking the kiss only to leave kisses from her jawline to ear.

"You've been the only thought that got me through this summer," he confessed.

She grabbed his face, and he met her gaze with raw lust and need that shot a jolt to his abdomen. The assault of kisses continued as he lowered to the edge of her bed, falling to his knees. She pulled him in, and he regained possession of her lips. Their kiss broke only when Aeron grabbed the hem of her shirt and pulled it over her head. Leaning his forehead against hers, they paused— breathless. His fingers ventured to her lower back, drawing tiny circles on the smooth skin. She shivered.

He could have her here, right now. But this is not how he wanted it. He wanted to wine and dine her. He wanted her to know without a doubt that he was all in. "We're moving too fast, Aeron."

Her head shook against his, and lightning sparked down his

body. Her fingers ran through his hair, and he took deep breaths, slowing his racing heart. She'd always been just out of reach—his best friend's sister.

"You are the only reason I came back this year," she admitted.

He took a steadying breath and forced himself back on his heels. This wasn't how he wanted to do this. "I'll be damned if this moment," he waved a hand between them and looked up at her with a crooked smile, "is going to be—"

The words choked in his throat. Dark spots stained her arms. He bounded to his feet and flicked on the lights. Rich bruises hollered at him from across the room. He raced to her, gently touching her arms—all his lust and need, gone.

"Where did you get these?" They were fresh, welted, and a nasty dark blue and purple. They could only be hours old.

"Training."

"With who? You didn't have these this afternoon."

"Some people I know in the area. I just went to blow off some steam."

He sat back on his heels again, eyes narrowed. "I thought you weren't feeling well."

She avoided his stare, a hand pressing to her head.

"Aeron."

"My father." She answered so softly he could have missed it. Moisture gathered in her eyes, and she covered her face.

Dave and Cage. His Granddad. Her father. Without a place to funnel his anger, he retreated and slammed his fist into the closest wall. A string of expletives escaped him as pain raced from his knuckles to his shoulder, and he cradled his right hand to his chest.

"Luke!"

She moved toward him, but he waved her off, filling his lungs slowly several times until his temper no longer raged just below the surface. After several minutes, he pushed off the wall. "I'm going to kill him."

"No. Luke—"

"Don't you dare defend him. I've always known that you were unhappy there. I didn't suspect that he was intentionally injuring you—until the funeral."

"He's never—"

"And Decius! Lying to me the morning after I'd buried my parents."

"That's not fair." She stood up now. "Decius has always protected me."

"So you do need protection!" The anger boiled over again, a plan to make Mr. Seward suffer formulating with a cool calculation he'd never have been capable of before D.C.

An aggravated sound escaped her. "Cut it with your damned interrogation techniques! There's something you need to—"

But he didn't want to hear any excuses. "If it wasn't for my parent's death, you wouldn't have been dragged back to that hell-hole. You'd be safe." The anger tapered out of him. She was in danger because of him, just as much as anyone else. "Why did you even go see him?"

She sat motionless on the bed. He sat down and wound the good arm around her, letting her look at his hand. Once she seemed satisfied it wasn't broken, she wrapped her forgotten shirt around the bloody knuckles and leaned into his shoulder—the perfect fit.

"It wasn't something I planned on doing. It just happened," she admitted.

"You should come stay with us." He could keep her hidden from her father and from the team at the mansion until he could figure out how to explain everything. Perry could keep her safe.

She raised an eyebrow. "At the mansion?"

He nodded.

"Your Granddad offered me something similar this morning."

Was that why the hit team was sent? Because she'd refused earlier? Or was it because he'd left the airport early. And the visit tonight...was that because they failed on the subway? "I may have mentioned something to him once, or twice, every day this past summer," Luke said, giving a small grin to feed the lie. He hadn't mentioned it. He'd begged, pleaded for her life. He hugged her close, kissing the top of her head. "Besides being an amazing asset —which is what he cares about—you should be somewhere you feel safe."

"I feel safe right here." She snuggled against his chest. The growing list of concerns the only thing stopping him from laying down with her right now and burying himself in her comfort.

"I need to go." It took every ounce of willpower to stand and walk away from her, only a single thought pausing him. "Is everything good between you and Dee? He was pretty pissed."

"Yeah. Just sibling stuff. We'll be good." The smile didn't quite reach her eyes, but it was a problem for another day. He kissed her forehead lightly and left.

The girls were just leaving the apartment when he returned.

"You're recon tomorrow," Shannon reminded him at the door. "Everything good?"

Luke nodded, ignoring her narrowed eyes, and slipped past her. He headed straight to Decius' door, knocking harder than necessary.

"Yeah?"

"We need to talk," Luke said, swallowing back the anger. The door swung open. Luke's fist connected to Decius' face, pain ricocheting down the already injured hand. "Damn it!" Luke reeled back, cursing the irrational impulse.

Decius stumbled back too; Luke remained just outside the threshold, hand still throbbing but not regretting the decision he made.

"What the fuck, Luke!"

"You lied to me."

"About what?" Decius' confused look met him.

"I buried my parents, and you lied to me about catching Aeron in the face. I knew I saw your father hit her. I let it go, thinking the grief and alcohol had me confused."

"Luke—you don't understand…"

"I just checked on her. Decius, she's covered in bruises all over her arms. I'll give you one guess where she got them." Luke fought the urge to jump over the threshold and start swinging again. "You made a mistake this summer, Dee. She's not safe at all."

Decius' crestfallen expression met Luke, his now black eye swelling with impressive speed. He dropped to the bed. "Come in."

Luke grabbed two icepacks from the mini-fridge. He tossed one to Decius before sitting on the desk chair and icing his own hand. "We need to discuss what we're going to do about your father."

"There's nothing to be done, Luke. I've tried. I've fought. Hell, I've challenged."

"Well, now you have me."

"What can you do that will change anything?"

Luke hesitated. He couldn't bring Decius into the fold yet, but they could make getting to Aeron a lot harder. "We can shadow her. Make sure she's never alone. You can't do it alone, but with both of us?"

"Shannon would help too." Decius added.

Hurt crossed Luke's heart. Shannon knew the truth? But he nodded. The more eyes on her, the harder it would be for her father, or his Granddad, to make a move. "Perfect. I have to handle some stuff with my Granddad." He stood, hope lingering just outside his grasp. He'd build his own army, if it meant keeping Aeron safe. He paused in the doorway on the way out. An apology sat on his tongue, but his anger denied its exit.

"We're good," Decius supplied. "Go be the next Senior Assassin."

Luke stalked through the Rose Way lobby, a single objective in mind: finish what Aeron had started on the train. It could have waited until morning, but Katherine had not returned a single one of his texts, and he was itching to do some damage. The suite door swung open before he could reach it, and two petite yet strong hands pushed him back into the hallway.

Kathrine's dark gaze and pursed lips silenced the questions burning him inside. A small shake of her head reminding it wasn't safe to talk.

"What's going on, Kat? Meeting a secret boyfriend?" Dave pulled the door open behind her. Luke sprang across the threshold. A mess of flying fists and cuss words broke out, Luke aiming for any part of Dave's body he could connect with. He'd touched Aeron. He'd laid his filthy hands on her. Luke had witnessed Dave's version of 'roughing up', and when it involved females, he had a hard time keeping his dick in his pants. Luke aimed for his face; the satisfying crunch of a nose beneath his knuckles would have to suffice—for now.

A small arm snaked beneath his chin and a body latched onto his back, but he dropped his chin and continued to throw punches as the black spots appeared. He could have defended the choke, but bliss came from each smash of his knuckles.

"They don't know," Katherine whispered in his ear. "They were following a direct order." Luke's movements slowed, mainly due to the loss of oxygen to his brain. She released the choke enough for the blood to resume, and it took the words a few seconds to register. They were being played against each other. Aeron was being used as a pawn, just like Katherine said she would be.

He put his bloodied hands up, and her arm slid from around his neck. Blood poured down Dave's chin as if from a spigot, and Kat pulled Luke toward the kitchen area.

"What the fuck was that about!" Dave yelled, catching the towel Katherine tossed at him. It seemed the question of the week.

"Just relax, Dave."

"Relax, Katherine? He re-broke my nose."

Katherine's firm grip stopped Luke's arm from throwing

another punch, which was a good thing, as his whole hand throbbed in pain. This was another test of Granddad's.

"And how did it get broken to begin with?" Luke seethed. Katherine's hand remained on his arm, guiding him to a chair and out of striking distance of anyone.

"On assignment," Cage said. "Like you would know if you weren't off playing delegate at that lame Institute."

"I'm sorry, is it my multi-mission that bothers you more, or the fact you're not trusted enough to be informed what it entails?" Luke responded—although the words were more geared to himself.

"Enough of the bickering and peacocking," Katherine spat.

"Peacocking?" Luke tilted his head, trying to forget about Dave's and Cage's hands on Aeron. "Seriously, did you swallow a thesaurus as a kid?" Her glare sent chills down his spine, and he fought a smirk.

"We're waiting for orders." Katherine sat on the arm of his chair, ensuring he couldn't make any more rash moves.

"Orders?"

"Hopefully, if Dave and Cage didn't screw it up already."

"I didn't realize saving your life was screwing up—don't worry, I won't make that mistake again." Cage turned on the television and crossed his arms.

"Why are you here?" Katherine asked under her breath.

"What the hell happened at my building?"

Her eyes scanned the room. "Dave was pissed about something that happened on their first mission, and wanted to…I don't know, honestly. I didn't realize who it was until we pulled up to your building."

"What was the original mission?"

"Recon, I think. Tonight was not legit. Dave said he needed backup to make sure they got what they needed to make up for the failure. I wanted to know what Granddad had them doing."

Anger coiled from Luke's stomach. "Why would he do that? It puts me right in the crosshairs."

She shook her head. "Because it's sunny out? Because the driver hit too many red lights? Luke, I—"

"Why?" The word broke as it came out.

"Because he can. I told you that. He's a sociopath who holds our lives in his hands and likes to squeeze his fist for fun. I thought if I could get in there, I could do some damage control."

He dragged a hand over his face. "She has no idea how much danger she's in."

"We have time. She's not in immediate danger right now."

"Bull—you know how those two operate. They never just look. I want to go over there and break every single finger…I don't understand why he brought that filth here."

Her face scrunched in disgust.

"Then there's her father. She came home covered in bruises today."

"Luke, we don't have proof yet that that's why their mom died. There are a million reasons people are killed." Katherine shook her head.

"Which is why I can't bring Decius in. I'd have to tell him about his mom. I can't. Besides, he thinks their father attacked Aeron—if he found out it was those two? She's lying. We've never lied to each other before."

"You've never lied to each other?" Katherine rolled her eyes.

"Never. It's what makes the Legacy teams unstoppable. Complete trust and," he swallowed the last word: transparency. Aeron and Decius *had* been lying to him for years. "Now my team is falling apart, and I'm running out of time."

The magnetic lock disengaged, and all heads snapped to the door. Granddad entered, followed by a petite blonde in crisp jeans and a low-cut shirt, and then Perry, dark circles under his eyes and clothes wrinkled, probably from days of travel.

"Good. You're all here." His gaze stopped on Luke—who shouldn't have been there. "What is it?"

"I need a word about…an asset," Luke said, buying himself a

few seconds to create a reason to be at the hotel other than to assault his own team. His Granddad nodded and waved him into the hall.

"You had her attacked?" The words slipped out before he could stop them. "You said she would be safe."

"Attacking is a bit harsh. I prefer tested. She is remarkably resilient."

Luke's fingers tingled. "Are you satisfied then?"

"You will know when I'm satisfied." His Granddad tilted his head to the side, a crease forming above the brow line. "What is the issue, Luke?"

"Why are they here?" He gestured his hand toward the room.

"To carry out our vengeance."

"They attempted to break into her apartment tonight. What if Aeron had identified them as the ones who attacked her on the train? What if my team wanted to reciprocate? Whose side would I take? The task force or the Legacy? And if they blew my cover? How would I explain to my team I knew the fools who attempted to assault her—something I had no idea about?"

A scowl answered him. "What exactly is it you are accusing them of?"

The image of Aeron storming into the apartment, her clothes askew, and buttons missing from her blouse. He swallowed hard. "You know what they do—what they thrive on." He couldn't bring himself to say the word.

The scowl morphed into disgust. Luke took an involuntary step back. "Those were not the orders."

He swept into the room, the door slamming open. Everyone inside jumped. Luke followed behind, the door closing with an audible click. He met Katherine's eyes across the room and shrugged.

"Cage—Dave. What were my instructions in regard to the brunette?"

Brunette. They didn't even know her name. Cage and Dave rose to their feet, weight shifting and looking anywhere but at the Senior Assassin.

"What were your orders?" he growled out.

"Follow." Luke's eyes snapped to the petite girl in the corner of the room. Who the hell was she?

"And?"

"And see how long before she intervened," Cage supplied. Dave remained quiet, eyes glued to the Senior Assassin.

"Tell me, where in those orders did that involve having your dicks take a test ride?" The chill in his Granddad's voice pulled Luke back to his first hours in D.C.; he backed up, putting at least three arms lengths between them.

"This is not DC," his Granddad continued, glare bouncing between Dave and Cage. "You are not the top dog here. The brunette you followed? She is a top dog, although I'm sure you got a taste of that."

Top Dog. Luke swelled with pride. His Granddad knew exactly how valuable Aeron was: to the Institute, as leverage with him, and with her father. His bubble popped—she was also a huge threat.

"And since you walked away, even after you attempted to…" A small laugh escaped him. "She let you walk; lord knows why. If she had an ounce of her father's temper, you would have been wearing your balls as necklaces. I don't know what you were thinking tonight—but it has jeopardized our mission, one you didn't even know about because you aren't privy to it."

"Sir." Cage's face paled. "We didn't—"

"Didn't what? Have the thought to stick your bits where they don't belong? Or think to follow up with me before chasing her down to try again?"

Neither one answered.

"Alexis, pull the feed up, please."

"Feed?" Luke's mouth went dry.

"Yes. The security footage I had Alexis record—offline."

Dave paled.

The blonde girl retrieved a small thumb drive from a bag and plugged it into the TV, pressing play: Alexis on the subway by herself; Dave and Cage entering. She fast-forwarded until Aeron appeared in the doorway and hit play.

Seeing Aeron on-screen was beyond uncomfortable. Watching her fight was sacred, something personal that he didn't want to share with all of them. But from the moment she appeared on the screen—the set of her shoulders, the ice in her eyes—he could see she needed the fight.

"You heard her, she doesn't have any money," Aeron's voice wound around him. He wouldn't have been able to look away if he wanted to.

"Hey sexy," the Dave said. "Want to join this party?"

"Not particularly." Aeron looked almost directly at the camera, toward Alexis, and jerked her head to the side. Alexis vanished, and Dave and Cage turned toward Aeron.

"You should have stopped there." His Grandfather's voice slid over the on-screen narrative. "That is what I needed to know."

Luke watched as Aeron dropped her gaze, and they both moved closer to her. He swallowed hard, nails digging into his palms.

"Or you could have left then…" His Granddad's voice becoming increasingly lower.

"He asked you a question." Dave moved closer to her, and Luke itched to wrap his hands around his neck.

Aeron's gaze snapped up, and everyone in the room took a step back—except for Mr. Wayward. "Ah…I see her father now."

"It's impolite to speak to a lady that way." Her hand shot out, grabbed the strings of Dave's hood, and yanked. Luke watched, mesmerized, his facial expression fighting to be more than mildly interested. In the short exchange, he moved from amusement at her quips to rage at Cage's hands on her to pride for how effortlessly she fought them. He couldn't hold back the smile when Aeron's knee smashed into Dave's face.

"Is that how you got the broken nose?" Luke asked, satisfaction winding around his soul as he recalled re-breaking his nose beneath his knuckles. He looked over to Dave, but he didn't answer. Sweat dripped from his brow, his hand tapping against his leg.

Even with Dave screaming and Cage squeezing her arms down, Aeron's smile warmed Luke, and a small laugh escaped as she continued to mouth off. Every nerve in Luke's body froze, though, when he caught the glint in Dave's eye on the screen as he ran a hand down Aeron's chest. He didn't want to see this. He didn't need to see this.

A soft touch on his shoulder—Katherine. He forced himself to meet his Granddad's gaze before returning to the screen. Luke's gut twisted, Katherine's hand giving him the strength not to look away —he couldn't show weakness.

When Dave's hand ran up Aeron's thigh, Katherine gave another reassuring squeeze on his shoulder, but as uncomfortable as watching Dave feel up Aeron was, for as much rage swirled inside him right now, Luke knew what she kept strapped to her thigh.

Aeron released a laugh that most people only heard in their final moments of life. Dave on-screen had been too preoccupied, but Luke didn't miss Aeron slipping the throwing knife from beneath her hemline and slamming the dagger into his forearm. She kicked away Dave's knife like swatting a fly and pulled out her mother's dagger, backing Dave against the side of the car, blade to his throat, pressing deep enough to draw blood.

"Damn," Katherine said, hand dropping from his shoulder.

"Why didn't she just kill them?" His Granddad wondered aloud.

"Body disposal," Luke said automatically. "She would have had to worry about body disposal if there was anyone on the platform. Plus, she's proud. She wouldn't have wanted to admit that she'd been attacked on her own *and* needed help." It felt like a betrayal to tell his Granddad, but he needed to stay in the best graces.

"She thought they were common Underworld thugs." Amusement colored his Granddad's words.

"They certainly fought like some," Katherine chimed in.

How much surveillance was there on Aeron? What about on him? His heart stuttered when Mr. Seward came into frame.

"Pause it." His Grandad pointed. "That man. That is our target. The girl's name is Aeron Seward." A vice clenched around Luke's gut as her name passed from his lips. "Her father is our enemy. He wants the Legacy for himself and will do anything to take it. He currently has no idea we are coming for him. I'd like to keep it that way. The task force is now fully in Luke's hands. The Legacy is too precocious to leave anything to chance, and after this display, I can't trust you."

Luke's eyes doubled, and he avoided looking at Katherine. "You need the ability to play both sides." He turned back to address the rest of the room again, and Luke dared a glance at Katherine, the small upturn at the corner of her lips at this unplanned victory. "You will report back to Luke. You will follow his every order, no hesitation."

"No," Dave said softly, shaking his head. "I came here to work for you, not some child. My loyalty is to you, and Katherine, and Rosemary. He has no—"

"He is the heir to the entire Legacy! You *will* answer to him."

A hard lump filled Luke's throat when Dave scowled and shook his head.

"Katherine." She snapped her attention away from Luke. "Do you have any issue answering to your younger cousin?"

"Absolutely not, Sir. Luke is a great leader, and we're lucky to have him. It's almost as good as having you here."

"Perry?"

Eyes moved to Perry, who'd been blending into the shadows since they entered.

"I think Luke is the best fit for the lead of this Task Force. He's the only one of us currently still active in Legacy training."

Luke caught Granddad's smile in the glass reflection from a picture hanging on the wall. "See, Dave? Nobody else has a problem with this. I would hate to think this is the best your family could afford to lend me."

Luke jumped as a muffled shot zipped through the room. Dave dropped to the floor, blood pooling around his shoulder. No one moved. Cage's hands trembled by his head, blood spatter across his face and chest. The lump in Luke's throat pulsed.

"Cage, do you have an issue with reporting back to Luke?"

"No, Sir. You have impeccable judgment, and I trust you to know what's best."

"Don't butter me up," Granddad said, humor in his voice. What he found so funny, Luke couldn't begin to fathom. Blood seeped from Dave's lip as he bit down, trying not to cry out in pain.

"Dave. I think you will serve me better in D.C., working with Rufus, or I could reach out to my contact in Interpol? I hear there's a lovely Villa in Greece that would spark their interest." His Granddad holstered his gun, pouring a glass of ice water and sipping it.

"Sir," Dave ground out. "I'm sorry. I'd be happy—to follow—Luke's lead."

"Marvelous! Now that we are all on the same page, Luke, go take care of your asset."

"Thank you, Sir." Luke backed out of the room, fear creeping in at the thought of turning his back. Dave and Cage had done some vile things, according to Katherine and Perry, but they were Granddad's favorite. Shooting your favorite pet—Luke wished he would have just killed him.

19

AERON

*A*eron bounced her leg under the table, tuning out Shannon's breakdown of medical terminology for Lesley. The kisses played out in her head over and over. *Why* had she taken her shirt off? It was so stupid. Of course he would see the bruises. She wanted to spill her guts to Shannon, talk about it, confess she lied to him. But training took precedent over everything else.

Then there was the conundrum of who had attacked her on the train and tried to break in last night. She wanted to assume it was Mr. Wayward—Luke looked spooked enough—but Kat was related to whoever set the attack, so did she just find herself on an Underworld hit list?

Her phone buzzed, nearly jumping off the table. An unknown number flashed across the screen, and Aeron flipped it open, hoping Luke had messaged her. But the ominous message could only be from her father:

'Now. —S'

Now. That's all he could give her? She slid out of her seat and took a few paces backward. Lesley hadn't noticed Aeron's sudden absence, but Shannon did. She looked quickly over to her with a raised eyebrow.

A simple line such as 'I've got something to do' or 'I'm not feeling well' would never work on Shannon. There was a rule not to lie to family or your team. She was breaking all the rules this year.

"I was going to try and call Luke and see what they've got." She used her best 'honestly, I swear' look.

"Will you be home for dinner?"

A twinge of guilt accompanied Shannon's resigned look and her decision to not push the issue.

"I'll try. Les—take good notes for me?"

Lesley looked up from the nearly full notebook that had been empty just hours before, eyes wide.

"She's joking," Shannon assured, not looking back up at Aeron.

Aeron found her father's apartment door ajar. Her threat assessment went into overdrive. She pulled the dagger from her boot and inched closer, her back against the wall, listening for any noise.

"For the love of...where the hell is it!" Paperwork rustled, and boxes moved beyond the door.

Inside, a taller, scrawny male stood in the middle of the room with one hand on his hip and the other running through his black hair. Slowly, Aeron pushed the door open. He hadn't noticed; she charged forward. A terrified scream left him, surprising Aeron long enough for a retaliation. Her feet were no longer beneath her. She hit the ground, but bounded back up, throwing a right hook. He stumbled back. Aeron grabbed his arm and swept his feet. The floor reverberated from the impact. Aeron held tight to his arm and placed a heavy knee on his chest, pinning him to the ground.

"Who are you?" She pressed the tip of her knife into his chest.

He looked up with wide gray eyes. "I'm...I'm..."

"That," her father called from the doorway, "is Ivan."

She looked over; a cross between annoyance and amusement danced on his face. She'd just attacked her father's apprentice.

"My mistake." She removed her knee and reached for him, the adrenaline still moving through her. "When my father said he was training someone, I expected something...else."

Ivan refused her hand and clambered to his feet. She re-sheathed the blade and looked toward the now closed door.

"I did tell you Ivan would be here, did I not? Ivan meet Aeron, Aeron—Ivan."

"Yes," she said, annoyed at his patronizing tone. "You also told me you were training him. The idiot left the door open. What was I to think?"

He raised his eyebrows at Ivan.

"I needed my hoodie. I swear I left it on the chair yesterday."

She laughed. "Darth Vader means that much to you?"

"You've seen it?" Ivan asked anxiously.

"I have it. I'll bring it back next time. I didn't realize my father's apprentice would have a security blanket."

"It's not a security blanket. Why do you—"

"I gave it to her," her dad interjected. Ivan opened and closed his mouth a few times before just nodding in response.

"What was so urgent?" Aeron raised her eyebrows at him. There didn't seem to be any drop-everything-and-run news waiting for her.

"Nothing," he said, confirming her suspicions. "I just needed to see how quickly you could get here if I needed you."

Annoyance flared in her chest for a moment, but she swallowed it. "Works out well then. Is Darth Vader over here in the loop, or do we need to wait for him to leave?"

Ivan glared. "I've wired the entire place with surveillance. I'll leave if you want, but I'll hear everything anyway."

She returned the look. "We had an attempted break-in last night masked by a fire alarm."

"Who?"

"Three who's. The two guys who jumped me on the train and a red-haired chick named Kat. My first thought went to Enemy Number One, but Kat is related to whoever their boss is, and there aren't too many people on the Wayward family tree these days."

"Kat?" Ivan moved to a stack of folders on the floor and sifted through them. "As in Katherine, perhaps Katherine Wayward?"

"Who is Katherine Wayward?" Aeron asked.

"Come look." Ivan opened the dossier and placed it on the kitchen table, which held a picture of a woman with fiery red hair, and an even older woman, with brown hair and sharp features.

"Katherine and Rosemary Wayward," her dad supplied. "Rosemary is Mr. Wayward's only daughter. She's been in D.C. since before you were born. Her daughter, Katherine, is a few years older than you."

Aeron pointed at Katherine. "That's her."

"What were they after?" her father asked.

She hesitated.

"Aeron—what did they want?"

She met the intense look across the small space. "Me."

"Excuse me?"

"I thought I had pissed off some Underworlders—the ones from the train. But if this is a Wayward, and she was trying to get into the apartment. She was looking for me. Why else would they be there?"

His eyes fell closed, a weariness sinking his shoulders.

"I assume the team knows since it was an attempt on your life?"

"No." She met his confused look. "It was a failed attempt on my life. Only Luke knows."

He let out a sharp laugh. "Great. Hours after your encounter with Mr. Wayward, and you're on his hit list."

"I don't think I was ever off the hit list."

He rubbed his head. "How much do you think Luke knows?"

"About...?"

"The attacks."

"He seemed genuinely shocked to see them there. And he had no idea they were sent after me on the train—he thought that was you."

He nodded and turned to Ivan. "Ivan—"

"Dad. Luke mentioned something along the same lines as Mr. Wayward—about me joining their Legacy. We need information. Twice I've been offered a place in the devil's den."

He glared at her. "No."

"Luke trusts me, and Mr. Wayward has no idea that we are—"

"My answer is no." His dark features deepened even more. He turned to Ivan again, and Aeron's insides deflated. The solution to their problem was as simple as letting her walk in the Wayward's front door. "Now that we have a location on Kat, can you track her?"

"What good would I be to you if I couldn't, Sir." Ivan moved to the computer, the whirling of hard drives and electricity crackled in the room.

"What's your plan, Dad?" Aeron crossed her arms and leaned against the table. The possibility of death was a product of the Legacy. Intel could be wrong, missions could go sideways, and pissing off the wrong person was an everyday hazard; being put on a hit-list, though…

He gave a measured look, and the intense urge to punch him tingled her fist if he didn't start talking.

"Ivan's been running traces through all Legacy finances trying to figure out where all the Jones' money has gone. In all accounts, it should have been returned to the Legacy pool—but it hasn't. Even the Jones' property has been liquidated, but there is no money trail —it breaches the bylaws."

"I haven't been able to find a link yet. Like all you spy-assassin types, he keeps his information in a fortress," Ivan said. "If—and I keep telling your dad this—*if* he has this information anywhere, I won't be able to access the location of a secured hard drive remotely. We'll need the hard drive in hand and be at the computer he uses it with in order for anything to be opened. Our best bet is to find the inside-man moving the money, which is what I'm working on."

"I actually understood that," Aeron said, surprised. She knew how to hack into systems, create diverting frequencies, and home-made bugs, but the last computer nerd she worked with talked circles around her.

"No point in having to repeat myself."

"I see why you like him," Aeron said to her father.

"Ivan, get the program started, and then join us upstairs. And lock the door."

Ivan gave a small nod and continued typing away at the keyboard.

"I thought you were training him," she said, looking back toward the apartment as they headed upstairs.

"Ha. You should have seen him before."

Aeron and Ivan went for dinner after the intense training session. She needed a reason to be gone all day, and he reluctantly agreed to be her alibi. A quick text to Decius would cover her: 'Have a trail on new techie. Be home late.'

"I'll throw you some work," Aeron said between bites of her burger. "All computer work, nothing combat related. I just need to keep this lie as honest as possible."

He sat with his glass of water to the side of his face, his meal untouched.

"It's not that bad. Move the glass. Let me see."

He sighed and removed the glass. It was bad. The entire left side of his face shone bright red. Three gashes extending from in front of his ear to just beneath his lip were barely held closed with butterfly stitches. He looked like he'd been mauled by a bobcat.

"I really am sorry," she said, stomach turning at the sight. "At least now you *look* like you could kick some ass."

He didn't respond and returned the ice-cold glass. They ate in silence. Aeron eyed the bracelet Luke had given her. She'd sliced Ivan's face wide open by accident—it really should have come with instructions. She traced a finger down one of the blades. Like a fish's scale, it would only catch the blade going back up.

"Ouch." She stuck the bleeding finger in her mouth.

"Serves you right," he muttered.

She stuck her tongue out, and he returned the childish gesture. A laugh bubbled out of her, but his phone chimed, interrupting the moment.

"Hey. Hey!" He put the glass down. "We've got it."

"Got what?" Aeron asked, confused.

"A name." He turned his phone around for her to read: Daniel Wilks.

Blood drained from her face. "No. That can't be right."

"The program is running a second time to be sure, but this guy is the common link to all the accounts."

The phone buzzed in her pocket. "Yeah?"

"Red flag on our mark. We're active." The line went dead. Bile burned in her chest, and it took pure willpower not to regurgitate her meal back onto the plate.

"I think you tripped a security trap."

"Impossible," he said nonchalantly, digging into his fries with more gusto than before.

"Not impossible." She ran a hand over her hair. "Our target—my team's target is named Daniel Wilks. I doubt there are too many Daniel Wilks who are targets for the Legacy and pop up on your most interesting accountant list. We just received a Red Flag."

His face fell. "What does that mean?"

"It means the execution date has been changed to the next six hours."

"Six hours!"

"I need to go." She released a long breath and stood.

"What do we do?"

"Call my dad. See if you can get to him before we do."

He nodded and stood too.

"Can you get home okay, Darth?"

"The force is with me," he replied. She raised an eyebrow. "The force...you have seen Star Wars, right?"

"No," she admitted. "But, be safe going home with it."

She dropped a few twenties on the table and left.

The reassuring scent of gun oil assaulted Aeron when she arrived home. Guns and knives were strewn across the breakfast bar where Decius and Luke sat cleaning them. Lesley stood next to the sink, measuring different liquids and powders into separate containers.

"Where's Shannon?" Aeron asked, moving over to see what weapons they'd taken out.

"Getting dressed. You should too," Decius answered.

She paused, catching sight of Decius' black eye. She raised her eyebrows and tilted her head to the right. His eyes flitted to Luke, who smiled at her around the greased rag he held between his teeth. They must have settled their differences last night.

She hurried to her bedroom and suited up in the familiar second skin—reinforced black pants and a lightweight carbon fiber reinforced sleeveless black shirt. The top protected all the major organs yet left her arms with complete range of motion. She glanced at her wrist and removed the bracelet. She needed to practice with it before bringing it into combat. Instead, she slid her dagger into her boot and returned to the living room.

The home atmosphere had been replaced with adrenaline and pre-assignment tension. Aeron looked to Decius filling magazine after magazine with rounds. "Where's the dossier?" He pointed to a thicker manila envelope on the counter—one with an official black Legacy seal, now broken. She thumbed through the contents.

"Why are they sending us in again?" Lesley asked, moving away from the chemicals she'd been dispersing. "Shouldn't they send in someone more experienced?"

"We are experienced," Luke answered, agitation coating his words.

"We have six hours to find and eliminate Wilks before the case is jacked from us and assigned elsewhere," Decius reiterated.

"No problem at all." Aeron scanned the file for Wilks' address. Mr. Wayward wasn't playing around with this guy. Ivan's program identified Wilks barely minutes before the Red Flag hit. Wilks must possess some serious dirt. She flipped through the pages. Dossier reading was an art form, deciphering a code inside a code. "A majority of this is blacked out—this…" She paused, spying Luke's handwriting in the margins. No one else seemed to have caught it or had said anything—but the scrawl of his A's was identical to the notes they passed over the years. She swallowed back the urge to look at him.

"Why would they black it out?" asked Lesley.

"A lot of reasons," said Luke. "We're still training. They give us what we need to know in order to complete the mission at hand. With the surveillance we've collected, he should be home."

Lesley nodded, her shoulders tense. But Aeron looked past her to Luke. This was blacked out because Luke had been working it, and he was trying to protect himself. She was sure of it. Shaun flitted into her mind, had Luke taken notes like this on Shaun?

"What are the specifics?" Shannon asked, walking over to take the file from her. Shannon's wild hair sat tamed in a tight twist atop her head. Long hair often became a weapon of its own, and most Legacy women chopped it all off. Aeron took her seat and pulled out her phone. Shannon dropped the file down and started on Aeron's hair, braiding it into submission.

She had a text from Ivan — 'Address?'

She relayed the coordinates, careful to keep Shannon from noticing.

"It's pretty clear like Luke said. Specifics: Dead accountant. Accidental. So, in and out—a robbery gone wrong?" Decius suggested.

"We should really just send a few of us," Luke countered.

His rough tone pulled Aeron's attention, but Shannon tugged her hair as she braided two large cornrows. "His apartment is in a prime location to not be robbed—away from the exits, several floors up. It's going to call attention to the fact he was targeted. Is that what they want? I say go with a female visitor—see if we can get him to leave."

"We haven't had enough time to establish any of you as assets," Decius said.

"What about poison?" Lesley asked.

"Calls attention to the death." Shannon answered.

"I can just…" Luke trailed off.

"You can? This is a team assignment," Aeron snapped. She hoped Ivan and her dad would get there first, and all the planning wouldn't matter—unless Mr. Wayward was waiting in the wings, watching to see if Luke could pull this off. A Watched Target was not a training assignment for the very reason they could not commit 24-7 to follow him.

Luke exhaled; she could feel the irritation emit from him. "So, what do you suggest?" he asked, coming to sit in front of her while Shannon worked; the sound of the clippers next to her ear hummed as her undercut was touched up. He rested his hand on her knees, his gaze hard.

"Multiple break-ins," Aeron answered. "Create chaos on all floors, and then handle Wilks. You're right—it's a simple kill, and we don't all need to be there, but we are a team for a reason. Plus, the chaos will add legitimacy to the escalation of force and be considered heat of the moment and not pre-meditated. Is there anything else that we need to make sure is done?"

Luke picked the file up from the floor and thumbed through it again, but his eyes didn't scan the pages.

"No."

At that moment, Decius' phone rang, and he placed it on speaker. "What do you have for us, Justin."

"He's home. The building has security, but it's minimal for a Watched Target. You have to be buzzed in by a tenant and get past the security guards. There are cameras outside and in—on all floors, and there aren't any blind spots. But, it's an easy over-ride of the alarms and cameras, and we'll be in."

"What about a roof entrance?" Aeron asked. "I'd rather run along the rooftops than walk in the front door."

"There's one. The building to the left is a bit of a jump, and there's a line of small market buildings to the right. I'm up here now. This is almost too easy, to be honest. I don't like it."

"Thanks, Justin," Decius said.

"Oh—" Justin added before Decius could hang up. "Luke—it's on the fringe of Brighton Beach. It's that tall brick building next to that diner we ate at. I sent the address to the system; blueprints should be loading on the table now."

"Brighton Beach?" asked Lesley.

"Little Odessa," Shannon said. "What were you guys doing over there?" Luke didn't answer. "You're good, Aeron."

"Thanks." She ran a hand over the smooth braids.

"Keep your eyes on him, and we'll check in soon, Justin." Decius hung up and leaned back in his chair, running a hand up and down his jaw. He had the final say in how the mission played out, and also the sole responsibility if the mission failed. They moved as a unit around the glass coffee table, and Aeron gripped the edge with her thumb and forefinger. The table glowed to life, and the digital dossier appeared on the screen.

Decius slid folders and images across the screen until the blueprints appeared. The building was ten-stories high and appeared to house seventy apartments. The layouts varied per floor, some single bedrooms some up to four bedrooms. Families lived in this place.

"When we go in for chaos—safety is top priority—ours and the tenants," Decius said. "We divide and conquer—there are five of us, so we hit every other floor and pick two. We don't have time to do backgrounds for weapons and children, so go in, scare them, toss the houses and take some jewelry and cash. If they look like they are going to fight, knock them out and get it done. Any other thoughts?"

"What is the response time we're looking at? Three minutes? Ten minutes?"

"Luke?" Decius asked. "You're familiar with the area."

He nodded and fingered through the physical file. "I would say under ten minutes, once units are alerted. I'll assist Justin with the cameras and rerouting of the phone calls to buy some more time. I had an informant from a previous case live in that building. It was a few years ago, but it runs a tight ship. There are heavily armed security guards, and they are not by any means mall cops—ex-military. However, their Polish is actually limited for being in that neighborhood, and they are bored. A pretty smile and a bit of Polish will get you in, Aeron."

"Am I distracting or disarming?"

"You distract. I'll disarm," Decius answered.

"So, the plan." Decius looked around the room at his team. "Luke and Justin on cameras. Aeron gets inside, goes straight for Wilks. Once she's secured him, Luke follows on the fire escape."

"What am I doing, exactly?" Lesley asked, her voice small. This was not a good first mission for her. There wasn't enough planning.

"You, me, and Shannon are going to do some breaking and entering, don't worry—I'll have your six the entire time. Justin will follow after. Everyone clear?" There was a consensus of nodding. "Alright. Sync your watches, grab an earpiece, and let's get moving."

The apartment building loomed overhead in the dark. Aeron checked her watch; they had less than three hours to finish the job. She checked the street for any sign of her father or Ivan. She'd texted the plan to Ivan, hoping they could get in before her, but hadn't been able to make contact since.

She passed by security with a small smile, heading up to the fifth floor. There was no sign of her father or Ivan. This would be a solo mission of her own. She touched her earpiece.

"Fifth floor is clear. Heading to the apartment now." She moved in silence toward Wilks' door and knocked. The door opened, and Aeron entered the open living room with caution. "Hello?"

Wilks pounced from behind the door, hitting her in the face. She stumbled back, knocking the door closed. With her back pressing against it, she reached up, slid the deadbolt in place, and looked up into the barrel of a shotgun.

"Don't move." Wilks' voice trembled. "I will kill you." Aeron held her hands up. The barrel trembled as badly as his voice.

"You don't want to kill me," she said. "You would have already."

"I could kill you if I need to."

"You're a Legacy." The pieces began to fall into place. Mr. Wayward would only trust a Legacy to move his money. It made sense, but it didn't stop Aeron from placing a hand on her head. How the hell did she end up on another Reaping mission.

"Hands up!"

"I'm here to try and help. My team will be here in minutes to kill you."

"You're—Maureen's kid?"

Her stomach jolted, and she nodded. He didn't lower the gun, though. "Is my…" her father? By using her mother's name, he was putting distance between them. Someone pounded on the door behind her—Justin.

"The person who contacted couldn't make it. Said there are too many eyes watching."

"Do you know why they want you dead?"

"No. I work in numbers. I've worked the numbers nearly fifteen years. I live here," he waved a hand around his high-end one-bedroom apartment. "I'm content. I have no reason to cross them."

He hadn't done anything wrong. Ivan had raised the Red Flag accidentally, and Mr. Wayward was simply cutting his assets before they could be worked against him. A cold fist wrapped her heart. How many other people had Ivan accidentally placed on the Legacy's hit list?

"Where's the information they're looking for?" she said as the door rattled behind her.

"I don't have any," he said. "I keep it all here." He pointed to his head.

"Where is the money going?" Aeron asked. Before he could answer, glass shattered from the direction of the fire escape, and Luke rolled into the room.

"Aeron!"

She grabbed the gun's barrel and pulled, knocking Wilks off balance. He looked up with shock as it slipped through his fingers, and she twirled it around to point it back at him. "Not another word," she warned, and unlocked the door, letting a battered, but still functioning, Justin inside. He nodded and carried in a small package.

"Secured," Luke said into the earpiece.

Wilks eyes found Luke and did not move. "I didn't," he pleaded. "I swear…" he dropped to his knees. "You have to believe me. Tell your—"

"It doesn't matter." Luke's eyes were ice. He pulled out his Sig and aimed.

"Luke," Aeron warned, moving in front of Wilks. "You said it yourself—accidental. Execution style is not an accident!" The ice in his eyes did not waver.

"Move."

"No. We're not blowing this operation."

Wilks attacked her from behind. She hip-tossed him over,

wishing for a moment she had just let Luke shoot him, and pinned him to the floor. He wrapped an arm around her head, pulling her down, they continued to struggle.

"He's dismantling it," Wilks whispered. Aeron stilled for a moment. "He's taking the money for himself."

Aeron broke the hold and swung her legs to the side of him, pinning him more securely. "How?" she breathed.

Wilks threw a crappy punch, and Aeron rolled with it, letting him get on top. "When a Legacy member is killed, the money returns to the Legacy fund if there are no surviving heirs." They struggled a moment more, buying a few more words. "I move it to a dummy account."

"What's the name?" She dug her elbow into his side.

A shot rang out. Aeron reeled backward from Wilks' convulsing body. She looked up at Luke standing over them, his expression unreadable.

20

LUKE

"Why did you..." Aeron's voice trailed off, staring at Luke, a small spatter of blood across her face.

Fuck. "I don't know," Luke said. But the instinct to protect his secret from Aeron had gripped him. He needed that man alive. It'd only been a few days since he'd flipped Wilks. He hadn't even gotten the access numbers yet, and if he didn't find something, the $10 billion Wilks stashed away for him would be gone.

Luke gave himself a small shake. "Burglary gone wrong. Help me trash this place." He helped her to her feet, avoiding Wilks' body. The man had done nothing to deserve death. Luke swallowed the knot in his throat. How many innocent people were going to die in this war? How many would be at his hand?

They overturned and destroyed anything their fingers touched. Luke headed to the bedroom, dumping drawers out and flipping the mattress. Nothing. He moved to the closet, looking for a hidden compartment. When he found none, he searched anything with a pocket.

He should have reached out to Wilks when the red flag came in. He should have—

"Find what you're looking for?"

He whipped around, heart slamming in his chest. "Ron."

Aeron leaned against the door frame. "Who is this guy?"

"Don't worry about it, Aeron."

She glared in response.

"Ron—"

"Don't 'Ron' me. Is this even an official Legacy mission?"

"Of course—"

"Because *he* was Legacy. And cleaning up Legacy messes is a Reaper's job. I didn't know we'd signed on to be a Reaping team. It's one thing to pull me and Dee into an off-the-books mission, and even Shannon. It's another to put Justin and Lesley at risk. What are you thinking?"

He exhaled hard. These lies were building, and if he wanted her to believe him later about her father, she needed to know some of the truth. "This *is* an official Legacy assignment—just higher up than normal. I requested this assignment from my Granddad. Wilks is connected to my parent's killer."

Her jaw dropped. "Killer? I thought it was an accident?" Her pure shock warmed him. Who would ever think she was working with her father?

"Granddad wanted to keep it quiet." Luke ran a hand through his hair. "It's complicated."

"You want justice. Not that complicated," Aeron said, shrugging her shoulders. "Why didn't you say something? Decius would have let you plan this your way—you know that. You could have questioned him. You could have beat the shit out of him. Give him Sin to get your answers for all I care."

Luke shivered. Wilks did not deserve a dose of Sin. No one deserved the torture the neurotoxin inflicted, except perhaps Aeron's father.

"It's not that simple. Aeron, no one knows about this. I'm handling it, though. I just need to do a quick sweep before this place blows." His gut twisted at the disappointment in her face, but he recoiled a moment later when his words processed, and the look turned into disbelief.

"Blows? What do you mean, blows?"

"I asked Justin to set up a small explosive."

"There are hundreds of people in this building, Luke! Children —seniors."

He swallowed hard. "I need this completely smothered. The fire will look accidental…"

Her mouth opened several times, but for the first time he could remember, she was at a loss for words. His Granddad couldn't know he turned Wilks. He needed to be sure no evidence was left behind, or Aeron would surely be dead. She kept her eyes on him when he slipped past her to the kitchen to join Justin.

"Luke." Aeron followed him, but he ignored her probing questions and dug for an accelerant.

She grasped his arm. "Luke! Stop it. You can't burn this place down. This is an entire apartment building."

"I have to, Aeron. You can't understand, but I need to do this." Her disbelief remained plastered in place.

"Do the others even know?"

He shook his head. "It was a last-minute precaution. I made a judgment call."

"You're really willing to risk all these lives?" Aeron glared at him, and his heart faltered. He hadn't thought that far ahead, but the fire alarm from the other night…the rush of people down the stairs.

"What do you want from me, Aeron?"

"Honesty, to start with. But I'd settle for giving the people in this building a head start."

He swallowed hard and brushed past her to the kitchen, hoping that he could track down the access codes another way. "Fine. Justin, go pull the fire alarm. We'll meet you in the hall."

Justin's eyes bounced to Aeron, but he nodded. "This will light up in about a minute. Be quick," he said and left. Luke paused by the body, sidestepped the growing puddle of blood, and crouched down to reach into Wilks' pocket. He pulled out a wallet and phone and tucked them away.

He swallowed around the ball in his throat before addressing the team on the headset. "Complication in Wilks' place—fire's been set. We need to get everyone out of here."

"Roger," Decius responded, not asking for any clarification.

They moved to the hallway. An explosion rocked the floor, and Aeron stumbled sideways, covering her ears. Luke pushed her along, wanting her safely out.

A young mother clutching a crying baby scurried past them toward the main stairwell as the fumes from the fire breached Wilks' door. Luke tried to grab Aeron, but she twisted away and rushed forward.

"Hurry," Aeron said, holding the door open. The woman gave her a grateful smile and rushed out. The twisting in Luke's gut snapped. What was he doing? He'd just placed hundreds of innocent lives at risk, and his team, just to cover his own ass.

"Let's make sure all these people get out of here," he said into the earpiece, guilt clawing up his chest. "Justin, you go up."

They banged on the other apartment doors, making sure everyone knew the fire was real. Smoke billowed into the hallway, and they checked the last door before the flames licked out of the apartment.

"Fifth floor is clear. Fire is moving fast, though," Luke reported. They could hear sirens in the distance. "Everyone else clear? We need to get out of here."

"Fourth is clear," Decius responded. "Give me a headcount."

"L checking in with A. Heading down north stairwell."

"J here. Top floors clear."

"L2, heading to the car. You've got company a half minute away. Flames are licking the sky."

Aeron pressed her own earpiece to join the conversation. "What's your status, S?"

There was no answer.

"S, head count," Decius ordered. The radio stayed silent. "Keep your eyes out for her. Third and fourth floors are clear," Decius said. "I'm headed to the second now."

Luke followed after Aeron as she raced down the last two flights of stairs and burst onto the second floor. He nearly crashed into her stock-still form and grabbed her shoulders, but she tore toward Decius, stooped over a figure with a tangle of vibrant red hair by his feet—Shannon.

Luke followed, each step a strike to the chest—if anything happened to one of them because of his selfishness…

"This isn't her," Decius said, rolling the girl over.

A breath of relief left Luke. The girl in his arms must be fourteen or fifteen with a busted lip and black eye. A crashing sounded from the apartment closest to them. Aeron shot inside, Luke on her heels.

Shannon's back was to them, but there was no mistaking the fiery hair tumbling around her shoulders. Fresh bruises decorated her pale upper arms, and a cut bled freely on her face.

The man entangled with Shannon looked worse. Cornered against the kitchen counter, blood leaked from his ears, Shannon's favorite technique of busting eardrums. He held his hands close to his face, trying to dodge her repetitive blows to his head and abdomen.

"Shan." Aeron moved closer. "The building's burning. We need to go."

Shannon didn't acknowledge her. Luke hung back as Aeron approached, tugging on her arm to break through her rage. The man collapsed to the floor, whimpering.

"I heard her screaming, banging on the door trying to get out." Shannon's crazed eyes looked wildly around. "He was going to leave her to die."

"C'mon. The fire department will be sweeping the building any minute."

"Aeron." Decius' voice rang in Luke's ear. "We're coming your way."

Decius entered, carrying the limp girl in his arms, Justin right behind them, weapon drawn. Luke drew his as well. Another small explosion rocked the building, and the lights went out. Justin shut the door and barricaded it.

"We need another way out," he said.

A gurgling sound came from the floor. The man's blackened eyes widened when he spotted Luke and Justin's guns. Luke lowered his—if anyone else was in the apartment, they would have a hell of a time getting past them. He moved to the fire escape window and pulled. It didn't budge. Aeron joined him and felt around the windowsill, finding where it could be caught.

"He nailed them shut," she said in disgust.

Luke grabbed a cast iron frying pan from the kitchen and swung. The glass shattered, and he and Aeron kicked out the remaining sections to make an exit. He stuck his head out and looked down. "Clear. The fire is on the front of the building." He climbed out of the window and dropped on the fire escape. Decius handed him the girl, and Luke cradled her close as Dee joined him.

"L2," Decius said into the earpiece. "We're coming out the back from the second floor. Bring the car two blocks east of us."

"Copy," Lesley answered.

Decius looked back in the apartment, waving them to hurry up. Shannon exited next.

"What about the douche in there?" she asked.

"He's not our problem," Decius said. "Get her down there. I've got the other two."

Luke hesitated.

"Go. That's an order," he said, pulling rank.

"She'll be fine," Shannon assured. Luke nodded, ignoring the urge to grab Aeron and run, and followed Shannon to the ground.

"We have company," Shannon said.

The firemen swarmed around them, and Luke rushed forward,

yelling, "Help!" A fireman pointed him to the side of the building. Luke looked back. Decius and Aeron carried Justin between them, blood drenching his clothes. What happened up there? A flash of blond pulled his attention near the ground; Alexis watched from beneath the fire escape. She signed '*Done?*'. He nodded, and continued forward with the girl, mind going blank. That woman— Alexis—had been sent to follow him, and he hadn't even noticed.

Luke handed the girl off to an EMT and slipped into the crowd. He put an arm around Shannon's shoulder, pulling her close to mask the cuts on her face and bruised arms. They didn't need to be checked out. They needed to get out of there.

"Headcount," Decius said into his earpiece.

"L and S clear. Heading to the diner," Luke answered.

"L2 clear. En route to diner."

"A and J are with me. Meet you there."

Debriefing was customary after every mission. Sally served them with big smiles and zero conversation, and Al's food hit the spot that creating mayhem tended to cause. Luke excused himself early to get to his Granddad on time. He avoided Aeron's piercing gaze and patted Justin on the shoulder. He'd taken a knife to the thigh but would be fine. He slipped out the back door, double-checking the worn piece of paper he'd taken from Wilks' wallet was tucked inside his pocket. He back-peddled when he spied Alexis leaned against the dumpster, waiting for him.

"Why are you following me?"

"I wanted to see this asset for myself," she said.

"What is your job on this task force anyway?"

She shrugged and pushed off the wall.

Luke rolled his eyes and kept walking. She kept pace with him, and they continued toward the Institute.

"You will have to choose between them and us." Her statement was matter of fact. It irked him, mainly because she was right. Only she didn't realize there was a third option he would be picking.

"They are family. I don't even know you," Luke countered.

She stopped, and Luke looked back, eyeing her. "I can't be seen within a block of the Institute. Who is she to you?"

Luke's wall built up around him. "Which one?"

"The asset."

"A friend."

"Is that all?" She rested a hand on his arm and leaned close.

"That's all," Luke breathed. Her face was closer to his than was comfortable, her blue eyes boring into him.

"Because I think I'd like to be on that list of what you choose from." She smirked and stepped back. "Wouldn't want you to be late. Catch you later, Luke."

He watched her saunter around the corner, her light touch still lingered on his arm. He tried to shake it off, but it clung to him the whole ride up the elevator to the office. The hallway echoed with emptiness, and the office door waited ajar. He knocked.

"Luke. Come in. I assume all is taken care of?"

"Yes, Sir." He chewed on his lip. "I found nothing compromising on him. Phone was clean, wallet empty." He placed both items on the desk, having checked them at the diner.

"Excellent. And the access codes?"

He hadn't recovered the access codes for the account. Even if he had, he would have lied. He, Katherine, and Perry needed that money. He bowed his head and shook it. "I tried to get them, but—"

A low laugh escaped the older man. "I warned you."

He'd made a grave error—how would Aeron pay for this misstep? "I know, and I should have listened," Luke said, controlling the fear in his voice. "But we were supposed to have more time. My team—"

"Failed to live up to expectation because you refused to take leadership, giving it to a Seward. Your new team, however, will not disappoint me. You *will* find me those access codes. Do you understand?"

"Yes, Sir." Luke nodded.

"Good."

"Sir?"

His Granddad looked up from his laptop.

"Thank you for this opportunity. I know I have let you down—and I didn't seem grateful this summer—but I am. And I will do better." The lie burned as he said it, but the almost genuine smile from his Granddad made it worthwhile.

"I have meetings in a few hours, but tonight you will accompany me."

21

AERON

Thursday evening rolled right into Friday morning. Aeron groggily made her way to the kitchen, a slight headache behind her eyes. She hadn't slept much—nightmares of finding Shannon slaughtered and Luke being killed in a car crash for disobeying his Granddad starred in her dreams. Those were only pushed away by a crumpled baby-blue car, her mother's screams startling her awake until she finally decided sleep wasn't worth it.

"Morning," Shannon called from the couch. Aeron redirected her destination to her best friend, laying with an ice pack on her face. They'd returned home just a few hours ago after unwinding at the diner and assessing injuries.

"Still hurts?" Aeron asked, sitting on the arm of the couch near her feet.

"Not too badly. I just want the bruising to go away."

"Yeah. Good luck with that." Aeron chuckled and resumed her trek to the kitchen for yogurt.

"We're excused from morning workout," Shannon said, sitting up.

Aeron nodded. That would give her a chance to catch up with her father and Ivan. "Did you get any sleep?"

"No. That coffee at the diner was a bad idea."

"That's why I don't drink the stuff." Aeron grabbed water and sat next to her. "Anyone planning on going in?"

"Everyone's knocked out. What's up?"

"I was thinking about training anyway," Aeron said.

Shannon shot a curious look, then grabbed Aeron's water bottle and stole a sip.

"I'm surprised you didn't kill that man last night," Aeron said, filling the silence.

Shannon gave a short laugh. "I'm surprised you did."

"I only did it to save Justin. Otherwise, I wouldn't have wasted a throwing knife."

"You were too kind. That man deserved to burn alive." Shannon let out a disgusted noise before they fell into silence.

"What do you remember about your dad?" Aeron asked suddenly, ignoring the sideways glance she received.

Shannon stilled. They knew intricate details about each other's lives and understood the complicated family dynamics of being a Legacy child—but it was an unspoken agreement that the dead stayed dead.

"He was kind," Shannon answered after a moment. "And loved us with everything he had." She looked down, her expression heavy. "What's going on with you, Aeron?"

What wasn't going on with her? "I had an interesting summer with my father."

Shannon waited for a better explanation. Aeron didn't have one. Guilt ate at her for the secrets that hindered their friendship.

"Tell me about him? Your dad?"

Shannon smiled and adjusted her posture, sitting up straighter. "My mother would tell my sister and me stories of his heroic deeds —computer hacking turned superpower, I guess. We have pictures of him all over the house. He lived on through my mom. To this day, we leave a place for him at all the holiday meals."

"I don't remember my mother," Aeron confessed, cheeks

burning with Shannon's eyes on her. She didn't think about her mother much, and it dawned on her why: because she couldn't remember her.

Shannon's hand rested on her shoulder, and Aeron locked her sight on the corner of the coffee table. Her father never spoke of her mother. He'd let her die a second death in their memories. Swallowing the lump in her throat, she pushed against the sadness threatening to slip in.

"I need to train." Aeron stood suddenly, not wanting to dive too deep into a hole she wouldn't be able to get out of, and beelined to the door.

Aeron found Ivan at the computer, his eyes locked on security footage.

"What do you have?" She pulled a chair to sit beside him. Surveillance from several different hotels, traffic cameras, and a corner store played on the multitude of screens.

"Not a lot," he admitted. He fiddled with a pen in his hands, not looking at her.

"Where's my Dad?"

"No idea. That man is like a ghost. Here and then gone." Aeron laughed. "Aren't you supposed to be in class?"

"Yes and no," she said. "Workout was canceled this morning because of—"

"Were you able to get anything from him before..." he trailed off and looked up. Her stomach spiraled to the floor. She'd completely forgotten. The cuts across his face had scabbed over, and his pale face only highlighted the broken skin.

"How's it feeling?"

He shrugged and fell silent, clicking through screens. She kept her eyes on the computers, unsure what to say. When he broke the silence, it was the last question Aeron expected.

"How do you become Legacy?" He didn't look at her but had stopped clicking away at the keyboard.

"What?"

"How do you get into the Legacy?" he asked again. "Are there rules? Tests?"

"You have to kill someone, Ivan."

"Yeah but, it can't be just that. I mean, you're the good guys."

She exhaled. "You have to save somebody. But in order to save them, you have to kill somebody else, and either you pass, or you don't."

He spun in the chair, his eyes widen with curiosity. "What about the Blood families?"

Aeron cleared her throat and straightened up. "Um, if you are born into, like me, you don't really have an option."

"So, you were taught to kill at a young age? Doesn't that fuck you up a bit?"

She laughed. "No. Well, yes, but not how you think. We aren't taught to kill. It's not like we had killing 101 at age 7." She hesitated. How could she explain a lifetime of experiences in a few sentences? She settled on, "It's a lifestyle. We grew up in a world that revolved around protecting people. We learned self-defense. We learned anatomy, chemistry, survival skills. It seemed like a natural progression from learning about these things, to how they could protect you, then to how they can harm you, and therefore someone else.

"It starts small. Catching a pick-pocket, then a thief. Move on to the kidnappers, and somehow it slowly, progressively, gets more intense, until one day you need to choose between the person you are saving and the person doing them harm. That's how you get into Legacy—civilian or blood. It's a scenario where one of them has to die. If you kill the perpetrator then you're in. If you let the innocent person die, you're out."

"And if you're killed?" Ivan asked.

"Then you're dead, so it doesn't really matter, does it?"

"When did you first...who was your first..." He couldn't get the words out, but Aeron knew what he wanted to know. The first time she killed someone.

She licked her lips, her mouth dry all of a sudden. She'd killed so many people since then. Some still haunted her, others she'd celebrated, but that first kill never leaves you.

This wasn't a story she walked around sharing; not even Luke knew all the details. But Ivan's fragile gaze pulled it from her. He needed to know because he wasn't built for this life.

The memory swirled around her, the weight of him crushing her even now: a 35-year-old man straddled over her and pressing down on her throat. The panic that had raced through her veins as she failed to roll him off of her chased her into every nightmare she had. It was a technique she'd executed thousands of times with men much bigger and more skilled than him—a simple trap and roll. But *he* meant to kill her. It was written in his light brown eyes: her death just seconds away.

Aeron had found her technique in that moment, toppling him off her like a rag doll. And when he sprung again, she had let him get between her legs because even at thirteen, she understood what he wanted from her, from the eleven-year-old girl tied to the bed frame ten feet away; a girl Aeron had practically begged Mason to let her go after on her own. The man had smirked, reaching his desired position, and Aeron played complacency.

'That-a-girl,' he'd said before reaching for her waist. Those words forever would send a shiver down her spine and spring the uncontrollable urge to wrap her legs around someone's arm and neck the way she'd done that night. He'd fallen unconscious within seconds, hardly a fight in him after a few well-aimed elbows to the face, and Aeron squeezed her knees together until the brain damage had set in. And then she held another two minutes.

She shivered again and looked directly at him. "I was thirteen."

His mouth fell open slightly. Questions pooled behind his eyes, and she cut him off before the words wanting to rush out had the opportunity.

"It was worth it. He was a pedophile and had an eleven-year-old girl chained to a bed. He would have raped and killed me and then her. Technically, it was self-defense, but that's how everyone's Legacy story starts.

"And then you start to realize there are real monsters in the world and make the conscious decision to do what 99.9% of the population can't. Any other questions?" She kept her voice steady, but her skin crawled.

Jeremy Ford—her first kill. He'd haunted her for many years before scarier monsters took his place, but every once in a while, she'd still wake up with the feel of his hands on her thighs, the tug of fabric on her waistband as he tried to rip the clothes from her body.

A shake of her head cleared the memories. Ivan had closed his mouth but sucked on his knuckle, wearing his discomfort. "Why did you want to know? Thinking of signing up if we manage to save the Legacy?"

He shook his head, shoulders slumping forward. "Is that even possible?"

"I guess we'll find out."

"So, what did Wilks say?"

She exhaled. "I couldn't get much before Luke crashed through the window. He admitted to moving money for Mr. Wayward. He claims—uh, claimed—that Mr. Wayward is taking the money returned to the Legacy after the last heirs are killed and moving it into a private account. That is all I got before Luke—well, you know."

Ivan clicked through a few screens of footage in silence. He looked years older, somehow, as if the building sat on his shoulders instead of him sitting inside it.

"Luke mentioned Wilks being involved in his parent's murder," Aeron said, trying to keep the conversation going.

"I thought he believed it was an accident."

"Mr. Wayward must be using their deaths to fuel his agenda with Luke."

Ivan exhaled harshly, his brow furrowed. "How many of the dead do you think your father and I found are that way because of me? Because I had this grand idea that working in computers meant I wouldn't be harming anyone?" He kept his eyes on his screens. "I'm doing this to save people, but instead…"

She placed a hand awkwardly on his shoulder. "You didn't pull the trigger."

"But I wrote the death warrant."

"No, Mr. Wayward did."

He grabbed an energy drink and took a sip. Aeron twisted her face with disgust, and she snatched the can from him.

"What the hell are you drinking?"

"Energy."

"No wonder you're slow when we train. You need water—and good eating habits." She took the can to the sink and dumped it out. "Seriously. This stuff is terrible for you."

"You know what else is terrible for you?" Ivan retrieved another can from a cooler beside the desk and turned to look at her. "Your father coming home and finding out I haven't tracked down Katherine yet."

"And the plot thickens. She slipped my mind."

"Yeah. You've had a lot on your plate. Once you gave me a general location, I was able to go through too many hours of video surveillance and triangulate most of her movements with Mr. Wayward's. I narrowed it to this area." He pointed to a screen on the left. "Best bet—here is where she's hiding out." He spread his fingers out on the screen and zoomed in on the entrance to a hotel.

"Would make sense. Security at all times—Mr. Wayward's most likely—and hidden in plain sight. Which hotel is that?"

"A newly acquired international asset that is looped through numerous dummy corporations and subsidies. I can't trace back to any single buyer, but I'm betting it belongs to Ms. Rosemary Wayward."

"Why would you think that?"

"Because it's called The Rose Way."

Aeron laughed. "You're joking right?"

"Nope." Ivan took a swig of his drink, and Aeron shuddered.

"How positive are you that it belongs to Rosemary?"

"Not one hundred percent. But with a name like that and being able to place both Katherine and Mr. W. there makes me feel confident."

"Confident enough to break-in?"

Ivan gave her a shifty look.

She checked her watch. "I need to be to class in about two hours."

"What are you doing here then?" Ivan leaned back in his chair and crossed his arms, studying her.

"I was going to…" She came to train, but the idea of going upstairs exhausted her.

"Want to learn how to play Forbidden Island?" He pulled a tin out from his bag. "It's easy."

"I'm not a—"

"I've been staring at these screens all night. And you owe me." He pointed to his face.

"Fair enough." She sighed and helped him clear a spot at the table.

22

LUKE

*L*uke drummed his fingers on the desk, eyes glued to the door. Worried glances shot between him, Decius, and Shannon—Aeron's whereabouts unaccounted for. Without a moment to spare, she bounded into the room and slid into the seat next to him as Dr. Finn wrote a list of regular household ingredients on the board. Luke's eyes roved over her, looking for any sign of injury.

"Where were you?" It sounded harsher than he intended.

"Tracking down more information on a new techie. Didn't Decius tell you?" Aeron whispered back.

He needed eyes on this techie, but didn't push the issue. It wouldn't be an issue much longer. He took a deep breath, his stomach jumping with anticipation.

"He didn't. But, I was wondering, if maybe we could go out this weekend?" Her eyes brightened, and his heart could have burst right there.

"Are you asking me out on a date?"

A foolish grin spread across his face. "Yes."

The brilliant smile he'd fallen in love with surfaced. He'd do anything to keep that look on her face.

"If you two are quite done," Dr. Finn called from the front of the class. "I'd like you all to come up here so we can practice creating explosives from household items."

Luke ducked his head, his smile still plastered across his face. They gathered around the laboratory table, Luke standing as close to Aeron as possible. She leaned into him, his body reacting with tingles of lightning wherever she touched. With an arm over her shoulder, it was perfection, and he wanted it forever.

Decius raised an eyebrow from across the room, and Luke nodded, Decius closing the distance between them.

"Dads in town," he whispered.

Her shoulders stiffened beneath his arm. "Is he here, here? At the Institute?" she whispered back.

Decius nodded.

Dropping a hand to her waist, Luke pulled her closer. He and Decius had discussed at length the best ways to protect her. It came down to reacting to Aeron's reactions.

"Don't worry. He won't be able to get to you," Luke said. "We won't let him." She shivered beneath him, and he placed a soft kiss to her head.

Luke remained glued to her hip for the rest of the day, barely allowing her to go to the bathroom alone—but she didn't seem to be complaining. The night ended on the love seat in her room, leaning against the window.

"What do you have going on tomorrow?" he asked.

"Training, with Mason. What about you?"

"Lesley and I have sky diving training."

"What about Dee? I thought he wanted to do that too."

Pressing his lips to her hair, he only half answered the question. "He's handling some Legacy stuff." She nestled herself beneath his arm, jaw flexing—holding back whatever she wanted to say. He threaded his fingers into her curls, playing gently with the ends of her hair until her breathing evened and she fell asleep.

Pulling out his phone, he dialed Perry.

"Yeah."

Luke kept his voice low. "Have you checked your schedule for tomorrow?"

"I just got in from Argentina. I haven't even showered yet."

"Damn."

"You good?" The weariness in Perry voice halted his annoyance.

"Yeah. Yeah, Aeron is working with Mason. Could you…"

"Of course. I'll keep you posted."

He hung up and dialed Decius—straight to voicemail. Hopefully he had luck tracking down his father. The light breathing deepened. Luke laid Aeron down, the intoxicating scent of her curls surrounded him when he placed his lips to her head one more time, calling him not to leave her side.

The family S.U.V. idled at the curb. He pulled the door open, Granddad in the driver seat.

"Ready?"

"Of course," Luke lied, and although he knew it was a private mission, he glanced in the back, hoping Katherine would be there. Empty.

A three-hour drive brought them just over the Massachusetts border into Mt. Washington. Luke sat straighter when the Woodsworth Compound came into view. Most Blood Families held two residences, a large compound for families and training, and a suite within the Institute for ease of meetings and elite training.

Luke hadn't been back to his Institute residence since his parents died, and never intended to again. He shook the thought away.

"What are we doing here?"

"Jeremiah doesn't want to concede the estate to us. We're here to change his mind."

"He's what…seventy and in a wheelchair? What's holding him back? I mean what did you offer him?"

"His life. And the lives of his grandchildren." The comment was off-handed. Luke's stomach turned, but he kept quiet.

The Woodsworth's Legacy suffered the death of all four Legacy adults during a mission last year. It had been a catastrophic loss to the Legacy, leaving old man Jeremiah to care for a handful of children between six months to ten years. Their mission had been successful, though.

"What about a place to live? A monthly stipend?" The suggestion sounded reasonable when he said it, but Granddad's knuckles tightened around the steering wheel.

"The Wordsworths were on the Seward's payroll. They have enough blood money stashed away. It's an insult to your parents to offer more. It is only out of respect to Jeremiah, who claims he had no knowledge of such nefarious acts, that I offered anything."

"Offered? It's no longer on the table?" Luke didn't receive an answer, and he rubbed his hands on his pants, trying to sort through what the purpose of this field trip truly was. He expected negotiations, maybe a few threats. This didn't sound anything like that.

They entered Woodsworth House without knocking, as if it belonged to them—which technically it did. The door creaked open acting as an early warning system into the silent house. For being nearly midnight, lights still shone throughout the halls, and Luke heard the pitter-patter of feet upstairs. He followed behind Granddad, shadowing his confident strut toward the stairs.

"Jeremiah!" His booming voice echoed through the tiled hallway. Luke fought the urge to shrink away, being pulled back to the mansion as a five-year-old, cowering in fear of the Senior Assassin. A high-pitched scream froze him mid-step; a child's terrified scream.

"Granddad," Luke half-whispered. "Stop, you're scaring the kids."

"Good. Keep quiet and watch. This is how we handle rouge members—we don't use the Reapers for such sensitive matters, and I need you to understand what is expected of you." He continued down the hall, and Luke forced himself to follow. A light, familiar voice floated from behind a door. Granddad waved for him to open it. Removing the gun from his holster, Luke held it ready to fire at the first sign of danger and entered the room. He stopped short, Aunt Rosemary in his sights.

"Put that thing away before you kill someone, Luke."

Movement to the right pulled his gaze from Aunt Rosemary sitting on a desk next to the growing pool of blood beneath the wheels of Jeremiah's chair. Based on the blood splatter, it'd stopped shooting in spurts from the deep cuts on his arms, and slowed to a faint drip, maybe dribble, like it fell through the filter in a coffee pot.

"You were supposed to wait for me."

"I got the information we needed," Rosemary replied.

The casual tone kickstarted Luke's reaction. He pried his focus away from the dead body, propped like a rag doll in the wheelchair, and turned around. "I thought we were coming to negotiate?"

"That's cute." Her lipped curled as she said it, and his face flushed with foolishness. Katherine had warned him this wasn't child's play.

"We will discuss this later, Rosemary. Let's go handle the rest."

Rosemary hopped off the desk, wiping the specks of blood from her hands on her black slacks, and followed him. Luke stayed frozen. The rest? As in the children? He forced his feet to follow, tripping when they refused to cooperate on the stairs. He bounded up two and three at a time; he didn't need to see them, just follow the bone-chilling screams. He crashed into Granddad as he pushed open the door. A blond woman, maybe in her thirties, stared at him with frantic eyes, the children shielded behind her.

"They're just children. Please. Don't do this."

"And you're just a nanny. I'd let you go, but…actually I wouldn't. Loose ends and all." Rosemary smirked.

"Enough." A shot rang out and the nanny dropped to the floor. Luke could see clearly now the four children. The oldest, Gabe, pushed his siblings into the wall, his chest heaving, and his blonde hair plastered to his face by tears. Gabe—who was so close to breaking the team's record for bombs diffused. What was he doing home?

The slight adjustment in the gun jumpstarted Luke. "Granddad—"

"What is it, son?"

"We don't need—I mean…"

"Don't you trust I know what's best for this family?"

"Of course, I do."

"Haven't I been perfectly clear of what happens when orders aren't followed." Luke swallowed back his reply, remaining quiet.

The shots rang out: one—two, three. Complete stillness followed. The feeling left his legs, and he was on the floor. Breathing became impossible. Had he gotten shot? Noise passed above, but Luke couldn't take his eyes off the dead children. No, not all dead. Gabe huddled in fear, somehow untouched by the bullets. His brown eyes met Luke's, terrified—begging for help.

"Get up, Luke." Rosemary grasped his arm, taking him to his feet. A warm metal grip pushed into his hand. "Finish it."

The world moved in slow-motion. It took a lifetime to look from weapon in his hand to Gabe, to his Granddad. He surely could have fired off the entire clip in that time. Gabe could have run away. Why wasn't he running?

"Excuse me?"

"The boy," Rosemary replied. "Eliminate him."

"No." The word escaped before he'd thought about it.

He stumbled forward, pain radiating through the back of his skull.

His hand came from his head red. He rounded on Granddad,

not sure if the blow knocked his self-preservation out of place, but he couldn't hold his tongue. He'd already killed one innocent person to protect himself. Wilks shouldn't have died. Gabe shouldn't die.

"I'm not killing him. I'm not killing an innocent child. What is wrong with you?"

"It's not that difficult of a decision, Luke. I did the difficult work for you. He is no longer a child, and he just witnessed us murder his entire family. What will be done with him if we spare him? Any of them? What of the young ones when they learn what really happened to their parents? When the children of these mutinous families find each other and learn they have a common enemy? Why are you here, Luke?"

Luke looked to Gabe. The pounding in his skull drowned out the question and he looked back, confused.

"Why are you training with me now?"

To protect Aeron, but he knew the answer he needed to give. "Because my parents are dead."

"Because your parents were murdered, and you want vengeance. That rage that drove you here? The injustice? If these children aren't eliminated now, they will come for you. This is how we keep the slate clean, Luke."

"There's got to be…"

"You want to run the new regime? You need to be willing to get your hands dirtier than everyone else. The first one is always the hardest, until you realize this isn't the first one. Don't think of him as a child. Once you start training, you're no longer a child, you're an asset. Every one of you. The reasons you kill don't make you a saint or a martyr. They make you a killer, plain and simple. All that changes in this moment, is you are protecting yourself, you are protecting this family, instead of someone else's interests."

"No." It was the only logical word Luke could form. The pounding in his head blurred his vision and he wrapped his hands behind his head.

"In five, ten, fifteen years they will be you. Out for blood. You can eliminate that threat now, prove to me you belong here. Or I will do it anyway and consider our agreement null and void."

Aeron.

His gut churned. How the hell did he end up here? In this nightmare? He'd wake up to his alarm at any moment. He could believe it, if it weren't for the concussion—the pounding pain at the base of this neck.

"Luke…" Aunt Rosemary's uncharacteristically soft voice mirrored Katherine's. What would Katherine do? Pull the trigger and add the casualty to her growing vendetta? His right arm raised of its own accord—no a soft hand held his. The gun trembled, a dark blur in his sight. This was not what he signed up for. But he couldn't turn back now. He tried to steady his arm with the other hand, unsure he'd even hit the trembling blur with his hand shaking. Maybe he could miss, grab the kid and run. They'd both be dead before Luke reached him.

Or he could turn the gun on his Granddad right now, but then Rosemary would kill him and Gabe anyway.

Soft hands moved from his arm to rest on his shoulders, the light pressure calming him. There wasn't another choice. Either he did this, or more people were going to die. Aeron, Decius, himself, the boy anyway, and how many others? It needed to stop. He could stop it, but not if he was dead.

"Take a breath," Rosemary whispered.

Two shaky breaths were all he could manage. If he did this now, then he could stop it from happening ever again. "Good. Now don't close your eyes." He focused on his sight, the blur beyond almost completely out of focus. *Forgive me.* He turned off his mind. It was easier than expected, and he focused on the soothing voice by his ear.

"That's it. Now, pull."

23

AERON

*A*eron waited in Central Park alone. People bustled past her still form, leaning against a light pole. Mason should have arrived twenty minutes ago. She'd texted and called, but no answer. Perhaps he'd been held up at the Institute, or she'd been given the wrong lamp post. What if Mr. Wayward was coming instead?

The overwhelming odor of stale alcohol crept from behind her, and she spun, coming face to face with Perry.

"Sorry I'm late!" His always cheerful smile masked the smell and eased the endless what-if questions. "I didn't realize the time. How are you?" His eyes did a very Luke-like once over on her—and not in a sensual way, but in the cautionary, is everything really okay, way. What had Luke been telling him?

He removed his hat, the dirty-blond hair clearly unkempt for a few days, and another whiff of liquor caught in the breeze.

"Were you up late partying?" she asked, half amused Perry would be irresponsible at all.

He rubbed the back of his neck and sighed. "No. I had some Legacy stuff to handle." When he looked up, some of the easygoing shine left his eyes. "We need to walk and talk." His eyes shot skyward and he headed east.

"So why the Central Park meeting?"

"I honestly couldn't tell you. Mason asked me last minute to meet you. Thought maybe you would know." She shook her head. "Well, want to just grab some lunch instead?"

Great. Her first report back to her dad would be she didn't even meet Mason, but a Wayward. "Sure."

They took a booth at the diner, Sally bringing their order without even asking. Aeron pushed the salad around her plate, the awkward silence sitting between them. Never would she think things could be awkward between them. "How's your food?"

Perry didn't say anything, lost in his own thoughts and checking his phone every three minutes, occasionally sending a text.

"Everything okay?" She'd asked more than once, but the top of his head answered her.

"Perry." Nothing. "Dickwad." He glanced up at that but stayed quiet. "What is going on with you?"

"Work. I'm going to use the bathroom. Meet you outside?"

She rolled her eyes when he stood. "Whatever." Instead of going outside, she stopped by the register handing Sally a hundred-dollar bill. "The food was delicious as always, Sally. Tell your father we appreciate it."

Perry walked right by her without a second glance, phone glued to his ear. She followed, not bothering to be discreet.

"Finally. I can't be texting you this shit. I need you to grab some Valium or something. I've got assignments I need to be covering the rest of the day. I left my mom with him, but it's not good. What the hell happened last night? I can't get a coherent word out of him, and he threw the bottle at me when I offered a drink."

Perry leaned against the bench in front of the diner. Aeron paused in the entranceway when his face paled.

"This is my fault," he said. "I'm the one—Yeah. I know, but that's not a decision. It's like asking someone if they want to be shot in the left foot or the right.—He wants him there when?! —I'll do what I can. Just get there—Hey Kat? Would you have done it?" Aeron's heart jump to her throat at Kat's name, but Perry blanched at her words. "Of course she is. Is Shay worth it? Even after everything?" He pulled the phone away from his ear and stared at it. Aeron backpedaled into the restaurant. That was not a conversation she should have been listening to. She counted to ten before exiting, and he somehow looked worse than before.

"Thanks for meeting me. You know I'm always up for hanging out, but you could've just texted if you're busy."

He nodded, but whatever Katherine had said stole the small glimmer of joy from his eyes.

A white envelope sat on her bed. She slid a finger under the flap and opened it.

Look forward to a magical night. Chef's table 8pm. —Lulu

She smiled. Perry may have been acting weird, and Katherine might be trying to kill her, but at least one Wayward had his head screwed on. She tugged on a modest black dress and looked in the mirror. She took it off and pulled on a floor-length purple dress with a deep slit. After several dresses had been abandoned on the bed, a knock interrupted her mini fashion show, a hive of bees invading her stomach.

"Just a second!"

She rummaged through the pile of clothes and pulled back on the first black dress. She picked a pair of heels from the closet and headed to the living area, running smack into Decius in her hallway.

Her knee came up instinctively.

"Whoa. I just need to talk to you before you head out." He raised his eyebrows at her outfit but said nothing. She'd worn less as bait on their missions.

"Sure." She noted his newly busted lip.

"Privately." He gestured back to her bedroom, and she turned around. He pushed her pile of clothes over to clear a spot for himself on the bed. She stayed standing and waited for him to start talking.

"Does this have anything to do with my date tonight?" Aeron finally asked. She and Luke morphed into something overnight, and she hadn't asked how Decius felt about that.

He looked up, shocked. "No. No, I came to terms with the fact my best friend and little sister would be an item years ago. This has to do with Dad." His gaze wandered around the room and found the hole Luke made a few days earlier. His eyebrows raised in question.

"Luke. Probably his warm-up to the black eye you received the same night."

"Yeah, well, I deserved it. I owe you an apology, Aeron."

She bit the inside of her lip. What could he know?

"I've always tried to protect you. Keep Dad's wrath to a minimum. But it's not just Dad I should have been worried about. I was thinking short-term. Get you through training. Get you somewhere safe. But there is no such thing as safe for a Legacy child, is there?"

"What did he say to you, Dee?" Too many variations of the truths and lies ran through her head to determine which Decius could know. She internally cursed her father for not giving her a heads up. A simple text would have sufficed.

"That you're training with him to earn your Legacy spot. Is it true?"

Aeron took a seat beside him, a small weight lifting from her shoulders. It was mostly the truth. "Yes."

"I thought you wanted out?"

She pressed the heel of her hand to her forehead, a headache beginning to form over her right eye. She had wanted in. She had wanted out. Then she didn't want out but pretended she did. Now she was in and had to pretend she was out and trying to get in. Her head throbbed thinking about it. "What do you think my chances are of surviving a Legacy hunt?"

"If they even declare one, Aeron." He dropped his hands to his lap. "He's got you terrified that if you don't win his approval, you'll be killed. But the only person who has the authority to activate a hunt is Mr. Wayward. Why the hell would he issue that? For one, Luke would never let him, and by that time, Luke could very well be the Senior Assassin. Bottomline, you aren't going to get run out of town."

Luke would never get a chance to stop the order if Mr. Wayward killed him first.

"Did Dad say anything else?"

Decius scoffed. "He tried telling me he's keeping your options open. That is the biggest pile of bull I've ever heard. There are no other options."

She looked up at the dark circles under his eyes, which were not because of his recent altercations. He lacked the carefreeness he'd held over the summer. That seemed to be a theme going around this year. This was her fault. She should have never agreed to lie to him—but it was too late to turn back now. "He's not actively trying to hurt me, though. You and Luke can ease up on babysitting duty."

He released a long breath. "I get that. We're used to Dad's… intense training tactics. But Luke isn't buying it. He's genuinely concerned for your safety, Aeron. He's not going to just sit back on this one. For some reason, he thinks you're in real danger."

She sighed. Her fault again. "He thinks Dad abuses me."

"Why would he think that?" Decius asked, shock coating his words.

"Because I let him. The incident at the funeral. The bruise on my arm from training with Dad. A bunch of other reasons. I was under strict orders to tell no one about the training—I couldn't chance Dad finding out."

He nodded.

"Dad's kinda right. I have options. Option one: win Dad's approval and be claimed. Option two: beg Mr. Wayward for my life. Option three: play it by ear." There was also the option of marriage, but she couldn't consider that yet. Marrying into the Wayward family would put her life directly in Mr. Wayward's hands.

Decius looked over at her. "You shouldn't have to win anything. It's yours by birthright."

A deep sigh came out, the bravado of having her life together slipping. "It's the cards we're dealt, Dee. Now, if you're done being a downer, I have a date." She got up and headed out but paused in the doorway. "I'm here because you've always protected me. Don't you let anyone—Dad or Luke—make you believe you owe me an apology. I should be the one apologizing for putting you in this impossible position between Dad and me." She left before he could answer.

Luke still hadn't arrived at the apartment, but Lesley and Shannon sat on the couch.

"Hey, Les—where's Luke?"

Shannon's eyes lit up when she turned from the television. "Damn. I don't know, but he's missing out."

Aeron blushed and shook her head. "No, seriously, Les, when did you guys finish training?"

"I finished a few hours ago, but he didn't show up. It was just me."

A cold fist gripped the buzzing bees, killing the feeling instantly.

"I'm sure something came up with his Granddad. He's been super busy with him, right? He'll probably meet you there."

"Yeah," Aeron agreed. It could be possible. After a few deep breaths, she pulled out her phone. No missed notifications. "I'm going to wait at The Chef's Table. If he shows up here, tell him I'm eating on his tab anyways."

Aeron drummed her fingers on the half-filled glass of ice water.

Luke was two hours late to their date. She checked her phone again. No messages. No calls.

"Ma'am, would you like your food to go?"

Aeron smiled at the waiter. She had ordered food, a Dragon Tail sushi roll, and seaweed salad. She'd only picked at both—where the hell was he?

"No, thank you."

She couldn't stomach food, worry filling her stomach instead. There could be a million reasons he was late. His Granddad needed him; he got caught up and lost track of time; he was dead in a ditch somewhere. No—she wouldn't allow those thoughts. There was no reason to think he was in imminent danger. But if he wasn't dead… She took a deep breath, rejection burning hard in her heart.

She downed the rest of the water and pushed back her chair. True to her word, she charged the Legacy account. It was 10pm, she could actually get to her father's early for training and recon before midnight.

24

LUKE

"I can't do this." Luke's hand shook as he straightened the tie. His hands hadn't stopped shaking since the Woodsworth compound.

"Cancel," Katherine said from his bed. He'd returned to the Wayward Compound, unable to face anyone back in the City. "I'm sure she'll understand."

He ripped the tie off and tossed it across the room. "I feel like it's strangling me." He unbuttoned his shirt, and it joined his tie on the floor. "We're hitting another compound tonight."

She stiffened on the bed. "This isn't about the date."

"I can't even think about that. Your mother is picking me up at nine." The shadow from the curtains danced on his wall, and Gabe's pleading face begged from the darkness. Pleaded with him to be spared. The tears that had kept falling on the boy's face, even after his body had hit the floor, seemed to never stop.

"Luke. Luke!"

He swatted Katherine's hand from in front of his face, shaking Gabe out of his head. Why wouldn't his hands stop shaking?

"If you're too drunk, she won't take you."

"I'm not drunk. I don't want to drink. Why is that yours and Perry's answer for everything?"

"At least you're talking. Perry thought you might have brain damage from the hit you took to the back of your head."

"I don't want him to know."

"Too bad. I told him."

Rocks formed in his empty stomach. "Why would you do that!" Breathing became hard again.

"Because we're a...a team. I was going to say family, but the family sanity ship sailed a long time ago."

She was trying to make him smile, but he refused. He should never get to smile again.

"We need to get you drunk— it's the simplest way to keep you home."

"Are you sure?"

"I may have done this a time or two to get out of an assignment after Shay."

"He's expecting me there."

"I think he's testing to see what you can handle. And if you handled this well, I'd be worried. You passed his first test, Perry said. He had to up his game. If you can't be broken—"

"Then I'm a threat," Luke said, recalling their conversation the day he agreed to help her. He let out a shaking breath. "He said we're all just killers. I mean yeah, but..."

"He says what he needs to in order to get his way. Haven't you learned that yet? Look how he uses Aeron as leverage."

Aeron.

All of this to keep her safe so they could be together. He wouldn't even be able to look at her now. She'd see his sins painted across his face. Time with her had been his sanctuary, but now... she'd never understand.

"That was the biggest mistake I ever made."

"Caring about her?"

"Admitting it."

She opened his nightstand drawer, and pulled out a bottle of Jameson, left over from the funeral. He caught it and spun the bottle in his hand. There wasn't much left, but it would be enough. He'd emptied his entire stomach last night.

"Well, you can't take it back now. Drink up."

He opened the bottle, inhaling the sweet scent. "For the record," he said and took a sip, "I don't condone drinking as a way to deal with this."

He took a few more sips, shuddering each time. "I just want to stop seeing his small face, staring at me in terror," he whispered.

"You didn't have a choice." The soft words should have been comforting but weren't.

"Kat, I can't do it again." His voice cracked, and he took a long gulp. "How could he just pull the trigger, no second thought? No remorse? He's going to do that to Aeron, and Decius, and then probably me."

"Not if you stay in his good graces." She pulled him to the bed.

They sat shoulder to shoulder against the headboard, passing the bottle back and forth. Each swig burning less and less, and his head feeling heavier and heavier.

"You would have done it. Killed that kid without hesitating, wouldn't you?" He needed her to say yes. Or maybe no. Neither would change what'd he'd done.

"I can't say what I would have done, Luke. I wasn't there. But you're now in a position that I could never dream of."

He readjusted from the slouched position he'd somehow ended up in. "What do you mean?"

"Give it a year, and you can crumble the Legacy. He's handing you the power to not only eliminate the people who killed your parents but to end the reign of terror he's had over all of us, and I think he thinks you're too weak to see it."

"The kids—"

"Are going to die anyway. Let them at least die for a reason. So Granddad can't do this ever again. And once the Legacy is gone, think of all the children who won't have to grow up like this—in this twisted place forced to do unspeakable things."

"You enjoy these unspeakable things," he half-laughed and then caught himself.

"Only when they really deserve it."

He took another swig, tilting his head back. The silence stretched on, the echo of terrified screams in his mind.

"What if they all didn't have to die?"

Luke sat up straighter, hope resounding in her words.

"What do you mean."

"Some of them, yes, will have to die, but what if he trusted you enough to handle them by yourself? They're children, for Chrissake."

"But I'd have to…"

Her face fell. "Yeah. You'd still have to." She took a sip. "But think of all the other children you could spare. This needs to end, Luke. You'd be a hero."

A hero? Would a hero wager the lives of a few children—for the freedom of all the other Legacy Blood? He took the bottle back, chugged the last shots, face scrunched up as they burned all the way down, and his stomach turned. Maybe he should have stopped on that last sip.

A loud burp escaped him. It tasted like vomit. "Ahem. So, how would we save them?"

"Dominic."

The techie popped into his head, and he imagined how many other people Katherine and Perry had working with them. Katherine could be more dangerous than their Granddad, given the opportunity.

"We'll take care of it. You get Granddad's trust; I'll work out the rest."

How many murders would it take to prove he could do it? How many innocent lives would stain his hands? As if summoned by his guilt, Gabe's voice echoed in his head. "Please. Don't kill me. I'll do anything you want. Please!"

"I'm so sorry." The words meant nothing. They never would again.

"Come here." Katherine wrapped him in her arms, and the tenderness now reminded him of his mother. Tears he kept at bay since last night fought their way down his cheeks, and he leaned into Katherine, repeating his apology over and over until darkness took him.

Rough hands shook him. The Jameson bubbled from his stomach, and he pushed the hands away as the liquid poured from him onto the bedspread, splattering across the blue pattern. He dragged a hand across his mouth. The room spun, and he tilted back and forth, trying to find Katherine in the tilt-a-whirl around him.

"I told you he was too drunk." Katherine sounded close, but he couldn't pinpoint her.

"Honestly, Luke." Aunt Rosemary's cold, leathery fingers slipped under his chin, her weary face bobbing to and fro. He groaned and tipped his head away from her fingers until she let go. "Should I inform your Granddad that you allowed this to happen?"

"You'll tell him if want you to," Katherine said defiantly. "It's not like my needs have ever come before Granddad's. Besides, it's not my fault. I found him this way."

Aunt Rosemary gripped Katherine's chin the same way she'd done Luke's, searching her face and sniffing as if trying to smell her lie. She released it roughly, an agitated sigh escaping. "I told him Luke wasn't ready."

"Is anyone ready to shoot an innocent child?" Katherine's head snapped to the side. He tried to reach for her, but the world wobbled around him, and he remained still, holding in his liquor with his fist pressed to his lips. He really liked this bedspread. His mother had bought it for him.

"It could have been you in that room instead of Luke."

The statement sobered Luke. Katherine's eyes doubled as she stepped back, her mouth open in horror.

"Why are you doing this anyway? Since when are we involved in Legacy matters?" Aunt Rosemary remained silent. "Mom?"

His aunt looked back at him before leaving. "Get him cleaned up. He has a board meeting in the morning, and attendance is mandatory."

The door swung shut. Luke pushed himself up again, snail slow, trying to keep the liquor he unwisely drank down.

"Kat."

"Shit." Her foot collided with a basket of clothes. "Shit. Shit. Shit." Items flew around the room, some breakable, most not.

"Kat."

Her fingers dragged through her red hair, eyes wildly searching for something. "I need my phone." He pointed to the nightstand, next to the empty bottle. "I gotta go." She snatched it up and looked out the window, probably watching for headlights in the driveway.

"Don't leave me here." The vomit pooled toward him as he tried to get off the bed. He gagged. But the vomit wasn't why he couldn't be alone.

Face scrunched against the foul odor, she yanked the blanket off the bed and balled it on the floor. "Sleep it off, call Aeron in the morning. It will help."

"This is all your fault," he spat. "You swore she'd be safe. Just get close to Granddad," he mocked. "Just sell your soul, right? She's not even close to safe and will never understand what I did. Must be nice to have a parent alive to protect you."

She froze by the door, the deep breaths visible to him from behind.

"I'm not forcing you to do this, Luke. You were drowning in D.C., and I tossed you a lifeline. She's still breathing, isn't she? She's still sane, right? I'm keeping my end of the bargain; you better too. Now sleep it off before you say something you'll regret." The door shook on its hinges as it slammed.

He dropped back on the bed. The silence overwhelmed his senses. Each creak echoed like the children's screams. He fumbled with the nightstand drawer until he found the remote to a surround sound he had to have but never used. Turning it on, rock music called out from the speakers, and he raised the volume to the point of deafness.

The children still screamed louder.

"Thank you for joining us this morning. I realize it is unconventional to meet at such an hour, but the news of the Woodsworth murder-suicide has come to my attention."

Luke glared at his Granddad from his seat at the conference table. Rosemary and Katherine had the privilege of being absent from the mandatory meeting, remaining tucked away as Grand-dad's little secret.

"With the increased number of deaths the last year, we have to start considering that this is not a misfortune we are suffering from, but a plague of a traitor in the Legacy ranks."

Luke sat straighter in his chair and looked around the table, realizing it wasn't a normal board meeting—several prominent people were missing, Mr. Seward being most obvious. It was impossible not to miss his huge presence.

"You may notice the absence of some of the other board members. This is intentional as I believe there is a usurp for the Senior Assassin position, and we are feeling it down to our foundations. It is time we take back the reins. I'm requesting my grandson be officially signed into the by-laws as the next Senior Assassin."

Chatter broke out amongst the Board members. The knot on

the back of his head thrummed, and he gingerly ran fingers across it to be sure it hadn't busted open.

"What do you think, Luke?" He met Mr. Franklin's blue gaze, trying to look pensive, but he'd completely missed the question. Anger came in waves across the room from his Granddad.

"May I have the room, gentlemen?" A calm, simple request. The chairs moved, and the old men filed out. Granddad didn't move until the soundproof door closed, and Luke jumped when his hands hit the table like a shotgun. "I'm tiring of this, Luke."

"Then why don't you just put a bullet in my head and be done with it." He didn't look up, eyes fixed on a knot in the oak table. Maybe he'd do it. Not even hear the shot, and it'd be done. The stress, the anxiety, the guilt.

The chair next to him moved, and Luke jumped, nerves frayed. But his Granddad took the seat, rubbing the stubble on his cheek.

"If you do not want this, Luke. I need to know. We can show no weakness, and we can show no compromise. You seemed so ready in D.C. Perhaps I made a mistake, and you're not ready to fill your father's position." There was no threat in his voice, just a simple statement.

Luke hated the pride that roared inside of him, bristling at the idea he couldn't fill his father's shoes. A small voice in the back of his mind reminded him his father never wanted him working with his Granddad and wouldn't have killed children. A slightly louder one asked how could he be sure? His father was dead.

"You weren't prepared for last night. Rosemary did not give me much choice; I needed local authorities to time stamp and sell the murder-suicide without any Legacy intervention. It was a message to Mr. Seward; we are coming for him. Have you talked with Aeron about her supporting us? We could use an inside man."

An asset. He needed an asset, and the cool demeanor was what he used to work a mark in D.C. Luke nearly forgot, his mind torn to bits the last few days. He'd been set up. He'd been marked and played by the master—he'd also learned from the master. The throbbing in his head ceased, and for the first time since he set foot in the Woodsworth compound, clear thoughts formed—he understood the game board.

"You're right." He tamped down the anger that wanted to lash out. He needed to be calculating. "I wasn't ready. But I wasn't ready to lose my parents, and I wasn't ready to learn about Mr. Seward. But I want to be. Tell me what you need me to do."

25

AERON

"Aeron!" Shannon yelled from the kitchen. Aeron rolled over in her bed and checked her phone. It was 7am, and there were no calls or texts still. Her gut clenched.

"Yeah?" she called, her voice hoarse from exhaustion. She'd trained with Ivan until 4am. A soft knock answered her. A groan left her as she sat up. "Yeah?"

"May I come in?" Luke's soft voice asked through the door.

Her stomach fluttered—he was okay—but then it filled with rocks. He was okay. She sat up, leaning against the headboard. "Sure." Her voice trembled, and she cleared her throat, preparing to give him an earful. How dare he stand her up. Did he even consider how she would feel? What she would think?

He pushed the door open, waiting in the doorway with a dozen roses wrapped in a gold bow, and the saddest face she'd ever seen. Bags hung beneath his eyes, his slumped shoulders punctured her anger, but fueled the rejection.

"Roses will not fix this."

"I should have texted. Granddad summoned me at the last minute. Before I knew it, hours had gone by."

She raised an eyebrow. That wasn't an apology.

"Can we start over? Try for dinner again tonight?" he asked.

"No."

Shock colored his face. "What?"

"No," she said again. "You stand me up, no explanation, no contact, and then show up with flowers and expect me to swoon for the opportunity to give you a second chance?"

"Aeron—"

"An apology." She hopped off the bed and moved to the door, aware she was wearing just an oversized t-shirt and the effect it was having on him as his eyes roamed her body. "What I need from you is an apology and contact. A text letting me know you're not dead in a ditch so I could get some sleep."

His breath hitched as she paused in front of him and looked up. "If you want to make it up to me, come running in the mornings. I leave at 5am." She plucked the flowers from his hands. "I do love the flowers, though." She smiled and brushed past him to the kitchen to get a vase, heart racing. She wanted to pull him into bed, to bury herself in him, explore his body head to toe, and take his mind far away from whatever hung so heavy on his shoulders. But once they decided to take the next step, it was a line that couldn't be uncrossed.

An alarm buzzed loudly in her ear, and Aeron silenced it, her exhaustion getting the better of her. The phone buzzed again—a phone call this time. She picked it up.

"Yeah?"

"Where are you?"

"I'm sleeping, Ivan." She kept her voice low.

"You're over an hour late."

"Tell my father—"

"Aeron. We found it."

She sat up; blood thrummed through her body. "What?"

"Get over here ASAP."

Aeron closed the phone and leapt out of bed, pulse racing. Ivan and her father had found just as many dead bodies as dead ends on the search for any information that could lead to Mr. Wayward. Exhaustion rushed out of her as she pulled on her black sweats and sneakers to move through the darkened apartment, as she had every night the past few weeks.

She headed toward the large windows which overlooked Central Park. The fire escape door sat to the far left, tucked behind the curtains. The first night it screeched and cried as she forced it open, but tonight it was as silent as her.

She ran and jumped her way toward the ground making as little noise as possible. An idling car in the alleyway froze her movement on the third-story, and she crouched down. A figure stepped out of the car. Her heart hammered—she had run her fingers through that soft brown hair just hours before. She continued down one more level, trying to catch the conversation between Luke and whoever was in the car.

"—told you," Luke said.

She couldn't hear the other side of the conversation. She inched closer, careful not to be spotted.

"Have I not proven my loyalty? I understand what's at stake. I *will* handle them."

Who was he talking about? Luke took a step back as a taller figure stepped out of the car—Mr. Wayward.

"You better. That man murdered my sons. He murdered your parents. He needs to feel the loss we feel before he dies."

"He wouldn't care if you killed her. I already told you that," said Luke. He raked a hand through his hair, causing it to stand on end. "Killing Aeron is not going to bring him any pain." Aeron swallowed a gasp, heart threatening to jump out of her throat.

"Then I'll settle for adding her to my arsenal and dancing her around for him to see. Convince her to renounce him. That leaves Decius."

Luke hesitated. A rock formed in her throat.

"He's not a threat either. He'd join—"

"Luke."

"They are my best friends." Luke's voice had risen. "They are family."

"Mr. Seward was your parent's best friend as well. You see how that ended."

"Granddad—"

"The entire Seward lineage will be eliminated. Not only are they a disgrace to the Legacy, but we need the assets. Aeron can become one of us—she marries in and severs ties. But Decius carries the name. It is a slap in the face every time we speak it. Do you understand?"

A few moments of silence ticked by. Sweat slid down Aeron's temple, even in the chilly night air, as she waited to hear Luke's answer.

"Luke."

"Okay."

"What was that?" Mr. Wayward's voice held a note of victory.

"If he becomes a problem, then I agree, under the condition she—"

"Is off-limits. Yes. I've heard you a thousand times."

Aeron's heart shattered, her breath frozen in her chest. She leaned against the brick wall, eyes falling shut as she bit back the emotional bubble trying to escape her chest. Luke would be willing to kill Decius—for what? For a load of bullshit? How could Luke actually believe him?

"Same time tomorrow." The car door slammed, and the footsteps faded. The lump in her throat pulsed while her mind spun circles in her head. Luke thought her dad killed his parents, and Mr. Wayward was gunning to kill them all.

Minutes ticked by before she could stand and race to her dad's apartment. Her hands shook at the door, the keys falling twice before Ivan pulled it open. He ushered her inside, her father looking up from blueprints on the table.

"What is it?" Ivan asked. She stared at him, the words unable to form. "Aeron."

Where to start? That Mr. Wayward was trying to eliminate their family? That Luke was willing to serve up Decius on a platter? That she might be the only one to make it out of the entire situation alive? She finally looked at her dad. "You thought the price on my head was because of what you and mom tried to do."

He put his pen down and nodded.

"Well, he's upped the game. There's a price on all of our heads. Mr. Wayward has convinced Luke you killed his parents." The statement hung heavy in the air between them. His face remained still, but she could see the thoughts swirling behind his eyes. Even Ivan remained completely still.

"How are you still alive?" Ivan finally whispered, breaking the uncomfortable silence.

"Because Luke is protecting Aeron, and as long as he's trying to protect you, Aeron, he will do what his grandfather says, effectively keeping him safe," her father answered. The lump in Aeron's throat formed again, and she tried to speak around it.

"Except he's plotting your death, Dad." And Decius'—but she couldn't bring herself to say it—or believe it.

"I'm a lot harder to kill than you may think." He said it with a smile, but she felt the tension in his words. "This doesn't change our current plan, though. Come look."

Aeron moved next to the table. She needed to focus on anything other than the conversation she'd just overheard. "What do we have so far?"

"We know that Legacy families are being eliminated, and their money funneled."

"How many families?" Aeron asked, stumbling over the last word. She looked up at his drawn face.

"Over half the founding families have either been dismantled with few surviving members or completely decimated."

Decimated. Aeron's mind reeled with the implications. Generations of Legacy Members—dead.

"Who? Where?" The questions poured from Aeron's lips.

"Start with the most obvious: ours, the Waywards', and the Gales' numbers have dwindled. Joneses were eliminated over the summer. Woodsworths just the other night. I've reached out to the Pallards and the Finches, but they are refusing to communicate. But that's not all." He shuffled papers around, pulling out another list. "Any Legacy members who hold a stake are disappearing. Some dead; most vanished. There is a paper trail, but nothing substantial."

"How have we not heard about this? Why has no one reached out?"

"They did. That's what John and Mary were working on when they…"

"And Mr. Wayward did all of this on his own? That seems impossible." She looked to Ivan, desperation in her eyes. "Anything?"

"I'm still focused on the Rose Way." Ivan pushed the papers aside and laid a new blueprint down. "We know we'll never be able to infiltrate the Wayward estate. And I don't believe there is anything of value there anyway. He spends a lot of time here." He smoothed the paper down. "I'd bet my life Katherine and her douchebags are operating out of here as well."

"Careful what you bet," her dad said. "That is what is on the line once we head in."

"You say infiltrate like it's a CIA operation. I can be invited in." Her father's ice gaze shut down her suggestion, though. "So, what is this plan?" She looked at the blueprint, trying to decipher the lines and chicken scratch.

"We," her father pointed to himself and Ivan, "are going to scout.

Ivan will message you when we are set. All we need is for you to show up."

"Dad—"

"You are going to have to trust me, Aeron. Ivan needs to do what he does best in the computer world. You need to stick to Luke like glue. He might be the only thing keeping you alive right now."

Aeron let out a long breath, thoughts returning to Luke's haggard appearance—what had Mr. Wayward demanded of him that night?

"Fine." She spun around and headed for the door.

"Where are you going?" Ivan called.

"Upstairs. Luke is expecting to meet me in a few hours to run, and I need to clear my head before I see him."

Aeron rested on the front stoop of the apartment building, her foot tapping on the bottom step. She checked her watch: 4:57. Luke should be down any minute. As if on cue, the front door opened, Luke appearing in running shorts and a gray hoodie. The overwhelming urge to cry or punch him fought below the surface, and she swallowed them back. She couldn't believe he would serve up her brother to his Granddad.

She gave a small smile, though, and he leaned in for a kiss, his warmth heating up her cold face.

"Ron, you're freezing." He wrapped her in a tight hug, and she leaned into his chest, not realizing how cold she'd been.

"Ready?" She stepped back and bounced on her feet a few times. He nodded, and she took off running toward Central Park. The cold air stung her lungs and burned away the emotional roller coaster that sat beneath her calm exterior. Her feelings for Luke ran deeper than butterflies and passionate kisses; she'd known this for a while. The encounter she witnessed just hours ago stamped out any doubts about his feelings for her. The only problems were the lies they told each other and the fact he may be willing to kill her brother.

They vaulted over benches, statues, and fences. They used a fire escape to get to a rooftop and jumped from building to building, before finding themselves in a parking garage and moving over the cars. Luke bumped her shoulder as they ran and, she looked up, but his focus was on the area around them. His gaze moved continuously as he looked for potential threats.

"Everything okay?" She touched his arm to get his attention.

A tight smile met her, and a quick "Yeah," before he turned away. The hour dragged by in a similar fashion—Luke's eyes roving and minimal words spoken. At last, they slowed to a walk and entered the lobby. Luke's flush face looked more relaxed.

"Ready for the finisher?"

"Finisher?" Luke raised his eyebrows.

"Race you to the top." Aeron pointed up the stairs.

He laughed and nodded. They started the stairs at a sprint, Luke taking three at a time in most spots. He reached the top floor and she glared as she finished the last flight.

"Your legs are much longer. That's an unfair race."

"Don't be a sore loser." He held the door open for her, and they stopped outside the apartment doors, the adrenaline and endorphins sparking between them while they stretched in the hallway.

"Thanks for letting me join you." He touched a hand to her sweaty face. "I really needed to just…run."

There was nothing like free-running, whether in the park or on the buildings, to release her mind. "How are things with your Granddad?"

His smile lessened, and his shoulders tensed. "Intense."

"That's it? That's all you can give me?"

"I don't really want to talk about it."

"Why?" she pressed.

"Because—he's asking me to do a lot. My days are split between training with him and training here. Now he wants me taking classes at Columbia, so when I'm MIA, I'll probably be there." His weight shifted.

"Columbia? What for?"

"I honestly don't know, and I don't care."

"You sound like you are thinking about not doing it." Her heart hammered against her chest.

"It's crossed my mind. I'm so busy. We are working side missions, and trainings, and meetings, and the Institute. Add in Columbia, and then what? I could be sleeping or spending time with you. Perry should be the next in line, not me."

"And why isn't he?"

"I have no idea." Luke sighed. "What about you? Any word from your father?"

"No." She kept his piercing gaze until he looked away.

"Do you smell bacon?" he asked.

"Turkey bacon, I'm sure." She let the subject change. "Shower and come over for breakfast."

He planted a kiss before disappearing into his apartment. Lesley waved and flipped the bacon on the stove. The smell, although appetizing, turned Aeron's stomach. Instead, she headed straight to her bathroom and turned on the shower. She pulled out her cell phone and dialed Ivan.

"Can't get enough of me, huh?" His voice held humor she could not return.

"Why would Mr. Wayward want Luke to take classes at Columbia?"

"Because he's a douchebag?"

"I'm serious," Aeron said, weary.

"Me too. I have no idea why. You guys don't normally do the college thing, right? Maybe it's just a test."

"Maybe, but he lied to me when I asked him why."

"And he's lied to you about knowing you were on a hit list and that he's currently plotting your father's death. And you're lying to him about knowing who really killed his parents and feeding into his lie that your father is an abusive bastard. Do I need to go on?"

His words smashed into her. "When you put it like that."

"I'm not putting it any way. I'm stating the facts. You may have genuine feelings for each other, but your relationship is built on a convoluted foundation, Aeron."

His words stung. "Just run the information by my Dad. And Darth?"

"Yeah?"

"You're a dick." She spat and clicked the phone closed.

26

LUKE

The Sig trembled in Luke's hand, the silencer slipping between his fingers, bouncing off the car floor twice before he managed to screw it in place.

"There are six." Rosemary checked her watch, the dull green glow indicating two minutes until the elimination of the Finch family.

"Two adults in the master bedroom, one adult in the guest room, and three children," Luke repeated for the third time. "I got it. The master bedroom first, since it's on the second floor. The guest room next as they would be coming up from the first, and finally the children." He kept his voice as even as possible on the last word.

"I'm impressed with the speed in which you've come around. Who would have thought you would be asking for these missions."

"My parent's murderer is still out there," Luke replied, checking the time. One minute. "I'll do whatever I need to do."

"Don't tell Katherine, but she would never have been able to handle this. Or Perry. He did right choosing you."

Luke swallowed the bile, aware of the invisible eyes always watching him from the shadows.

His watch hit the hour. "Let's go." They slid out of the car, silent on the gravel driveway. Rosemary punched in the security code for the basement door. It whined when she pulled it open, and Luke flinched, waiting for the sound of footsteps and gunfire. It opened enough for the two of them to slip through, and she propped it with a doorstop for an easy escape—not that they would need one. Everyone would be dead.

He'd memorized the blueprints, so even in near darkness, his foot hit the steps exactly when he expected. Once on the first floor, lights peeked out from unattended rooms—he checked to make sure. He paused by the guest room—ear pressed to the door. A light, easy breathing could be made out.

"Why don't you just stay here," Luke whispered. "I take them out upstairs, and you handle this one?"

She gave a harsh look. "You know why."

Yeah—she needed to see him not flinch as he pulled the trigger. He nodded and continued upstairs. The master bedroom door was open a crack—probably so they could hear if the children called out. The knot grew in Luke's chest, Gabe's ice-cold stare ever growing with each step. He slowly opened the door. Shelby Finch lay draped across her husband, Joe.

The floor creaked beneath his step, and Luke swore—a security measure designed into the floor but not in the blueprints. Genius. Joe shot up, pistol in hand, and froze before pulling the trigger. Shelby jumped up, covers falling to reveal more skin than Luke was prepared to see, and his cheeks burned.

"Jesus, Luke," Joe said, rubbing his eyes. "What the Hell?"

"Oh, you will be there soon enough," Rosemary said from behind him.

"Who's with you?" Shelby asked.

"Let's not pretend you don't know, Shelly. This day has been a long time coming. I'm just sorry I can't pull the trigger." Rosemary stepped up next to him, and Shelby paled.

"Luke?" Joe asked again.

Luke swallowed hard, not sure what Rosemary meant. These were his parent's colleagues. They'd mentored him. They'd scolded him, and praised him, and consoled him. They'd betrayed him.

"For my parents." Luke released two shots before they could react—at least the element of surprise was on his side. Adrenaline raced at the sound of footsteps. "I hear the other one." He pushed past Rosemary and looked over the railing, reeling back as two bullets sped past him. "Damn it. There are two, not one, Rosemary." The wall next to Luke exploded, and he dropped low.

"My mistake," she said, dropping next to him.

"Mommy!!" The call from a little girl. "Daddy??"

Luke was definitely going to vomit. Rosemary nudged him hard. "Not here, you don't. We weren't here. Can't pull that off if you puke."

He nodded and swallowed hard, willing his stomach to cooperate.

"It's okay, Olivia!" a male voice called, in between shots. "Stay in your room. Uncle Steven will be there in a minute."

"Steven?" Rosemary called out. The gunshots paused.

"Rosemary?" The voice held a note of disbelief.

"Stay there," Steven said, Luke assumed to his companion. Footsteps raced up the stairs, and Luke raised his Sig, ready to fight.

"No need." Rosemary stood up. "Steven is an…ally."

A man rounded the corner, neatly trimmed brown hair on top of a square face. His brown eyes smiled when they fell on Rosemary. "I'll be damned."

He turned and fired a shot, a thud followed by a series of muffled thuds followed as his companion tumbled down the steps. His eyes found Luke, who stood, Sig still gripped to fire.

"Luke, would you be a doll and finish what we came here for?"

His throat was dry. "Excuse me?"

"The Finch Legacy. We need it. Go."

"But what about…" he waved a hand in the direction of 'Uncle Steven' because there was no record of a Steven Finch.

"This is one of those moments you show how smart you are and keep moving. You know how he gets when we're late."

Luke swallowed the sandpaper his mouth had become and nodded, walking past Rosemary and the mystery man.

Luke caught sight of the twisted body at the bottom of the stairs as he passed, the face covered by auburn hair as the blood surrounded her head like a cartoon halo. He released an absurd laugh as he headed to the children's rooms. *Don't think. Just point and shoot. Don't think. Don't think. Don't think.*

He pushed the first door open. The closet door was not fully shut. Luke hesitated, the soft sound of conversation coming from just down the hall, there would be no way to save them. Maybe the next family he could.

His feet moved through invisible mud, Gabe tugging his body to not take another step forward. He pulled the door open, and the sliver of light from the hallway fell on two young girl's faces. Identical terrified blue eyes looked up at him, and then for a moment, relaxed when they recognized him. Sarah and Olivia Finch dressed in pink pajamas with ponies on them. *Don't think. Breathe.* Shots sped out, and Luke jumped, looking around for Rosemary. But the smoke rose from his silencer.

Swallowing hard, his feet moved him to the next room, Ben's room. The sheets hung off the bed, draped to cover the bottom. Luke shook his head. Ben Finch. Why couldn't you have hidden better? There were rooms in this house designed to hide in. Places in this very room to tuck away safely. Did they never teach their children? They probably never thought they would need to be protected from the Legacy.

Luke inched closer and squatted down, a shaky breath leaving him. Words would do nothing for either one of them. *Don't think. Don't think. Don't Think.* He pulled up the sheet, finding Ben tucked in the corner. His shot sped out before they could make eye contact, and he dropped the sheet back down.

Clapping from the door stung his ears. "And there it is," Rosemary said. "Exactly what this industry needs. No hesitation. No reservations."

Luke stood, his hands shaking uncontrollably. He holstered the Sig and stuck his hands in his pockets. "Where's Steven?"

"Dead. Shot himself in the head after killing this poor family." Her eyes shone with pleasure, and he just didn't care enough to ask for clarification. He needed a shower and a drink.

He stopped next to Steven's body and unscrewed the silencer from his Sig. He wiped it for prints and attached it to the dead man's gun. Luke's bullets would be tagged in the coded system and swapped out for whatever model needed to be put in. Tonight? It would be for a Glock. He retrieved a bullet from the wall to drop off at coding.

"You did good work here," Rosemary said. "He'll be very pleased indeed."

The knot in his chest grew with each step away from the house, and he concentrated on breathing around it. In. Out. In. Out. But it didn't matter. He would never breathe freely again, and he didn't deserve to.

27

AERON

*A*eron stared at her phone, foot bouncing off the floor. She hadn't seen Luke in over a week, his Grandfather's tasks keeping him off the grid for days at a time. The last text came almost two nights ago: 'Night'. If it wasn't for Perry's random updates and Ivan's constant surveillance picking him up every twelve to sixteen hours, she would be sure Luke was dead.

"Would you knock that off?" Shannon snapped, kicking Aeron's leg. "It's like a damn earthquake in here."

She looked up from the phone. Shannon scanned medical files on the other end of the couch, feet resting next to Aeron. "Sorry. I haven't heard from Luke in days. Our sudden relationship went from late-night make-out sessions to doorway kisses to single word texts."

"I'm sure he's fine," she said, eyes not moving from the pages. "It's got nothing to do with you, and you know that."

"I do." She tucked the phone away and turned to Shannon. "What are you looking at?" An uncomfortable veil had fallen over them. Aeron would take a hundred bullets for Shannon and vice versa, but the strain of hoarding secrets had left them unable to talk about much.

"Dr. Sherwood's medical reports. She's been the head of the Medical Department for almost a decade, so I don't want any of my notes to fail in comparison to hers."

"How long is she out?"

"Indefinitely."

Aeron raised an eyebrow. "Really? I thought she just broke her arm."

Shannon shook her head. "No, she slipped in a pool of blood in the O.R. and shattered her elbow into too many pieces to fix. They said it felt like a bag of marbles."

Aeron sat a little straighter. "So what? You're taking over her classes? What about the advanced medical students who are training for that?"

The team had been split up across multiple assignments the past week and had left a knot in Aeron's stomach. Luke stayed busy with Senior Assassin duties, Shannon stepped in to help the medical ward, and Justin and Decius were immersed in a mini assignment, which they'd been tied up in for about four days. Add in Ivan and her father doing recon, and Aeron had too much time to contemplate the many ways they could all be killed before dawn. Even classes couldn't hold her attention—not that they ever did. But with Legacy lives disappearing by the day and Luke planning her family's deaths, Explosive Chemistry and Decoding Tactics just didn't compete.

"It hasn't gone over all that well, to be honest," Shannon said. "I'm younger than all of the trainees and they don't think I'm capable of running surgery, but the Board didn't give much choice. The head medic must be a Legacy descendant. I've been sure to dole out jobs accordingly, and it's only for a few weeks until my mother comes back, but…"

"Don't worry about it. You were born to be a medic. It's in your DNA," Aeron supplied.

Shannon smiled and put the files down, hand running over the back of her neck. "I know. How are you doing? This has been a crazy start to the year."

"I'm good," Aeron lied. "I just need something to do. It feels wrong not having an active assignment. The boys are off on their own, Luke's off becoming our next boss, you're saving lives, and I'm here: attending training. I'm bored."

"What about Lesley? Is she still training with Mason?"

"Every free moment she has. I tag along, make sure she'll be able to keep up with us on the rooftops. I never pictured myself the mentoring type, though." But that was only half the truth. Mason provided insight into the upper workings of the Legacy she wasn't privy to and that her Father had been excluded from.

"I guess we're all finding our superpowers this year."

Aeron laughed. "I guess so." In all fairness, Lesley *had* been chosen to be a part of this team. Not only was it a huge honor, but they'd also needed her. But that was before the team was falling apart, and half of them were on a Legacy soon-to-be-killed list. "What time are you heading back?"

Shannon glanced at her watch. "An hour, did you want to—" A knock interrupted her. Their gazes snapped toward the door. No one ever knocked before nine p.m. Either their retinal scan was in the computer, or they didn't know this place existed. It was only eight. Aeron jumped up.

"Who is it?" she called through the door.

"Mason."

Aeron's heart skipped several beats, and Shannon's wide eyes must have matched her own. A house call from Mason meant one thing: Something happened in the field. Aeron yanked the door open and hesitated. He leaned nonchalantly against the door frame, his bright smile faltering.

"What happened?" The words spilled from her as a million scenarios played out in her mind, but the only one to warrant a visit this late and formal was a death notice.

"What?"

"What happened?" Shannon reiterated, coming from behind the couch, phone in hand. "Who died?"

"No! No." He stepped into the apartment. "Shit. I didn't mean to —nothing's wrong. Shannon, I—ah, I thought you were living at the Institute for the time being."

Aeron's racing heart eased up a bit, and Shannon gave Mason a bewildered look. "I am. I'm back in the family residence while acting Head Medic. I know I'm not supposed to leave the grounds. I just needed to clear my head. Is that why you're here?"

"Not at all. I honestly agree that being locked to within a half-mile of the Institute is an absurd and unreasonable stipulation. Your secret is safe with me."

But Shannon's face had already paled. "No. You're right. Had they needed me, I would have been cutting it too close. I'm going to head back." She retreated to the pile of files and returned them to her bag before heading to the door. "See you later, Aeron. Mason."

Aeron nodded in her direction but didn't miss the raised eyebrow sent her way. Mason showing up to the apartment, where he assumed Aeron to be alone, at night, was not normal.

"So, what are you doing here?"

He waited until the door was closed to answer. "How is it going with your father?"

Her mouth suddenly went dry. Was he in deep with Mr. Wayward like her father suspected? "Would you like some water?" She stood, needing space and a moment to think. He grabbed onto her wrist, spinning her back around.

"I'm concerned, Aeron. There are whispers…an upheaval. His name has passed through many closed-door meetings, none of them good. I stay on the outskirts, but I can't sit back on this. Your family is in trouble."

"How do you know what's going on in these meetings?" A moment of contemplation passed before he answered.

"I know much more of the inner workings than any non-blood should. I don't do what I do without being beyond discreet.

It's often forgotten about—because I'm pretty damn good at my job and I stay in line—but my entry into the Legacy was anything but smooth." His fingers slid to her hand, turning it over. The light danced over the pale scars on her palms and inner forearms from various fights and falls. He rotated it, exposing a patch of minuscule scars by her elbow you'd have to know were there, and ran his thumb across them; remnants of a nasty fall from a single-story roof into a windshield; Sarah had died that night, Mason racing to their aid and by default becoming their next Guardian.

"Luke's father vouched for me, your father backing his statement. I was hours from elimination, but they secured my place here. I'll never forget who I owe my life to. And who's lives I'm responsible for: yours—and Luke's."

A chill ran through her. They *did* have an ally close to Mr. Wayward if her father would just accept his help.

The door swung open. Lesley froze in the doorway, eyes bouncing between the two of them, Aeron's wrist still in Mason's grasp.

He let go of her, the reassurance of his grasp suddenly gone. "He's shut me out. If you could pass on that message…Great training today, Lesley," Mason said, suddenly out of the apartment before Aeron could respond.

Lesley looked from the closed apartment door to Aeron and smiled. "Wow."

"What?" She sounded defensive and rephrased. "What's the big deal."

"He's just so…"

Aeron laughed, aware of just how hot Mason was and how that may have looked. "Yeah. How has training been?"

"Exhausting. I'm actually going to shower and then head out with Justin for food. Did you want to join us?"

"I actually have to meet Luke," she lied. "You know Justin is a player, right?"

Lesley nodded. "Trust me. I'm not into him like that. He's been helping me with the surveillance equipment."

"Well, be safe." Aeron retreated to her room, mind filled with a million questions. She needed to reach her father, but the only contact in the past week had been Ivan sending a thumbs up on spotting Luke alive on surveillance. The line rang and rang. Ivan wasn't going to answer. She tossed the phone to her bed and closed her eyes. A good night's sleep would do wonders.

A scream broke the silence of the apartment. Aeron bolted up, scanning the dark room. The scream continued, high and long. She tossed the blankets off and raced down the hall, following the sound. The living area was dark, the sound coming from Lesley's room. Aeron slammed open the door, looking for an attacker—but Lesley sat bolt up in her bed as the door bounced off the wall, drenched in sweat and gasping for air.

A nightmare.

"Stop! Stop!" Lesley yelled out.

Aeron moved next to the bed, hand hovering near Lesley. "Hey! Hey! You're good. You're safe."

Lesley's wild eyes landed on Aeron, who gave a reassuring nod.

"I'm sorry," Lesley said, panting as if she'd sprinted up the building's stairs. "I, ah—did I wake you?"

"It's okay." Aeron handed over a bottle of water from the nightstand. "How long have you been having nightmares?"

She took a long swig of water, her breath slowing. "Since the first assignment. It uh, it brought up some memories of my entrance into the program."

"The man you killed," Aeron clarified. It was dangerous to talk around the harsh truths—it buried them deeper. "He deserved it. You wouldn't be here otherwise, nor would the girl you saved."

"I know." She pushed her hair back from her face. "I know. But one of the apartments I broke into, there was a man who looked so much like him."

"What was it about him?" Aeron asked, moving to sit next to Lesley on the bed. "His eyes, his nose?"

"His eyes. Light blue—it was like he was staring right through me, and…" she shivered.

"That's a good thing. It means you're human, Les."

"How do you mange? You've must of killed…" she trailed off.

"Many," Aeron supplied. "I've killed many people. But the nightmares, the ghosts are worth it."

"How do you know?"

Aeron adjusted herself. "The first girl I saved—really saved from a horrible life—her name was Sammie. She's a freshman at Yale this year. She's studying law." Lesley relaxed beside her. "There was Brian, a boy older than me, who was being held as a bargaining chip by a foreign diplomat. His dad had access codes to some research the diplomat wanted. Brian just got married, his wife is pregnant with a baby girl.

"That little girl wouldn't exist without us. And who knows what change she'll bring. The nightmares are a small price to pay. They are worth it."

Lesley laid her head on Aeron's shoulder, and Aeron stiffened but didn't move. She kept her breathing even, coaxing Lesley back to sleep. Keara had been so much better comforting them: hot tea, a warm blanket, an ear to listen. Aeron didn't know how to do any of that. But Lesley's even breathing matched her own, and Aeron readjusted her on the pillow before slipping out and returning to her room. She paced a few minutes, spinning the phone in her hand. She needed to tell her father Mason *was* loyal. She knew it in her soul. She took a deep breath before dialing Ivan. He picked up on the third ring.

"Darth."

"I can't talk." The line went dead. Aeron stared at the phone. That was unexpected. She dialed her father instead.

"Everything okay?" His voice was hushed like Ivan's.

"I'm fine. I just—"

"I told you. Sit and wait." He hung up too. Her body flushed in irritation, and she tossed the phone down to the bed.

Sit and wait—what he'd been telling her since the summer, and she had. But too many lives hung in the balance, and she had found them their ally. If he refused to give answers, maybe someone else would. She checked her watch, two-forty-five. Justin and Decius wouldn't be home, but maybe Luke would be.

She slipped into sneakers and pulled on a sweater before heading over to the boy's apartment. She knocked softly on the door and then knocked a little harder. Movement stirred on the other side and the locks slid back. Luke squinted against the hall light, his hair standing up in all directions and wearing only sweatpants.

"Hey, Ron." He yawned and pulled the door open wider, inviting her in. She didn't say anything, her hand running across the fresh bruises on his ribs on the way inside. He gave a small flinch, and her anger began to ease up. She headed to the kitchen to retrieve a bag of peas, tossing it to him. In the light, she could see the mixtures of sleeplessness and the remainder of bruises beneath his eyes. The rest of her anger fizzled out, and she sat next to him on the couch.

"What the hell happened to you?" She took the cold bag from him and repositioned it.

He sucked in a breath but wrapped an arm around her shoulders and didn't answer.

"Luke."

"Have you ever been to Japan?" he asked. She looked up, but his eyes were closed, head leaning back against the couch.

"No. Do you have a concussion?" She reached for his head, smoothing his hair down.

He chuckled and shook his head. "I was dreaming about getting away, from here, from all of this." He gazed down at her, his eyes intense. "If I just left, would you come with me?"

Yes. This was the year of impossible offers. She'd been given opportunities of a lifetime—to leave the Legacy, to be in the Legacy away from her father, to run away with Luke. Asked barely six months ago, her answer to all of them would have been yes, yes, yes.

"What about Decius?" she countered. She'd held on to *that* part of the conversation, and it tore like a beast to get out. She wanted to believe that he had lied to his grandfather. She had lied over and over for good reasons—she was lying now for a good reason. Her heart quickened as she waited for his answer.

"If he wanted to, of course." An unknown pressure flew from her shoulders. He raised an eyebrow. "Why?"

"If you're whisking me away forever, I wouldn't leave him behind."

He kissed her forehead, and she removed the ice pack—her hand now freezing. "That's why I love you." His voice so soft she could have missed it.

Aeron's cheeks burned as the beast inside calmed. Deep down, she could never believe that he would hurt Decius, but his reassurance ignited a fire inside instead. "Did you just say—"

He leaned in to kiss her again, and she met him halfway, closing the small space between them. He wrapped a hand around her waist and ran the other up her back to cup her head. He tugged gently, and she shifted from next to him to on top of him without breaking their kiss.

Her hands trembled as she touched his shoulders and adjusted herself in his lap. They hadn't been alone in weeks, their relationship surviving on doorway kisses and scattered texts. His arm tightened securely at her waist, pulling her closer, hand slipping beneath the back of her shirt. Fingertips traced her spine, and she broke the kiss, shivering. They stilled, both breathing deep, their foreheads pushed together.

"Not yet," he whispered. "Can we just be?"

She nodded, breathing heavily too. She slid her hands down his arms, pulling them from around her to hold hands. Without his arm around her waist, she felt vulnerable and wished she'd kept them there.

They laid quiet, wrapped together on the couch. Luke leaned to the side to lie down and pulled her with him, pulling her back in his secure hold until she fell asleep.

"Hey." A rough shaking woke Aeron up. She bolted to her feet, blood racing through her body. Justin took several steps back. "Whoa. Just waking you up. Luke said I'd find you here."

Luke. Aeron looked at the empty couch. He'd left without waking her. "What time is it?"

"Six a.m. Get dressed. We're drug testing today." Justin's intense bronze gaze met her. Seven years of missions allowed for Aeron to look past the gaze to his intentions.

"Shit. All of us?"

"Well, not Shannon because of obvious reasons. And I'm not sure about Luke. But Dee and I wrapped up earlier this morning, so it's us three and Lesley."

"What time?" She dragged a hand over her face and wiped the sleep from her eyes. She needed food if she had any chance of surviving a drug test.

"Meeting in the Battle Room in three hours." He moved to the kitchen. "Dee and Lesley are already at the Institute. I just came home to get you and to eat. Carbs?"

She nodded. "Please. I'm going to change. Don't eat it all."

The apartment was empty as usual. After brushing her teeth and pulling on the carbon fiber under-protection, she tugged on jeans and a t-shirt. A blinking light on the bed grabbed her attention on the way out. She'd forgotten her phone last night.

Backtracking, she flipped it open. Fifteen missed calls and twenty texts from Ivan. She dialed him back.

"About damn time."

"What's going on?" She asked, irritation biting to come out. They hadn't had the time to listen to her last night, but because *they* had something, she should be jumping through hoops.

"Tonight. Our first-date dinner. 21:00."

Her heart jolted, irritation forgotten. "Fuck."

"What's wrong?"

"I can't." There couldn't be a worse day.

"What do you mean you can't? There's an impromptu fundraiser tonight at the Rosey Way. The whole Wayward squad is on the guest list. It's our best shot to get into their room for the next month."

"If he would just let me go on the inside, I'd probably already have access," she snapped. "Tell my father I'm being drug tested in a few hours."

"What's the big deal? You pee in a cup."

"Just tell him. If he changes the plan, let me know."

28

LUKE

*A*eron, Decius, Justin, and Lesley stood in line in front of Mason, a slew of Legacy members dressed for battle in the shadows. Luke looked on from the observation room, anger radiating through every pore.

"I should be down there. That's my team."

"To be technical, it's *Decius'* team. But you will have your drug test another time. I need you focused on the fundraiser tonight," replied his Granddad. "Besides, there are other drugs we will need to test you with. You will hold centuries of secrets and the identities of hundreds. Your conditioning will be much more in-depth."

A cold vice gripped Luke. "You're talking about Sin."

"We can't use it against our enemies if it can be used against us. Before you officially take over the Senior position, yes, you will have to successfully fight through multiple doses of Sin."

Luke wiped the cold sweat that formed on his brow and looked back out to his team. Sin: the neurotoxin created for the Legacy, which left enemies broken without ever physically touching them. He'd seen it used once and never wanted to again. Movement in the Battle Room pulled Luke's attention to Lesley—Decius had already been dosed and had dropped hard to his knees. She back-peddled from Mason, but Justin gripped her upper arms, holding her still so Mason could inject the poison—a frown on his face. Lesley dropped nearly immediately, hands covering her head. Justin stumbled, falling to his hands and knees after his shot, and finally, Aeron —her jaw set as the other three held on to the floor as a safety net. Whatever cocktail they'd chosen for the test was not normal, but Luke didn't dare ask. He kept his eyes on Aeron, who'd dropped to one knee.

Nails dug into his palm as the first bell rang and the lights dimmed. Legacy members dressed in black descended on the drugged participants. Lesley screamed, scooting back into another black-clad member. He could see, even from above, the panic in her eyes.

"Did Lesley get the same dosage?" Luke asked, concern for the youngest team member's mental stability. "She's never been through one of these before."

"She is on an elite team, Luke. All new members get the same dosage."

He bit back the reply. He knew that to be false— Justin had received half the dose of a completely different cocktail his first time. Luke scanned for Aeron in the near darkness instead. It wasn't hard to find her. Bodies flew, making a clear path toward Lesley. Why were there so many people?

"What's the objective?" Luke asked, searching for Justin and Decius. He glanced at the computer monitor to find their tracking bracelets; it showed them deep within the scaffolding, on opposite sides.

"Don't be killed."

"Don't be—what kind of testing is this?" They were usually given a dossier and had an asset to retrieve or eliminate. They'd battle against two or three Legacy members each, whose goals were to engage but keep everyone safe. A battered and bruised team member could still function. A broken team member was no good to the Legacy.

"A new kind. It's perfectly safe. They are using paint guns and dulled knives. No harm will come to any of them."

Luke didn't answer, swallowing back the urge to punch his Granddad in the throat. It'd been an urge that grew every day and egged on by tiny voices that haunted him. Aeron incapacitated three more Legacy members on her way to Lesley. She ducked beneath the punch of another, slipped around to his back, and brought him crashing to the floor. Her legs whipped around his head, locking him into an armbar with such force Luke flinched when the arm dislocated. This was not normal or safe training. An involuntary gasp left his throat, his feet propelling him closer to the viewing window. The glimmer of a knife shone in Aeron's grasp. Dull or not, she'd kill a man with it.

"Granddad…"

"Let's just see where this goes." The older man stood beside him, a slight bounce in his stance.

Luke's heart beat against his ribcage. She would kill them. Who knew what she was really seeing right now. What drugs and toxins had been combined for this test. He scoured the computer screen for Decius—he'd stop her. But Decius' tracker hadn't moved—the vitals on the tracker reading normal. Returning to the Battle Room, the knife flew from Aeron's hand as two members attacked. Lesley managed to get to her feet, fleeing her aggressors.

Involuntarily jumps continued to make their way from Luke as Lesley slipped on a landing twenty feet up, or when Justin, who'd materialized looking completely dazed, was shot twice in the chest, orange splatters declaring him dead. He was escorted from the room, followed by Lesley moments later: they'd lasted a total of fifteen minutes. Decius finally reappeared, wild eyes searching the room. The remaining members flooded between him and Aeron.

The door to the viewing area opened. Mason poked his head in, a grimace on his face. "I'm going to take Lesley and Justin to the infirmary. The Sewards are all yours."

Panic spread through Luke's entire system. Had he misstepped?

Was he about to witness the death of his best friend and girlfriend in a single swoop, and have it declared a training accident?

"Granddad—I've done everything you've asked. No hesitation."

"I'm aware."

"Then what is this?" He scanned the massacre of Legacy members unfolding in front of him. There had to be at least fifty masked people in the room, a third already indisposed. It was too many.

"Those people aren't Legacy," he realized aloud.

"Why don't we just watch? I'd like to know what they are capable of." His Granddad stared intently out the window. Luke took a stance next to him, crossing his arms and eyes bouncing between Aeron and Decius. Decius squatted low and swept feet from beneath one of them and bounded into a single hand back handspring, ready to defend again. They attacked two at a time. He dropped to a knee, eyes glued on a single spot on the ground, holding base as they attempted to move him, he swayed slightly, and Luke's head throbbed in sympathy. Fighting drugged determined the elite from ordinary assassins. It took extreme self-discipline and mental focus to fight against your own mind and through the disorientation of a world no longer steady beneath your feet.

"C'mon," Luke whispered. "Get up." With a surge of energy, Decius bounded into the air, a spin kick landing squarely to one of their jaws. He was back in the fight.

"This is an audition," Luke realized, turning around, the vicious nature making sense. "What are they on?"

"They will be fine, Luke."

The words didn't comfort him, and he pushed his luck. "Granddad—"

"I need to know."

Know what? How well they fight? Or how hard they were to kill?

His foot began to tap as his eyes moved to Aeron. She looked skyward towards the observation room—a feral look on her face. A kick to a knee, and her opponent collapsed. Luke cringed as they rolled around grabbing their leg—without a doubt useless for the next six months. "Who are all these people?"

"Legacy Inc. recruits—auditioning, as you put it—to see which one can eliminate them. It doesn't look like many will be making the cut."

Luke wanted to be appalled by this type of recruitment, the you're in, or you die approach. How was this different than the Legacy?

After what could have been a lifetime, Aeron and Decius crossed paths in the chaotic environment. A clear look shot between them, an eyebrow raise, a tilt of the head—whatever cocktail had been given, they'd mastered how to work around it. He glanced at the timer on the wall and smirked: thirty-seven minutes to reach a clear thought process. Not a record, but who knew what really coursed through their veins right now.

Decius tossed Aeron a gun, which she caught with deft fingers and initiated the beginning of the end. Any black-clad person who'd been lucky enough to avoid bodily injury during the drug-induced panic now fell as bright paint splattered their clothing. With no shots left, the siblings retreated into the shadows again, only five opponents remaining.

"Are they retreating or planning?" his Granddad asked, curiosity in his voice.

"Both." He turned back to the monitor to track their movements. Slow, precise. Something whizzed across the field. Heads snapped as a puff of lime green exploded when it struck the chest of a Legacy Inc. recruit. The remaining four people scattered, but Luke smirked; it was too late. Aeron and Decius were hidden within the scaffolding, scouting. Two more knives flew, the green dust exploding against a wall. A black-clad person raced toward the other end, catching an exploding knife to the head from Decius.

Three left.

Aeron threw a knife in one direction and then jumped from

above, landing in front of her target. Kick to the abdomen, knee to the face, arm beneath the chin…out.

Two left.

One appeared behind Aeron, gun raised as she gently laid down the unconscious person. Decius appeared behind them. He struck the gun from their grasp and caught the wrist-lock. The guy dropped to one knee. Decius snatched another gun from their belt, pressed it to their temple, and moved toward Aeron in the middle of the room, where she held the last attacker in a similar fashion.

Decius' mouth moved, but no sound came from it. His Granddad clicked on the speaker so he could hear.

"…without any direction. Should we shoot them, or can this be called a pass?" The clipped tone caught Luke off guard.

His Granddad pushed another button and answered. "I'd say you exceeded my expectations, Mr. Seward. But you can shoot them if it makes you feel better."

Decius' dark complexion paled. "My apologies, Sir. I hadn't realized you were the one administering the test." He released the wrist-lock and cleared the gun before dropping it to the ground. Aeron followed suit. Both swayed as they moved toward the exit, the adrenaline dying down and the drugs taking back over. Luke didn't wait to be excused. Racing down the stairs, he caught Aeron as she missed leaning against the wall and dropped to the floor.

"Ron."

Glazed-over eyes looked up. The cuts to her face were minimal, a single cut over her eye the worst of the damage. A quick body assessment assured him there was no real damage. He placed a kiss on her wet forehead and turned to Decius. The same glazed-over look met him, but he too looked to be in one piece.

"You alright?" Luke asked.

Decius gave a quick nod, looking as if anything more and his breakfast would end up all over Luke.

Footsteps echoed down the hall, Mason returning from the

infirmary. "C'mon. The quicker we can get fluids in them, the faster this debacle will be over."

"Yeah. Let's go, Aeron." Luke tried to scoop up Aeron, but she pushed him off.

"I need to walk. Go help Dee."

Decius' eyes had fallen closed as he swayed side to side. Mason swam a hand under Aeron's shoulders, Luke doing the same to his best friend, heading swiftly to the elevator.

"Luke!" His name rang out before he could step on it.

"Shit," he mumbled and then looked back to his Granddad, eyebrows raised. There was no need to ask 'what' when the Senior Assassin summoned—you just went. He looked back to Mason, already inside the elevator, pleading for a way out.

"I'll handle this. Lesley and Justin are already on the mend. Whatever it was, it moved through their system pretty quickly after the antidote was given. Go."

There was a direct order in Mason's tone, and Luke followed it without hesitation. He pushed Decius forward, Mason easily supporting the siblings in each arm, then turned before the door closed. He headed down the hall to his Granddad, taking several deep breaths to calm the storm, but his rage swirled below the surface.

"I think that went well, don't you?" His Granddad turned to the stairs.

It could have gone worse, Luke thought, but he followed without uttering a word. *Breathe in. Breathe out. In. Out. In. Out.* They descended to the parking garage, and Luke stopped dead in his tracks. A black Audi R8 parked in their spot.

"Whose car is this?" He looked around for the Navigator.

"It's yours."

He caught the keychain tossed at him, looked at the car, and back to his Granddad. Not that the thought of driving it didn't excite him, but a race car didn't fit well in the city—nor did gifts ever come without anvils attached.

He meant to say, 'Thank you, Sir' but instead, "Why?" slipped out.

"Why not?" His Granddad smiled and opened the door, dropping into the passenger seat.

Luke rotated the key fob around a few times. He slid into the driver's seat, the leather invading his senses. It was a magnificent car. Sleek. Dangerous. He wouldn't be bought, but he couldn't appear as anything but grateful. It purred to life, and a smile filled his face—Aeron was going to love this.

"Where to?"

"The hotel. We have a fundraiser to get ready for."

A general rule existed that smaller rooms gave an advantage. They could be cased in a single glance, not many hiding places, and any intruder would be heard. Right now, Luke wished they'd converted the penthouse suite to their home base instead of a random room on the fourth floor. Five grown assassins and the Senior Assassin needed more room than a king-sized deluxe room with a kitchenette.

"Cage, go find another room to shave in," Katherine complained, tugging at Alexis' hair and pushing Cage from in front of the mirror. "There are about twenty other ones on this floor."

"And only one where we will all learn to trust each other," Luke said, dropping into the desk chair. It was actually so he could keep tabs on the unwanted crew members. He opened up the Burn Book—a laptop where the financial records were stored. Foreign characters moved across the screen as he scrolled—Japanese so he could work without the fear of someone reading over his shoulder.

"What are you looking for?" Katherine appeared at his elbow, hands tangled in her hair, taming the wild frizz.

"There's missing money," he whispered. "From the last one." He couldn't bring himself to even think the name of the family he'd massacred.

Katherine's hands fell to his shoulder, skilled fingers working the tense muscles. "What do you mean?"

"I mean, I'm going to have to report that not all of the Legacy was returned. It'll open an investigation into all the other Legacies, Wilks' included, and we know where that'll end."

The grip on his shoulders tightened for a moment. "One issue at a time. The trail to you is pretty thin. If you're leading the investigation—it gives us leeway. Better to show good faith, then risk losing the sweet babysitting gig."

Luke spun around, surveying the group. He needed fewer people to babysit. The buffoons just added an extra obstacle. He'd dispose of them if it wouldn't piss off his Granddad. As Cage attempted to tie his tie in the TV reflection, Dave stumbled back from the bathroom, clutching his shoulder.

"It was meant as a compliment!" he said, a smirk on his face.

Alexis stepped into the room, and Luke did a double-take. The blonde hair had been knotted at the nape of her neck, and a sleek black dress clung to her body.

"Wow," Luke said, moving to his feet. He could do without all of them, especially Alexis. But Granddad insisted he play extra nice with her, his motive unclear, but instructions clear: Let her believe she has a shot. It felt like adultery each time he spoke to her. "You look stunning."

Pink tinged her cheeks, a smile lighting up the room. "Thank you. Are you going to be getting dressed or…"

"Yeah. I have a few more things to attend to, but I wouldn't miss this date for anything." He reached out, bringing her hand up for a kiss. Her eyes fluttered as he won her over.

Dave made a gagging sound, and Luke wasted no time wrapping fingers around his throat. Taking charge of the team had been easier than he'd imagined. A little flattery, a little violence, and everything ran smoothly—but there was no trust. His fingers tightened, the pulse beating beneath them as the pale complexion reddened by the second—but Dave didn't fight back.

Katherine tugged on his wrists. "If you leave bruises on his neck, he won't be able to go tonight."

The grip loosened, his heart slamming into his chest. "Are you all clear on your assignments tonight?" he asked, not moving away from Dave. He could've cleared a player right there. "Alexis?"

"Yes. I'll be taking notes on the interactions of the major leagues. Particularly Winston and Bryce."

Luke nodded. "Cage?"

"I've already infiltrated the kitchen staff. I'll be working the nightshift, supervising all people who move through the kitchen who are not staff."

"Perfect. Kat?"

"Bed the Senator's son, if possible. At least make him feel he has a chance." She smirked, but Luke couldn't return it.

"And Dave." Luke returned his gaze to Dave still pinned beneath his hand.

"I'll be shadowing Mr. Wayward through the fundraiser."

Luke nodded. "Do not take this job lightly. It should have been Perry's, but he is currently running another operation. This is your second chance. Now, there will be many, many beautiful, sexy, wanton women there tonight. Your dick stays in your pants tonight. Your eyes remain on our Senior Assassin." He shoved Dave back against the wall and turned to Katherine, the set of her shoulders reminding him he'd almost gone too far.

He returned to the computer, dropping hard into the chair and running a hand over the back of his neck. $5.5 million was missing from the Finch account. He'd need a Legacy server to run the traces on the accounts, but couldn't because it would raise too many red flags. Not to mention it would take him hours, that he just didn't have, to sit in front of the computer running the programs and tweaking them. He really needed a new safe techie.

A small pair of hands rested on top of his—Alexis' gaze met his in the reflection of the screen. "It will go smoothly tonight. Trust me," she said.

He moved his hands and let her massage his shoulders. The firm pressure pushed through the tension, and his mouth fell open in relief. "It better. Dave and Cage are—"

"Fully capable. Don't underestimate them. They play folly, but he didn't select them for their grace. He selected them because they're vicious."

Much like at the drug testing that afternoon. He sat straighter and spun to face her. "You're right." He'd been looking at the recruiting for Legacy Inc. all wrong. Granddad wasn't recruiting the best—even Mr. Seward wouldn't have lasted ten minutes drugged against thirty training assassins—they weren't being trained, they were being systematically eliminated. Less Underworld to contend with. It was genius—and dangerous.

"Thank you," he said, giving a coy smile to her, which she returned. The door opened, Rosemary barging into the already crowded room, her ballgown sparkling in the dim-light. Alexis took a step away from him as she marched toward them.

"Everyone out," Rosemary said, her lips set tight and her "kill-you" stare boring into him. "Except you."

Cage and Dave didn't need to be told twice. They grabbed their jackets from the bed and bolted. Alexis gave a curt nod and slid past Rosemary. Katherine leaned against the wall, arms crossed. Rosemary turned on her. "Get out."

Katherine's mouth fell open. "Excuse me?"

"I need to speak with the leader of this team, and unfortunately, that's not you. Get. Out."

Katherine glared at her mother and then Luke. He threw his hands up in surrender and shook his head—he had no idea what his aunt wanted.

"Fine." Katherine spat. "I need to get ready anyway." She stomped out of the room, but Luke had already turned his attention back to Rosemary.

She waited until the door closed before speaking. "Did you find it?"

He raised an eyebrow. "Find what?"

She looked at the Burn Book on the desk and pushed past him. With a few clicks of the keyboard, the characters turned to letters and numbers on the screen. She scrolled, wild eyes searching the document.

"You did." She spoke more to herself, but Luke peered over her shoulder—the missing $5.5 million. "Could you trace it?"

Luke remained rooted to the spot, afraid this was another of many tests.

She slammed a fist to the desk. "Did you find it?!"

The impatience of her words propelled him forward. "No! I-I just realized it was gone today. Do you know where Mr. Seward would hide it?"

Moving past him, her gown shimmered in the dull lighting as she paced, heels clicking against the floor. "Are there..." she waved her arms around, a universal sign for surveillance.

"No. I sweep it every time I come in. So do Perry and Katherine. And he certainly doesn't want any evidence from what happens in here."

"Good. It wasn't Andrew. I need to know if you can find it."

The use of Aeron's father's first name caught him off guard. He shook his head, forehead creasing, unable to control the words coming out. "And when exactly would you like me to camp in front of a computer and run these traces? I hardly have time to take a shit between killing Legacy families and running dual operations. Why don't you tell me what the hell you are hiding?" He swallowed the ball attempting to lodge into his throat, pulse hammering. He'd seen Katherine lash out at Rosemary before, and the ramifications of those encounters lasted days.

She hardly noticed, though. "Good. No, that's good. You *can't* do it. Katherine isn't skilled enough. And Perry, well, Perry might be able to, but you can convince him it's a bad idea."

What the hell was she talking about?

"Aunt Rosemary?"

"If I can get it back before he realizes…"

"Rosemary."

"I need you to make this go away." She looked up at him. "You need to make this go away."

"What?"

She tapped her fist against her lips, sizing him up. "I need you to keep this quiet until we can get the money back."

"We?" Luke laughed. "I didn't steal that money."

"Neither did I. Steven did. I thought…" she waved her hand in the air as if brushing aside a bad idea. "Well, I made a misjudgment, and if that money doesn't reappear before it's missed…"

He laughed again, his brain on overload. If this wasn't the icing on the cake. If he didn't need to report the missing $5.5 million from the last raid, then there would be no reason to look into Wilks. "Why should I help you? What am I getting out of this?"

"What do you want? A Villa? Head of Legacy Inc? Katherine wouldn't be pleased, but I could make it happen." Of course, she would think he wanted power. And he did… just not that kind.

What did he really need at this moment? With ice spots on his back, he said, "I don't want to be babysat anymore. I need breathing room. I want to be trusted to eliminate families on my own."

She studied him, looking for a weakness in his armor. She wouldn't find any—he'd built his walls up high enough to keep even Aeron out.

"I can arrange that, but I would need more than you just staying quiet on the Finch's finances. If I'm putting my name on the line for you, I need to know you have just as much at stake. You agree to help me find that money—no questions as to why I need it or what must be done to retrieve it. You give me *that*, and I guarantee you solo missions."

"What if I can't find it? What if he figures it out before you put it back. This isn't chump change, and my integrity is on the line. If I do this—and that's a big if—I'll lose it all."

Pushing past him, she dropped into the chair, scrolling through the documents again. Numbers flew up the screen. Boxes popped up, numbers went in, more boxes popped up. Rosemary opened Wilks' file, Luke moving closer behind her, heart breaking through his chest. No one knew the account as well as he did, and the money he stole never even hit the Legacy's account. It would be near impossible to trace.

"Do you think Steven skimmed off of Wilks too?"

"No. There's no connection. Wilks had been our money handler for over a decade. It was a shame we had to take care of the threat." She closed the laptop and spun in the chair, leaning back. "I don't envy you, Luke, having to handle these finances. That's a lot of money to be responsible for."

"It is. And I've never lied to Granddad when dealing with it. Even when I had to admit I couldn't recover over 6.5 billion from Wilks' account without the access codes—my blunder completely—I've never held back the truth, no matter what it cost me." Aeron's ripped outfit fluttered into his mind.

"How much is your freedom to fly solo worth to you?"

If he could fly solo, saving the Legacy children would be worth the possible death sentence for lying—even Aeron and Decius would agree to that if they knew. But agreeing to go off book with Rosemary did not sound like a good deal. In fact, it could be an entire set-up. The cold spots on his back answered for him.

"I keep this under wraps and help you find that money, and I get to fly solo. To be clear, Steven is connected to you from the original report. If I go down, I'm taking you with me," he said.

She reached out a hand. "I wouldn't expect anything less." They shook on it, Luke suddenly feeling he'd given his soul to the devil. "Go get that handsome tux on. We have a Fundraiser to attend and politicians to rob."

29

AERON

*A*eron looked around the diner she had taken Ivan to the first time they'd met. He said 21:00. Only ten minutes to go. She took a booth with her back to a wall and a clear view of the door. Her head pounded from the drug test, and her body felt as if it had fallen from a second-story window.

"Can I get you anything?" The waitress looked at her expectantly.

Aeron pulled out a hundred and held it out. "A glass of water and privacy."

The waitress took the money and quickly walked away. Aeron watched the clock on the wall. 21:01. 21:02. Where were they? The water burned her raw throat as she tried to stay hydrated. The aftereffects of the cocktail left them groggy, so slipping away from Decius had been easy, at least. She'd said she was going to pass out for the night, and that would normally be what happened.

Silver shone from beneath her sleeve, and she tugged it down, the bracelet Luke had given her for her birthday peeking out. She couldn't pinpoint why she wanted to wear it, but the weight reminded her of his strong arms wrapping around her. The bell above the door rang, and she snapped her head up. Ivan and her father entered. Ivan's attire matched her black reinforced outfit. Her father wore a black-on-black suit and tie. Knots formed in her stomach, and she couldn't tell if it was nerves or another round of vomiting about to happen. She pushed the water away as they sat across from her.

"What happened to your face?" Ivan asked, running a hand over his eyebrow.

"Drug-testing," she responded. The semi-concerned look on her father's face made her smile. She never thought she'd be on the receiving end of that look.

"Are you okay to do this? It's only reconnaissance. In and out, they won't even know you're there."

Aeron nodded slowly, picking apart her straw wrapper and making it into a pile in front of her. "As long as I don't need to be physical, I should be good."

"Which vial did you get?" he asked, raising an eyebrow. "Last year, I asked them to give you #25."

"That was before you liked me." She gave him a half grin. "I don't know. It was nothing like last year—this was…it wasn't a normal test." Her muscles ached, and the pounding in her ears had eased only an hour ago.

He scowled. "What do you mean?"

"It was four against at least forty, Dee and I handled almost 30 ourselves. I can't even compare what the sensation was like—is like. Our systems were flushed, and counter-meds given, but I feel off."

"Wait, wait, wait…so they like actually drug you?" Ivan asked, eyes wide. "Like with actual drugs."

"Yeah. We've had opioids, benzodiazepines, stimulants, and a whole slew of others."

"Marijuana," her father added.

"That's right." Aeron shook her head. "I almost forgot about that —that was a bad trip. They did edibles that year….it was awful."

A wrinkle between Ivan's eyes appeared. "Are you sure you're okay to go in? I can do this by myself."

"They'd never administer anything they couldn't, without 96% certainty, counter. But knowing how to function under the influence of a variety of states of minds is a huge asset." Her father checked his watch. "This fundraiser ends at midnight. That gives us two hours." His confident voice did not ease her in the slightest, but she kept quiet as the room tilted.

"I have a woman on the inside. She will delay the security footage and alarms for exactly ten minutes. That is all you have to get from the parking garage to the room. He's not staying in a penthouse. He's visited the same room three times in the past two weeks. Now, he's either got some important information in there, or you are going to find where he's keeping his girlfriend." He smiled, but Ivan looked sick.

"What are we going in for?" Aeron asked.

He hesitated.

"Dad?"

"Information—any information. Like I said, this is strictly a reconnaissance mission."

"Ah, spying, the only thing I'm suited for, right?" She smirked at him, but he remained serious. "Can I do this alone?" she asked, crinkling her nose at Ivan's paling complexion.

"Aeron—"

"No." Ivan met the questioning gaze. "We are looking for documents, hard drives that will be in a safe, most likely. I'll need to crack that and then make sure it's what we're actually looking for. No offense, but I need you there for muscle in case we run into those other people we are looking for."

"Well, in my current state, let's hope we don't."

"Aeron, are you sure?"

She met her father's gaze. "I can do this," she assured.

"Alright, set your watches. Our opening is in fifteen minutes. Ivan?"

Ivan removed three earpieces from his pocket and two sets of night vision goggles. "The earpieces are on a secured frequency. Don't lose them, please. And night vision for the room."

The trio headed out the rear of the diner and toward the Rose Way Hotel through dark alleys. Once in the parking garage, Aeron pulled Ivan back twice to avoid the security cameras. They stopped behind a large cement pillar and waited, watching the seconds tick by. Her father nudged her with his elbow and held out a small firearm.

"Dad, you know how I feel about guns."

Ivan gave her a curious look.

"What? Just because I kill people doesn't mean I'm a gun fanatic."

"Just take it. It will make me feel better." She eyed the weapon warily and shook her head. "It's too loud. I have my knives." Aeron patted her forearms where she kept her throwing knives sheaved. He didn't push the issue, but she caught his disappointed frown.

22:00.

"How do we know if it worked?" Aeron looked around. She expected the lights to cut out or something.

"We trust I paid the girl enough. Go!"

Aeron and Ivan pulled down their masks, moved from behind the cement pillar, and raced up the stairwell. They took the steps two at a time. Ivan kept pace with her up to the fourth floor. They pushed the door open and headed straight to the far-left corner room. They did not have a key card, but Aeron stood guard as Ivan did whatever it was that he did.

The door clicked open behind her.

"We're in," she said for her father to hear, and they entered the dark room, pulling on the night vision goggles.

The room was set up similar to the layouts given on the hotel website. They had hoped this was the case and had planned possible hiding spaces accordingly. Aeron searched the bathroom, the kitchenette, and the closets. Ivan checked the bed, the office area, and the entertainment center.

"Jackpot." Ivan motioned for Aeron to join him by the television. The flat safe was bolted into the entertainment center beneath the T.V. shelf.

"Can you crack it?" Aeron's palms sweated. She checked her watch: 22:15. "We're running out of time."

"I have no idea." Ivan began turning the dial, his stethoscope pressed into the steel.

"You two need to get out of there, now." Her father's voice was loud in her ear.

She touched the earpiece. "We're working on the safe now."

"Katherine was spotted in the lobby. Get out now!"

A click of a lock sounded from the door. Aeron whipped off her night vision goggles. "Too late," she said.

Ivan shouted as the hallway light hit the night vision goggles, drawing the intruder's attention to them.

"What the—" The lights turned on, and Aeron froze. Katherine Wayward stood in the doorway. Her red hair had been pulled neatly into a French braid. She wore jeans and a black hoodie—a purple dress slung over her arm. She dropped the dress, and a pistol materialized from behind her, aimed directly at Aeron.

"Who are you?" she demanded, her green eyes holding Aeron in place.

Aeron remained silent. She put her hands up near her head in surrender. They'd failed to retrieve any information. Katherine could have a multitude of people here in seconds. If they could get past her, they might make it out unscathed. Katherine twitched the gun at Ivan, directing him next to Aeron. He visibly shook—adrenaline and fear coursing through him, no doubt—but he kept quiet and moved.

"Report in." Her father's voice sounded in her ear. "REPORT IN!" he yelled. Ivan flinched.

She watched Katherine's eyes flick over to the entertainment center, and Aeron deftly hit the switch on her earpiece so her father could listen in on their side.

"Who sent you?" Katherine demanded.

Neither of them spoke.

She moved closer, the gun still pointed at them. "Masks off. Now."

Aeron and Ivan remained still. Katherine fired a shot into the wall near the window.

"Last chance." She pointed the gun inches from Aeron's face.

Aeron moved with purpose pushing Katherine's wrists up and dropping low to land a kick to her abdomen. Katherine stumbled back, and Aeron lunged, tackling her to the ground, her first focus getting on top of the fight while trying to get a grip on the gun. Ivan hadn't moved.

"A little help?" Aeron yelled. Her words broke through his haze. Ivan's foot swung. Aeron released the grip on Katherine's hands before he connected, sending the gun skidding across the floor. Dropping low and heavy, her feet found purchase beneath Katherine's thighs, but her muscles would not cooperate, and Katherine flipped her off. They were a mess of punches and kicks for a few minutes. The distraction allowed Aeron to remove her earpiece. Katherine had no idea if they had gotten what they came for or not.

She gave up the struggle and let herself be flipped over. Katherine slammed her knee to Aeron's ribs, pinning her down. Aeron sucked in a breath as the weight bore down—there would be a bruise there, for sure. She tossed her earpiece at Ivan, who'd been knocked to the floor.

"GO! Get it safe."

He looked down at it for a second, and she prayed he could go with her improvisation. His eyes met hers, and she nodded for the door. He sprinted. Katherine tried to stand, but Aeron reached up and grabbed onto the strings dangling from Katherine's hood and yanked hard, pulling her back down. She clawed at the tightening garment allowing Aeron to wrap the string around her neck and pull. Katherine rolled off of her, and Aeron jumped to her feet, avoiding the reaching arms.

"Let go of me!" Katherine yelled.

"Not today, sweetheart." Aeron slid behind her, sliding her right arm beneath her neck. She locked in the choke and slowly squeezed.

A shot rang out, buzzing past Aeron's ear. Luke's large frame blocked the doorway. The sight of him in a tux with his Sig in hand would have been sexy if the gun wasn't pointed directly at her.

"Release her," he demanded. His cold eyes bore into her, none of the warmth from last night visible. She fought backing up—she'd never been on the receiving end of that look before. He was terrifying.

Her hands moved near her head in surrender, and she stood, letting Katherine drop to the floor. He remained in the doorway, eyes locked on her. A petite blond girl in a sparkling black gown stepped around him and hurried toward Katherine. When she looked up, her bright blue eyes forced Aeron to retreat a few paces, stomach churning. She'd saved her on the train or thought she had. Bile burned in her throat—it'd been a setup. What the hell was she doing with Luke? Did Luke know about the train?

"Stay where you are," Luke demanded, the gun still pointed at her. "Who are you?"

There was nothing she could say. He'd know her voice.

The blond managed to untangle the strings around Katherine's neck.

"There's another one," Katherine gasped, taking several deep breaths. "He might have something."

"Then why are you still here?" Luke said. "Go." Katherine glared at him but raced out the door.

"Go help her, Alexis," Luke ordered the blond in a softer tone.

"You can handle this?" she asked, pausing next to him. Aeron glared as her fingers lingered a little too long on Luke's outstretched arm.

"Yes. Go." He nudged her playfully with his elbow before

returning his full attention to Aeron, who nearly gagged, swallowing her rage.

"I'm only going to ask nicely one more time. Who are you? And who sent you?"

The sweat dripped inside Aeron's mask. He was going to kill her because that is what they were trained to do. What she would do if it became a necessity. He moved closer, the gun now an inch from her chest. She looked down—the safety was still on.

"I'll just find out for myself." He reached for her mask.

She had the smallest window before he clicked the safety off. Aeron kicked hard to his knee and pivoted away from the muzzle. He dropped instantly. She whipped up her leg and scrunched up her own nose as his crunched against the knee. Kicking the gun out of his hand, she bolted for the door. Just a few feet away, a figure larger than Luke blocked her exit. A moment of relief hit; her father had arrived.

Instead, she reeled back. Mr. Wayward towered over her. His furious expression pushed her back several more steps.

He surveyed the room. Luke pulled himself up off the ground, blood pouring from his nose and bruising already appearing around his eyes.

"Where are the girls?"

"Went after another one. About two minutes ago."

"Go help them. I'll handle this." The ice in Mr. Wayward's voice created a pit in her stomach. She wanted to call out for Luke. Beg him to stay. But he nodded and raced out of the room.

She continued to back away as he entered. "Who are you?" he asked curiously.

Again, she didn't answer this question, but this time she couldn't form the words. The blade hidden beneath her sleeve slid into her hand as she readied to attack, the only goal to get past him and out the door.

She lunged, knife out, expecting him to step to the right, out of her way; instead, he stepped left. His hand closed around her outstretched wrist, and she ran into his solid body. Her arm twisted behind her, the knife dropping uselessly to the floor. He jerked her arm, and Aeron barely managed to spin with the twist to prevent it from breaking, and dove under his legs. She kicked the back of his knee. It buckled, and she made a break for the door.

A hand caught her ankle, and her body rebounded off the floor. "Ugh." The breath left her, and the room spun, spots dancing in her vision. Her muscles refused to obey her command to move. The side-effects of drug-testing needed sleep and hydration to recover, not a covert op and a fight to the death with the Senior Assassin—because she was definitely going to die tonight.

"Not so fast." He knelt over her and reached for the mask.

A boost of adrenaline hit. No. she was not going to die tonight. Her free leg snapped across his jaw, and she spiraled out of his grasp, bounding into a fighting stance, ready to attack again. Mr. Wayward returned to his feet and swung. She ducked. He swung again, and she sidestepped it and grabbed the back of his tux jacket. She pushed with his momentum and brought her knee into his abdomen. An attempt to sweep his standing leg failed, and he only stumbled. With lightning speed, he spun a roundhouse. The bruised ribs snapped, and Aeron screamed in pain. There was no hesitation when he lunged again, and she fended off only half the blows from his fists and legs. There was no fury behind each blow. He could end this at any moment, rip her mask off, damn their Legacy for treason. However, the glimmer in his eye foretold a brutal beating was in store for her.

Bruises formed as they landed. With arms too heavy, they dropped for a moment—long enough for two solid hits to the face. Consciousness danced in and out— the copper taste in her mouth urging her to stay awake. Where could her father and Ivan be? Had Luke caught up with them?

Mr. Wayward laughed, his fingers wrapping around her throat. She pressed her chin down and clawed at his hands with little success.

"Let's see who you are."

She kicked out, but like her arms, her legs fought against her request, becoming sluggish. She tried to back away and backed herself to the wall for support. Her bloodied hands grabbed his wrists and kicked again. She couldn't rotate, her body completely fighting against her. The tingling sensation of losing consciousness crept in. With a last-ditch effort, she hung on to him, kicked toward his hips with all the energy she had left. The grip broke, and she dropped like a rock to the ground, but not before he latched his arm around her ankle. The tangle of arms and legs fell in two different directions.

A pop sounded. Searing pain nauseated Aeron in an instant—she couldn't even tell where it came from at first. When her ankle bounced off the ground, a scream broke from her, and she reached down to support it. A large, expensive leather shoe pinned her chest back down. Stars appeared when he dropped to his knee, weight bearing down on her broken ribs. She half heartily pushed at it, and he smirked in triumph. With enough weight on his knee to crush her broken ribs, his fingers dug beneath the bottom of her mask. She reached toward his face with her left hand, and he leaned away, his attention on grabbing the mask. She brought her arm down with as much force as she could muster.

A strangled yell rebounded around the room. Long, deep cuts appeared from his temple to his chin, and blood poured between his fingers when he reeled back. The sight reminded her of Ivan. She hoped he'd gotten far away. Laughter bubbled up. Even though her ribs screamed in agony and her useless ankle shook, she laughed. He was going to kill her anyway.

His presence vanished from her immediate surroundings, and Aeron wondered if he was going to torture her first. A loud commotion near the door pulled for her, but she couldn't move. Her eyes refused to open—and maybe it was better she wouldn't have to see Luke's face when she was unmasked. A foul odor hit her senses. Someone was coughing hard. Was that a body hitting the floor? Then her lungs began to burn. Had he set the room on fire? She was going to die, unable to save herself, let alone Luke. The burning increased, her skin itched—it wasn't smoke, but gas.

Someone knelt down beside her. She tore against the dried and swollen skin to open her eyes again. A blurry shape was all she could see as the chemical hit her eyes, and she closed them again.

"No!" She tried to push away, but they ignored her, pulling her to her feet. A hoarse scream escaped her, and she collapsed. Strong arms scooped her up.

"Hang in there." The air became easier to breathe as the man moved them out of the room, but her lungs still burned. Every hurried step radiated throughout her entire body. She couldn't distinguish where the pain in her body resonated from anymore. It was everywhere. Cool night air filled her lungs, and she struggled to gulp it in.

"Is she…" Her dad's voice trailed off.

"She's alive, but…" Was that Ivan? The person holding her bent over, and a sound of pain escaped her as he moved them into the backseat of a car. He laid her out across the seat and carefully cradled her head. Two doors slammed, and she rolled back as the car took off.

"Wake her up." Her dad's voice sounded heavy with concern.

"I'm. I'm up," Aeron whispered. The movement of the car rocked her body, and she moaned, the pain past the point of screaming.

"She's up." Shaking fingers worked at her neck to remove her mask. She did scream as a new pain registered when the fabric pulled away from her face. The material buried into her cuts and felt as if he were filleting her face.

"Ivan! Stop!" Her father yelled.

"I have to get her mask off! Aeron, I'm really sorry. I'll go slow, but I need to get this off."

She made a sound of agreement and gritted her teeth. He worked quickly, swearing every time she let out an involuntary gasp of pain. The air stung every pore. A wet cloth caressed her eyes until she could open them again. The blurriness subsided, and she could make out Ivan's face. He sported a few cuts and bruises himself, but his pale complexion and wide eyes alarmed her.

"Darth."

He gave a tense smile. The light from the streetlamps accented the scars on his face. She reached up a shaking hand to touch them.

"I gave Mr. Wayward a matching one," she said, letting her arm fall back down. He didn't say anything, but she spied moisture in his eyes.

"What hurts the most?" her father asked from the driver seat.

Everything—she wanted to say. But he needed to know where the most damage was.

"My ankle." It was all she could manage to say as the car turned a corner.

"Broken?" he asked.

"Not sure."

"Anything else?"

"Ribs. Broken."

"How many, Aeron?"

She closed her eyes and tried to take a deeper breath. The pain shot down her entire side. "At least two. Probably three or more," she said, the memory of his roundhouse returning.

"Where are we going?" Ivan asked. She didn't care where they went, as long as it was away from Mr. Wayward and Luke. Luke. How could she explain this to him?

"Dad," she said, but it came out more of a whisper. "Luke was there."

"I know."

"He'll put it together."

Her father stayed quiet for a few minutes while the car idled in traffic.

"I know. I have a plan, but you're not going to like it. It's our only card at the moment." She remained silent, waiting for him to continue. "We bring you to your apartment and make it look like I did this."

No. She tried to sit up. "Dad, no."

Ivan pushed her back down, and she let him, agony racing through her body. "This doesn't sound like a good plan, Sir."

"Mr. Wayward will put together Aeron's injuries with the attack tonight unless we can give a viable witness to her being attacked elsewhere. The apartment should be empty tonight. We put Aeron there, make it look like an altercation went down. Ivan, you text both Luke and Decius to get them home so they can see me leaving."

"There is a lot of room for error in this plan," Ivan said.

"It's suicide, Dad. Luke will shoot you on sight."

"He'll be too worried about you."

The car came to a halt, Ivan holding on to keep her from moving too much. Aeron looked out the window at the tall skyscraper. Home. She wanted to argue with him, but when he opened the back door, his expression deceived his calm demeanor.

"Oh, Aeron. C'mon."

Ivan helped get her out of the car—a more painful experience than getting in. She bit her lip to hold in the complaint as her father cradled her into his chest. The lines in his dark face, once barely visible, looked cavernous.

He held her close to him the ride up the elevator and while Ivan unlocked the apartment door—bypassing the system and reprogramming it to look like Aeron had been home hours ago. Darkness met them when they entered, and Aeron sighed in relief.

Ivan flipped on the lights, and her father laid her on the floor near the couch. His eyes darkened, and he refused to meet her gaze as he checked her injuries. A gasp escaped him when he reached her ankle.

"Ivan, I need you to brace Aeron's leg."

"Dad?"

Ivan held her leg steady but looked away from her foot, his face tinged green.

"Is it really that bad?" she asked.

He touched her cheek with feather lightness, and she flinched, which shook her ribs and ankle. "It's worse."

"Ivan."

Ivan returned his hand to her leg, and Aeron screamed as her father pulled her shoe off. Ivan let go and took a few steps back, his face scrunched up in disgust.

"Aeron, it's dislocated," her father said. "Do you want me to try and re-align it or wait for…"

"Fix it." A dislocated ankle could be worse than a break—it could mean losing full function of her foot if not realigned in time. He nodded and summoned Ivan to hold her leg again. Her father's eyes roamed the room before he pulled out his leather wallet.

"Bite on this." Ivan placed the smooth, brown leather between her teeth. It tasted sour, but the material melded to her teeth, and the smell reminded her of the leather shop they used to visit as children. Her yell was muffled against the wallet as her dad moved with slow, agonizing precision. It took only a minute for her ankle to slide back into place, but it could have been a lifetime. The pain spiked, and she fought the blackness until it eased, just marginally. Ivan removed the wallet, a clear indent from her bite visible, and she motioned for him to take the bracelet off.

"Are you sure?" he asked, eyeing the weapon with distaste.

"Yes. I marked him with it."

He nodded and gingerly took the offending weapon off her wrist.

"Ivan, send the messages. We need them here now." He disappeared into her bedroom and returned with a shirt. "This is going to hurt, but we need to put something else on you."

She nodded. He pulled out a knife and sliced through the laces holding her protective chest gear in place. Darkness threatened to take her as her ribs shifted without the support.

"Dad!" She cried out.

"I know. I'm sorry." He gingerly slipped a black t-shirt over her head and removed her sheaths from her arms. He took the throwing knives and tossed them, embedding them around the room.

"You're signing your death warrant, Dad."

"And for sending you in there, I deserve it. I should have never —Aeron. I thought—"

"Done. We will have barely eight minutes before they get here." Ivan kneeled next to her.

"Don't you get sentimental too, Darth. I'm not dying."

He kept his mouth tight and nodded. She laid her head back. The room began to spin again like a tilt-a-whirl, and she closed her eyes.

"Ivan, I need to you hit me," her father said.

"What?"

"We need to create the appearance of a fight—more specifically, a fight with Aeron."

She tried to open her eyes. This was something she wanted to see but couldn't manage to move her eyelids. She was having a hard time moving anything at all, as crashing and slamming sounded on around her.

"Go, now. Before they get here. Take the elevator and send it back up. They will take the stairs or the rooftops."

Something shook. An Earthquake? Should she wake up?

"Aeron. You need to wake back up. C'mon." Her dad again. Light kept going on and off. Where was it coming from? "Aeron Seward, if you do not open your eyes right this instant, I swear... Wake up!"

Aeron tugged against the heaviness of her eyes. He was inches from her face.

"Don't ever do that again." His left eye held a cut and bruise, and blood dripped down his lip. She nodded, and the world spun. "Luke should be here in moments. Do *not* fall asleep." He placed a light kiss on her forehead and left.

Confusion bubbled in Aeron's mind. She couldn't remember her father ever kissing her. She must be dreaming. Silence followed his absence. Deep breaths pulled at the pain in her ribs. Pain. It wasn't a dream, not even nightmares hurt the way reality could, and she needed that pain to keep her conscious. Voices stirred in the hallway, and the door banged open against the wall. She tried to sit up, fear coursing through her. Mr. Wayward had found her.

30

LUKE

*A*eron's 911 text burned in Luke's brain as he rushed toward the apartment, shoving people out of his way unapologetically. He had no idea what threat she faced, but it was 100% his fault. He took the stairs two at a time, and burst through the hallway door, and froze.

The elevator stood ajar, Mr. Seward leaning inside with a busted lip, and blood covering his clothing, gloating. He'd waited for Luke; he was sure of it. Luke's trembling hands itched to wrap themselves around his throat, and he started forward. He was going to end this right now, be damned what his Granddad wanted.

"You'd better hurry, Luke. She doesn't look well." Luke hesitated, eyes glancing toward the door, and the elevator slid closed.

Aeron's still form was visible through the doorway; his heart skipped several beats. His feet moving faster than his brain, he slid to her side without knowing how he got there.

"Aeron!"

She looked at him the best her swollen and bruised face would allow. The bruising and cuts contorted for a moment as if she wanted to smile at him.

"Oh, Aeron. What did he do to you?" His fingers hovered over her, afraid of inflicting any more pain.

"Lulu."

"Shh, don't say anything."

"Luke!"

His head snapped around, the sight of Decius fueling his anger.

"I got the message—oh." Decius froze in his tracks. "What the fuck happened?"

"Your father," Luke spat, returning his gaze to Aeron.

"He wouldn't…"

"I saw him, bloodied up, the elevator doors closing when I got here. I swear he waited, just to taunt me."

"What did he say?" Decius moved next to them.

"That I'd better hurry." His voice held pure menace. "He's dead when I see him, Dee. Fucking dead."

Decius didn't argue with him. Instead, he turned his attention to Aeron, taking full stock of the visible injuries. "Give me a stat report, Aeron." But when he squatted down, Luke noted the pain in his eyes.

"I—I don't know," she said.

Luke's heart cracked at her barely audible voice. He lowered his hands to rest on her core before moving them over every inch of her body, pausing to probe with each flinch and groan of pain.

"Ribs. Possible internal bleeding. Ankle. Knuckles." He continued to report each injury to Decius, who spoke rapidly to Mrs. Gale on the phone. She looked like she had gone to war.

"I'm going to meet Mrs. Gale downstairs," Decius said, looking down at Aeron. "Keep her awake."

The note of command in his voice irked Luke. "I know how to deal with this." Tension flew between them, and Luke returned his attention to Aeron. Her eyes had fallen shut.

"Hey, Aeron?" He kept his voice light, biting back the rage best he could. "Do you know what I realized? We haven't talked about our favorite things."

"Yes, we have." Her voice missed the conviction she normally spoke with.

"Humor me until Dee gets back, alright? What's your favorite color?"

"Green."

"Which gun is your favorite?"

"I hate them."

"I know. Which do you like more? Summer or winter?"

"Spring and fall—the two seasons I spend most with you."

His chest tightened at the brief smile she tried to offer, but the moment only contorted the large gash down her cheek. He blinked back the moisture in his eyes.

"Pizza or ice cream?"

"No hard questions," she joked. A small laugh escaped her but morphed into a cough, and then into a cry of pain, which would keep her awake. He moved to support her head in his lap instead.

"Shh. I'm sorry," he said.

"It's not your fault." Her eyes drooped closed.

"Yes, it is," he admitted. He should have never left her side.

"Luke—"

"I should have been with you tonight. Not with my Granddad at some stupid function."

"Is that what happened to your face?"

He raised a hand to the dried blood on his face, pain shooting through his skull at the slight touch. He'd forgotten about the broken nose.

"A scuffle afterwards. Not a big deal." But it had been a very big deal. Someone tried to break into the vault, and that someone slashed his Granddad's face pretty nicely too. His eyes darted to Aeron's wrist. The cuff he gifted her had a similar attack pattern, but Aeron was here, a victim of her father's tonight.

Her head lulled to the side. "Aeron? Aeron!" Her eyes rolled back. "Hey! Wake up!" But no movement jarred her awake.

Decius reappeared, Mrs. Gale at his side.

"You let her fall asleep!" Decius joined Luke, trying to rouse her.

"This is not my fault," Luke said, in stark contradiction to his confession to Aeron. "Where were you tonight?"

"I—I was—"

"I told you how dangerous he was!" But Luke hadn't, really. He'd kept that secret to himself, and Aeron paid the price.

"Enough." Mrs. Gale's pale face stopped Luke's next words. "If we don't get her into the medical ward, she will be dead within the hour. Now stop bickering and help me."

Luke slipped his arms beneath Aeron's limp body, cradling her to his chest. He followed Mrs. Gale to the elevator, unable to look at Decius. Aeron's swollen face looked ten times worse in the elevator light, and it was a relief when the darkness outside engulfed them. He slid in the back seat of Mrs. Gale's four-door sports car, Aeron securely on his lap.

The flash of streetlamps illuminated a trickle of blood on Aeron's chin.

"Mrs. G? She's bleeding." His voice sounded hoarse.

"I know, Luke."

"No. She has blood dripping from her mouth."

Mrs. Gale didn't respond, but the car sped up and weaved between traffic. His gaze remained fixed on her chest. Up. Down. Up. Down. Decius yanked the door open, holding his arms out. Luke hesitated but passed Aeron to her brother. His legs wouldn't have allowed him to get out of the car anyway.

"Go," Luke said, eyeing Mrs. Gale rounding the front of the car. "I'll move the car."

"No," Mrs. Gale said, leaning in. "Call Shannon. Find her. I need her here."

Luke nodded before closing the door and clambering into the driver's seat. He gripped the wheel, steadying the shake of his hands. He needed to call Shannon. He wanted to find Mr. Seward and rip his throat out. But he needed to find Shannon. Reaching a still shaking hand into his pocket, he pulled out his phone and dialed.

"What's up, Luke?"

"How far are you from the Institute?"

Her voice faltered. "About three blocks."

"Run. I'll meet you out front." He cut the engine and jumped from the car. It seemed to take Shannon a lifetime to round the corner, her face beet red.

"What's happened?" she gasped.

"Aeron—her father." He couldn't form sentences. "Your mother needs you—upstairs."

Shannon paled beneath the flush of her face. She raced through the front door, Luke on her heels. Security stood when they entered but said nothing when they spotted him. Whether it was because he was a Wayward or covered in blood, he couldn't be sure. Shannon slammed her finger repeatedly into the elevator button until it opened.

The short ride to the fifth floor took an eternity.

"How bad is it?" Shannon asked, removing her jewelry and handing it over to him.

He pocketed the rings and bracelet; his voice lodged in his throat. Only a desperate sound escaped.

"Luke—" The doors opened, and Shannon gave no backward look as she raced toward the emergency room. Luke followed more slowly, taking the vacant seat beside Decius. He stared at his hands, running through the night again. The stupid fundraiser. The break-in. His Granddad's attack. Aeron's attack. There had to be a connection. Maybe the threat came from the outside? The Underworld? Granddad's recent decimation of their numbers would make them the number one contender.

"Mr. Wayward?"

Luke looked up. A female doctor smiled at him.

"Would you like me to set your broken nose?" His hand moved to his face, the pain flaring again once he thought of it.

"Go." Decius patted him on the back. "I'll come for you if anything happens."

Luke followed the woman into a procedure room and stopped short. His Granddad leaned against the counter, butterfly stitches holding together a set of nasty cuts down the side of his face.

"Did we catch them?" Luke asked.

"Mr. Wayward, would you please take a seat?" She directed him toward the table. He obeyed, keeping an eye on his Granddad.

"The intruder managed to get away. Tell me, what is wrong with the Seward girl?"

"Ah!" Pain shot through his head as the nurse touched his face. "Stop!"

"Don't be such a baby," his Granddad's voice taunted. "You will survive. Tell me."

Luke did not want to have this conversation right now. "None of your business."

"I have to disagree with that. Legacy blood is certainly my business." Luke slid off the table, squaring for the inevitable confrontation. A light hand eased him back.

"With all due respect, Sir, I need to set his nose."

His Granddad smirked and waved a bloodied hand for her to continue. Luke returned to his seat and gripped the table, bracing for the pain. It didn't come, though, and he glanced up.

"What's the matter?"

"Would you like some local anesthetic?"

The image of Aeron, bloody and beaten and fighting for her life, still sat seared in his head. "No. Just fucking fix it already." The words sounded harsher than he intended, but he bit back the apology waiting to come out.

With diligent fingers, she moved along the crack in his nose and snapped the small bone back into place. Blood poured freely from it again, and she handed him a towel and taped his nose to hold it in place. Once satisfied with her work, she disappeared, leaving Luke alone with his Granddad.

"Is Katherine alright?" he asked.

"If you remained behind, you would know, but she is fine for the moment. Now tell me, how did you come to find your lovely pet in such a state? Nearby the hotel, perhaps?"

Luke bristled at his suggestion. "In her apartment, her father leaving as I arrived."

"Andrew did that?" Disbelief echoed in his voice.

"What are you suggesting?" Luke's voice wavered with anger.

"One of two scenarios." He began pacing the small room. "First, it was Ms. Seward in that room with us tonight. Ah!" He cut Luke's protest off. "Her injuries are eerily similar to the slight woman I encountered in the hotel room. I see you're ready to defend your damsel, so I'll lay the second scenario for you: assuming that Ms. Seward was nowhere near the hotel tonight, why did he choose tonight of all nights to reveal himself? How did he even gain access to her?"

Luke lowered his hand, anger shaking the blood-drenched towel. "How was he able to murder his best friends without raising any flags? How has he turned so many people against us? I saw him there, wiping her blood from his hands. There is no way she was in that hotel, and no way in hell she'd ever work with him."

He'd somehow moved within inches of the older man's face. They stood toe to toe, Luke's temper rising with each passing moment of silence. He wanted—no, needed—to fight.

"Watch that temper, son. I would hate for you to put her life in even more danger."

Luke bristled at being called 'son'. If he treated his father this way—no wonder they kept Luke far away. He swallowed the rage, though. Mr. Seward wasn't the only threat to Aeron.

"What is your plan?" He continued the conversation as if he hadn't just threatened Aeron's life.

Luke shook himself, playing along with the charade. "Mr. Seward? He'll be on the run. Not easy to track down. My best bet is Decius."

"What if he's working for him?"

"He's not."

"And what about our breach?"

"I'll start scanning the surveillance around the hotel. See if I can get a lead on whoever did that." He waved his hand at the deep red slashes across his Granddad's face.

"Check the apartment too. Who knows—maybe you will kill two birds with one stone."

Luke nodded, the motion causing a domino effect of throbbing throughout his skull, and he grabbed it.

"Bring me Andrew or bring me the culprit of tonight's break-in. You have a week."

"And if I can't?" Luke said in defiance, his patience drained.

"Then she will be no more use to me. If you need clarification on what that entails, ask Katherine." He strode out of the room.

Luke didn't need to ask Katherine what he meant, the look of torture on her face as clear as the day she asked him to help her kill their Granddad. Luke left the room, heading straight toward Decius. This was not only his fault.

"Where were you tonight!" The words left him in a half yell, half plea.

Decius stood, surprised by the sudden verbal attack.

"I—I was…."

"You were supposed to be with her! You said you would make sure that nothing—" he choked on his anger, unable to believe Decius would leave his own sister vulnerable in her post-drug-test state.

"She was home!" Decius screamed back, his voice echoing in the near-silent wing. "She was home. She was safe."

"Obviously not. Where were you? Huh?" Luke shoved him. "How the hell did he get in?"

"He shouldn't have been able to. She told me—"

A rapid, high-pitched beep sounded from the emergency room as the people rushed in and out, followed by the unmistakable sound of a flatline. Blood drained from Luke's face, feet rooted to the spot, and eyes pulled to the now-closed door. Decius pushed past him, two nurses wrestling with him before he could open it.

"No!" Decius's broken scream propelled Luke forward. He muscled past anyone in the way and pushed the door open.

The operating room sat behind glass doors. Shannon and Mrs. Gale, covered in red, didn't notice he'd breached the first entrance. The alarm continued to blare while Aeron lay motionless on the table. She couldn't die. She couldn't leave him too.

"Aeron!" His voice cracked.

Shannon glanced up. Her head shook slightly, and her fingers resumed whatever work they did inside Aeron. People moved about the room in a blur. Decius' hands settled on his shoulder, and only left it to swing at anyone who tried to move them.

They watched for an eternity, the paddles charging and her body jumping in response. Charge. Clear. Jump. Repeat. The flatline jumped too, and resumed to a steady beep. Luke released his breath as he visibly saw Shannon do the same.

He turned and swung, fist connecting with the side of Decius' head. Every ounce of anger he'd swallowed since his parents died fell on his best friend. Decius blocked the blows, but Luke wasn't aiming, just releasing.

"This is all your fault! I told you! Why didn't you listen to me!"

Security tore the two boys apart. Decius dropped to his back, his hands covering his face, not allowing the nurses to take a look at him. Arms wrapped around Luke and dragged him from the emergency room area.

"Let go of me!" He wrenched free, chest heaving, and vision blurred. He wiped the moisture from his face and turned ready, to swing again, but Perry's crinkled brow paused Luke's arm midswing.

"Katherine called." Those words tamed Luke's anger for the moment.

Katherine. Luke searched his pockets for his phone and came up empty.

"Give me your phone."

Perry handed it over. Luke ran a hand over his hair while he paced the hall. After two rings, she answered.

"Is he alright?"

"I'm fine. I need you to pull all the security tapes surrounding my apartment and a four-block radius of the hotel."

"Is she alright?"

He swallowed around the lump in his throat. "I need to find out where her father was tonight and where he is now."

"Alexis is going through the security footage here. I've already collected DNA samples."

"I want you personally on the apartment," Luke said. "This cannot be screwed up."

"Luke, is she—"

"I have to go. I'll find you when I can." He hung up and handed the phone back. "Go help her."

"No."

"I don't need you here."

"You need someone, seeing as you just bludgeoned your best friend."

"I need to find Mr. Seward or find the person who broke into the hotel tonight."

"And if you don't?"

His gut tightened. "It would have been better for her to have died on the table." Perry nodded, hand resting on his shoulder.

The emergency room door swung open. Decius walked back to his chair in the waiting area and dropped down. A bandage held the cut over his eye closed, and he held an ice pack against the large knot on his head. He avoided Luke's gaze.

Perry caught Luke's eye. "Do you want me to…" He gestured to Decius.

Luke shook his head. "Go help Kat. That will help more than

anything." Perry pulled him into a quick hug before leaving. Luke rubbed his sore knuckles, watching Decius. The anger subsided, but Decius allowed Aeron into their father's path tonight, and Luke couldn't forgive that just yet.

When the emergency room doors opened for what seemed like the 100th time, Shannon exited, scrubs covered in blood. Luke pushed off the wall, and Decius jumped to his feet.

"Is she—"

"Please—"

"She's alright." Shannon's weary voice cut them off. "Broken ribs, fractured ankle."

"What happened in there?" Decius' voice barely rose above a whisper.

"Punctured spleen. We caught it as it ruptured, thankfully. She'll live."

The breath left Luke like a popped balloon, and he sunk to the floor. His head pounded, the bruised knuckles ached as if he'd been punching a wall, but Aeron would live.

"Luke?" He ignored his name and forced himself to slow his breaths.

"What the hell did you two do to each other?" Shannon's voice pierced his head. "Aeron died on that table. This isn't the time to fight. What the hell is going on!"

He met her piercing gaze. If there was ever a moment to tell Decius and Shannon the truth, it was now. They would believe him in an instant. He clambered to his feet, but catching sight of Decius landed a blow to his gut harder than any physical hit he'd taken. He turned on his heel and left the infirmary. He'd call Shannon. Bring her into the fold with Katherine and Perry.

But if Decius had any information on his father, he'd have to get it later. Luke couldn't look at him without reliving the brief moment Aeron had left him alone in this world.

31

AERON

*L*ight shone in Aeron's eyes. She had heard about following the light when you die, but how could you follow something that kept moving back and forth and then disappearing completely? This couldn't be death, though. There was pain —pain everywhere. She shot her eyes open, and she released a hoarse scream.

"Aeron! It's okay! You're okay. Here, lay back."

The room blurred around her, a red blur attempting to push her back down. "Shannon?" Aeron croaked.

"Hey there," Shannon answered. "Lay back down. I'll give you some more morphine." Aeron obeyed, and slowly the room came into focus: white bare walls, ugly polka dot curtains, unflattering fluorescent lights: the infirmary.

"What happened?" Aeron asked. The monitor next to her beeped furiously in time with her racing heart. The sound pierced her skull, and she reached up, turning it off.

"Damn it, Aeron." Shannon turned it back on and pressed a button on the side. "There is a mute button." Shannon's normally impeccable hair had been pulled into a messy bun, and deep circles sat beneath her eyes.

"What happened?" Aeron asked again, concern touching her voice.

"You don't remember?"

Aeron shook her head, which made the room spin and her head throb. She grabbed her temples with her thumb and middle finger. "How long have I been out?"

"About a week. We weren't sure you would come out of it—"

"A week! What the hell happened to me?"

A low sigh escaped her, the horrid lighting accentuating her pale and drawn face. Ignoring Aeron's question, Shannon checked her vitals. "How's the pain?"

"Manageable. Stop avoiding the question. What. Happened?"

Shannon's eyes flicked to the flashing monitor, picking up on Aeron's irregular heartbeat, and checked over Aeron's vitals again—busy work. Aeron didn't miss how her hands shook as she did and reserved her questions for the moment, eyes beginning to get heavy again. A knock interrupted their silence. Decius stood in the hallway, the entire right side of his face swollen with bruises and cuts and a slight lump on his head. "May I come in?"

"Of course!" Aeron sat up and ignored the wave of dizziness. He didn't come in, though, until Shannon gave the nod.

"How is she?" He picked up the clipboard, reading over the medical sheets.

"I'm fine," Aeron said, annoyed. He barely allowed his gaze to fall over her as she spoke.

"Does she—"

"Hey!" Aeron yelled hoarsely. "I'm right here. You can talk to me. I'm not dead."

He looked from Shannon to Aeron, and when their eyes met, shame creased around them. They looked exactly like her father's eyes had when…memories of the attack flooded back to her—Katherine. Luke. Mr. Wayward. Her father.

"Oh." She sunk back to the bed, dizzy. He knelt next to her, grabbing her hand.

"Are you alright?"

She nodded. "Just remembering a bit."

"It's all my fault." His voice hitched, and she pushed past the disorientation to look at him.

"No, it's not. Why would you say that?"

"I wasn't there, Aeron. Luke warned me, and I didn't listen." The lies she'd told in order to keep everyone safe flew through her head. No, this was her fault, but she couldn't tell him that. She looked to Shannon for help, but she'd left. She'd never seen her brother this distraught. You would think she had died.

"Decius, what happened? Why was I out for so long?"

"I should have been there. I should have helped!" He stood up and began pacing. "Dad—I *knew* he was in town. I didn't think he would go to the apartment! I never dreamed he would…"

"Decius—"

"And when we found you." He stopped. Unable to get the words out without choking. "Aeron. I—I thought you were dead. And then we lost you once during surgery, and Luke nearly killed me—I didn't even fight back. I was hoping he would…"

"I died?" Aeron said, shocked. The fight with Mr. Wayward returned to her. Every painful blow. But she hadn't been hurt that badly, had she?

Decius whipped around, face drawn, the horrid lighting highlighting the moisture in his eyes. He nodded mutely then sat down on the bed, head dropping to his hands. "This is all my fault."

"No, it's not, Dee. Look," she moved her arms, "I'm fine!" For the first time she could remember, he needed her. "It's not that bad. Really, what do I have, a concussion and a few broken bones? I'll heal."

"You shouldn't have to. I should be in that bed, not you. You don't deserve this."

"You don't deserve this either." She leaned into him, and he gently pulled her close. They sat, letting the minutes tick by.

"You died." His voice shook.

"It will be a great story to tell my nieces and nephews." They sat in silence a few more minutes, Aeron running over the series of events again and again.

"Where's Luke?"

"Legacy stuff," he said, not meeting her eyes.

"Where's Dad?"

"Gone."

Her heart stopped. "Did Luke…"

"No. No, he's just laying low, I guess." He gave Aeron a hard look. "Why did he do it? Never in a million years would I think that…"

"I can't remember," Aeron lied. There wouldn't be a good enough reason to justify the beating he didn't give her.

Shannon returned to the room, folder in hand. "You have three fractured ribs which punctured your spleen—don't worry, we saved it. A nice concussion, and by nice, I mean it lit up the imaging in a horrid way. And luckily, only a few fractures in your ankle."

"Yeah, lucky," Aeron said, remembering the sound and agony of the dislocation—which Shannon seemed to be unaware of.

"Dee, you're needed in the boardroom."

He placed a kiss on Aeron's forehead—and she was pulled back to when her father placed a kiss before he left. Was that the last time she would ever see him alive?

"Rest up. We already have an active case, and it's not as much fun without you," he joked. Aeron gave a half-hearted laugh as he left.

Shannon stood at the end of her bed, glaring.

"What?"

"Now that I know you are going to live, mind telling me what the hell is going on?"

Aeron looked at her best friend, taken aback. "What do you mean?"

"All of it. Luke, your father, Decius…"

"Has Luke been in?" Aeron asked, tackling the topic she wanted to know most about.

Shannon shook her head. "He was here during the surgery, and then he and Decius went to blows—I've never seen them fight like that before—and then Luke left. No one's seen him since."

"Has anyone heard from my father?"

"You're safe here. Don't worry about him."

"Shan—"

"I'm not having this conversation with you, Aeron." Hurt tinged her voice. "Twenty years—we've buried parents, teammates, a Guardian. We've nearly died. We've fought over boys and who should be the lead on assignments and patched up broken hearts. But never in all that time have you ever lied to me about your father. When did it become physical? We could have protected you!"

"I don't need protection—"

"Really? I guess dying on the operating table while I try to patch up your spleen because you've taken a beating of a lifetime doesn't qualify!"

Aeron's chest constricted, and it had nothing to do with her injuries. "It's complicated." The words echoed hollow as she said them, and she wanted to take them back immediately.

Shannon's face fell. "So I've been told. I need to go home, shower. I have a medical ward to help run."

"Shannon."

"I expected things to get weird once you started dating Luke. But I never expected you to lie to me." She left without looking back. The door to her room closed with a resounding *click*, which Aeron felt in her core.

When the door to Aeron's infirmary room opened a few minutes later, she was relieved to see Mrs. Gale.

"How are you feeling, Aeron?" Unlike Shannon's fiery hair, her mother's long curls were light brown with a tinge of gray. It'd been years since Aeron had seen her, but the motherly warmth in Mrs.

Gale's eyes still shone. She moved around, checking Aeron's vitals again.

"Mrs. G," Aeron began, but the older woman shook her head and put a finger to her lips. Mrs. Gale shut the door and locked it.

She took a seat on the edge of Aeron's bed. Aeron kept her eyes locked on her movements. She reached into her pocket. Irrational panic overtook Aeron, and she tried to back away, but her injured leg did not allow her to get very far, and a hiss of pain escaped her from her ribs.

"Aeron!" Mrs. Gale's voice was full of concern, and Aeron paused in her retreat. She held out a black business card. "I've spoken to your father."

"You—you what?" Aeron's heart raced, the lights on the machine blinking furiously. She waved the card between her fingers and held it out for Aeron to take. Aeron turned her father's calling card over. A single 'S' scrawled on one side, *Safe* on the other.

"He called me after your attack at the hotel, and luckily he did. If I had waited until Decius' call, you wouldn't be with us."

Aeron looked at the card again. Her face warmed with relief. Her father was safe.

"Where is he?" Aeron whispered, unsure of who was sitting outside the door.

Mrs. Gale's smile didn't reach her eyes. "He is safe—and will stay safe." She hesitated a moment. "I must apologize. I am partially at fault for this mess. I refused to aid in the fight, and it has put you right in the crosshairs."

"Mrs. G."

"Please—I knew what the leadership was doing, but once I saw what he was willing to do to his own children, and after he took your mother and my husband…I retreated to protect my own."

Anger began to boil, but not at Mrs. Gale, at the injustice of the whole damn situation.

Mrs. Gale stood and moved to the window. "It was selfish of me to only think of my children."

Aeron swallowed the anger. She could have walked away, but having someone to fight for, someone to lose, pulled her in deeper to the Legacy life than she ever wanted. For Mrs. Gale, it had been the opposite—she had people to lose if she entered in any further and chose to back away.

"You did the right thing," Aeron assured.

"Did I? He took my best friend. Then he took my husband. And he's destroyed half the Original Legacy families."

"Half?" How many more families had been eliminated?

"I may not have agreed to help your father, but I wasn't going to sit around and wait to be finished off. I did my own research. The Board meets so infrequently these days it was easy to slip in to grab medical records and leave with…other files."

Aeron smiled despite herself. "Breaking the rules, Mrs. G…"

"The point is," she continued, waving off Aeron's admiration, "this should have never happened. I should have gone to your father as soon as I had my leverage against Mr. Wayward. So yes, Aeron, I'm sorry. I'm sorry you had to pick up my weight. I'm sorry it took you dying on my table for me to step up. Your father and that nice young man are currently working through all the files I acquired."

Ivan was okay. Her father was okay. They had an ally—they had two. Mrs. Gale and Mason. Their fight wasn't over—it was just getting started.

A knock at the door interrupted their conversation. Mrs. Gale looked over. "That will be Decius." She slipped a cell phone to Aeron, which she tucked under her pillow. "To keep in touch." She opened the door again and left, letting Decius back in.

Aeron sat in silence, waiting for him to say something. In the fluorescent lighting, the bruises on his dark face looked worse than she knew them to be.

"What is it, Dee?"

"I've been granted temporary control over the Estate."

"Temporary?"

"Until Dad can be found, I'm taking over Legacy responsibilities and any active missions he had—which aren't many."

"And what will happen when he resurfaces?" She found a loose thread on her blanket and started to tug at it, not wanting to know the answer to her question.

He didn't answer.

"Dee—"

"I don't know, Aeron. I'm still trying to wrap my head around the fact he would…" he waved his hand in her direction and let it fall, heavy on his lap. His face fell. "How did I not see this coming? Why didn't you say something to me?"

It was Aeron's turn not to answer.

They sat in silence. Aeron leaned back and closed her eyes. All she had wanted to do was save Luke. How had it spiraled so far out of control?

Aeron woke to a hand on hers, a thumb making soft circles against her palm. She didn't remember falling asleep; Mrs. Gale must have given her a drip cocktail. She pulled her eyes open a crack and recognized the top of Luke's head. Her stomach fluttered.

"Hey, Lulu," she whispered—it was all the sound she could make. Her throat was sore as if she had been screaming in her sleep.

His head snapped up, and she could see the dark bags beneath glassy eyes. "I didn't mean to wake you."

"You're here." She twined her fingers in his. His touch alone made her aches ease, and she wanted him to crawl in bed next to her and wrap her up.

But he pulled his hand away instead. "I shouldn't be here."

"You're leaving already?" Aeron's heart began to race, causing the monitor to beep. She didn't want to be left here alone—what if Mr. Wayward discovered the truth, and she was just a sitting duck?

"Relax," he said, reaching over to turn the machine off. "I just stopped in to check on you, and if Shannon finds out I upset you, she'll kill me. Besides, I shouldn't be here." He sat back in his chair, creating more distance between them.

She folded her hands in her lap. "Why not?"

He flinched at the hurt in her voice. Good. "Because this is my fault. This is all my fault." His voice caught on the last word.

"Luke, wait." She needed to tell him the truth—it was only a matter of time before her father was caught and killed, or Mr. Wayward figured out it was her in that apartment and killed her. But how the hell did she even begin to explain?

"I can't, Aeron. I need to fix this so you, and so many others, aren't in danger anymore." He sounded lightyears older all of a sudden. He leaned forward and gently kissed her hair. "Please, just trust me. I'll come to you when I can." He left without giving her a chance to respond.

Her pulse pounded in her ears, each thump a blow to her composure. What could he fix—her father? He had it so very wrong, and she couldn't tell him. She couldn't tell anyone. The fissures in her composure cracked. It started behind her eyes, the tears forcing their way out. And then, like a failing dam, her chest ached, and she started to drown in a flood of loneliness.

"I was starting to suspect you had no heart at all."

Aeron choked on a sob, swallowing it down and scanning the room. In the darkest corner, a figure pushed off the wall. If the monitor had remained on, her heartbeat would have sounded alarms as Katherine Wayward materialized from the shadows.

Her red hair was pulled to the top of her head, and she wore a hoodie—without strings, Aeron noted. There was nothing in reach for Aeron to defend herself with, but Katherine poured a glass of water and held it out. Aeron's fingers were buried into the sheet, holding her upright. Katherine raised her eyebrows and shook the glass, but Aeron mutely shook her head.

"Okay then." She set the glass on the nightstand. "I know I need to rehydrate after a good cry."

Arms giving out, Aeron slumped a bit, her fingers tingling, and she shook them out. "What do you want from me?" Her eyes glanced to the door.

"No one will be coming to check on you for a bit." Katherine pulled a chair over and took a seat, propping her feet on the bed, bits of mud falling onto the sheet. "Luke made sure he had a few hours alone. He didn't plan on you waking up."

"Does he…"

"Know I'm here? No." She gave a dry laugh. "He's been a bit distracted. You. Your father. Our Granddad."

"Why are you here, then? If you were going to kill me, it would have been easier to overdose me. Or smother me in my sleep."

"You didn't even ask me who I am."

"I know who you are," Aeron said, tired of lying.

"Then my assumptions are correct—you're working with your father."

Aeron's parched mouth somehow went drier.

"You're not denying it." She nodded and sat up straighter. "I don't care, really. He's trying to kill my Granddad. I'm trying to kill my Granddad. If the circumstances were different, I'd reach out to him myself. But as Luke is hell-bent on killing him…you can see where there is a conflict of interest."

She wanted Mr. Wayward dead too. Another ally—if she or her dad even lived through the week. "Then you know how much danger Luke is in. You're in."

"I don't care." Katherine held up her hands. "He said, she said, they did. It doesn't matter to me. What does matter to me is finding your father's tech man—or woman. Where are they?"

Aeron forced her face to remain neutral. She might be an ally—or she might be trying to set Aeron up. "I don't know."

"I know they tampered with the DNA collected from the Rose

Way and blacked out surveillance. An impressive feat—an outsider beating the Legacy at their own play."

"I don't know what you're talking about." And she didn't, although she could envision Ivan hopped up on energy drinks furiously beating away at a keyboard.

"Oh c'mon. That hoodie surprise?" She tugged on her own hood. "I witnessed you do it over and over, but to have it done to me? I didn't even see it coming."

Witnessed it? Aeron shook her head. "I don't—"

"I've seen your fight—the one on the subway? Impressive, really. But the icing on the cake? Using that cuff to slash the old man's face. Man. I wish I could have seen that." She picked up the water and took a sip. "Sure you don't want some?"

Aeron's throat begged her to say yes, but she shook her head, remaining quiet.

"I helped Luke pick out that bracelet."

Heat flooded her face. The implication of Luke buying her that weapon never even registered. "Does he know that it was me?"

"Granddad suspects. Luke, on the other hand, is in complete denial." She took another gulp of water, and Aeron licked her lips. "I don't blame him. Your father gave you quite the alibi. Me? I'm not as emotionally invested, nor does your life have any particular meaning to me, other than it's important to keeping Luke on task."

"Good to know," Aeron said, voice barely audible. Another pawn in someone else's game. "I don't know where to find my father's tech person or my father."

She released a long breath. "I actually believe you. I figured it was worth a shot, and I wanted to let you know—I know. Your secret is safe with me, though. I need Luke on task, and your lies keep him there. Luke is doing everything in his power to protect you. But if you decide you want to save Luke? Let me know." She dropped a piece of paper on the bed next to the pieces of dried mud. "I know from personal experience, what my Granddad wants, my Granddad gets. And right now, it's your father's head on a silver platter, and Luke is tasked with delivering." She refilled the glass, handing it to Aeron. "You can't even imagine what happens to people who don't deliver."

The glass of water trembled in Aeron's hand as Katherine pulled her hood up and slid into the hallway. She placed the water on the nightstand, wiping the spilled moisture from her hand before opening the paper: A phone number. Memorizing the numbers, Aeron dropped the paper in the glass of water, the ink turning the water blue.

32

LUKE

*L*uke balanced the bags of take-out in one hand, giving two sharp knocks and a whistle to the door in front of him. Two whistles and a sharp knock answered, and he pushed the door open, pausing just inside the threshold and before the tripwire.

"I'm here with food," Luke called out. He stepped over the wire and rounded the corner. Dominic, Gunnar, Perry, and Katherine sat around the kitchen table of the safe-house. Luke dropped the food off on top of the mounds of paperwork and went to wash his hands. No matter how many times he washed them, they never felt clean anymore.

It'd been weeks since the fundraiser, and they were no closer to finding Mr. Seward or determining who broke into the Rose Way. His secret deal with Rosemary, however, had granted him the freedom to move about the city and check-in more with Katherine and Perry.

"Good news?" Luke asked, joining them at the table.

"Well, no bad news," Perry said. "We need more information and have zero leads."

"How are you on the D.C. side?" Luke asked Katherine.

"I'm going to have to return to secure my authority. My mother has been back and forth every few weeks, but I need face time with my contacts there."

"Anything on surveillance?" He looked over to the computers.

"Nothing," Dominic replied. "There is a four-mile black zone around the target areas for three days leading up to the attack until two hours after."

"How the hell did the world go dark and no one noticed?" Luke asked, but he knew the answer. The same answer to every other question: Mr. Seward's techie.

"Add that into the Legacy facial recognition software basically erasing any Legacy blood that shows up on camera, and it's an impossible Where's Waldo."

"I was hoping, with the kill order out on him, we would get some kind of hit." Luke rubbed his neck. "It's okay, though. I managed to buy us more time by convincing Granddad I should hit more families to weed him out. Bad news, I have a family to hit within the next few days." He pulled out a file from the inside pocket of his jacket. His deal with Rosemary gave him mission freedom to secure the children and get them out of danger. But he still needed bodies at the scene. "Not a blood family, but a newer one—the Smiths."

"Why them?" Katherine asked, opening the file.

"I've stopped asking, to be honest," Luke admitted. "He won't always tell me, and I run the risk of pissing him off."

"What do you need?" Dominic asked, retreating to the computer with his food.

"White female, 6 years old. Brown hair. White female, 1 year." Luke answered.

Katherine lowered her fork and pushed her food away. "You couldn't have waited until after we ate?"

He raised his eyebrows. "He asked."

A disgusted look answered him, and he shrugged, moving next

to Dominic. "I will see what I can do. No promises on the infant—I'll pull up the medical records."

"No need." Perry moved to the door. "I have them here."

Shannon stepped over the tripwire, handing a pile of files to Perry. "Did you get me lunch?" she asked him. "I'm starving."

Katherine held out an unopened container. "Here you go."

"Thanks."

"How is she?" Luke asked. He pulled a chair out for her.

"Stable," Shannon answered, taking the seat, and opening up her chicken salad. "And tired of the bodyguards at her door. She's being discharged tonight."

Luke nodded. After his visit last week, he and Mason created a rotation of guards to keep almost everyone out of her room. He needed to get a few steps ahead of his Granddad and her father before she'd be safe again. "Thanks for the files. I know this has been an unimaginable week."

"Having Aeron die beneath my fingers was unimaginable. Finding out the truth about her father? It's almost a relief. I can hate him with conviction now." Perry pulled a chair next to her, stealing some of her food. "Get your own," she joked.

"Yours looks better," Perry countered but pulled his own food toward him.

Luke exhaled deeply, surveying the group he trusted almost as much as Decius and Aeron. Dominic's fingers moved across his keyboard, food untouched. Gunner chowed down on his grinder, nose deep into a stack of papers. Perry and Shannon laughed, conversation flying between them. And Katherine met his stare, arms crossed. Leaving the table, she moved beside him.

"You doing okay?"

"I wish you'd stop asking me that," Luke said, biting the inside of his lip. "I stopped being okay the day I pulled the trigger on a ten-year-old."

"How are you managing," she rephrased.

"As long as I keep the priorities in check and I have something to focus on—I'm managing."

"And these 'assignments'?"

He scrunched his nose, the ball in his chest expanding at the thought. He sucked in air, trying to force it back down a manageable size. "As long as I don't think about it—I'm good."

"That will only work for so long."

"It only needs to work long enough. Plus, I have you to keep me from cracking." He shot her a smile, but she shook her head. The phone buzzed in his pocket: Rosemary.

"It's your mother." The ball fought against his chest again.

Perry and Katherine's phones buzzed next. Katherine pulled hers out and showed him the screen: Cage. Perry held his up too: Senior Assassin.

"Why does he call you instead of me?" Luke wondered.

"Because Rosemary refuses to call me," Perry said. "My voice reminds her of my mother."

"Then why does Cage call me?"

"Because no one else wants to call Luke—he's not just the pretty boy anymore."

Luke ignored him. "We gotta jet. Dominic— let me know if you're able to get the bodies for me."

"Not a problem," he answered around a mouthful of food.

"Shan, are you good here?" It'd been two weeks since he'd brought Shannon on board. He feared she would tell Decius or her mother, but witnessing Aeron die—even for a moment—was an experience neither wanted to repeat.

"Yeah. I need a break from the Institute anyway. As soon as Dominic confirms, I'll grab the thumb drive. Perry can come collect it from me when he brings me roses later, and he can get started with re-coding the files."

"Roses?" Katherine pretended to hurl, and Perry turned a slight shade of red.

"You don't have a romantic bone in your body, Kat." Gunnar grinned, looking up from the mountain of papers.

"Shut up, Katherine," Perry replied. "I remember the days when roses from a suitor in D.C. were basically a proposal for you."

"Yeah…on an undercover assignment where a serial killer left roses as his signature."

"How many hearts did you break?" Perry asked, full smile in place.

"Twenty-seven hearts before we caught him," she replied, eyes glistening with glee. "Those men fell for me so hard. Remember Joshua?"

"Was he number twenty-four or twenty-five?" Perry looked skyward as if counting.

"Twenty-four," Katherine said, unable to keep from smiling. "He proposed ring and all after the second date. Jackson, may he rest in peace, was so pissed. I don't even remember why. I just remember him showing up on the third date. The poor man pissed himself and apologized for not asking for permission." Katherine and Perry laughed.

"Jackson?" Luke asked—the conversation a stark reminder they'd lived an entire life without him. It hardly felt that way, though.

"Our handler," Perry said, laugh subsiding. "He was our Mason. Great man."

"What happened to him?" Shannon's voice was soft.

The laughter died down, and Katherine replied, "Our Granddad."

"Well, he placed the hit. Your mother executed the order," Perry corrected.

Silence descended the room, even Dominic's typing had stopped. "I'm very sorry," Shannon replied.

The three cousins headed out. But Luke didn't make it to the Rose Way.

He stopped halfway to the hotel. "Decius is calling." He hadn't heard from him since the night… "I should take this. If they ask where I am, I'm following up on Mr. Seward."

Perry nodded, patting him on the back. "Be safe."

He let the phone ring a few more times before answering. "Yeah?"

"We need to talk."

"I know," Luke said. Decius' voice brought a tidal wave of emotions through Luke, anger, regret, calm. The ball in his chest decreased, though. He missed his best friend. "Where?"

"I'm at the Institute. Family Residence?"

"Yours or mine?"

Decius was quiet for a moment. "Yours? I tore mine apart looking for anything on my father."

Luke swallowed hard. He hadn't stepped foot in his family home at the Institute since before his parents were killed. "Does an hour work for you?"

The Wayward family residence had been left untouched, the layer of dust over every surface confirming the fact. Luke didn't go past the main living area, though, taking a wet cloth to the countertops to clean them. His mother hated dust. The place sat too quiet. He needed the noise of other people. A fissure in his wall began to appear, and he fought to ease the pain seeping in. He'd laid them to rest a long time ago, and if they could see him now…

His stomach lurched when Decius knocked. "Come in," he called, clearing his throat.

The lock clicked open to Decius' retinal scan, just like it always had, but Decius looked nothing like he did the last time the two of them had been in the residence together. They had completed the last task of the year before his Granddad had requested him for the assignment that changed everything.

Decius had shown up with celebratory beverages, bright eyes, and his contagious smile, insisting Luke's parents join them for a drink—just one more year of training. Decius, their second son—they never said no to him. It'd been one of the last happy memories he had of his parents—drinking Johnny Walker Blue and talking about the upcoming trip to the Maldives. But they never made it on that trip.

Decius frowned, looking around the room. A beard covered his chin now, and his normally tamed hair was almost long enough to pull on top of his head. The Legacy duties didn't seem to be suiting him.

"Hey," he said, nodding at Luke.

Luke couldn't answer, a storm churning against his logic. Dee had let his father nearly kill Aeron, and that rage still burned deep. But being in this room—where he'd been the happiest of his life with his parents and Aeron. And with Decius—the one who up and took over the Team Lead when Luke refused to do so, afraid of making the wrong call. The person he'd trusted to call when shit hit the fan, no questions asked. The best friend who helped bury his parents.

Luke glanced to the counter—the bottle of Johnny Walker Blue sitting half-empty near the sink where his father had left it. He grabbed two glasses from the cupboard and poured them both a healthy amount. Decius accepted, clinking cups before downing the liquid. Luke followed suit, the taste and slight burn a relief to his system. He poured two more, leaning against the counter.

Decius swirled the drink. Luke continued to sip his, the liquor continuing to calm the storm inside.

"I'm sorry—" They both started and then laughed.

"Me first," Decius said. "I should have been there with Aeron that night... I'd returned to the Institute for a second round of fluids. Whatever we had that morning took a rough toll on my system. Aeron told me to go. She was going to sleep, and we all needed the rest. I was on my way back when I got the text."

The image of Aeron alive, the pink tinge to her cheeks, eased

Luke's anger. The rest melted away with another sip of scotch—he'd forgotten they'd been drug tested that morning. And in all fairness, Luke had believed for more than a moment that same morning that a misstep on his part had signed an execution order on both Aeron and Decius. What a fucked up situation.

"It's not your fault," Luke admitted. "You're not him—you're not your dad. If he was able to get past the security measures, then there was nothing we would have been able to do anyway."

Decius nodded—apology accepted. He placed the glass on the counter and leaned next to Luke, hand deep within his pockets. "I have no idea where my father is. I've checked the safe houses I know of and found nothing of value. I found one more I didn't know of and confiscated a slew of computers, all of which have been wiped."

Computers. "Do you think I could get a look at them?" Luke asked. Dominic and Perry were two of the best IT men he knew. Maybe they could find something Decius had missed.

"Yeah, that's one of the reasons I'm here. I was going to see if Perry could take a look—pull something I missed."

"Of course. Want me to pick them up?" Luke fought the smile coming to his face. Another break. "Are they here or at the Manor?"

"The Manor. Being in the family residence—it was always his domain. I can't be in there." He sniffed. "I'll bring them to you."

Luke nodded, eyes jumping around the room—he'd avoided this place for the same reason.

"How is she?" Decius crinkled his brow looking over with a tilted head.

"You haven't been to see her?"

He shook his head. "I've been neck deep in cleaning up my father's messes and trying to find him. Shannon's kept me updated though. Said she's heading home tonight. I was going to pick her up. Want to join me?"

He couldn't. So many of his decisions kept her in danger—he

couldn't control her father, but he could have killed him a long time ago. "No. I've got Legacy stuff that I have to attend to."

"You haven't seen her either, then."

Luke shook his head. She would be pissed with them both—leaving her alone to heal. But he saw his pain of losing her that night mirrored in Decius's eyes. "I can't unsee—unfeel that night. I wanted to protect her. Instead, I was off at a fundraiser, playing diplomat. I was useless."

"Running the Legacy isn't useless."

"But I don't want to run it," Luke admitted out loud for the first time in a while.

"The cards we're dealt," Decius replied, quoting his father.

It sparked the short fuse in Luke. He stood straight, turning to face Decius. "You *really* have no idea where to find him?"

"No, Luke. I don't." The weariness in his voice was clear. But Luke couldn't accept it.

"You're the heir to his Legacy—you're telling me with all the access you have—you've turned up nothing?"

Decius straightened up too, standing toe to toe with him. "Your parents were his best friends—you're telling me with all the access you have to their stuff, you can't find my father either?"

Luke's cheeks burned. He'd never thought to look through his parent's stuff. He tried to not think of his parents at all.

"With all the Legacy resources at your disposal? With a kill order out and not a single peep from the Underworld? The fucking Legacy can't find their best assassin—how the hell am I supposed to?" His breath had become labored. "I'm doing everything I can to find him. Are you?"

Not everything. He could be spending hours in the Cold Room, helping sift through surveillance while Perry skimmed codes. He could dig through the boxes in his parent's room. But he needed to uphold deals with Rosemary and pretend to kill children—if all went according to plan—and continue to protect Aeron and Decius from his psychotic Granddad.

"Of course, I am," he spat. They stood toe to toe, each as tall as they could possibly be.

"Then why are we even arguing?" Decius asked, deflating.

Luke answered with a short laugh, rubbing the back of his neck. "Extenuating circumstances?"

"And my temper's short. I'm just exhausted." He ran a hand down his face, eyes fighting to stay open. "I'm going to nap on a bed in the infirmary for a bit until she gets out." His stance relaxed, but the slouch betrayed him—he was defeated. "Want me to bring the computers here tomorrow or somewhere else?"

"Here will work." Luke would have to figure out a way to get Dominic in or the computers out without raising any flags. But having Decius working with him again, hunting his father on his own terms without having to tell him anything…"Why don't you sleep here for a bit," Luke offered before he could think his way out of it. Being home brought up memories he'd long-buried—happiness and parental expectations. Katherine was right—he couldn't keep up running this lie forever. "Aeron will be released in a few hours. Get some shut eye in. Shower. Shave."

Decius raised an eyebrow at him. "Are you sure?"

"It will be just like old times. I have no idea what my room looks like, though. I haven't been in here since…"

Decius pulled him in for a hug, the embrace so familiar the ball in Luke's chest expanded for a second before nearly disappearing. Luke hugged back, hanging on to him like a lifeline. There was no ulterior motive. No threat if he failed. Just the confidence that they could conquer anything together. "Don't worry," Decius assured him. "We'll find him."

Decius' embrace clung to Luke on the way to the Rose Way, but each step off the elevator, cold stares of the dead stripped him of the comfort. What would Decius say if he knew the truth of what

Luke had been up to the past few months? The door swung open before he reached it, Katherine's wide eyes forewarning that things were amiss within. He stopped short in the doorway, all thoughts of Decius and his parents fleeing his mind.

Rosemary knelt in the middle of the room, the barrel of his Granddad's Sig pressed to the middle of her forehead.

"Took you long enough," Rosemary snarled, but a tremble in her hands gave away the fear she tried to mask.

"What is this?" Luke looked around. Katherine stood stock still next to him, Cage materializing from behind her, gun in hand. Perry sat at the desk, Burn Book open and leg bouncing, Dave behind him, aiming at the back of his neck.

The chill of metal pressed into his neck. *Shit.*

"More money is missing, Luke. I thought we had an agreement."

"Yes," he said slowly. Which money was he talking about? "I didn't realize Wilks' money was still top priority. It's on my radar, but I've been on the trail for Mr. Seward."

"I said *more* money. The Finch account came up short: 5.5 million dollars short. Dave brought it to my attention, that the money was taking longer to move than necessary. I had Perry pull the records to see why it hadn't been moved yet since you seem too preoccupied to come when called. Imagine my surprise when the numbers didn't match my records. Do you think I'm a fool?"

"No, Sir. I think you trusted me to be one-hundred-percent sure in my actions and information. May I ask why everyone has a gun to their head?" He didn't particularly care if his aunt was shot—one less queen on the chessboard—but why his Granddad thought he cared was curious. There was no love lost between the two of them.

"Because until I brought you aboard in D.C.—I had zero insubordination issues or financial problems. Now?" He looked around the room as if it explained his logic. Luke tried to talk around the knot in his throat. He was supposed to be the leader—the next Senior Assassin.

"That explains the gun to my head—and perhaps Perry, maybe

even Katherine. But why Rosemary? You can shoot her, and it would only make my life easier."

Rosemary sneered. "I had the audacity to suggest that you couldn't lead this team, Luke, and that Katherine should be reassigned back home—where she belongs, training to lead Legacy Inc. Not chasing rogue assassins."

"Who murdered your kin," Granddad said. "Who threatens to take the Legacy from us and has stolen billions from beneath our noses!" He turned to Luke. "Who tried to kill his own daughter—a Legacy child. These are not small infractions."

The fire in Luke's belly roared—the accusation he was as bad as Mr. Seward burning into him, that he almost missed the implication that his Granddad had just let Aeron off the hook for his attack. Fingers itching to pull a trigger, Luke looked for a reason. Dave's smirk from across the room would be enough—had Luke smirked at his Granddad that way...

"Do you find something funny, Dave? Remove the gun from Perry's head," Luke commanded.

Dave didn't move, eyes jumping to the Senior Assassin for confirmation. Luke had been given full power over the team, and it hadn't been stripped away—yet.

"Now." The command in Luke's voice rang through the room. Dave still didn't move. Luke pivoted away from the shaky barrel at his neck, knocked over Alexis, and pulled out his Sig. The shot rang out. Dave dropped to the ground, Luke's bullet finding purchase between the eyebrows.

"Cage. Stand down." He did, and Luke turned the gun to Alexis, but she'd already lowered her weapon. Facing his Granddad again, he re-holstered. "This team wasn't working because you didn't trust us—your *kin*—to work together. Having outsiders not privy to all the information, who thought they were equal to the Wayward name, was your mistake.

"Dave looked for every opportunity to sabotage this team. I had to plan for his every pushback and constantly reminded him he wasn't a Wayward—no matter what he did, he never would be. It was getting exhausting, quite frankly." Luke took a breath before continuing. Once he said his next thoughts, his deal with Rosemary might be null, but he had to do something to save face with his Granddad. "The Finch money isn't missing—I know who took it. Would you like me to report every time someone sneezes, or do you want results? Until you say otherwise—I'll lead this team my way and get you your results." Luke's chest rose and fell rapidly, the word vomit coming to an end. "Have I completely failed you at all so far?"

A smile spread across his Granddad's face, and he removed the gun from Rosemary's head. "I wondered how long it would take you to find your balls."

"Seriously." Rosemary stood, rotating her head, neck cracking. "I didn't think he was going to kill anyone, though."

"Excuse me?" Luke said, legs suddenly threatening to give out. Perry and Katherine looked equally confused, which comforted him only slightly.

"You passed," Rosemary said, clapping him on the back.

He shifted away, her touch making his stomach churn. His Granddad extended a hand, and Luke shook it, unsure what was happening. "The beginning of your Senior Assassin trials starts here; your loyalty to this family—though I did not see you shooting anyone today. I am impressed. The team remains yours, but I will be sending Katherine back to D.C."

Luke looked over to Katherine. "I'd like her to stay. She's my right-hand."

"And I knew she would guide you, but it's time she resurfaces in D.C."

Luke nodded and swallowed the panic back. They weren't ready for her to go. "What about Cage and Alexis? I meant what I said about not wanting non-family involved."

"You will soon learn that having non-familial contracts are a necessity; loyalty to the purse is sometimes more objective than the loyalty of blood. Alexis and Cage remain on the team."

"And Perry?"

"Perry replaces Katherine, for now. We've globe-trotted enough. I want the Smiths dealt with tomorrow.

Luke nodded, his mind trying to catch up to what just happened. Katherine was leaving. He hoped Dominic had found bodies for the Smiths—his timeline to save the children just got moved up.

33

AERON

*A*eron glared at Shannon from the bed. It was nice to be back in her own room—on her own bed, but the order of house arrest dampened the excitement.

"Why," Aeron complained.

"Because you're still healing, and my mom thinks it's best. And because we still don't know where your father is," she added, a bit softer.

She was so tired of everyone coddling her. She should have been released a week ago. "If he wanted me dead," Aeron said with disdain in her voice, "I wouldn't be alive."

"You did die." Shannon's words hung in the room, and Aeron paled. As far as everyone knew, her father had attempted to kill her and succeeded—even if for the briefest of moments.

"You're right. I'm sorry. I'm just tired of being laid up and alone."

Shannon dropped onto the bed beside her, leaning against the pillows. "You're not invincible, you know."

"I'm also not incapable," Aeron responded. The phone chirped from the nightstand. She dragged herself across the bed, grimacing with the movements, and flipped it open.

"Who is it?" Shannon asked.

Aeron hesitated. "One of the guys from the garage," she lied. "I was really bored in the infirmary."

"We've been spread pretty thin," Shannon supplied, closing her eyes. "But I'm not needed in the medical ward for the next few weeks. Told my mom I needed the break—get you settled back in. Try and bring the team back together."

"Is that even possible? Luke won't even…" Aeron exhaled sharply. She hadn't seen Luke since the night she'd seen Katherine. He wanted space, and that was what Aeron was giving him. It would be a lie to say that it didn't hurt worse than her broken ribs.

"He'll come around," Shannon assured. "I think he's just trying to figure out what he can do, where it can all fit in—being the next Senior and all."

"Have you been talking to him?" Aeron scooted to a straighter position.

"Our paths crossed a few times, but I see him as much as I see Dee."

"That was nice of him to bring me home. Too bad he couldn't stay."

"I can't believe I'm going to say this," Shannon said, eyes still closed. "But I miss the good old days."

Aeron chuckled. "Straight and narrow Shannon is missing the rule-bending?"

"Breaking. Rule-breaking. And yes. At least when we were causing havoc, it was together. Remember Justin's first year? We went out so much he nearly failed every class."

"Yeah. And then Mason would drill us for hours the next morning, and we'd puke our brains out."

"We never did learn our lesson."

"No," Aeron agreed. "We learned how to hold our liquor better."

"Remember the night Perry tried to stop us from going clubbing with Keara?"

Aeron cracked a grin. "And we almost got him arrested for stalking?"

"He was so mad at us," Shannon said, laughing.

"What about the time we borrowed a limousine to bring us back to Connecticut and snuck into that boarding school your cousins go to—Taft?" Aeron laughed. It had been so long since she laughed. Shannon joined in, but it was quickly cut off by a yelp of pain as Aeron's ribs shook.

"Oh, gosh," Shannon said, sobering up and checking Aeron's ribs. "I'm sorry. I should know better."

Aeron brushed her off, still chuckling. "So, what happened?"

Shannon's smile faded, and she laid back on the pillow. "Luke's parents died, we were thrust into an unusual and uncomfortable case the first week home, and you changed."

"Me?" Aeron said, shocked. "What do I have to do with anything?"

"We've had fun every year because we went out together, all of us—even when we didn't want to. But now, you barely make it home for dinner most nights; Luke is too busy with his Grandfather; Decius…well, he's got a lot on his plate now." Aeron's heart sank—she was right.

They lapsed into silence, and Shannon's light breathing soon regulated into a sleeping pattern. Aeron couldn't sleep. She'd spent too much time laid up in bed to do it anymore, and now her mind raced with the unanswerable questions of what happens now. She opened the phone Mrs. Gale had slipped to her to see what Ivan had sent.

'Settled in?' —I

'Sucks' she wrote back. 'House arrest.'

'But safe. :)'

'Any more info?' She chewed on her lip waiting for the reply. So far, three more families had been found murdered, children and all, the money still unaccounted for.

'No.'

'Any luck with that number?'

It took him several minutes to reply, but finally, the screen lit back up. 'Clean.'

Aeron didn't expect anything different, but the disappointment still stung. Shannon snored softly beside her, the sound bringing Aeron back to the days of sleepovers and late-night chats. This year had really gone off the tracks. She leaned back against the pillow and imagined for the briefest of moments what saying no to her father might have been like. Annoying music. Delicious, bad-for-you food. Always pretending to be less-than she was to keep everyone safe. Everyone except Luke.

Shannon dropped a handful of pills into Aeron's hand and then passed the pillbox over. "Here. Be sure to take them with food—"

"I know, I know. These aren't my first broken ribs, Shan." Aeron reminded. The team gathered in the living room, prepping for their next assignment, which Aeron was not a part of.

"This is a smash and grab. We'll be home before you know it," Decius assured, lounging on the couch next to Mason.

"Doesn't mean I like being stuck home."

"I think you should feel grateful to be alive, Aeron. Not pouting because you can't smash skulls at the present moment," Mason scolded.

Aeron glared at Mason, but he ignored her. The special assignment was designed to get Lesley used to fieldwork.

A low whistle left Decius, and Justin cat-called from the kitchen. A moan escaped Aeron when she tried to turn to see what the fuss was about. "Damn ribs," she muttered. But what impressed the boys soon came into view. "Whoa." Lesley sported a short, black halter dress that stopped above mid-thigh.

"She looks hot," Justin said.

"She looks the part," Mason clarified, his sharp look directed at Justin. "Lesley, are you clear on the assignment?"

Lesley tugged her skirt down and nodded. "Guard-distraction duty while Justin and Shannon go in for the kill."

Shannon cleared her throat. "I want to make this clear—so you don't get the wrong idea, Les. This is sexist as fuck. However—men think with their dicks and are heavily influenced by their testosterone, making them predictable and easy to manipulate."

Aeron chuckled. It was a long-standing tradition in the Legacy to make sure the new girls realize the power they hold, simply because the male population decided that they had it.

"I'll be there as your cover. Nothing will happen," Decius assured. "We've worked this club on many occasions—it'll be a second home to you before you know it."

Lesley nodded, but the fear stayed plastered on her face.

"Ugh," Aeron said, trying to stand. Mason stood, helping her. Aeron tried to look appreciative but having her Guardian help her stand only demoralized her more. She pulled out one of the throwing knives from her cast and held it out to Lesley.

"Even if you don't need it, it's better to have it than not," Aeron said, slipping the knife into the hidden pocket along the ribcage of the dress. "And it doesn't matter if it lands. Throwing it is enough of a distraction to get you some space. But you'll be safe at Sapphire."

"Thanks," Lesley said, running a hand over the concealed weapon.

"If things go south, Decius, pull her out. This man works for a trafficker I've been tracking for over a year. Don't compromise this."

"Got it."

Decius, Justin, Shannon, and Lesley headed toward the door. Lesley gave a backward glance, and Aeron nodded at her. "Kill 'em good!" she called. Lesley nodded back and left. Being broken sucked.

"How are you, really?" Mason asked once the apartment door closed. He headed for the kitchen, pulling out veggies and meat.

"Ready to snap," she said. "I can't train. I can't participate even in an observational capacity. And I haven't heard from Luke."

"Any word from your father?"

She shook her head, propped her crutches against the counter, and pulled the cutting board and veggies closer to her. "No. I haven't heard from him since that night." It wasn't a lie; she hadn't spoken *to* him at all. He passed her a knife, and she began dicing up the carrots.

His eyes looked up from under his brow. Her double talk would never fly with him. "Anything you want me to pass on? I'm going tonight."

Jealousy rippled through her. She'd been the one to risk her life for nothing. She'd been the one to lie over and over to everyone she cared about. She was the one left in the dark, again.

"Wouldn't matter if I did. He would dismiss it as childish." The knife in her hand moved more aggressively, a carrot flying off the cutting board.

He caught it and handed it back to her. "His loss. I think your ideas are usually the best ones. This team follows your lead."

She raised an eyebrow.

"Decius never holds back information in his reports. Neither did Perry. You pretty much have the final—and most useful—suggestion for the operations. Your father is a great assassin, but he's short-sighted when it comes to you."

"Well, if I have such great ideas, why can't I figure out how to piece the team back together?" She pushed the diced carrots into a bowl, starting on the cabbage. "Luke is completely gone doing the devil knows what with his Granddad. Decius is burning the candle at both ends. Shannon…well, we're not the same team we used to be."

"I can't believe I'm going to say this," Mason started, stabbing his knife into the cutting board, and putting a hand on his hip. He smoothed his hair back with his wrist. "Perhaps you should get everyone together and go out. I'm sure there's a Halloween Bash coming up."

Aeron cracked a smile, the memory of Mason dragging Perry out of the club by his collar last year—Perry too intoxicated to even stand. "I thought we were banned from partying?"

He nodded, laying the chicken out. "I didn't think you'd actually listen."

"Weren't your exact words, 'The next time you decide being intoxicated is more important than the Legacy, I will leave you for the police to find, and your parents can bail you out'?" A slight shiver ran through her, the FBI raid and her father showing up to bail her out last year surfacing in her mind.

He dislodged the knife to chop the meat. "I might have been a little harsh. It's no picnic reporting to the founding families that their children are too intoxicated to attend training. It worked, right?"

She laughed. "We just partied closer to home. Besides, my father wasn't *that* mad."

"No, but it's when he's not furious I get nervous." He pushed the chopped chicken into a bowl and moved over to the sink to wash the cutting board and knife. He dried his hands on the towel tucked into his front pocket and turned on the stove, placing a large frying pan to heat. "Get the group together. Go out. You guys need to bond. After Shaun, and then John and Mary...this shift in the Legacy can be felt all the way through the Underworld. If we start falling apart on the elite level—there's no hope for any of us."

"Have we managed to save any families?"

"It's impossible to save anyone when you don't know who the next target will be. If we reach out and it's to the wrong family...we lost the Peters just last week."

"They're not even a Blood Family." She sat back, propping her foot up on the next stool, a dull ache creeping into her ankle.

"I know. Which means either the rest of the families are on board with Mr. Wayward, or he's just cleaning house at this point."

"Shit."

"Yeah. Shit." They continued to prepare dinner as they lapsed into silence, the chicken and vegetables sizzling in the pan. Mason's phone jumped around on the counter next to Aeron. She slid it across to him, and he picked it up, flipping it open. "Go."

His eyebrows crinkled, and he turned off the pan of the half-cooked meat. When his eyes met hers, Aeron stretched across to the utensil holder, spinning it until she found the scissors. She began cutting at the cast around her leg. Nothing good was coming from this conversation, and she needed to be ready to assist. Mason joined her. He took the scissors, though, and placed them aside, shaking his head.

"Understood. A taggy?"

He was talking about her. A taggy—tagalong. She bit her lower lip, her good leg shaking, waiting for him to give her some sign.

"I disagree. I think she is more than able to handle it." Her mouth went dry. "Will do." He clicked the phone closed and tossed it back on the counter. His fingers inspected the slight cut in the top of the cast. "What were you thinking?"

"That I am more mobile with this thing off my leg."

"And useless if it doesn't heal properly. It comes off in a week—give it a week." He sat on the stool previously occupied by her foot. "There's been another hit—the Smiths."

Aeron swallowed the bile rising in her throat. "The whole family?"

"We're going to find out. Grab your gear."

The Smiths' small-town, two-story home swarmed with police. The crime scene tape encircled the entire lawn. Mason flashed a badge at one of the detectives and pointed to Aeron. The detective smiled and they waved them in.

"Clear out," the detective called as they followed, Aeron

awkward on the crutches. The first responders filed out. "Looks like a home invasion. Nothing to suggest otherwise."

"How many dead?"

"Four."

Aeron's throat tightened. Entire families had been eliminated, children and all. This was the first with an infant—she couldn't wrap her mind around it. How? Why? How?

"Thank you. We will take it from here," Mason said. The detective nodded, relief to leave the case clear as his shoulders relaxed.

Aeron's scanned the room for surveillance as she followed Mason through the small house—but there wouldn't be any. Mr. Wayward would be sure of that.

He stalled on the threshold to the first room, swallowing hard enough for Aeron to see his Adam's apple move. "I don't know if it's better or worse to start with this room." Aeron moved behind him. She saw the mobile hanging over Mason's shoulder and the white sheet hanging over the crib, blood-soaked with spatters upon it.

"Well, it can't get worse than this."

"You wait here. I'm going to…"

Aeron hovered in the doorway, silently sending thanks she didn't need to follow. She didn't think she'd be able to handle what was beneath that sheet. Mason moved slowly, as though afraid to disturb the scene when a sudden thought came to her.

"Mase—who sent you here to check this." She hadn't questioned when he invited her, but she should have reached out to her father —what if it was a trap? Her pulse quickened, and she peered down the hallway. There were no cameras to record them, but there could still be eyes on them.

"Don't worry, Aeron. This is sanctioned." That didn't answer her question. He reached the crib and used a gloved hand to lift the sheet. His face paled, and he turned away, still holding the sheet up. After a steadying breath, he scrunched his face and looked again. For Mason to turn away—he'd seen some vile things in his time.

Aeron backed up, looking back down the hall. This was pure

calculated chaos. Broken picture frames littered the floor, a house plant knocked over, the vase broken and dirt peppering the hallway, disturbed by the police that had come and gone. Mason rejoined her, slipping a tiny trinket into his jacket pocket.

"What's that?"

"Might be our first lead. I gifted them a nanny cam when Ryan was born. Because it doesn't transmit a signal, it's harder to detect."

"That's good then," Aeron said, following him to the next room, "all things considered."

"Let's hope so."

34

LUKE

"*P*our me some coffee?" Decius called.

Luke looked up from the eggs he was frying. Decius had brought the computers as promised. He pushed around the dirty dishes until he found one not as dirty for the eggs. The coffee maker hissed when droplets of water splashed on it as he shook out a freshly rinsed mug. He poured the liquid gold, carrying it over.

"Anything?" he asked, Decius accepting the scalding gift as he sat down.

"Perry definitely opened some more doors for us, but I can't pinpoint anything new. Maybe he will have more luck when he gets back. Have you found anything?" Decius glanced to the stack of half-empty storage containers pulled from Luke's father's office. Journals and spreadsheets open across the floor, none telling him how to find Mr. Seward. A few had pointed to some off-shore accounts with a gracious amount of money set aside, though.

"Not yet. If they did have information on your dad, it's not stored here." He took a bite of eggs, his stomach thanking him for feeding it anything other than black coffee.

The door to the apartment swung open, Perry with his phone

glued to his ear. "I don't have a say in this, and you know it. Stop yelling at me. K—" He froze, eyes falling to Decius. "I'll let him know, mom. Okay."

"Everything good?" Luke asked, eggs halfway to his mouth.

Katherine's return to D.C. left him on edge. Perry didn't know the extent of the work he did for their Granddad. He knew that Luke disposed of families, but he'd been gone while Luke fought through the agony of each kill, Katherine piecing him back together—for better or worse. She'd witnessed his breakdowns and breakthroughs; she'd anchored him. Both of them had people they were trying to save—or in her case, avenge. Perry didn't have the same at stake as they did—the life of someone you love in constant danger based on your reactions and words—it's why he wasn't slated for Senior Assassin: he didn't have enough to lose.

"Yeah. My mom just wanted to tell you to check in once in a while. She worries about you."

"Your mom is so nice," Decius said, sipping his coffee. "Want to be just as nice and take this over? I've flagged several files that look promising, but I wasn't going to try and open them."

"Not a problem. Where are you off to?"

A weighted sigh escaped him. "South America."

"South America?"

"I have a plane leaving in about two hours."

"We don't have outposts in South America," Perry said, forehead crinkling. "What are you into, Dee?" The concern that made Perry the best team lead seeped through.

"I was assigned to complete my father's outstanding cases. Most of them are out of the country. Is that not normal?"

Luke and Perry exchanged a look. They had no idea what constituted normal—and keeping Decius busy and in danger gave his Granddad another leveraging angle. "I'm sure for him it is," Luke assured. "Did my Granddad say anything else?"

"Don't get caught."

"Isn't that the unspoken Legacy motto?" Perry joked, taking the now vacant seat in front of the computer.

They waited until Decius had cleared out before speaking. "Katherine wants to know how you're holding up. You haven't called."

"And I don't plan on it." Luke took a seat on the side of the couch near the computer.

"Where are the kids?"

"Kids?"

"The Smiths kids. You did…"

"Yeah," Luke said. "I got them out. I moved them into a safe house with Dominic in Jersey."

"So fat chance of us getting Dominic in here then to help with these."

"One issue at a time, Perry." He rolled his neck a few times.

"Was it easier this time? Since you didn't actually have to…" Perry trailed off, not looking at Luke, his eyes on the screen. Katherine would have asked if he hesitated. What was he thinking? What could have gone worse? She dug into him, pulling out answers he didn't want to give.

"Yes, and no. It gets easier each time," Luke said, pulling back the chill from running down his spine. The logistics of moving dead bodies and saving the kids, but killing the parents, and then making it look like he killed everyone… the thought crossed his mind it would have been easier to just kill everyone and be done with it. The balloon in his chest throbbed at the thought. For half a second, he considered just killing those kids.

"But they're good?" Perry asked again.

"Alive, yes. Out of immediate danger, yes. But good? No. Those kids will never be good. I don't even know if…"

He stopped himself, unable to voice to Perry his real fear: What if Granddad had been right? Was it really better to save them? They were going to grow up alone, with vengeance seared into their small hearts. The infant would have no idea, but six-year-old Eliza? She knew he was up to no good when he swept her away from the house. She will remember that he saved her and let her parents die. What if she ever found out what he'd really done? Fake her and her brother's deaths and then murder their parents.

"What have you pulled from the files?"

"Well, Mr. Seward was definitely watching the accounts of every Legacy member. I have found ghost traces of names and partial account numbers I've managed to cross-reference. However —all this says is that he was keeping tabs. There is no trace of him touching any of the money."

"Keep digging. We know what he's capable of and what he's been doing. What I need is a link to him now. Or a link to the techie so we can find that money."

Luke took a seat on the living room floor amidst the boxes. He hadn't told Perry or Kat about the money he'd found—not until he knew if he could even access it. And it didn't seem like too bad of an idea to have grab and go cash off the grid. He pulled out a stack of papers from one of the plain gray filing cabinets and then put them right back in.

He didn't want to be doing this, sifting through his parent's papers. He needed to get out and do something. His phone bounced in his pocket: Alexis.

"Shit." A call from that part of the crew meant he'd neglected them for too long. "Hello?"

"Hi." Her voice was light, almost musical. "I have the unpublished schedules for the senator for this weekend."

"Good. Where's Cage?"

"He's on his way to the Institute now with them. Elij—Mr. Wayward wanted them hand-delivered."

"Nice work," Luke said. But hadn't missed her near slip calling Granddad by his first name. She was closer to the inside than was comfortable. It was time for Alexis and Cage to find themselves off his grid.

"Is there anything else I could do?" He could hear the eagerness in her by the light lift of her words.

"How about drinks?" She didn't answer. "Ali?" he prodded, using a nickname to pull a yes out of her. Bring them close, then throw them out.

"I'd like that," she finally answered.

"Good. I'll call you later." He hung up.

"I'll be back," Perry said, heading for the door.

"Where are you going?"

"Mason asked me to step in for him with Aeron. Did you want me to…"

Luke shook his head, waving Perry out. He couldn't think about Aeron. Too many lies blocked him from being with her how he wanted to be—how his parents had been. He pulled his phone out again and called Katherine back.

"Make it quick," she said.

"Two." They'd created a code before she'd left. Make it quick=not safe to talk. And a number would mean how many kids they saved. "It's been nearly two days, and you haven't even tried to call," he covered.

"Being back home reminds me a lot of what I can and can't do. I can't control the weather, but I can control not having to talk to you on a daily basis. It's been nice."

Luke laughed. "I'm taking Alexis out for drinks."

Her tone became serious. "That's a bad idea."

"I didn't ask for your opinion on it."

"Then why tell me?"

"Do you think she will be dragged back to D.C. anytime soon?"

Hesitation met him. "No. I asked for them to come back. He likes them right where they're at."

Crap. Luke picked at his nails, looking around his bedroom. He'd wandered in without realizing it.

"Have you located the package?" she asked.

"No," he admitted. "I think it's time."

She sucked a breath in. "Not yet, Luke. You only just began. To be honest, I think you have a few more in you. You're a star, now. Shine for a bit."

A groan escaped him. Of course, she was right. They'd only saved two children. By their estimate, there were about ten more families with a chance of being eliminated with children too young to be at the Institute. He was really just getting started.

"I know." But what he really wanted was to confess to Katherine, confess his fears about how close he'd come to throwing the mission last night. How much easier life would be if he just quit fighting everyone. If he just took his parent's money and ran far away with Aeron. But he couldn't do that over the phone.

"Just handle it," Katherine said as a replacement for goodbye and hung up.

"Hello? Kat?" Irrational anger seared through him. She couldn't talk. Of course, she couldn't talk, she was running Legacy Inc., and he was stuck in this shithole mess. "You've got to be kidding!" he yelled and tossed the phone across the room. In. Out. In. Out. He reeled the emotions back into place, something that was harder to do each time he lost hold of them.

*A*eron leaned against the half-pipe in the training area, waiting for Perry or Mason. She couldn't train like she wanted—running the rooftops, high-intensity knife fighting drills, and full contact sparring with Mason, but she could still strength train and go to the range. The training area echoed around her, unusually empty for a Tuesday afternoon.

"Aeron?"

Her head snapped toward Perry's voice. She adjusted her crutches and met him in the middle of the room. "You're late."

"I didn't expect you to show," Perry admitted. "I was in the family residence when they paged me."

"Well, with all things considered, I don't have much else going on, and I've been cooped up since the accident." The words tasted sour in her mouth.

"Bull." Aeron looked up at him, and his eyebrows pulled together. "I'm not sure what happened that night, but I know you well enough to know that it was no accident." She didn't answer. "What you should do is go upstairs and talk to Luke. He's been pretty torn up since—"

Aeron's breath caught in her chest. "He's here?"

"Of course he's here—he lives here. Where did you think he sulked off to? Aruba?"

Where else would he be? She thought maybe he'd gone back to the mansion or had bunked with Katherine at the hotel. But she didn't think he'd be here since no one had seen him around.

"Listen, he's been moping around for weeks and is driving me insane. If you ask me, he's a little overdramatic."

Aeron's lips twitched at the idea of Luke being overdramatic. An image of Luke at last year's Halloween party crept into her mind: thick, black eye-liner, with matching lipstick; netted black tank and matching wings. He had been the dark angel to her white one. Had that only been a year ago?

"I've never seen him like this," Perry said, whisking the image away. "And he'll kill me for saying this, but I think you should go see him."

"He doesn't want to see me."

"Right now, he doesn't know what he wants." Perry dug his hands in his pocket, his eyes begging her to help him. The worry lines by his eyes were so far from the laugh lines he had at the end of last year. What had they been doing? "Please?"

Luke asked her to wait for him to come for her, but she was done waiting around. "Yeah. Okay."

She hesitated outside the Wayward Family residence. Knocking felt weird. She'd never knocked before. Not knowing if it would work still, Aeron stepped in front of the retinal scan. It whirled to life and the door unlocked. She pushed it open.

"Hello?" No one answered. She stepped into the entryway, closing the door silently behind her. The house was a mess. The kitchen counter on the left had plates and coffee cups scattered everywhere. The living room had boxes strewn across the couches and floor, and by the TV sat a very familiar computer. Her pulse jumped as Darth Vader bounced around the screen. Ivan's missing computer.

Luke's voice pulled her down the hallway, though. Pictures of his parents and their families together on vacation still hung on the walls, dust clinging to the baseboards for dear life as her crutches sunk into it. He'd been staying here, but not living here. She neared the door, Luke's words becoming more distinct.

"Hello? Kat? You've got to be kidding!" She reached his room.

He stood at the window, the afternoon sun silhouetting him. He released a frustrated yell and chucked the phone across the room. It hit the wall near the door and fell at Aeron's feet.

She cleared her throat, announcing herself, and he snapped his head up. His face softened for a second before becoming clear of any emotion at all, sending a chill down her spine.

"Is this why you haven't gotten any of my messages?" she asked, moving the broken phone with one of her crutches.

"What are you doing here?" The question sounded accusatory.

"Well, you see, I have a class downstairs, but I needed to pee, so I'm looking for a bathroom, and I got lost."

He gave the smallest hint of a smile. "How's your ankle?" he asked.

"Still broken," she said, hovering in the doorway. "How's the fixing?"

Confusion flitted across his eyebrows.

"You know, this big mess you created that you need to fix before you can talk to me again?" Sarcasm coated her words. "You just left me there to fend for myself against—" she stopped herself. She'd almost said Katherine.

He raised an eyebrow at her. "Aeron—"

"Listen." She exhaled sharply, getting back on point. "I'm not here to fight or even ask you why you abandoned me when I really could have used someone over the past few weeks."

"Then why are you here?"

She entered the room uninvited and dropped down on his

unmade bed, tossing her crutches to the ground. "The team is falling apart. You're gone. Decius is gone. I'm broken. You wanted something to fix—fix this. Fix us. Fix me."

"I'm trying." He stepped out of the shadow. Purple bags hung beneath his eyes, and Aeron wondered if he had lost his razor weeks ago and was just too lazy to look for it.

"You look like crap," she said bluntly. "When was the last time you showered?" He paused and looked as if he were actually thinking about it.

"I'm not sure. What day is it?" he asked.

She scrunched her nose up. "The big Halloween bash is tomorrow. Please tell me you haven't decided to go as a bum. I don't do bum well."

His lips twitched, but he managed to keep his face serious. "What is it you want from me, Aeron."

She wanted a lot from him, but she'd settle for getting everyone in the same room again. "I want you to come to the party."

Luke didn't say anything. Instead, he picked up her crutches and walked to the door, holding them out. She raised her eyebrows.

"I'll think about it."

"Excuse me?"

"This isn't a good time. I have business to take care of, and my Granddad is expecting me at a meeting tonight."

"Does this have to do with who killed your parents?" She hadn't broached the topic since their first mission.

"Yes." His answer was short, clearly his end to the conversation.

"And my father? You're still looking for him?"

He didn't answer.

Aeron stood and gimped to the door, the rejection cutting into her chest. She took the crutches as her cheeks and eyes burned. She ducked her head to hide her face.

"Luke..." What could she say to him? She had come up here to get him to come home. But rejection never crossed her mind. A hand slipped beneath her chin, and she allowed it to lift her face.

"Aeron," he breathed, his face inches from hers. At least he still managed to brush his teeth. She closed her eyes and leaned into his kiss. Warmth spread through her body. She dropped the crutches again and wrapped her arms around him. Her hand reached up, tangling in his messy hair, and she found the additional facial hair roughly sexy.

She missed the security of his arms around her. He broke the kiss and placed another one in her hair, holding her tight.

"What are you wearing tomorrow?" he asked, lips still pressed against her head.

"Hmm?"

"The Halloween Bash. I could use some fun. What's your costume? We always coordinate."

She smiled into his chest. "How does a banana sound."

He chuckled. "Sexy."

He walked her back out to the main door, her eyes lingering over the mess. "What's going on in here?"

"Research."

"And the computer?" She peered around him, and he turned to look.

"Decius found it at one of your father's safe-houses. We can't seem to crack it, though." His eyes lit up like a light bulb when he turned to her. "But that techie you've been chasing down. Did he work with your father?"

Aeron slid her unsure face into place before answering. Another opportunity to get them close to Mr. Wayward. She'd just have to convince Ivan to go along. To hell with her father. This was no longer his call. "You know, I'm not sure, but it's possible. Want me to bring him in?"

His smile broadened. "That would be extremely helpful."

She lifted her face, and he leaned down for the kiss. "I'll see you tomorrow."

She dialed Ivan on the way back to the apartment, mind racing with the possibilities. Her dad would never agree, but who knew what they would find when they cracked the computer.

"Darth. What are you doing tomorrow night?" She was bursting to tell him, but this was a face-to-face conversation.

"Hello, Aeron. How are you doing? Good? That's great. Me too," Ivan said rapidly. "Any progress decrypting the files and piecing together anything useful? No, Aeron. I haven't—thanks for asking, though. I know how important it is to you. You know what's important to me? Caffeine. Did you know that my energy drinks are like contraband in this house? I'm losing my mind."

"Wow, Darth," Aeron laughed. "I'm sorry to hear that."

"Was that laughter I heard from the serious Aeron Seward? What's up with that?"

"I have some really good news for you. Come to the Halloween costume party at Club Sapphire tomorrow night. Be there or be square."

36

LUKE

A loud knock pulled Luke from sleep. He pushed the pillow off his face and caught himself from falling from the couch. When had he fallen asleep? The loud rap on the door sounded again.

"Yeah, yeah," Luke mumbled. "I'm coming!" He rubbed the sleep from his eyes and tapped the monitor by the door to see who it was. Mason waited, eyes boring into the camera and hands deep into his jeans pockets. A visit from the Guardian. Either his Granddad was pissed, or someone was dead. He yanked the door open.

"We need to talk." Mason brushed past him, not waiting for an invitation.

"Yeah. Come on in," Luke said under his breath, closing the door behind and following him to the kitchen, where Mason scoured the cabinets.

"Can I help you find something?" Luke crossed his arms and leaned against the counter. No one was dead—surely that would have been breaking news.

"Booze."

"Whiskey is above the sink." Luke watched as he redirected for the whiskey. Mason rinsed out two coffee mugs and poured liberal amounts of liquid into them, holding one out to Luke.

"Drink."

Luke stared into the dark mug, the whiskey looking like coffee, but the intense scent not allowing his mind to be fooled. "No, thank you."

"Suit yourself," Mason said, and took a long gulp before his blue gaze bored into him. "I know you've been killing Legacy families and children."

Luke's heart froze in his chest. The mug slipped from his grasp, cracking against the floor, whiskey drenching his sweatpants. His eyes stayed glued on Mason.

"The Jones. The Pallards. The Finches. The Woodsworths. The Peters. The Smiths." He ticked them off on his fingers. "Just to name a few."

"I have no idea what you're talking about," Luke lied, icicles boring into him from every direction. He focused on the living person in front of him.

Mason poured another mug of whiskey and held it out to him. "But not all the Smiths. Where are the children?"

Luke accepted the cup but again refused to drink. This was a trap. How could his Granddad know he didn't kill all the Smiths? He'd been meticulous in the planning, Perry and Shannon ensuring the blood samples and the records matched the new bodies. Unless they hadn't…

"Words would be wise, Luke," Mason advised. "I can only help if you are clear with me. I'm not here for your Granddad. I'm not here as a Legacy member. I am here as your Guardian."

Luke swallowed around the ball forming in his throat and put the mug down. This was another test. Like Dave. Like Rosemary.

Mason downed his drink and slammed the mug on the counter. Luke jumped, his heart kick-starting. "The Legacy is dying, Luke, at your hand. I think I deserve an answer."

"I think you need to remember who you're talking to," Luke

said, finding his voice. He placed the mug down gently. If this was a test, he needed to pass. Aeron was too vulnerable right now. If this wasn't a test, then he had fucked up somewhere along the line, and it wouldn't be long until Rosemary or his Granddad found out. "Those are some big accusations you are making against your next Senior. I'd think twice before saying anything else."

A soft laugh left Mason. He rubbed the back of his neck, the tell-tale sign he had so much more to say but would keep it to himself—for now. "You are too smart to be in his pocket, Luke. You are also very alone right now. If your parents could see you, they'd be rolling in the graves."

The jibe at his parents slammed his gut. "Get out!"

"Not until I know what you did with those children."

"I didn't do anything with them," Luke denied, but his pulse continued to race. He needed to call the others. Warn them they'd messed up. He had to call Katherine—Aeron. What if it was too late? Too late to save her, too late to tell her?

"You need to—"

"Yes. I need to go. I heard you. But I'm not leaving. Killing for him will only keep Aeron alive for so long. What you're doing now? It will get her killed. And probably Decius. Once they're dead, how long do you think you'll last without any leverage over you? The only reason Perry is still breathing is because his mother is alive."

Luke's brain went into overdrive. Of course—Perry's mother was his reason, but not nearly a strong enough motivator to his Granddad to force someone to kill for. And Rosemary kept Katherine just shy of despicable, in her own caring way.

"I swore an oath to your parents, Luke. I intend to pay my debt, be it with my soul. However—I'm more interested in salvaging what is left of yours. Where are those children?"

"How do you know it's safe?" Luke's eyes roamed the room.

"Because I trained you," Mason said with a smile. His eyes finally roamed the room, too, falling on the piles of boxes and the computer. "Where did you get that?" He moved toward the computer. Luke hopped over the counter and intercepted him, standing between them. He wanted to trust Mason. He wanted a lot of things right now. "Confiscated it. It's for a case for my Granddad."

"And you're hiding it here?"

"Storing it," Luke answered too quickly, but Mason dropped the subject.

"Luke, please let me help you."

'Yes' seemed too easy an answer to give. "Why? And don't talk to me about debt."

"Because there are other options besides killing your own for your sociopathic relative." Mason moved to the vast amount of boxes in the living room, glancing in each one. He'd been close with Luke's parents; maybe he knew where Mr. Seward was.

"Do you know where Aeron's dad is?"

Mason spun around, hands deep in the pockets again. "What is that worth to you?"

"I'm not in the riddling mood, Mason. If you know where he is and are withholding, you are guilty of treason against the Legacy. He is priority number one."

"And I'm sure our Senior Assassin would find it interesting Perry visited the coding room the day the Smiths turned up dead. I wonder what he could unearth with a little direction."

Luke stared daggers at him.

"I didn't come unprepared, Luke. But I'm not here to manipulate you or make your life harder, or put any of you in danger. I want the opposite. I want to help. Where are you stashing the children?"

Luke could tell Mason everything. He could have an ally—and even a connection to Mr. Seward. But too many lives rested on his shoulders at the moment, and he just shook his head.

Mason gave a disappointed laugh. "Perry does not know I know. And as far as he is concerned, I'm diligently working angles for your Granddad. I made an oath to protect a young boy and his two best friends until the day I died. But you're no longer a young boy,

Luke, and the deeper you go into the darkness, the less I can do to save you." He looked around one more time, the flitting glimpse of regret on his face before he walked past Luke and left.

Luke pulled out his phone, dialing Katherine.

"What is it?" She asked, sleep in her voice.

"We missed something. How safe is it with Dom?"

"What?" Katherine's voice was more alert.

"Someone knows about the body switch. I need you here. I need you back here." His pulse raced at this confession because with Katherine in D.C., he really was alone and toeing the edge of right and easy. The thought again crossed his mind that saving the kids was not worth the danger—but he knew that was wrong.

"You don't *need* me. What's really going on?"

She was right. He needed a favor. "Can you make me a promise?" He squeezed his eyes shut, envisioning Aeron in her favorite jeans and white tank laughing, carefree, and breathing. He took her silence as a yes. "Promise me that Aeron will live, no matter what."

"I've already…"

"Because she *has* to. I don't know that I can keep going like this —the pressure, the fear." He swallowed, sure Katherine could hear his heart pounding.

"Luke? Is everything okay?"

"No. No, it's not. If you hadn't left Gunnar…I would have…" He could see Katherine's face in his mind, fingers pinching the bridge of her nose, eyes scrunched closed, deep breathing to keep her voice level.

"I'll be back as soon as I can," Katherine said. "Keep your shit together until then."

37

AERON

*A*eron tugged at her yellow mini skirt and adjusted the matching cropped blazer.

"Stop moving," Shannon ordered, pushing bobby pins into Aeron's head to hold the banana-peel-hat in place.

They waited outside the back entrance to Club Sapphire—one of their more frequented clubs in the city. The bass shook the metal door while they waited for everyone else.

"Do you think they will show?" Shannon asked.

"They better," Aeron said. "I didn't wrap my ankle this tightly to sit around and watch TV."

"Done."

Aeron reached up and felt it. "Thanks."

"So, what are we doing here?" Lesley asked.

"You didn't fill her in?" Shannon raised an eyebrow.

"Fill me in on what?" Lesley scanned the area nervously.

"On the crazy amount of fun you're going to have tonight!" Justin yelled behind her. Lesley jumped, spun around, and landed a kick to his knee. "Ow!"

"Oh, I'm sorry!" Lesley tried to help him. He laughed and shook her off.

"I'm fine. You've got a wicked kick, though." He stood and straightened his ripped pants.

"What are you?" Shannon asked.

"Zombie…" Justin slacked his face and lethargically headed toward them.

"Where's Dee?" Aeron looked around in the shadows. As if on cue, a figure dressed in a black ninja suit entered the alleyway. Decius dressed as a ninja every year since he was five. He pulled off his hood just feet from them.

"What are you supposed to be?" he asked Aeron.

"I'm a banana! How come no one can figure it out?"

Justin laughed. "I just want to see what you have Luke in this year."

"Well, I don't know if he's coming." Aeron's heart sank, and she checked her watch.

"He'll be here," Decius said. "We should head inside."

Aeron banged on the door three times and waited. The muffled music blasted clear as Marcus, the club owner, pushed the door open.

"If it isn't my favorite group of deadly killers. It's been a while." He stepped aside and let them in. "Let's keep the kidnapping and mayhem to a minimum tonight?"

"We're here just for the party, Marc," Decius assured and handed him an envelope. Marcus peeked inside and then nodded.

"Enjoy your evening."

They headed to their private room next to the bar, Aeron taking each step slowly and deliberately. The last few years, they'd become acquainted with Marcus after using Club Sapphire multiple times as a rounding area for targets. The chaotic scene made it easy to corner and kidnap someone before anyone noticed. The bartenders waved at Justin as they entered.

"I'll get drinks," he said. "Any special orders?"

"Virgins, please," Decius said. Justin's smile faltered.

"What did that mean?" Lesley asked Shannon.

"It means Decius just pulled rank, and we're not allowed to drink yet."

Aeron sent Decius a questioning look, but he avoided her gaze. The music dulled when the door shut in the sound-proof room. They piled onto the couches in the rectangle room. A long one-way mirror created a moving picture of moving bodies on the dance floor.

Justin placed the drinks on the low table and sat next to Decius, who they turned to expectantly.

"Drink," he said, sitting back and not touching his own. "We're missing one person."

Aeron sat and watched the people through the window. The mass of bodies moved as one, but each small group inside the mass told their own story. The woman dressed as a fox tugged on a larger man's arm, but his attention stayed focused on the lady he was talking to—but there wasn't a physical connection between them. The fox-woman was jealous over nothing.

The door opened, and Aeron looked up. Her stomach lurched as Luke entered. He wore a brown suit and managed to look gorgeous in a pair of monkey ears. His apprehensive look around the room drew Aeron's gaze to Decius, who stood, grabbing Luke's forearm and pulling him into a hug.

"All right, guys, listen up." The team gathered around him. "Firstly, thank you, Aeron, for getting us all here. It has been too long since we just went out." Aeron nodded in response but said nothing. Something was off. "Next, I want to tell you that I am stepping aside as Team Lead."

"You're what?!" Aeron said, standing before she realized, pain shooting down her leg. All eyes turned to her. "Thank you for the heads up." She crossed her arms, but he ignored her.

"With my responsibilities to my family Legacy growing overnight, I cannot, with a clear conscience, lead you. My focus is too divided."

Everyone started speaking at once, except for Aeron. She stared

at her brother, mouth open. How could he make that kind of decision without telling her? He waved his hands again for silence.

"I'm passing the Team Lead over to Luke." The attention
swerved to him. His apprehension deepened. He never wanted the
position. Aeron remembered Luke handing it to Decius, begging
him to take the Lead before they'd broke for summer.

Justin stood up and patted him on the back, but Luke did not
share his enthusiasm. Decius picked up his drink, the group
following suit.

"To Luke—may you lead our team ferociously, fearlessly, and
freely." They all raised their glass and took a sip.

"So, what now?" Lesley asked.

"Now," Decius said smiling, "I grab us some real drinks, and we
enjoy the night. Except for you, Les. Just one drink. C'mon."

Lesley laughed and followed Decius out of the room, the music
blaring for a moment before the door closed again. Aeron stared
after them, and Luke moved beside her.

"Not the costume I was envisioning," she admitted.

"Well, I figured I'd be taken more seriously as the Lead dressed
like this than a full monkey suit." He put his arm around her, and
she leaned into him. "Plus, I can't stay long. I have stuff to do
tonight."

"Stuff?" Aeron asked. Luke's schedule was busier than Decius'.
How did him taking the Lead make any more sense than Decius
staying on? She kept quiet, though.

He checked his watch. "Yeah. Last-minute things for my
Granddad before I take the full reins from Dee tomorrow. Want to
sit?"

She nodded, and they found a spot on the couch. Music
blasted for a moment when Perry entered. He waved and then
looked past them. Aeron turned to see Shannon blush as he
approached.

"About time," Luke said in her ear. The sensation sent chills
down her body. "I've been telling him for months if he wanted to

ask her out, he should just do it already. You know, since we're breaking all the dating rules."

Aeron watched Perry lead Shannon out, leaving the room to her and Luke. She leaned into the nook of his arm.

"Where's your cast?" Luke asked, placing a hand on her leg.

"I had it taken off after I saw you."

"How about a walking cast?"

"You sound like Shannon," Aeron said, rolling her eyes. "It's at home. I'm wrapped tight, have a little faith."

"I'll always have faith in you." She could feel the tension beneath his words. "I'm sorry about the other day."

She shook her head against his chest. "No apologies," she said. He hugged her closer, and her body relaxed the way it always did around him.

His fingers drew absent-minded circles on her shoulder, and Aeron relished the calm and security and comfort of the silence. A flash of blond hair in the window caught Aeron's attention. She stiffened. The pixie-blond from the hotel. The faded memory of her returned in sharp focus—the coy touches and playful looks that passed between Luke and her. What was her name? Alexis.

Luke looked at his watch and placed a kiss on the top of her head. "I have to get going."

Aeron tore her eyes from the girl, now using the mirror to fix her hair, and looked up at Luke. "Are you moving back home?" He helped her to her feet.

"I'll be home for breakfast tomorrow. I told my Granddad I need to concentrate on this. The team."

"And he was okay with that?" Aeron doubted Luke told his granddad much of anything.

"Not really," Luke laughed. "But what's he going to do, kill me?" Aeron's face paled. "I'm more than ready to run the Legacy. I just have loose ends to tie up. Are you alright?"

A wave of dizziness swept over her, and she swayed. They needed to take down Mr. Wayward—yesterday.

"Yeah. We'll be fine if your Granddad needs you. Senior Assassin and all—I'm sure he's got a full plate."

"He's got more help than you think," Luke said. He kissed her, gently at first, the kiss deepening until she could hardly breathe. "I'll see you in the morning." She watched him go, the music piercing her eardrums as he exited. Alexis looked over and moved toward him, disappearing from view.

Her stomach heaved as a jealous wave raged through her. She'd forgotten about Alexis. No longer in a partying mood, she headed for the door. Shannon caught her as she passed the bar, heading for the back alleyway.

"Where'd Luke go?" Shannon asked in her ear.

"Finishing business with his Granddad. Where's Perry?" Aeron replied.

"He followed after Luke but didn't say much. Where are you going?" Her voice held an accusation in there. "This was your idea."

Aeron looked around the crowded club. It had been her idea.

"I'm going to—"

"Don't leave." Shannon's eyes pleaded with her. Aeron looked back. She'd never be able to follow them at this point.

"Get me a drink," Aeron said and dropped in the seat beside her.

Shannon's face lit up, and she leaned forward, getting the bartender's attention.

Aeron shook her head and turned to find the rest of the group and bumped into a tall, hooded figure. Hands reached out, and Aeron automatically attempted to twist away, but the hooded figure countered each move, almost before she made them.

"AERON!" the figure yelled. "Stop! It's me!" Ivan let the hood fall off his face for just the slightest moment.

"Darth! What the hell."

"You invited me, remember?"

"I know."

Shannon tapped her on the shoulder and handed her a drink. Ivan retreated a few paces as Aeron turned, Perry by her side again.

"Why don't you guys go dance? I'll wait here."

"No," Shannon said.

"Yes," Aeron insisted. "I can't do much with this foot anyways. I'm not leaving."

"Okay, but just one dance." Shannon pulled Perry toward the dance floor, and Aeron sat down, motioning Ivan to join her. Once Shannon started dancing, they'd have to drag her home.

"Nice costume," she said. "What are you supposed to be anyways?"

"A Dementor," Ivan said, gliding to the seat next to her. She scooted her stool closer.

"Tell me you found something."

He shook his head. "Nothing substantial."

"And the outcast members?"

Ivan leaned in close to her ear. "Most won't talk."

Aeron's pulse thumped in time to the bass. She took a sip of her drink and grimaced, looking to the dance floor. The group congregated around Shannon and Perry, laughing and looking like normal people.

"I found your computers," she said. The room seemed to mute as Ivan meet her gaze. "They're looking for you to help them, Luke and Decius. There's a window if you want it."

Ivan shook his head. "I have to run it by your dad. I won't do it without him."

Aeron nodded, jealousy grappling with her heart. Ivan was closer to her dad than she could ever be.

"One last thing. I need you to run a check for me. On a female named Alexis."

"Last name?"

"I don't have one. She was at the Rose Way that night and here again tonight. And the very first night back, she was on the train with me. She's working with Luke."

"Description?"

"Petite, pixie-cut blond hair. If you hack the footage from

tonight," she drew a circle in the air, "you might find her." She could feel the contempt in her voice and hated it.

Ivan stiffened and stood. "I'll let you know what I find." He left without warning, gliding through the crowd until he disappeared.

38

LUKE

*L*uke looked around the safe house, pizza boxes strewn about and computer monitors placed throughout the living room. The kids he'd managed to save puttering around on the upper level with Gunnar. Six in total under the age of ten. He hoped to add the remaining five without incident. Kids over the age of 10 were already training at the Legacy and already dead: training accidents that tracked over the past three years. Granddad had been planning this dismantle for much longer than he wanted Luke to believe.

Dominic pushed the newest files from Katherine toward him. He flipped them open, scanning the reports.

"What is this?" he asked.

"Our very own hit list. These are the most influential players in Legacy Inc. All Underworlders. All vile as shit. They're who we're up against."

"This is who took out Legacy members?" Luke asked, scanning the crimes associated with each initial and set of numbers. Rape. Murder. Torture. His gut turned. At least he was giving quick, painless deaths when he needed to. But the rap sheet on these people… Luke would eliminate them on principle.

"Rosemary handled that. No. These are the top paid assets at the moment. They get the job done, no questions asked."

"Making that much, I can see why. Some of these people are making seven figures. Where is that money coming from?"

"Whoever paid for the hit. Legacy Inc. is only taking 30%; the rest goes to the killer."

The Legacy took care of every need Luke ever had. Clothes, cars, food, expense account. When he needed money to break out from beneath his Granddad, it proved more difficult than he expected. He thought a few slips of the keystrokes and they could fund their project—but it hadn't worked that way at all. Instead, he was entangled with Rosemary and worried every second of the day Aeron would pay for the $5.5 million that was missing.

"No wonder Legacy Inc. took off. I should go to D.C. and take a few hits. We'd have no problem funneling money then."

Dominic laughed. "You wouldn't make a dime. The family doesn't get paid—it's why Katherine needed your help, to begin with."

Of course not. The first family was kept on a short leash. Money meant the ability to get away…and no one got away from his Granddad.

His phone buzzed. Perry calling from the family residence at the Institute. "What's up?"

"I found the money."

Luke's stomach jolted. Speaking of money. "Which set?"

"Finchs'. It's gone, Luke. Long gone."

"Damn." He knew finding it would be a long shot, but now he had nothing for Rosemary. "What happened to it?"

"Looks like it was gambled away. Steven was a Legacy Inc. asset, according to what I've found."

Luke scanned the file in front of him. The assets were coded, initials and numbers; FB7463; GG8896; AK9987. There were easily two dozen of them with stats and financials listed for each. But only one on the list had an 'S': SD6498. The last hit, they made $800,000.

"Steven D?" Luke asked.

"Dempsey," Perry confirmed. "You got the latest file?"

"Yeah. We're not going to be able to stop what Legacy Inc. has become. I don't think Katherine realized what it had become. We'll have killers hunting us for the rest of our lives. We're going to need a new plan."

"So, we focus on stopping it here first and worry about D.C. later. How are the little assets?"

"They aren't little assets," Luke growled. "They seem content. Dominic has a few people taking care of them. If my numbers are right, I have two more families to complete in the next few weeks, and that's it. Everyone else is either single or just married, no kids." Luke hated how casual those words left him. But the numbness had taken over. He'd killed innocent people—children—and he couldn't get any lower than that.

"Speaking of," Dominic interrupted, "I need the medical records ASAP."

"I'll call Shan," Perry said over the phone.

"What about the money?" Luke asked, returning to the origin of the call.

"We aren't going to get it back. However, I can move money around and make it appear that Rosemary has been skimming. There are amazing programs on this computer." Perry had finally broken the last firewalls on the confiscated computer. They'd found little data, as it had been wiped with the first attempt to breach the firewall—but the programs that had been written were still intact.

"No," Luke said immediately. He was done moving money around. "She can dig her own grave without our help."

Luke left the safe house, never putting eyes on the children. Hearing them move in the rooms above eased his soul and reminded him it *was* worth it.

He found Shannon at the coffee shop, his steaming mug already waiting for him. He slipped into the booth, his eyes flicking to ensure no one took particular interest in them.

"You're late." She sipped her chai tea, eyes narrowed.

"Dom needs the files." Luke nodded, wrapping his hands around the mug, his flesh burning at the touch. Shannon made accessing the medical records and switching them out a breeze, and a small nub of guilt ate away at him. Yes, she decided to join their coupe. Yes, she knew that once they were discovered, she would be an enemy of the Legacy, but she was an enemy already—on a list, waiting to be killed like all the others. But they hadn't spoken about that part, where her family would eventually come across his list to eliminate.

The files appeared on the table. Luke folded them and slipped them inside his jacket. He didn't need to read them. He already knew they needed two bodies, African American, ages 8 and 10. The files were more for Dominic to be able to add on or remove any glaring birthmarks or scars to the bodies before Luke switched them out. Small details like blood type or height were easy to manipulate in the system. Even eye color could be doctored. But memorable features must remain the same, such as Penelope's birthmark on her left cheek. One would think it wouldn't really matter—the Cleaners handling the cover-ups—but he knew better than to be sloppy in any aspect. A single thread out of place would unravel the entire tapestry.

"What are you going to do if your luck runs out and he can't find a match?" Shannon asked.

"Improvise." Luke refused the notion of not having a match, afraid the thought alone would make it so. Instead, he changed the topic. "The money is gone. Gambled away. I'm going to have to come clean to him about it."

"What about the money from your parents?"

Luke turned his gaze outside, watching the people bustling to wherever their simple lives took them. What would they do with six million dollars? He'd squirreled it away in an offshore account. Only Shannon knew this fascinating fact because having someone not blood-related or in immediate danger know about his triple life gave him perspective. She called bullshit on his excuses and reminded him more than just Aeron mattered.

"It was an escape fund. I've thought about just giving it to Rosemary briefly, but if we need to buy off Legacy Inc.'s most deadly? We're going to need a lot more than six mil."

"I think it's time to tell Dee." The piercing stare she sent held his tongue for a moment. His automatic answer was no. He and Decius worked miracles together, and he couldn't destroy his best friend that way.

"Not yet. I need—"

"This isn't just about what you need!" Shannon slammed her fist down. "We're a fucking team for a reason because the interests of the whole—for each other—are more important than our own. You've seemed to have forgotten that." She grabbed her bag from beside her and stood, lowering her voice to a whisper. "I've always trusted you with my life. I have blindly jumped from buildings on your word that I wouldn't be impaled upon impact. I have been willingly shot—by you—while playing hostage so we could get the information to eliminate a diplomat responsible for trafficking children. We trust each other, Luke."

"This isn't the same," Luke shouted a bit louder than he'd intended. He looked around. The coffee shop had filled, and with Shannon standing over him, he imagined people would be listening to hear what the intense couple might be fighting about. He grit his teeth. "This is like me telling you I've known for a while now your mother killed your father, and I need you to help me kill her."

She rolled her eyes. "Yeah, except he has a much longer history of this type of behavior than my mom. It's not that far of a stretch."

Luke disagreed but kept the objection to himself. It didn't matter if Decius hated his father—it was still family, still blood.

"I'm not keeping this secret forever. They are my best friends too."

Panic stirred in his gut. The moment Decius and Aeron found out the truth—he'd lose them both forever. "Give me a month. Dee's not even in the states half the time." He softened his eyes, and his head suddenly flew forward. He braced the table, halting the impact, but the sound of Shannon's smack to his head drew almost every eye in the building.

"You've forgotten who taught you to perfect that look. Get me what I need." Shannon stalked away, the swish of her hips telling him just how pissed off she was.

Luke followed after her, ignoring the shouts to 'Go get that fine ass!' and 'Good job, buddy' and 'I'd beat her if she hit me like that!' Luke glared, and the room fell silent. He wouldn't dream of laying a hand on Shannon. She was raised by a Medic and trained to be an Assassin. She could save your life or end it, and the torture that woman could bestow upon the human body…

She was gone before he'd reached the sidewalk, but he'd expected nothing less. He headed back to the Institute to pass the files to Perry and meet with his Granddad for the weekly Board meeting.

39

AERON

A stack of half-filled magazines and a manila envelope sat on the coffee table next to Aeron's propped foot. Shannon dropped down next to her, eyes on the large screen ahead of them. Maps and photos and timelines skidded in and out of view as she scrolled on the tablet in her hands.

"Perry wants to know if you are going to show up to training this weekend or if you're blowing it off since he's running them for Mason for the next few weeks." Aeron looked over at her. "If you're blowing it off, he promised to take me to Broadway."

"Shannon Gale, are you actually encouraging me to skip training?" Aeron asked in mock surprise, but she slipped the bit of information about Mason aside. What was Mason doing that he wasn't training her? "In that case, I'm blowing them off."

The apartment door opened, Justin and Luke loaded down with bags of groceries.

"You went shopping?" Shannon called from the couch, suspicion in her voice.

"Ever since Decius moved out, we've been living off of leftovers and take out," said Justin. "We need someone to cook for us."

Aeron and Shannon exchanged surprised looks.

"You can't cook?" Aeron held back her laughter.

"I think that's a deal-breaker, Aeron," Shannon said and looked over to Luke. "If you can't cook, the two of you will starve."

"My cooking is not that bad," Aeron countered.

"It's okay, Ron, I'll buy us a chef. Problem solved."

Justin and Shannon burst into laughter, and Aeron shoved her best friend but didn't hold back her smile. Her cooking would probably kill them.

"Where's Les?" Luke asked. He and Justin joined them around the coffee table, and Luke pulled the envelope toward him.

"Should be back soon," Shannon answered. "Is Decius joining us tonight?"

Aeron looked expectantly at Luke. She hadn't heard much from Decius in the last three weeks. He'd moved back to the Manor and remained radio silent.

"No. You haven't opened it?"

Aeron shook her head. "Waiting for you, Team Lead." The door opened again. Lesley, with bags overflowing with chemicals.

"Get everything?" Luke asked. She nodded and placed the bags in the kitchen. "We have an early morning and a long day tomorrow, so let's review one last time. Target: thirty-year-old Adrianna Kolb. Husband is Matt Kolb. They're Defense Intelligence Agents, so not small fries at all."

He opened the envelope and pulled out a small drive, and slid it home on the side of the coffee table. The latest information for the assignment scrolled across the screen.

Target: Adrianna Kolb
KOD: M/V
EXP: 0200 – 2400

"Violent murder," Aeron decoded for Kind of Death, taking note there was a time frame to work in. "Any notes?"

Luke tried to scroll the page, but it didn't go anywhere. "That's weird," he said. "There's no specifics." Usually, the assignments came with specific instructions on the type of murder or crime scene. Aeron's stomach began to get uneasy. Another unusual assignment.

"Well, creative freedom then. They will be at the National Museum fundraiser until 20:30, which gives us options. We can catch them on the way back to their yacht or, if there are too many civilians, we can do this on the yacht. Decius is running security—he's there tonight, getting our cameras into place. Justin and Shannon, I want you two already in place on the yacht." They nodded, fist-bumping across the table. "Lesley, you, me, and Dee will be eyes and ears at the fundraiser."

Lesley nodded, a small smile crossing her face. Aeron shook her head. She was too young for Decius at the moment, but give it a few years...

"Aeron, you are manning home base and the getaway boat, should we need it."

Aeron raised her eyes from the table to look at him.

"What do you mean?"

He hesitated.

"I'm doing good on my ankle." She rotated it for effect.

"We can't risk it," Luke said. "The uneven footing will put you, and therefore everyone else, at risk."

Aeron let out a growl of annoyance. "No offense, Shannon, but I should be the lead. This is my area."

No one argued this statement, but Luke met her glare with his own. "My answer is no." She glowered in defeat.

"Everyone clear?" Luke asked. A wave of nods around the table answered him. "Alright. Get some sleep. We've got an early start."

The group dispersed. Shannon tapped Aeron on the shoulder and leaned over the back of the couch. "I'll be fine tomorrow. It's four on one, two at most."

Aeron nodded, but the pit forming in her stomach did not agree. Luke returned the drive to the envelope and clicked off the screen while the room cleared out. She couldn't be mad at him for pulling rank—Decius would have too, although she would have argued a bit more with him.

He dropped beside her on the couch and laid down, his head in her lap. She pulled her fingers through his hair, the peaceful moment making life seem normal.

"How is it," she asked, "being Team Lead?"

"Stressful," he admitted. "I don't know how Dee did it."

"He had an amazing right-hand man."

He laughed softly.

"How is that other thing you're working on?"

His laughter subsided. "Not going as well as I expected."

"I know we don't talk about it, but if you want to…"

"Will you come stay with me at the mansion for a few weeks?" Aeron stilled her hand, and Luke looked up. "You don't have to go home. Your father's gone. And Decius is busy with Legacy stuff, so I thought you might finally be able to take me up on the offer."

Her stomach did a small flip. She *could* go with him. Not going would be far more suspicious.

"Yes. I didn't know it was still an option."

His smile erased the heavy stress he'd been carrying, lightening her own heart. "You will always have a place wherever I am."

Their lips met halfway for a too short kiss. A moan escaped Aeron as he pulled away. "We have a long day tomorrow, and I will stay up all night with you if I don't leave now." He placed another kiss before heading across the hall.

She sat back and closed her eyes. She had planned to stay at the Gales' estate with her father for the holidays—he would not be happy. Especially since Mrs. Gale had agreed to tell Shannon the truth. Aeron wanted to be there, to ease the anger that would roll off Shannon. But going with Luke was an opportunity she did not want to pass up.

At six p.m., Aeron sat on an empty boat in front of the computer, monitoring positions and communications. She bit at her knuckles and watched the blinking dots on the screen, the rocking motion lulling her into a daze. This had to be the most boring job on the team. At eight o'clock, Lesley called over the transmitter.

"Headed to sea."

Aeron glanced a few boats down. The Kolb's yacht was not enormous but large enough that hiding on board in one of the three cabins would be easy enough. She started up the engine and headed down the river ahead of them. The further down the sound she got, the closer the darkness loomed.

"A-go," Shannon said, confirming they were in place.

A few minutes of silence went by while Aeron maneuvered the river in near darkness.

"Luke, you've got company!" Decius called in the earpiece. Aeron slowed down.

"I see. L, back off. He's not letting her out of his sight. We will need to get on board before them. A, meet us at the rendezvous point."

"Copy." Aeron raced to the meeting place, the boat jumping against the current. The sudden silence unnerved her when she cut the engine. "In position," she said into the transmitter. Radio silence followed and the half-hour ticked by excruciatingly slow. Finally, the low rumble of a yacht in the distance echoed across the water.

The engine cut off, and the boat glided into view. Aeron stood, every nerve in her body buzzing. The radio had been quiet too long. A blue flare went up—the distress signal. She pressed her earpiece.

"Feedback." Silence. "Feedback!"

She started the boat and pulled alongside the dark yacht. Cutting the engine as fast as she started it, Aeron grabbed the security rope and launched herself onto the yacht to tie the boats together.

She ran for the cockpit. The lights from the main deck flickered, and she slipped on something slick. She steadied herself on the deck railing, and a thick, wet substance coated her hand. The coppery smell of blood assaulted her nose before her eyes could adjust. She looked around for a body—hoping it wasn't one of them, but there wasn't one. Aeron continued on. No noise sounded around her. Who had sent the flare? She raced up the stairs to the cockpit and peered in. A body lay sprawled on the ground. She pushed on the door, but it didn't budge. Locked. Her fist beat furiously against the door.

"Hey! Lesley!!" The body moved. "Open it up!"

Lesley looked up at Aeron. Blood leaked from a contusion on her forehead. Slowly, she pulled herself up and unlocked the door, pushing the unmoving Adrianna Kolb out of the way, allowing Aeron in.

"What happened?"

"Ambushed. They were waiting for us."

"How? How would they know?"

"I don't know."

"Alright—let's get you to the boat." Aeron pulled Lesley up and half carried her down the stair and to the escape boat. Something caught Aeron's foot, and she nearly dropped Lesley as she spun around. Justin looked up at her from the deck.

"Whoa," she crouched and found no immediate injuries, but he looked at her through hazy eyes. "Justin." Her voice pulled him into focus. He blinked a few times. "Are you okay?"

"Yeah. Yes. Confused, but unharmed I think. You saw the flare?"

"Yeah. C'mon, we need to get you to the boat." She pulled him up and directed them toward the speed boat, balancing between the two edges to guide them over. Aeron checked the bleeding wound on Lesley's head. Injuries to the forehead lumped quickly and bled a scary amount but normally looked worse than they were. She placed the medical kit next to Justin.

"Do you need help with this?" she asked.

"No. But they do," Justin said, motioning to the boat. "There are the two we knew about and then two we didn't. They are all locked in the cabins below."

Aeron didn't look back as she vaulted back onto the boat, her ankle trembling beneath her. She headed straight for the below decks, picking the small lock. The boat swayed beneath her as she silently moved down the curved stairwell. A commotion grew louder with each step.

Aeron removed the dagger from her boot. The door to her left burst open, and Aeron flattened herself against the wall, ready to spring forward. But Decius toppled out. She caught him, steadying them both.

"What are you doing here?" she breathed, thankful she hadn't stabbed him by accident.

"We lost contact with you—a frequency jammer," Decius panted. He clutched his side, and blood oozed between his fingers. "I managed to get on board right before it took off."

"Where are Luke and Shannon?"

"I have no idea. They got me in the side, and I took a hit of chloroform, and that's the last thing I remember." The boat shifted. He stumbled and gasped for air.

"Lesley and Justin are in the boat, banged up but alive. Go." She pushed him up the stairs and made her way toward the noise.

A door near the end of the hall rocked open a crack with the motion of the boat. Luke knelt on the floor with a gun to the back of his head. His pale face dripped sweat as he tried to stop bleeding from a wound on his thigh. He caught sight of Aeron and somehow paled further. He gave the tiniest of head shakes, which she ignored.

"How many?" she signed. He didn't answer, and she signed again. He coughed twice. Just two people managed to do this? Was Mr. Wayward on the boat?

For the first time she could remember, Aeron wished she had a gun.

40

LUKE

*H*ow did he not see this was a setup? Rosemary had been too complacent about the missing money. AK9987, otherwise known as, Adrianna Kolb. Legacy Inc. operative. Damn it.

Luke's leg burned beneath him, shaking as the blood seeped out the bullet hole, but he needed to keep Rosemary focused on him and not on the fact the Aeron was creeping just outside the door. If Aeron had made it on board, then everyone else must be…

"C'mon, Luke, where is it? I will slice her neck right open." Rosemary's voice radiated anger. Cage held Shannon, arms pinned around her middle, while Rosemary moved from behind Luke to trace her knife back and forth along Shannon's arms, the tip slicing a little deeper each time. Shannon bit into the gag, holding back her protests. Luke shot Aeron one last look before answering, a silent apology for what she was about to hear.

"I told you, it's gone."

Shannon's scream burned in Luke's ears, and he swallowed a sob. He should have come clean to Rosemary and his Granddad about the money as soon as Perry had told him.

"You're lying. You think I don't know what you and my manipulative daughter are up to? Stealing from Wilks was ballsy—but stealing from me? Tell me where it is, and you can all walk away."

How did she know he'd stolen from Wilks? "It's gone, Rosemary. You made a bad gamble on Steven, and he threw it away on hookers and card games."

An insane glint reached his aunt's eyes, and Shannon screamed again, the knife piercing beneath the collar bone.

"Alright!" Luke yelled, eyes flying to the door. Aeron was sure to burst through it at any second. "Let her go. Please! Your money is gone, but—but I can replace it." He thought about the funds tucked away by his parents. $5.5 million would nearly drain him, but he'd rather be poor and on the run than tangled up with Rosemary's panic any longer.

"The entire amount?" She smirked and stepped back a bit, the knife in one hand and Glock in the other. "Are you robbing Peter to pay Paul? What will Granddad say when he finds out his protege is no more than a thieving fraud?"

"Do you want the money replaced, or do you want to start up a witch-hunt?" Luke gambled, hoping she would settle for saving her own skin.

She paced back and forth, mumbling to herself and waving both weapons around—a mad sight. "I want that money in my account. To hell with everything else."

"No. That wasn't the original deal." Luke shook his head. "We agreed to put the money back. It's the only reason I helped you." What was her angle? She'd recruited Cage; what about Alexis? Had he been marking her while being marked? Did they even work for his Granddad?

"No, you agreed to help me because you wanted a little freedom. To be a little bit more ruthless without an audience?"

"I'll put the money where it belongs, Rosemary. Nowhere else."

"No. I think I'd rather take your untraceable money and leave." She drew the knife down Shannon's arm, and a whimper barely escaped her.

Leave. She wanted to be free. Agitation crept into Luke's words. "You will take what I'm giving you and be happy." He swallowed hard, ignoring the burning in his thigh, and kept his face free from pain. "If you chase this anymore, Rosemary, I will fucking bury you. I swear on my parents' graves, Granddad will have nothing on me. I will kill you, nice and slowly, layer by layer, just the way you like it. You want out—find another way." He glared at her, and all the cold spots on his back merged into a central fire in his gut. He pulled himself up to his feet, his bleeding thigh shaking under him. "You think he's scary? I've done more damage to this world in the last six months than any single assassin before me. You wanted ruthless—well, here I am."

Rosemary licked her lips and nodded. The shift in power between them was almost visible, and a small victory swelled in his chest.

"Fine. I want it done tomorrow—backdated." Cage released Shannon on Rosemary's nod, her body dropping like a sandbag. But Luke just nodded as Shannon stirred slightly on the ground. Weakness and concern for others were no longer an option.

"Like I'd be dumb enough to slip into the records from my personal account? I wanted nothing to do with this from the beginning. You will get the money when you get the money."

"Have it there tomorrow, Luke, or so help me God."

"Yeah, you'll need God's help because I'm just getting started." He stepped toward her, and a jolt of excitement shot through him when she stepped back. Rosemary would no longer be his problem…. Or Katherine's. "We're leaving," Luke said, waving his index finger between him and Shannon. "If any of my team are hurt, you'll have a whole new world of problems. Pick her up, Cage."

Cage hoisted Shannon up again, his gun in hand, walking ahead of them. Luke picked up his own weapon from the ground and followed him out, hoping to intercept Aeron before the situation escalated.

He lurched forward, however, as Rosemary attacked from

behind. Luke spun, fist connecting with the side of her face, the impact warming his heart. The scuffle in the tight hallway made it impossible to see where Aeron was, but Luke heard her. He tried to call out to her, but Rosemary jammed her gun into his gut, and he grit his teeth. She wouldn't kill him. She needed him to get the money.

"You are a menace, and I told him you would bring down the Legacy."

"I think he's doing a great job of that on his own," Luke ground out. A gunshot echoed around them. Luke sucked in a breath, glancing down, but Rosemary's gun hadn't gone off.

41

AERON

*A*eron's blood drummed in her veins, and she backed only halfway up the stairs before the door burst open. She froze. Muscles—from the train and the apartment—led the way, a gun near Shannon's head. He had a broken nose, and blood oozed from his ear. Aeron smirked.

"Hey!" he called. "Who's there?"

She jumped the last stair and stood up. "Muscles, looking good since the train. How's your buddy?" Aeron took in Shannon's state —gagged, with long gashes on her arms and beneath her collarbone —a pulse of rage moving through her. How dare Muscles touch her. She'd kill him like she should have on the subway.

A struggle broke out behind Muscles, and he lowered the gun momentarily to look back. Aeron ran forward with the intention of disarming him. She grabbed the gun. The boat rocked hard. Aeron's ankle gave way. A shot rang out.

Shannon's face stilled in horror. Her wide eyes dropped to her middle—blood steadily seeping through her shirt. Muscles released her, and she sank to the ground.

"Shannon!" Numb to the pain in her ankle, Aeron sprung forward. She ripped the gun from Muscles' hands and aimed it back at him. His eyes widened with her furious movements, and he put his hands up.

"I didn't mean to," he said. "I didn't."

No words came to her. She kicked at his abdomen. He doubled over, and she brought her knee up, breaking his nose. He fell to the ground. Aeron fired a single shot to his head, and then dropped beside her best friend.

"Shannon!" A sob racked Aeron's body as she pulled Shannon to her lap.

Grunts and thuds of a struggle sounded somewhere behind her, but Aeron tuned them out and gently tugged the gag from Shannon's mouth.

"Shan." She pulled up Shannon's shirt and found the hole below her lowest rib. Aeron ripped part of the shirt and tried to pack the wound, and Shannon cried out in pain, and Aeron cried with her, not releasing the pressure.

"Aeron," she gasped, but Aeron shushed her.

"Not now. You can tell me later."

"Luke," she breathed. The blood poured around Aeron's hand, and this time, Aeron didn't stop her.

"What about him?"

"He's in trouble."

"I know. I know! I'm working on it."

"No!" Shannon coughed, blood splattering Aeron's face; she didn't wipe it off. "He's," cough-cough, "his Grandfather" cough-cough, "Kat...Help her."

Her words made no sense. "Shannon," Aeron said, the tears streaming down her face. "You can't die."

Shannon smiled and closed her eyes. "You're...a bossy...pain in the ass."

Aeron laughed through her tears, hugging Shannon to her chest. The muffled sound of several shots happened behind her, and Cage's body jerked beside her.

"Ron," Luke said, pulling her arm. "Aeron," he said again. "We have to go. C'mon, get Shannon up."

Aeron clung to Shannon, sobs racking her body. "I can't…She's…"

Luke stilled. His eyes moved from Aeron's, down her blood-drenched clothing, to Shannon's unmoving body. Someone moved above deck, and Aeron heaved a deep breath. They had to go, and they needed to take Shannon with them.

"Luke, help me carry her." A calculated calm took over, her emotions wrapping themselves into a knot until she could look at them. She stood and fell right back down—her ankle the size of a softball.

"Luke," Aeron pleaded, "she's too heavy. And my ankle…" How could she have been so stupid?

His eyes snapped into focus. He hastily scooped Shannon's body from the floor, his footing faltering slightly. She hung limp in his arms. Aeron looked away and took the lead back up the stairs, grabbing on to anything that could help keep her upright. Justin met them on the deck.

"I was coming to get you," he said. "I disabled the jammer. Coast Guard is on their way." He reached out a hand to help Aeron, and his eyes fell on Shannon. He swallowed hard, escorting Aeron to the speed boat.

Decius grabbed her trembling hand. He helped her over the small gap, but she slipped and collapsed to the deck. "Good gracious, Aeron. Here, elevate that thing and let Shannon have a look at it," he said, motioning to her foot.

She didn't respond but let him lead her to the seat along the back of the boat. Luke appeared at the edge of the yacht, the blood-ied, motionless body in his arms. Decius' dark complexion paled in a way Aeron never thought imaginable.

Lesley cried out and lurched forward, Justin grabbing her as Luke passed Shannon gently over to Decius and climbed into the boat.

"Get us out of here," Luke said to Justin. He released Lesley, and she collapsed into Decius and Luke's arms—concussion, stab wound, and gunshot all forgotten as they consoled each other.

Aeron closed her eyes and embraced the rough movement on the water as it jarred her useless ankle, each jolt of pain nowhere painful enough to dull the harsh reality. Decius wrapped his arm around her shoulder but said nothing. There were no words to say. Shannon was dead.

The smell of lilies wafted across the Gales' Connecticut estate. Early morning frost crunched beneath Aeron's feet as she walked to the cemetery toward the dark oak casket. She held a Claddagh pin grasped in her hand, the sharp points digging into her palm. The Claddagh's two hands clasping a crowned heart also adorned a flag next to the casket. Aeron stopped beside Mrs. Gale and took the older woman's hand in hers, giving a small squeeze.

As Irish tradition called for, the wake had lasted all night, and the decision to bury Shannon at daybreak only seemed logical. Neither of them had slept, and they wore the same black dresses from yesterday. Aeron glanced to the empty seat on the other side of Mrs. Gale, the one reserved for Shannon's sister, Keara.

"I can't reach her," Mrs. Gale said softly. "She's on assignment." Tears stung Aeron's eyes, and she clutched the pin in her other hand, focusing on the points digging into her palm. If she gripped it hard enough, the pain would wake her up from this nightmare.

Aeron didn't care to hear the priest's words. They were insignificant. They could not console the hurt and rage that battled within her. But silent tears fell from Mrs. Gale's eyes after he concluded, and person after person placed flowers in the basket on top of the wooden box.

Aeron looked away. The repetitive gesture became more irrelevant with each passing person. She looked past the coffin to Mason. He looked out of place in a suit, his somber gaze on the casket, and Aeron was sure the clothes didn't even belong to him. Decius stood in front of him, Lesley tucked beneath his arm as her red eyes searched for stray strings on her hemline and she tugged at them absent-mindedly. She caught Justin wiping at his eye with the edge of his black jacket. And Luke—a sob caught in her throat. He stood beside a devastated Perry who clutched onto a dozen roses—he'd loved Shannon for years and waited to act on it until he was out of the program. Luke's hand sat firmly on Perry's shoulder in solidarity, but his gaze remained fixed intently on her.

After the procession of people had finished, Luke gave Perry a small nudge. He approached with the dozen roses, each of the team filing in line behind him. Aeron pulled herself away from Mrs. Gale's side and joined them around the casket. Perry placed the roses gently down and removed the Claddagh pin from his jacket. He placed a kiss upon the heart, hand, and crown before slamming it down, stabbing it into the wood. The sound echoed like a gunshot in the open cemetery. Each member of the team, one by one, followed suit—each pin a solitary shot. Aeron licked her lips, her pin the last to land—their tribute to Shannon's heritage, representing the friendship, loyalty, and love they held for their fallen comrade.

She returned to the seat beside Mrs. Gale as her best friend was lowered to the ground.

42

LUKE

"Aeron!" Luke called, but she remained still, fixated on the ground. Not even a year ago that had been him—could it really be less than a year? It felt like a lifetime. "Aeron?"

"Let her be," Mrs. Gale said behind him. "She needs to grieve in her own time."

"She's been a zombie for days."

"And she will continue to be until her heart heals. You cannot shake her from this—you can only be there when she wakes up."

Luke looked back at Mrs. Gale, wanting to wrap Aeron in his arms, but that hadn't helped at all the last few days. "I'm so sorry, Mrs. G."

"No need for apologies, Luke. We know the dangers. We accept the dangers when we chose to marry or have children."

Luke took a swig from his flask, the liquid trickling around the knot in his throat. They'd reported Shannon's death as a Legacy fatality on mission, and there was no one to counter the claim except Aeron—and who knew what she'd heard on the yacht.

"Go inside, eat something. Aeron will be okay."

He took another swig.

"Food, Lucas, will do you better than anymore from that flask. Let me have it."

He bristled at the use of his proper name, hand tightening around his father's flask. She reached out, the cool metal slipping from his hands. She shook it, the few shots left sloshing around. A small smile lit her face when the scotch hit her senses. "We can't be wasting this." She tipped her head back, finishing the rest of the reserve stock he'd taken from his Granddad. She shuddered, handed back the empty container, and gave him a gentle push.

The gray Victorian home welcomed him as he walked up the garden path, the turrets reaching toward the bright, clear sky. Shannon loved days without clouds. Luke shook the thought from his head—he shouldn't get to think about Shannon.

He scanned the massive windows, trying to remember which one had been her bedroom. It'd been almost ten years since he'd set foot on the property. After Aeron's mother and Shannon's father died, Mrs. Gale withdrew from the group. The view had definitely been over the garden and cemetery, but had it been more left or center? The movement of curtains on the second floor pulled his attention. Luke's heart jumped, almost leaving his throat altogether. It looked like a young man, with scars like his Granddad.

His pace quickened. The cool air of the house latched onto him as he rushed through the doors. The rear entryway was empty, the sound of guests in the ballroom directing him to where the food was, but food was the last thing on his mind. He headed away from the noise, the house echoing around him the deeper he moved through the halls. He needed to get to the second floor. He took out the flask, habit at this point, and sighed, the lightness reminding him he needed to refill.

He found the second floor just as abandoned as the hallways and began peeking into the rooms. Most were deserted, large sheets over the furniture, covered in dust. The house was just a shell of the greatness that once operated here, much like the mansion, and like Seward Manor, he'd wager. He opened the door to an abandoned study—a full bar stocked and untouched by the years. He ventured in, dragging a finger across the bottles, leaving a trail in the dust. Vodka, gin, whiskey. He paused at the whiskeys, tipping each bottle back to get a good view of the labels. He picked the Green Label Jack and cracked it open, the intoxicating aroma encouraging him to just drink from the bottle. No. He refilled his flask and took two large sips, shivering, and then topped off the container again and pocketed it. Footsteps in the hall called his attention.

Luke chased the sound down the hall, coming up on a man—lanky with dark hair. "Hey!" Luke shouted.

The man froze and looked over his shoulder—a long scar matching his Granddad's met him. The man's eyes widened, and he ran. Luke followed, closing the distance in unreal time, considering the world wobbled around him. The room spun, but he pushed through, tackling the stranger to the ground.

He rolled over and fought Luke from getting on top, sliding a foot under Luke's knee and elevating. Luke teeter-tottered and reached out to catch himself but toppled over. The man sprung to his feet and fled again.

"Seriously?" Luke muttered, clambering to his feet and following. He caught the man around the middle again but didn't give him a chance to roll over. He snaked an arm around his neck, but he was too slow, and the scarred man countered. Fists flew, and a new set of footsteps hurried toward them. Luke looked up—Mr. Seward rounded the corner.

Clear thoughts escaped Luke. A solid elbow to the man beneath him, and the body went limp. He sprang on Mr. Seward, rage and pain pushing past the alcohol and focusing completely on ripping the monster limb from limb.

"Aeron!"

Aeron looked up from the fresh grave dirt, her neck stiff. The sun sat high above her, and she squinted to see who was running toward her.

"Aeron!" Mrs. Gale's frantic face came into view, and Aeron shot to her feet, her heart hammering in her throat. "Your father! I don't know how Luke found out— "

Panic rose inside her. Aeron slipped off her low heels and dashed for the house.

"Where?" Aeron called, passing Mrs. Gale.

"His guest rooms!"

Aeron sprinted, ignoring the rocks that stabbed her feet and the throb in her ankle. If Luke had found her father—she didn't want to guess what he'd do. Aeron burst into the sunroom and took the back stairwell to the guest rooms. Yelling and slamming echoed down the hall. A figure lay sprawled in the hallway. She slid to her knees and turned the body over—Ivan.

Relief washed through her as a pulse beat faintly beneath her fingertips. She moved to the double doors of her father's living area. Paper and broken glass littered the floor around the overturned furniture. She carefully made her way to the next room following shouts of anger and sickening sounds of flesh-on-flesh blows.

"You are a cowardly—" punch "good for nothing—" punch "waste of fucking space." She pushed open the door as a desk lamp shattered beneath her father. Deep lines accentuated his drawn face, his movements lethargic.

"Luke!" Aeron yelled. He paused. "What are you doing?"

"I am fixing the problem."

She moved closer, alcohol assaulting her nose before she even reached them. She would have assumed her father was the intoxicated one, but Luke's bright red eyes made her second guess.

"How is this fixing anything?" She moved toward him. He towered over her father sprawled out across the desk. "Think this through."

"I am thinking. I've been thinking about doing this since my parents' funeral. He killed my parents. Did you know that? He killed my parents and your mother. He killed you. He may as well have killed Shannon too. If you hadn't been injured…"

Aeron sucked in a breath. He must be drunk.

"That's not fair, Luke," Aeron said, pulling the attention away from her father. "Shannon's death was not our fault."

"I know!" he yelled. "It was his." Luke landed a punch to the side of her father's face, and Aeron flinched.

"Please," she begged.

"I thought you, you out of everyone, would be glad to have him dead." He released the hold of her father's shirt and turned to Aeron. "I'm doing this for you. So you can be free."

He father rolled off the desk, and Aeron held Luke's attention the best she could. "I do, of course, I do. But I don't want you shit-faced while you do it. We've found him. Call your Granddad. Let this be handled the Legacy way."

Luke laughed. "The Legacy is dead, Aeron. It's only a matter of time—"

Smash. A vase of roses broke over Luke's head, and he dropped to his knees. Her father lunged for her, grabbing a fist full of hair. He placed a knife to her throat, speaking rapidly in her ear.

"I was wrong. You on the inside was always the better plan. I wanted vengeance for the deaths Elijah has caused. I should have worried more about the lives he could still take."

Luke clambered to his feet, swaying slightly.

"Ah, ah, ahh," Her father said loudly. "We shouldn't play with the big boys until we're ready, Mr. Wayward. Stay where you are." Luke glared at him but didn't move. Her father continued to speak quietly into her ear. "You are going to disarm me and drive this dagger right through my heart."

The color drained from Aeron's face, and she shook her head.

"Yes," he whispered. "I am already dying, bleeding out as we speak, so you must do it swiftly."

Tears burned Aeron's eyes.

"Let her go!" Luke shouted. "You're hurting her. Please." He raised his hands.

"Not so fast, young man. I'm having words with my daughter." Luke stepped forward, and her father dug the knife deep enough to draw blood, halting Luke's movements. "There's a good boy."

"Dad," she said aloud. "Please, don't do this."

"I gave my word," he whispered. "I'd do everything I could to keep him safe. If Luke kills me, when he learns the truth…" He didn't need to say it. Luke would hate himself. "But killing me will get you an open invitation. Get in. Finish our mission—the original mission—to save Luke. Do you understand me?" She nodded, unable to speak around the ball lodged in her throat. "Do it."

She grabbed his wrist and twisted. It was too easy to remove the knife and turn the point on him. He dropped to the floor, and she pinned him down. He looked up and smiled—a genuine smile that reached his hazel eyes and shattered her heart.

Footsteps caught her attention, and she glanced back when Luke spat, "Who are you?"

Ivan froze in the door, eyes locked on Aeron and her father.

"No!" Ivan's strangled cry jump-started Luke into action. He dove at Ivan.

Aeron looked back at her father. "I can't," she whispered, fighting back the panic.

"It is a mercy kill, Aeron. Even if I live—I would never be able to work again."

She looked over her shoulder at Luke, pinning a struggling Ivan against the wall.

"Don't do this. Please! Don't!" Ivan pleaded. "You don't have to."

"He killed you once, Aeron. I won't let him have another opportunity. This needs to end."

She met her father's gaze. "Katherine knows the truth about us. She came to see me at the infirmary," she confessed.

"Then you have an ally on the inside."

"He'll never forgive me for lying to him," Aeron choked out, tears blurring her vision.

"Take care of Ivan for me. I'm sorry I didn't trust you."

"I could have said no. I was *free* to say no." She closed her eyes, trying to shake herself into focus.

"What did you say? How far?"

"I—"

"Aeron. How. Far?"

"I'd do anything."

"Then do it," he said loud enough for Ivan and Luke to hear.

Tears fell freely down her face. She placed the blade over his heart. He put his right hand over hers and gave a weak push. Aeron held his gaze and pushed down. He smiled again.

His body convulsed beneath her, the smile staying on his face, even after the spark faded from his eyes. A heart-wrenching wail escaped her, and someone pulled her away from his unmoving body. Luke cradled her into his chest, the wail subsiding as she struggled to breathe. The door bounced off the wall. Aeron continued to gasp for air as Decius's wild eyes moved back and forth from Luke and Aeron to their dead father.

"What did you do?" He ran to their father's side, sliding to his knees in the growing puddle of blood. "What did you do!" A sob racked his words.

"I—I killed him," she said. He looked at her hands. They shook violently—the dagger still clutched in one.

"Let it go." Luke pried the dagger from her fingers. "This was my fault," he said softly. "I should have waited." He looked to Decius. "I should have called you."

"How did you know he was here?" Decius asked, eyes focused on the body.

"I, I didn't. I followed someone else. That man—"

A sharp intake of breath pulled Aeron's eyes back to the door. Mrs. Gale stood, a hand to her mouth.

"Mrs. Gale—" Aeron tried to get to her feet.

Mrs. Gale's eyes moved around the room. "Out," she said softly.

No one moved.

"GET OUT!"

Decius rose to his feet, now covered in blood, and backed away from the body. Luke pulled Aeron to her feet.

"Not you." Mrs. Gale pointed to Aeron.

"I'm not leaving her—" Luke started.

"I noticed your Grandfather could not make it to the funeral. Perhaps you could inform him we were disappointed with his absence." Her voice held a chill in it.

Luke's eyes widened. "Would you like to explain what the Legacy's most wanted man was doing camping out in your home?" Luke retorted. "There was a kill order on him. I had every right to—"

"But you didn't—Aeron did. And a kill order does not necessarily mean beat on sight. There is still a process to follow, or have you come so far from your roots you forget the laws your parents fought to uphold?"

"That man tried to murder her. He succeeded once—you should

be glad to have him dead on your floor and not your daughter's best friend."

Her mouth tightened. "Out. All of you." Mrs. Gale kept her saddened eyes on Aeron as they walked by, but Aeron could not return her gaze. She could only see her father's final expression, one of genuine happiness, dying at her hand.

LUKE

"*H*e's dead?"

"Yes," Luke said for the fourth time, standing in front of his Granddad's desk. He was still covered in blood, his, Aeron's, but mostly Mr. Seward's. "Dead. That was your wish, was it not?"

"I wanted him to suffer. This was not what we agreed on."

"I didn't anticipate her killing her own father," Luke ground out. "However, I hope her loyalty can be verified now." He clenched his fists, Aeron's anguished scream still echoing in his mind.

His Granddad nodded. "And their Legacy?"

"Decius will hand it over. Give it a week."

"And if he doesn't?"

Luke fought the urge to roll his eyes, closing them instead and taking several long breaths.

"If he doesn't?"

"I don't see that becoming an issue," Luke reiterated. "You will have the Seward's property in a few weeks at most. Which leaves the Gales. Are you planning for me to murder them too?" He was being sarcastic, but the sourness in his voice came through, and he found he just didn't care anymore. Mrs. Gale had been harboring

Aeron's dad for who knew how long. Had Shannon known? No. She couldn't have.

"Well, Eileen won't leave voluntarily. And we need to know what she knows." His Granddad leaned back in his chair, pressing a thumb into his temple. "This man—the one with a similar scar to mine. Who was he?"

Luke had no idea, the altercations a blur in his head, his hangover coming on strong. But he couldn't forget that scar. "I'm guessing the techie we've been searching for."

"And you let him walk right out the door?" Irritation rang through the calm exterior.

"I was a bit preoccupied. I searched for him after but no luck. Thought it best to respect Mrs. Gale's request and leave the premises."

"You thought wrong. Now you will have to make a return trip."

Luke bit into his lower lip. Mrs. Gale had been harboring Aeron's dad, but she was still Mrs. Gale—Shannon's mom. Who just had to bury her daughter because Luke had…No. He couldn't think of it.

"You haven't explained yet," Luke redirected, "what happens to everyone currently here at the Institute."

"What do you mean?" He raised a single eyebrow. The attempt to look confused was not lost on Luke. He'd come to know his Granddad too well to think he'd be confused about anything.

"The families here, the assets and instructors in this building are still loyal to the Legacy. What happens to them?" The silence that followed grew heavy.

"My boy, have you not walked the halls of this building lately? It's quiet. Dead quiet."

He'd not walked the halls of the Institute in what felt like months. The only path he took was from Lobby to Penthouse to his living quarters. The fire in his gut extinguished, returning to the ice cave it'd become, and he swallowed hard.

Was he insinuating everyone was dead? No. The Board still met, and the Medical ward still ran. And there were hundreds of people who lived within these walls. Children and Assassins alike.

But surely someone, Mason, or—the thought stopped his breath. When had he last heard from Mason? When he'd thrown him out of the residence, of course. When he begged Luke to be honest with him. To let him help. Was Mason at the funeral? Luke racked his soggy brain; he'd been focused on Aeron, not bothering to take note of anyone else.

"Where is everyone?" He dropped into the wooden chair beside him, elbows on knees, and his stomach thanking him—as it wanted to spill out onto the carpet. "With Mr. Seward gone, and his coup de taut extinguished, it is possible to continue with Legacy and Institute business as usual." That was what could happen. Luke could run it the same as always. No need to kill everyone. The snake's head had been cut off.

"Don't be naive." His Granddad poured a glass of water from the glass pitcher on the desk and placed it in front of him. "The end goal has always been to eliminate the Legacy. True to my word, those who had made the transition are training in D.C. Those who still have potential are training here—the impressionable trainees."

"The non-blood trainees," Luke clarified. He ignored the offer of water and sat back. "The ones who only know what they've been taught in this building with no outside ties."

"Not all made it. But the ones that did…"

"What about the Gales?" Luke asked, the thought of all the lives lost defending Mr. Seward churning his stomach. One last family. One last betrayal.

"Gale. Just the one. The oldest is not an issue. She was sent to D.C., and we have eyes on her. I need you to retrieve Mrs. Gale and bring her to interrogation. She'll answer what I need answered; I bet her daughter's life on it." The glint in his Granddad's eyes boiled Luke's stomach, and he chugged the glass of water to keep the vomit down. "That's not going to be an issue, is it, Luke?"

"No, Sir," he managed to push out. But that was a lie. Mrs. Gale had suffered enough at his hand. Shannon was gone forever—that was punishment enough. Never again would she hear that musical laugh or catch the wicked glint in her eye when Shannon was about to pull off the impossible. Never again would he see her face light up when she finished a disguise so good, facial recognition wouldn't stand a chance, even if it had one.

"—Tonight. Understand?"

Luke looked up, meeting a look that people saw the moment before they died, and asked, "What was that?"

A fist landed loud on the desk, the pitcher of water reverberating from the impact. But his words were as calm as ever. "I want Eileen Gale in this building tonight."

Something inside Luke broke with this request. The beast was slain. The murders avenged, but somehow life did not feel better. Life did not make any more sense. Eileen Gale saved Aeron's life on the table that fateful night. How could she harbor the man that did that? How could she bury her daughter while protecting that monster? The only person who knew the answers was her.

"Of course," Luke agreed and stood. "I'll need back up. Alexis and Cage left with Rosemary, back to D.C." He hadn't spilled the beans on Rosemary's deception just yet, more because he hadn't had the time. She and Alexis fled after Shannon was killed, and Cage's body was never recovered from the yacht. Probably fish food at this point. "Can I borrow Mason for this task?"

Mason knew he'd been eliminating families and saving them. Luke also suspected he know where Mr. Seward was the entire time, so where did his loyalty lie?

"What about Perry?"

Perry's echoed cry at the news of Shannon's death revisited Luke, and he shivered. He wanted to keep it under wraps, but Perry would be of use to no one at the bottom of a bottle. "He took Shannon's death hard," Luke said. "I don't know he would be the best man for the job, right now."

His Granddad inhaled deeply, nose crunching up in distaste.

Emotional weakness had no place within his rule. "Yes. Mason will be fine. He's as loyal as money can buy."

She won't leave voluntarily. What an understatement. Mason and Luke looked up at the flames billowing from the Gale estate. The smoke invading their lungs and scorching their throats. Mason had not said a word since Luke had confirmed their mission. He'd simply asked, 'You're sure?' and then nodded and followed him out of the Institute.

Luke had always thought graduating the program would allow him to work side by side with his mentor as equals. He was disappointed, however, as Mason was under orders from up top to follow Luke without question. But right now, he didn't want to be in charge. He wanted Mason to tell him that this was wrong. That Mrs. Gale was confused, and there was no need to capture his dead friend's mom. His gut was a constant wave of fire and ice. One minute he would know this was right, but then Shannon would smack his head, ice shivering down his body, telling him he was wrong. But she *had* kept Mr. Seward safe. So she *was* guilty.

They stood in the cemetery behind the house, Mrs. Gale rooted over Shannon's fresh grave. Her impeccable hair now a mane around her soot smudged face, but the pistol pointed at them was what concerned Luke the most.

"Eileen, just come with us," Mason bargained, a firm grasp on Luke's bicep, stopping him from vaulting over the headstones and tackling her to the ground. Luke needed this over. He needed to go home and drink a bottle of anything to quiet the noise. He shivered.

"I'm not walking to my death, Mason."

"Then I'll settle for dragging you out of here," Luke called. "One way or another, you are coming with us tonight. The Board demands it."